The Shakespeare Incident

Other Books by Jonathan Miller

Rattlesnake Lawyer and Luna Cruz Thrillers:
Rattlesnake Lawyer
Crater County
Volcano Verdict
La Bajada Lawyer
Conflict Contract
Lawyer Geisha Pink
Rattlesnake Wedding
Navajo Repo
A Million Dead Lawyers
Luna Law
Rattlesnake & Son
Rattlesnake Funeral

Other Books:
Amarillo in August: An Author's Life on the Road
Law and Loves: Part 1
Laws & Loves: Real Stories of the Rattlesnake Lawyer
Twilight in the Twelfth; A Ruidoso Romance

THE SHAKESPEARE INCIDENT

A Rattlesnake Lawyer Novel

By

JONATHAN MILLER

Artemesia
Publishing

ISBN: 978-1-951122-21-8 (paperback)
ISBN: 978-1-951122-29-4 (ebook)
LCCN: 2021933844
Copyright © 2021 by Jonathan Miller

Cover Design: Ian Bristow
Cover Photo: Jonathan Miller

Artemesia Publishing
9 Mockingbird Hill Rd
Tijeras, New Mexico 87059
www.apbooks.net
info@artemesiapublishing.com

"The views expressed herein are not necessarily those of the author."
Arthur C. Clarke *Childhood's End*

PART I

MUCH ADO ABOUT NOTHING

Chapter 1
Tuesday, July 7

"Have I ever told you the story of how I got my name?" Denny Song asked Cordelia Dunsinane. A ritual between them, he always asked her this question when he was nervous. Almost midnight, they stood on a desert ridge, next to a cylindrical water tower, just south of Lordsburg, New Mexico. If they looked to the west, they could see the outline of the "ghost town" of Shakespeare, an abandoned mining camp. To the south, they overlooked a squadron of heavily armed sheriff's deputies and a mysterious black van on her family's property, the New Shakespeare Ranch. Hell, the small-town deputies down below were distant relatives and might as well be her family, and that made it much, much worse.

Now was a good time to be nervous.

Denny was twenty-seven but looked years older. Off the drugs for a few weeks now, tattoos of flying saucers adorned his lanky arms. He wore a black tank top that read STRAIGHT OUTTA ROSWELL. It recreated the famed album cover of the rap masterpiece, *Straight Outta Compton*, but sported aliens instead of rappers glaring at the viewer.

He absent-mindedly played with an old Tek 9 semi-automatic handgun. Cordelia put her hand on his and slowly took the gun away from him.

"You might as well tell me the story while we figure out how to get the grail," Cordelia said. She wore a black western cut shirt and rattlesnake cowboy boots like a back-up singer in a country band about to go to rehab. Her phone tucked in her shirtfront pocket beeped, indicating a new message. She almost used her right hand to check on it, before remember-

1

ing the gun. "This damn game has me messed up."

When the CEO of Cygnus Moon, an Asian tech conglomerate, set up the 24 Grails Contest, the players couldn't predict it would become a matter of life and death. Initially, the world viewed the game as a cross between *Pokémon Go* and *Forrest Fenn Treasure Hunt*. For the silver grails that mysteriously appeared all over the world, the prizes were astronomical. And when Cygnus Moon announced that if someone, *anyone*, touched the Omega Grail—the one currently located on the Dunsinane family ranch—the sky itself could be the limit.

"A grand prize beyond your ultimate desires." Cygnus Moon's company website specified few details on the contest. "Find the Omega Grail and have it verified."

Finding the grail was no big deal. Having it *verified* might prove fatal.

No one knew how or when the final grail appeared on top of the boulder at New Shakespeare Ranch. No one knew how *any* of the other twenty-three grails magically appeared all over the world on random properties. And now the endgame had come here to the bootheel of New Mexico at the end of the earth.

Denny and Cordelia had discovered the Omega Grail two days ago, but they had to wait until it was "verified"—whatever that meant. Probably they would have to touch it in the presence of whoever was in the black van parked by the grail.

Leaning on a leg of the water tower, Cordelia looked at the dusty expanse of New Shakespeare Ranch. The cattle, the sheep and even the stray dogs were long gone. She wanted to touch the grail herself, more than anything, but somehow, she knew that Denny needed to be the one who did it. She sensed that touching it could kill her, but she didn't quite know why. There was a lot about her past that she didn't know or understand.

The Sheriff's office had seized the ranch the night before, her father's corpse still warm. Sheriff JC Diamond had shown an alleged warrant for bad loans from the bank on her late father's estate.

"Your daddy owed a shit load of money to the wrong

people before he died," the sheriff said. "If you challenge the validity of the 'warrant,' you gotta hire a lawyer and take it down to the courthouse. And as you know, *my* county, *my* courthouse."

"But what about the grail?" Cordelia had asked. "What about the prize?"

"You want to touch that grail and win that prize, you gotta go through me. Well, you gotta go through *us*."

Sheriff Diamond and his crew had set up a perimeter around the boulder, while the black van waited with its motor running, a few feet from the grail itself. When did that van get there?

New Shakespeare Ranch was her family's land, her birthright, but the other members of her family were dead or lost to the wind. Her father had always said that his family was "special," but they were vulnerable to meth, opioids and alcohol, just like everyone else. Maybe more so. Still, losing the ranch was like losing part of her soul. She wanted it back.

Denny reached up and put his hand on her shoulder. She was far taller, especially in boots.

"You gotta listen" Denny said. "It's important."

"You're right, Denny." She patted his hand. "You've told me the long-lost-sister-story like a million times but please, please tell me the story again if it calms you down."

"We were twins," Denny began. "Before I was even born, my real mother asked her sister, my aunt, for naming suggestions. My aunt said it should Denise if it's a girl..."

"And *De-nephew* if it's a boy," Cordelia piped in on cue. "And your real mom said to just call you *Denny*. And that woman who took you overheard that and went with it. That's how you got your name. But then you got taken away by that bad bitch before you even met your real mom, the saint."

"My stepmom said my real mom was so beautiful. If only we could have been together as a family."

"I'm sure your *real* mom would be proud of you," Cordelia lied. "Your *real* sister too. If she's still alive..."

"I wonder if my sister looks like me—half Korean, half-Hispanic and half-something else."

Denny always made that same joke about his ethnicity.

At least she hoped that it was a joke. Meth had ruined his math skills.

The ritual over, Cordelia moved on. "That's a great story, honey. Now we gotta figure out what to do about the grail. You gotta be the one to touch it in front of whoever's in the van. I don't think they can shoot us in front of the judges."

Denny wasn't finished. "I don't know what happened. I've got a feeling I'll meet Denise real soon. Maybe my real mom even. I can sense that they're on their way here. I'm kinda psychic you know. I'm sure Denise is a psychic too. Fifth dimensional consciousness and all."

"That's the first time you've told me that," Cordelia said. "I sure hope you're right. We need all the help we can get." She looked at her watch. It was her late father's watch. It had stopped but the second hand was vibrating in place.

"I should look her up like right now," Denny continued, not noticing Cordelia's distress. "I think she's a lawyer or something. She must be really good, especially if she's psychic like me."

Denise Song was a psychic lawyer? That was also new. "Uhm... can't she just reach out to you with her mind, if she's like psychic?"

"Maybe she doesn't know I'm alive. She doesn't know where to look."

"Whatever. We got to worry about the grail."

"I still say that the grail was put there by aliens as a portal through that black hole, Cygnus X-1," Denny said. He had now switched to another ritual between them—the grail-planted-by-aliens one. "You know Cygnus Moon probably has a connection to the Cygnus X-1 black hole."

"Aliens don't offer grand prizes if you find their artifacts," Cordelia said. "It was probably put there by one of those stealth drones you worked with on base before you got discharged. They dropped it down while we were asleep."

"Maybe we can get Denise to help us. Who knows, she might not be that far away," Denny said. "You can look things up with your phone, right? Maybe we can find her that way."

He didn't own a phone; he had traded it in for drugs last year.

"Well, we got to make a choice right now," Cordelia said. "We can stay up here and try to find your psychic sister, if she even exists, or we march down onto the ranch, you touch the grail and pray that the cops don't shoot us."

Denny looked down at the ranch—at the grail, at the black van and at the cops. He then looked at Cordelia. Her phone in the breast pocket of her shirt was still glowing from the unread message. She held the gun in her right hand.

"What should I do?" Denny asked. "Maybe I should just try to find my sister with the phone. What do you think?"

Cordelia could hand him the phone or the gun. She took another look at the grail on her family's ranch and at the vibrating second hand of her father's watch. Time was an issue right now. A grail in the hand is worth a lot more than a Denise in the bush. "That bitch Denise probably doesn't exist. Denise and De-nephew? Sounds like a bad joke your stepmom told you. If this Denise is alive *and* if she's a psychic, she would have found you by now."

"Are you sure?"

"Fuck Denise! Let's just get the damn grail," she said. "It's not like they're going to shoot you on my property in front of the prize committee, especially if you let them know you have a gun. Just don't point it at anyone."

"You're probably right. Give me the gun. Let's just get the grail. I'm sure I won't have to shoot anyone. Maybe Denise is just some silly-ass story my stepmom told me."

She handed him the gun.

Denny took two steps away from the water tower. He held the gun in his right hand as his left hand curled into a fist of anger.

Cordelia knew of Denny's hatred toward the sheriff, his hatred toward this whole county. "Promise me you're not going to shoot them," she said. "We got to play this cool."

"I won't if I don't have to. I'm going to sneak around the back. There's a ditch under the fence behind that boulder. I pop up from behind the rock, touch the grail and then we win the prize."

Denny took a third step toward the ranch and seemed to cross an invisible tripwire over a fault line. The earth rumbled beneath them and then intensified when he took another step.

"What's going on?" Denny asked.

"Look!" Cordelia said, pointing up. An object in the sky appeared directly above their heads. There was a blinding flash of light and then a pink glow in the darkness. It took a moment for their eyes to adjust. Blood now trickled out of her nose and ears. Whatever was up there now floated directly over the water tower and focused a spotlight on the grail.

"I told you it was a UFO!" Denny said. "It came through the black hole from another dimension."

"Not even. It came out of the ground," Cordelia said. "Like from right under the water tower."

"It could still be a UFO."

By definition, the thing above them was a UFO, as it was unidentified, flying and an *object*. It didn't matter where it came from. The object wasn't a flying saucer, more like a globe with stingray wings. It was impossible to tell its size in this light or whether it was metal, fiberglass or something extraterrestrial. The UFO was emitting the pink light, a pink from beyond the normal spectrum—not ultra-violet, but ultra-pink?

It made a sound like a dog-whistle that was barely audible to the human ear. The grail shimmered in the vibrating pink spotlight, like a mirror ball in Satan's disco.

"He's up there!" The sheriff was pointing right at them.

"We've got to do this now!" Cordelia said to Denny. "The cops know we're here!"

The lights above them grew brighter.

There was another flash. Lightning emerged directly from the grail, then ricocheted around the canyon. Cordelia heard a high-pitched noise that sounded like a dog whistle— for a dog from another dimension.

Denny screamed. Had he been hit by lightning? He froze.

Cordelia's whole body ceased to exist and then reappeared. Had all the pieces come back together correctly? Everything felt a little bit off. She fell to her knees and vomited. When her vision cleared, she checked her father's watch. The second hand was now rocking back and forth between twelve and six. At least she'd stopped bleeding...

While she still felt insubstantial, Denny now looked more solid, bigger even. He began walking directly down to the entrance of the ranch.

Cordelia stared at Denny and saw even his walk was different, like a zombie. He had "broken bad" before, and drugs made him do strange things, but now he might as well be someone or *something* else. While he had been hesitant to seek out the grail, now his eyes were locked on it.

Or maybe he looked so different because she felt even lighter, like she would float away at any moment. "Denny!" she yelled.

He didn't reply. He continued heading toward the cops.

"Denny, stop or we'll shoot!" the sheriff shouted. "We'll take out Cordelia too."

Denny kept walking. He lifted up his gun stiffly, as if he was a marionette and someone—or *something*—above was pulling the strings.

Damn. Instead of the gun, she should have given him the phone.

Chapter 2

"Looks like we got air support." Sheriff JC Diamond frowned at the flying object hovering over the big water tower on the ridge above New Shakespeare Ranch. He always claimed in public that he didn't believe in flying saucers and offered "logical" explanations to the press. He kept his real beliefs to himself.

He was the old-timer here. He could pass for a muscular fifty but was much older. He wore his standard crisp desert khaki. His shiny silver star badge was so sharp that it could draw blood. And of course, even though it was night, he wore his usual sunglasses.

"Did you call that in, Sheriff?" Antonio, one of his deputies, asked. "That sure don't look like one of ours."

"Maybe it's like military or something, sir," Beatrice said. "They got drones like that over at the missile range."

"Should we shoot at it?" Claudio asked.

The sheriff turned around and frowned at the three twenty-something deputies in their ill-fitting khakis and dull badges. The new generation failed to live up to their potential, that was for sure. Drugs, video games, modern permissiveness. These deputies weren't much different from the criminals they were supposed to be arresting.

Antonio Smith was the youngest. He had been hit in the head with a football a few too many times. Beatrice Baca was supposed to be the smart one. She was hoping to transfer to a higher paying job at Border Patrol once her twin daughters were a little older. And then there was Claudio Johnson, the only one who'd actually been in combat. He still had PTSD. Sheriff Diamond never knew whether Claudio would shoot the perp or shoot himself.

The only person he could really trust was Earl, the German Shepherd sitting calmly on his right.

"We'll just have to wait and see," the sheriff said. "And hope that it's on *our* side." His deputies didn't know what was really going on, and he wasn't about to tell them.

This unidentified object above the water tower was a wrinkle he hadn't been expecting on this night of all nights. Did that change anything? Somehow, he knew that it would change *everything.*

All of a sudden, his deputies shimmered in the lightning, covering their eyes. He was glad he wore his sunglasses. Then the three of them vomited, as if on cue.

"I'm bleeding," Antonio said.

"I don't feel so good," Beatrice said.

Claudio said nothing and threw up again.

"Damn rookies," the sheriff said. "Man. The. Fuck. Up."

They wiped their faces and tried to man up—whatever that meant. "What's your secret? Why didn't you throw up, Sheriff?" Beatrice asked.

"You're not bleeding either," Antonio said.

"I'm *grounded,*" the Sheriff said. "One of the benefits of being *old school.*"

"Well, Sheriff Old School, you better watch what's going on below the drone, on the ground," Beatrice said, "I don't know how you see anything with those glasses."

She pointed at two figures on the ridge. She would be a good border patrol agent—if they survived the night.

"He's up there!" the sheriff yelled, pointing a powerful flashlight at the ridge. "By the water tower. It's Denny and Cordelia!"

Lightning ricocheted around the canyon again. Earl whined. A scream came from the direction of the ridge and the sheriff saw Cordelia collapse to the ground. Denny started marching toward the sheriff and his crew.

"Are you sure it's him?" Beatrice asked. "He looks funny."

"Funny how? Like a clown?" the sheriff asked. He hated the word "funny" on principle. Nothing was funny to him.

"No, like funny *scary,*" Claudio said. Claudio had already drawn his gun.

"He's like a zombie," Antonio added. "He's walking so slow, like he weighs a million pounds."

"Alert the ambulance, just in case," the sheriff said. The ambulance was at the fire station over the ridge, less than a minute away. A hearse was parked in town if it came to that.

Denny kept coming.

"Denny, stop or we'll shoot!" the sheriff yelled. "We'll take out Cordelia too!"

Denny walked more like a robot than a zombie, his steps precise as if on a balance beam. He held the gun straight out from his body and his slow steps were in perfect beat.

"Try to take him alive," the sheriff said to his team. "But if you shoot him, take him out, he sure has it coming. Do NOT let him touch the grail under any circumstances!"

He directed the beefy Antonio off to the right. Beatrice Baca stood behind him; she was a mom after all. The wiry Claudio guarded the left flank. The canine, Earl, was still at his side. Earl was still spooked by something they couldn't hear, he continued whining softly.

"Good dog," the sheriff said, patting Earl's forehead. The dog didn't stop whining.

"Should we wake whoever's in the van?" Antonio asked.

"No," the sheriff said. "They don't need to see this."

The black van's doors were closed tight. At first the sheriff had thought the device on top was some kind of extraterrestrial transmitter, but it turned out to be a mountain bike. The man inside had claimed to be from the agency who "verified the prize." The man had shown the sheriff some fancy ID that had a military logo.

Why would the military be in charge of a silly grail contest? The answer was obvious to the sheriff—it was all part of the greater plan. No one told him anything, other than a text that Denny must not reach the grail, but they shouldn't kill him. He didn't know who sent the text, but knew he was supposed to obey.

But then again, if Denny died *accidentally*, that was on Denny, not him.

The van had darkly tinted windows. Did the man inside know what was going on?

Earl now started barking, in a slow but rhythmic pattern, as if keeping time with some cosmic metronome.

Denny kept coming. He was heading straight toward the grail, staying in the middle of the dirt road as if guided from above. Cordelia screamed his name, but he didn't respond.

"Denny, stop right there!" Sheriff Diamond yelled. Denny was now forty yards away and the Sheriff noticed that Denny had his eyes closed. Had they been closed the whole time? "That's an order. The grail ain't worth dying for. It's all some kinda bullshit."

The sheriff could now arrest Denny on a trespass charge alone. With another step, the sheriff could hang a "refusal to obey a lawful order" on Denny which would give them grounds to shoot to wound at least. With a second step, they had grounds to shoot to kill, despite what the text had ordered.

The UFO was still hovering above the ridge, the screeching sounds of the UFO were now at an audible frequency that made their skin crawl. The sheriff turned and shouted at Antonio, "Tackle him!"

Antonio had played middle linebacker for the Lordsburg High Mavericks. Antonio holstered his gun and headed toward Denny from the side, going for a tackle, just as they'd done in practice on that dirt field. Denny continued the robot-like slow march toward the grail. He ignored the beefy deputy on his flank.

Antonio dove toward Denny's legs, but it seemed like a switch was turned on from slow to fast. Denny whipped around and shot at him. Antonio went down face first, not moving.

Eyes still closed, Denny silently turned back toward the grail and kept walking. Earl now barked wildly. The Sheriff didn't want to release Earl and put his dog in danger, so he turned to Beatrice and told her to take the shot. "Phasers on stun," he said. Their code for a shot in the leg.

She fired.

Distracted by the barking dog and the glare of the drone's spotlight, her shot went wild. Denny, without missing a step, pointed his gun directly at Beatrice and fired. She went down

11

hard. Was she dead? What would happen to her daughters? The sheriff didn't have time to find out.

"Claudio!" the sheriff yelled. "It's all you. Take him out!" Claudio fired. He was supposed to be the sharpshooter of the bunch. Every shot missed Denny as if he had some kind of a force-field that deflected the bullets. Eyes still closed, Denny fired a single shot at Claudio's general direction. Even though it hit him, Claudio took another step from sheer momentum and then fell to the ground.

Denny didn't change his expression.

No, Denny definitely wasn't funny anymore. It was now just Sheriff JC Diamond and Earl the German Shephard.

"You don't want to do this, Denny," Sheriff Diamond said. He gestured to Earl to stay and put both of his hands on his weapon. The dog stayed but didn't stop barking. He could live without his deputies, but he couldn't live without Earl. He had been Sheriff for years, and while he had drawn his weapon before, this would be his first shoot-out. About time.

He had always thought he would take Denny down for good, sooner rather than later, and now it would be his chance. It had to be part of the plan.

Denny kept walking toward him, his weapon out...

The sheriff lifted up his gun, ready to fire...

The sheriff heard the door of the van open. He heard footsteps behind him but dared not take his eyes off Denny. He sure hoped that the guy in the van was on their side.

The sheriff took a final deep breath as he stared at Denny, this was it.

Suddenly Earl stopped barking and the UFO vanished, disappearing back over the ridge. The pink spotlight was gone from the grail. Even the water tower went dark.

Before the sheriff could squeeze the trigger, Denny dropped the gun and collapsed. If he was the marionette, the puppeteer had loosened the strings.

"Denny!" Cordelia's wail echoed through the rocky hills. "You killed him!"

The sheriff had a clean shot, but Denny was clearly on the ground, his hand off his gun. The sheriff could no longer claim self-defense if Cordelia was somehow recording this.

"I didn't do shit," the sheriff said as he hurried over to Denny and slapped cuffs on the prone man from behind.

He looked over at his deputies. They were still breathing. That was a good sign. "Hang in there! The ambulance is on its way!"

Right on cue, an ambulance pulled into the compound after speeding from the other side of the hill.

"Three down," he shouted to the two EMTs as they emerged out of the ambulance. Denny was down too, but he didn't count.

"Nothing happened," said a voice behind him.

The stranger was in his late twenties, Asian, and dressed in a black jacket over one of those tight black cycling jerseys with a small icon over the left breast. His black hair was long, and sweaty, as if he'd just run a mile.

Now that he had a good look at him, the sheriff noticed the stranger had a scraggly beard, and a lanyard with some kind of picture badge featuring a blurry photo. If he worked for the military, he was clearly not active duty. The nearby bases—Holloman Air Force Base, White Sands Missile Range and the ones over in Arizona—all had civilian employees. This guy must be one of them, and not one of *us*. The sheriff hated him at first sight.

"Nothing happened? What the hell are you talking about?" the sheriff growled at the stranger.

"Nothing happened with the *grail*." The stranger was talking into his oversized phone. He finally noticed the sheriff's deputies down on the ground. "Oh my God! This wasn't supposed to happen! Are your deputies all right?"

"They're going to be fine," an EMT said. "None of these wounds looks fatal if we get 'em to the hospital."

The stranger listened to someone on his phone. "All right, I'll let you know. I'll put the sheriff on."

The stranger handed the phone to the sheriff. "You better take this, it's the big boss."

The sheriff frowned and took the call. This stranger wasn't one of them, but he had a line to the big boss and that bothered the sheriff. The sheriff himself hadn't talked to the boss in years. Who was this guy?

13

"We're gonna say it's a military drone, right?" the sheriff said and then nodded at the response. He recounted the story into the phone, nodded again and handed the phone back to the stranger, who listened for a moment and then hung up.

It still didn't make sense, but it was becoming a little clearer. Just a little.

"What was supposed to happen?" the sheriff asked, his attention torn between his squad and the stranger. "Who the hell are you anyway?"

"That's not important right now." The man moved to the grail and looked puzzled. He hadn't noticed Denny's body on the other side of the ambulance.

The EMT shooed the sheriff away, so the sheriff walked closer to the stranger and the grail.

"I'm so sorry, this wasn't supposed to happen!" the man said again. "None of this."

"Was that one of *our* drones up there over the water tower?" the sheriff asked.

"We do a lot of work with drones," the stranger said. That didn't really answer the question of course. "That guy was supposed to trigger the grail. Are your men all right?"

The sheriff winced by the man's use of the word "trigger." This stranger obviously didn't get it, whoever he was.

The EMTs attended to his downed troops, but the immediate crisis was over. The deputies were alive, for now, and probably would survive. "They're stable," an EMT said.

"Do you want us to take the shooter to the hospital?" the other one asked the sheriff.

"No, Denny can die right here."

"*Denny?*" The stranger knew the name. He walked around the ambulance and saw Denny lying in the dirt. "Oh my God, you've got to help him."

"He wasn't shot," the sheriff said. He just fainted. I don't care who you are, he shot my men and that wasn't part of no plan, text or no text. It's my bust. He dies, he dies."

"Sheriff, that guy you want to let die was clearly affected by the grail." The man was really upset. He clearly wasn't one of *them.* "He didn't know what he was doing. This wasn't supposed to happen!"

"I don't care," the sheriff said. He took off his sunglasses at last, if only to make eye contact with the stranger. "The big boss says I've got to keep him in custody and make sure he never comes close to here again. He might trigger the grail for real next time and the whole world will go to hell."

The stranger nodded as if he finally understood. The sheriff put his glasses back on.

The EMTs loaded the fallen deputies into the ambulance and sped away.

"What was supposed to happen today?" the sheriff asked the stranger. "No one tells us anything way out here at the end of America. You can tell me the real truth now that everyone else is gone. I won't tell the big boss."

The stranger was trying to revive Denny. "Is there any way you can release your prisoner to me?"

The sheriff pointed his gun directly at the stranger.

"I don't care who the hell you are. You're alone. My county, my courthouse. Unless you have a court-order taking custody of *my* prisoner, he's going to Hidalgo County Detention Center, here in Lordsburg. Text or no text. We do things differently out here. This is Lordsburg, baby."

The man looked at his phone one more time, and then back at the gun. "Your bust, sheriff."

Still on the ground, Denny finally revived. He strained to lift his neck, opened his eyes and stared blankly at the sheriff. "Did I win?"

"You won a life sentence. You shot three cops," the sheriff said. "I should shoot your ass right now."

"I don't have any *recollection* of that."

"That makes sense," the stranger said.

Denny stared at the stranger, recognizing him. "You!"

"Not now, Denny," the stranger said, putting a finger to his lips indicating silence. He glanced at his phone one last time. "I'm going to do everything I can to get you out, but it might take a while."

"Do you know him?" the sheriff asked the stranger.

"He used to work with me on base."

"This piece of shit mether? I just know him as Denny. He's one of the usual suspects that somehow never gets popped for good even though we know he's dirty. Gonna do a little search incident to arrest if you don't mind."

The stranger nodded. "Like I said, your bust sheriff. Denny, I'm going to try to get you out."

The sheriff holstered his gun, came over to Denny and put a foot on his back. He gave a look over at the stranger and realized that he'd have to do this by the book. "You have the right to remain silent. Anything you say can be used against you in court. You have the right to talk to a lawyer..."

"I want my lawyer!"

"Who's your lawyer?" said the sheriff.

"Call my sister, Denise Song," Denny said to the stranger. "Find her for me. She's my lawyer, I'm not saying shit without her, I know my rights."

"*Denise Song?*" The stranger smiled a knowing, guilty smile. "It all makes sense now, why the grail didn't trigger. Sheriff, you can hold him for the moment, but I'll find his sister. Denny, I promise you. This wasn't supposed to happen!"

The stranger tapped on his phone. "Find Denise Song," he said out loud to his large phone that looked like it could be used as a laser. He smiled when he saw the result.

Chapter 3
Wednesday, July 8

"Young lady, I'm sorry, but no unaccompanied minors can be here at the memorial wall." Hotspur, the cemetery guard at Encantado Gardens, scolded the petite woman in front of him. The memorial wall was littered with pebbles, flowers and toys—usually toy arrows for some reason. Had this girl left such an offering? Hotspur was still hoping to become a real cop someday. He needed to prove himself here on the literal graveyard shift this afternoon. "Is your mother around?"

"I'm not a minor," the girl said. "I'm a lawyer. *Kinda.*"

"What's your name?"

"Denise."

Barely five feet tall, this Denise probably didn't weigh over a hundred pounds in her goth clothes and matching black running shoes. She had an accent of pink on a few strands of her long black hair which was tied into a bun, and a similar streak on her shoes. In her dark colors and round glasses, she could be the someone who hung out at cemeteries for fun. He noticed the barest hint of crows' feet around her eyes; perhaps she was older than she looked.

Hotspur made sure his Taser was activated; in case Denise was a modern-day witch on a scavenger hunt. She might seem mild-mannered, but there was definitely something suspicious about her. People shouldn't wear black in the heat of the afternoon in Albuquerque. It was almost a hundred degrees out.

"Who are you here to see, miss?" the guard asked, probing.

"My cousin Marley Cruz Shepard," the older-than-a girl said. "He's right up there in the corner."

The guard looked at the shiny white brick. "You don't look like a Cruz," he said. "Or a Shepard. *What* are you?"

This big white cop was asking about her ethnicity, his racism painfully obvious. "I'm part Asian. Korean. I'm also part Hispanic. And some other stuff I'm not sure about."

Hotspur looked up at the brick with vague recognition. "Marley Cruz, he was a school shooter or something down south. The one with the crossbow, right?"

That explained the toy arrows then. His supervisor had warned him about the "Marley Fan Club." Like the graves of the Columbine shooters, Marley's memorial brick had become something of a beacon for the lost souls of New Mexico. He was an unlikely hero, and possible role model to losers everywhere. A weird girl in black coming to see this memorial certainly aroused his suspicion. Hotspur flipped on his lapel cam.

"He's a bad guy," Hotspur said. He looked down at the various offerings on the ground. "Did you leave this stuff here? Are you a groupie or something?"

"This stuff was all here before me."

"And you want to see him? This crossbow shooter?"

"He was innocent," she said. "I was there.

"You were there for a school shooting?" This girl was more than a mere groupie. His lapel camera now on, Hotspur now fingered his taser. "Were you and this Marley Cruz kid close?"

"I lived with the family. I was his nanny. He was at a talent show when they gunned him down. He didn't kill anyone."

Was she lying? Hotspur liked to play detective. He *detected* that something wasn't quite right with the girl. He usually worked guarding Walmart parking lots, checking IDs to bust the convicted shoplifters who'd been banned for life. He loved trading his lapel cam videos with the other guards and Denise was clearly more than the typical banned shoplifter. Still he wasn't sure what she was trying to *lift*.

She was staring at the brick in the corner, mouthing a few words.

Was she casting a spell? "What's your full name miss?"

"Denise Song."

"Are you trying to talk to him over in the great beyond, or something, Miss Denise Song?" he asked.

"Kinda," she said.

"What are you going to talk to him about?"

That was a rude question, but Denise forced a smile. "He's going to tell me how to find my long-lost twin brother, Denny."

"Denny and Denise Song? That's funny."

She turned to look at him directly, as if playing lawyer for real. "It's even funnier than that," Denise said, not laughing. "My Auntie Luna named us—me Denise and my brother De-nephew as a joke and my mom went with it. I think he's calling himself Denny. I've never met him."

That was an original answer all right, thought Hotspur. "Your dead cousin knows about your long-lost twin brother, *De-nephew*?"

"*Denny*. My cousin Marley knows a lot now that he's passed over."

"And you can communicate with him? Your dead cousin?"

"Kinda."

Hotspur pounced, feeling a "Gotcha" moment. "But you *can't* talk to your long-lost twin brother, De-nephew or whatever?"

"He's lost, somewhere in New Mexico. I've never met my brother. I need my cousin to help find him."

"Find him in that?" Hotspur pointed to a black Lexus on the side of the road. The girl wasn't dressed nice enough to have a car like that. "Is that your *daddy's* car?"

"My *mommy's*," Denise said.

"Is your mommy here?"

"She's in Korea," she said. "But I have her permission."

That definitely was a *tell* for the guard. And this girl said she was a *lawyer*, right? He had testified in enough trespassing cases to sniff out a real attorney-at-law. "Could I see some identification, *Counsel*?"

The young woman handed him an ID card, listing her name as "Denise Song, Clinical Law Student." He was amazed

19

to see that she was indeed not a minor. The ID listed her as twenty-seven years old.

He was confused. "So, you are a *lawyer*?"

"Clinical Law *Student* pursuant to Rule 5.110.1 of the New Mexico Rules for Criminal Procedure for the District Courts."

Before he could ask her anything more, Hotspur suddenly had an intense headache and the overpowering urge to get on with his rounds. His lapel cam shorted and the Taser was suddenly too hot to touch.

"Shit!"

Had this bitch, this *witch*, cast a spell on him?

The girl stared at him. "This is a public place, I don't need authorization to be here," she said. "I might not be a lawyer. Yet. But I *work* for a lawyer and she will be pissed if you keep wasting my time."

He didn't like lawyers, or the people who worked for them. He shrugged, turned around and then he talked into a walkie-talkie to the main office downtown which finally worked on the third try once he was a hundred yards away. "Some Goth girl seeing the school shooter's brick or whatever."

From the other side of the cemetery, he gave Denise one more look. She was standing still, as if lost in thought. Suddenly his headache came back. He turned away and the headache went away. Was this girl casting a spell on him or what?

If she wasn't a lawyer, maybe she was indeed a witch. Then again, lawyers and witches could be the same thing. Kinda.

Chapter 4

Denise let out a deep breath when the guard finally walked away. Satisfied that the coast was now clear, she closed her eyes and touched the brick in the top corner. She had to stand on her tip toes.

"Marley," she said out loud to the brick. "Is there anything new with Denny?"

Even though she was visiting Marley's brick at the cemetery, Denise Song knew this visit would somehow be about her brother, Denny. For the last few months, it was *always* about her finding her brother.

She'd indeed been Marley's nanny and had watched the boy die during an incident at his high school over a year ago. Like many young people lost before their time, Marley could still reach out to the living. Denise was one of the few people who could reach back.

Still, what she called her "spark" wasn't all that impressive, at least in Denise's mind. She certainly wasn't worthy of a lesser Stephen King novel or becoming an X-Men trainee. She could "read" people here and there, but only if she had direct contact with an object associated with them. Maybe a trinket or a strand of hair. She couldn't see dead people, but she could *hear* them if she touched something personal to them. Her psychic powers had something to do with electricity. Or DNA samples. Or both.

She sometimes had issues with electricity and occasionally burst a small lightbulb unwittingly in times of stress. And like today, she could make a Taser heat up, but certainly not make it fire. She could even give people like Hotspur a mild headache, but that could be cured by an aspirin or two. No, she wasn't much of a psychic.

21

Still, her current was flowing smoothly today. "Go see that client in Roswell," Marley said, as if talking through the brick. "Right now. She knows the location of your brother. Time is running out!"

A fighter jet roared overhead from nearby Kirtland Air Force Base. That must have upset her telepathic link to her cousin because the brick stayed silent after that.

Hotspur was now walking back towards her from the other side of the cemetery after nodding at his walkie-talkie. Denise had subtle powers of persuasion on people like Hotspur, but they wouldn't work against a Taser, and not against a gun which he probably had somewhere nearby. It was time to go.

As she turned to leave Marley's wall, her phone beeped indicating a text.

NEED TO SEE YOU IMMEDIATELY! MEET ME AT ROSWELL MUSEUM AT 5.

She recognized the number of her new client, Nastia Kowalski. Marley thought it was important to see Nastia, so Denise would go. Roswell less than three hours away by car.

ON MY WAY!

She stared at the brick one last time. "*Hasta la vista, Marley.*"

Marley didn't respond.

The black Lexus sat alone in the far corner of the dirt cemetery parking lot. It started at her touch. Inside the car, she turned on some K-pop music with sappy vocals in Korean about lost love.

She left the lot and quickly took the Lexus past the turn-off for the Albuquerque Sunport. She would be traveling by land.

On impulse, she voice-dialed the number for her mom with its long international prefix and let it ring a few times.

"Can I take the car to Roswell, mom?" she asked the ringing phone.

It was her mommy's car all right. Her mother, the famed lawyer Jen Song, had rented this Lexus for the family when she'd flown in for Marley's memorial services a year ago. In her Asian haute couture, Jen always made a statement. She didn't really know her nephew. Jen was there ostensibly as emotional support for her sister, Luna—Marley's mother and Denise's aunt. Since her mother's rapid ascent into high society, Jen Song always made a grand entrance and an even grander exit.

Before that, Denise hadn't seen her mother since her grandmother's funeral, which seemed like another lifetime ago. After her grandmother died, Jen had returned to Asia and Denise had moved in with Auntie Luna's family for the duration of high school as Luna became her only slightly evil stepmother while her mom was overseas.

"Boy are we a close family," Luna had said whenever the extended family went on trips. But Denise never felt close to anyone.

To Denise, her mother was a half-Korean Jackie Kennedy—beautiful, but distant. The beautiful Jen Song had exhibited some mental illness issues when Denise was growing up. Her mother was the one who had steered Denise into the whole "laser geishas" thing and had actually told her that the animated show was "real."

Denise knew that her mom had been diagnosed with schizophrenia, which had caused her to lose custody of her daughter in those early years. Jen Song eventually became highly functional with medication, but Denise was never close to her mom. Perhaps it was a good thing that Denise was mainly raised by her grandmother and then by her Auntie Luna—her cousins Dew and Marley's family—for much of high school.

The very last moment Denise had seen her real mom in the flesh was that day a year ago, at the car rental return parking lot at the Albuquerque International Airport ("Sunport") a few blocks from this cemetery. Running late as always, Jen showed up with the Lexus sporting a very recent and very visible dent on the driver's side. Jen had great fashion sense, but lousy depth perception and had scraped a parked car with said Lexus in the rental return parking lot.

"Why did you do that mom?" Denise had asked. "Aren't you paying attention?"

"I've got something important in Seoul!"

Denise had hoped that she could reconnect with her mother on the trip back to the airport and then Uber home. Unfortunately, her mom had been on the phone the entire time.

"Got to run, dear," her mom had said as she left the door open, kept the motor running and hurried toward the bus.

"What do I do with the car, mom?" Denise had asked. A running car with the keys in it was strangely tempting. Denise didn't want to take another Uber home to the ghetto.

"Here. Just keep the corporate credit card," her mom had said from the doorway of the shuttle bus as it lurched forward then stopped. Her mom motioned her over and gave her the card. "And *deal* with the dent in the car."

The shuttle door closed. There hadn't even been a hug, there had never been a hug during any of the good-byes between her and her mother.

Deal with the dent? After her mom was safely out of sight, the keys still in the car and the motor running, Denise sat in the passenger seat as she observed the customer in front of her talk with a rental agent in a crisp green uniform. The agent hadn't noticed the dent on the passenger side of her mom's Lexus yet.

"Something came up," the man said in the car up ahead. "Can I keep the car *indefinitely?*"

"We will just keep it on the card," the agent had said to the man. "You're good to go." He drove off.

Extend the agreement indefinitely? That sounded better than hailing an Uber during peak hour and explaining a dent in the car on the passenger side. At that moment, Denise moved to the driver's seat, and smiled at the agent.

"Are you returning the car?" the agent came over to her on the driver's side.

"Something's come up. I'd like to extend it *indefinitely,*" Denise said and handed the agent the magic card. The agent smiled as she took the card and put it through a Point-of-Sale device. "You're Ms. Song?"

"Kinda," Denise said. Her mom's pin was always 66666 after her attorney number. She punched in the code and smiled back at the agent.

The card was black, as if the plastic had been coated with a sleek metallic alloy. It was issued by the Korean Swan Bank with a logo of a black swan etched in gold on the front.

"You're good to go," the agent said.

Good to go indeed. Denise took the card and had driven off from the lot without another word, or the agent noticing the dent.

Automatic payments on the magic card for the Lexus rental had led to fifty-two weekly rental extensions, but still no stop at the body shop. Denise was always terrified that the mechanics would check on the rental's uncertain status and she'd lose both the car and the card forever.

Denise had tried calling her mom, using the Bluetooth connection on her phone. Her mom didn't pick up. Within a week, her mom's number was *unavailable*. That was just as well. The next month Denise had traded a studio in the UNM student ghetto and moved into an "extended stay" hotel that she paid for weekly thanks to Korean Swan Bank.

If her mom really didn't want me to have the magic credit card, she would have said something right? Someone was paying the credit card bills, so her mom or *someone* still loved her. She could sense things from her dead cousin from beyond the grave; why couldn't she ever sense anything from her living mom from across the Pacific?

Back in the present, Denise put her finger over the red icon on the car's console. "Last chance, mom?"

The phone rang again on the other side. *Unavailable.* Denise pressed the red icon and hung up.

The Lexus raced down the six lanes of Gibson Boulevard and merged onto Interstate 25. Denise always carried a garment bag with three interchangeable charcoal outfits, and a small suitcase with toiletries and underwear, in the trunk. She also had a gym bag with two pairs of workout clothes and a martial arts staff as well as a computer bag that contained her laptop and accessories. In the cupholder she kept a skinny silver thermos usually filled with an energy drink. Along with her phone and its charger, everything she owned was here in this car.

She stepped on the gas, heading north toward the cross-

25

roads of the *Big I*—the massive intersection between Interstates 25 and 40. Although they couldn't communicate directly, she sensed that her brother was alive, somewhere in New Mexico, and that after all these years he wanted to connect. New Mexico was a big state, and she hadn't seen him in twenty-seven years. Her spark regarding Denny was a vague ping or two on her forehead.

A few miles east, now on Interstate 40, the Lexus entered the unfriendly confines of Tijeras Canyon—the gap between the towering granite Sandia Mountains to the north and the wooded Manzanos to the south.

Her phone rang on the Bluetooth connection to the Lexus. Unknown number the screen announced. Was it her mother? Was it her brother?"

"Hello?" she asked.

"It's me," her cousin Dew said. "I've got a new phone. Did Marley say anything to you about the client in Roswell?"

"Not much. Just that I should go there right away."

"Your being psychic is like the least interesting thing about you," Dew said.

"You've never told me what the most interesting thing about me is."

Dew didn't respond. It was always *Dew and Denise*, never Denise and Dew. Dew was also half-Hispanic and the half something else, but certainly nothing from Asia. They looked the same except Dew was an inch taller, a pound curvier and her green eyes lacked Denise's Asian influence. Dew also favored a wide variety of styles—from sloppy prep to glamorous Lolita, depending on her mood and her bank account balance. Around Dew, Denise was the red-headed stepchild, except her hair was often pink.

They had gone to the same high school, the same college, the same law school. But after they both failed out of law school together, Denise feared that they were drifting apart as Dew had moved down south to Las Cruces. With Marley gone and her mom in Asia, Dew was her only family. Other than her friend from high school, Rayne, Dew was the only person who even knew she was alive.

Rayne and Dew, she laughed at the moisture implied in

their names as she drove through this desert.

The Lexus vibrated over the rumble strips on the side of the road before Denise jerked it back into her lane. She had better concentrate on the road.

"I wish I was psychic like you," Dew said.

"I'm a psychic who can't even locate my own brother without help from a fake website."

"Well, I told you this lasergeishalaw site would finally work," Dew said, referring to their web site. "It would be a way to focus your powers or whatever they are."

Now that the car was firmly back in a lane, Denise could drive and surf the web on her phone at the same time. Well, she hoped she could. Still going ninety, Denise clicked on the bookmark for their site.

The home page had a motif of "Laser Geisha Pink"—the most powerful of the Laser Geishas—holding a lightsaber in one hand and the scales of justice in another. Underneath the animated laser geisha lightsaber gif, the site boasted a photograph of Jen Song standing next to Denise in front of her law school, taken the first day of school.

LaserGeishaLaw.com was perfectly kosher as it promised free legal work from the legendary (and *licensed)* attorney Jen Song, New Mexico bar number 66666, winner of the billion-dollar verdict. Well, the verdict wasn't a billion after taxes and costs, but a newspaper had used the "b word" and a legend was born.

Jen had won the verdict for their cousin Susie, the famed golfer, after a near-tragic auto accident. The Song name was famous around these parts, and hopefully the residual glow would envelope Denise Song as a clinical law student under Jen Song's direct supervision.

"I just hope this really works like you said," Denise said. "All those other calls were BS."

"Well third time's the charm. I told you that if you promised free legal work by the world-famous Jen Song people will call because of the 'law of attraction' or whatever. Then you get to use your shine or spark or whatever to find your brother. You're feeling a spark from this new client, right? Marley confirmed, no?"

27

Denise touched the screen and it sizzled. "This woman can take me to Denny. I just know it, but..."

"You're worried that she'll learn you're not a real lawyer."

"Since I freaked out in Professor Kang's class and walked out of law school, I'm *not* really a lawyer. I don't know the rules of evidence without a cheat sheet, much less the twenty-three exceptions to the hearsay rule. I don't know if I'm ready for this."

"You're still reeling from the *cheetah mom*," Dew said. "I was there, remember?"

Professor Marie Kang was indeed nicknamed "cheetah mom." This professor demanded student answers to legal questions at the speed of light, or she would pounce on the slowest of the herd.

In that fateful criminal law class in that first spring, Professor Kang had made Denise cry with a series of questions about the insanity defense.

"If you agree with Judge Cardozo in this case, Ms. Song, surely you must be saying this, this and this..." After Kang's fifth question, and Denise's fifth wrong answer, Kang had Denise stipulating to her own death sentence.

Dew and Denise reminisced for the next few miles about their brief stint in law school. She would draw closer to her brother with every passing exit sign, and with every sip from the thermos. The Lexus made incredible time on Forty East, heading toward the sharp turn-off onto Route 285 southbound at something called Cline's Corners.

"I still don't know about this, Dew," Denise said. "Law school wasn't much fun. Law isn't much fun."

"It was once," Dew said. "Remember Team Turquoise back in *high* school. We were great. You were great. Just pretend that a real trial is like mock trial."

"*Team Turquoise!*" They chanted in unison. In the beginning they had both excelled on the mock trial team at Albuquerque Academy. They caught the notice of the powers that be and were invited to be on the state's mock trial all-star team, Team Turquoise, along with some scientist's kid from Los Alamos named Hikaru Yu, and Denise's best friend, Rayne Herring.

28

Team Turquoise was a big deal, at least to them. They'd become really close and sometimes it felt like Team Turquoise versus the world. Their coach, a cop turned law student name Bebe Tran had to channel their energy, channel their anxiety. Despite her law enforcement roots, Ms. Tran soon became more of a camp counselor than a coach, and sometimes practice would turn into a singalong.

Team Turquoise went to an invitational tournament and beat the best mock trial lawyer in the country, a tough-as-nails Native American woman named Jane Dark. Denise and Hikaru had played witnesses; Dew and Rayne had played the lawyers. In an auditorium filled with hundreds, Denise and Dew had made a strong case for the judges in five minutes of direct examination. Then Denise had endured relentless cross from that damn Jane Dark, but had held her ground. It was the first happy moment of her life.

A car honked from behind. Startled, Denise swore under her breath. She probably shouldn't flashback while driving, much less being on the phone as well.

"You OK?" Dew asked.

"Fine," Denise said. She slowed to seventy-four, sensing a cop right ahead. She was right of course. "I'm just a little on edge playing lawyer."

"You have never been scared of courtrooms."

"I think I can play lawyer," Denise said. "But what if they won't let me play?"

"Paranoid much? You are a clinical law student at an online school according to Rule 5-110.1. I even had the dean of that online school sign off on it. You still owe me for the contribution I had to make to the dean's discretionary fund," Dew said.

"But suppose they find my mom and she tells the truth?" Denise asked. "She's supposed to be my online supervisor."

"They won't check these days with the lawyer scarcity in rural areas. They'll just be happy you're a warm body."

"Even if I am ready, I don't really know this case."

"You should call your girl, Rayne. She's doing the background check on the client, right and she'll be able to help you fake it."

Rayne—her former Team Turquoise teammate and only other confidante—had become a private investigator. She was supposed to be looking up this Nastia woman online. If Denise knew the case at least, no one would give her a closer look.

"I'll call her when I'm done with you."

Dew and Rayne didn't like each other much. For a psychic, Denise could never figure out why.

"Maybe your girl Rayne the private eye can even help you find Hikaru," Dew asked, dismissively. "You still have a crush on him?"

Hikaru, the fourth and final teammate, had been an immature eighth grader, possibly with Asperger's. Dew used to tease Denise for being soft on the kid.

"I don't know."

"He's probably still single..." Dew said. "And so are you. You'd be perfect for each other. The two weirdos."

"Talk to you later," Denise said and hung up. Time to call her only other contact in the world, Rayne.

Still, Denise hesitated to call Rayne for a moment. She wanted to give the two women some breathing space in her thoughts. Maybe she was hesitating about this whole "lawyer" thing. She passed a few more ranches and ominous "testing stations" on the road to Roswell. And then she saw them, a series of political billboards for Rayne's mother, Regan "Big Red" Herring, who was running for Congress. Her slogan was WORKING TOGETHER TO KEEP AMERICAN STRONG! GO BIG RED!

The candidate's billboards were filled with missiles and flags, indicating Big Red's military background. There was even a flying saucer in the background. Certainly not a bad thing on the way to Roswell, as it showed respect for the local legends. Were aliens liberal or conservative?

Regan was such a great first name for a Congresswoman in the red part of a blue state; a nickname like "Big Red" Herring made it even better.

The last billboard before Roswell had an invitation to see the BIG RED HERRING UPBOUND TRAIN WHISTLE STOP TOUR. There was a picture of Big Red, Rayne and Rayne's nine-year old daughter, Rita.

Denise dialed and Rayne seemed to pick up before Denise had finished. "Hey Denise. I was just thinking of you."

"I'm almost to Roswell to meet Nastia Kowalski. Just saw your mom's billboards."

"I wish my mom wasn't running for anything," Rayne said. "She made me feel like an underachiever back in high school when she was only a colonel, I can't imagine how bad it will be when she's in Congress."

"I know how you feel. Any news on the Nastia woman? I'm heading to Roswell."

"This chick Nastia did live in Albuquerque the same time your mom did, and they worked together. Nastia was a stripper at a place called the Ends Zones."

"My mom told me that she was just a *waitress* there to pay for school."

"I can picture your mom working at a club as a waitress," Rayne said. "She's beautiful. I sure couldn't picture anyone wanting to see my own mom in a sexy outfit."

Rayne was probably the only person who had bigger mommy issues than Denise. Denise didn't want to imagine Rayne's Amazon mom in anything other than military garb and quickly changed the subject. "What about Nastia?"

"Nastia got busted like ten times, so I was able to read up on her cases online. I checked with some old sources on Vice who told me that she claimed to be an Eskimo, but I couldn't find that she was an enrolled member in any tribes."

"I don't care if she was a stripper or an Eskimo, what did you find out about her and my mom?"

"And here's where it gets weird. Right around the time you and Denny were born, there's border patrol records of her going to Mexico, staying there for a while, and then ending up in Lordsburg. There are some sealed records of her on Nmcourts, the New Mexico courts website mentioning an *adoption,* but the records don't say who was being adopted and from whom."

"Sealed?"

"Certain adoption records are sealed. You should know that; you're the lawyer."

31

Denise bit her tongue. "Is there a way to unseal them?"

"I can't find out anything else without a court order."

The lights flickered on and off in her car. It was probably Denise's spark acting up in both frustration and excitement. She was getting closer to Denny.

"Anything else?" Denise asked.

"That's all I could find on such short notice before my mom calls me back onto the campaign trail," Rayne said. "This case is just a restraining order against her loser boyfriend. She got a restraining order and he visited her at the museum where she works, like five times. I'll send you his priors."

Denise's phone beeped indicating that she'd received some files. "It shouldn't be that hard to get the restraining order against this jerk. Anything else?"

"I had some extra time, so I looked up someone else for you..."

"Hikaru?"

"He was working for his dad's company," Rayne said. "But they got bought out and as far as I know he's still working for them. That's all I know."

Denise knew that Hikaru's dad was a successful military contractor, so that had to be a good job, especially if they got bought out by someone bigger. "Thanks."

Denise heard some giggling on the other end.

"There's somebody who wants to talk to you," Rayne said. "I'm going to put you on speaker."

"*Auntie* Denise!" a girl's voice shouted. In New Mexico, it was common for young girls to call adult friends of the family "auntie," even though they weren't related by blood.

"*Lovely Rita Meter Maid,*" Denise sang out loud.

Denise had never met the nine-year-old Rita in the flesh, even though Rayne was pregnant with her back during their mock-trial days. Rayne had never revealed who the father was, presumably a one-night stand intended by Rayne to piss off her mother the colonel. Then again, Denise hadn't seen Rayne in person for years either.

"*Nothing can come between us,*" Rita sang back. It was a ritual between them.

"I knew you before you were born," Denise said.

"What was I like?" Rita asked.

"My daughter really wants to meet you for reals," Rayne said. "She's lonely being homeschooled, and tired of being used as a prop on her grandma's campaign."

"Hopefully, we'll see each other this trip," Denise said.

"Promise?" the young girl asked.

"I promise. Got to run. I'm coming into Roswell pretty soon. Hopefully Nastia can lead me to my brother."

"Good luck Auntie!" Rita said.

Denise hung up. She drove past a gigantic black and white sign at the rest stop that warned her to "Watch for Rattlesnakes" which was visible from the highway. She laughed. Her cousin, Marley, had been the son of Dan Shepard, the self-proclaimed Rattlesnake Lawyer. Was this the sign he had seen that supposedly inspired him to take the name? No, there were a dozen signs like it all over New Mexico. Still, she didn't stop, just to be on the safe side.

There were rattlesnakes everywhere, even in her head. Denise didn't like guns, so she carried a six-foot wooden staff for protection. A screw in the middle of the staff allowed it to break down into two pieces, so she could store it in her gym bag.

Talk softly and carry a big stick, even if you had to take it out of a gym bag and screw it together.

It was five o'clock sharp and Roswell had the slightest hint of a rush hour for a small city. Denise slowed down as she hit the city limits at a WELCOME TO ROSWELL sign with a glowing 3D UFO colliding with a corner of the signpost.

Unfortunately, the sculpture had been tagged with the letters CTR. *Crazy Town Roswell.*

Crazy Town Roswell, indeed. Roswell had survived off oil and agriculture for decades but then hit the motherlode with extraterrestrial tourism. All those tourists were on the Main street right now.

Unfortunately, sometimes her spark wasn't really like radar; more like *sonar* and the water was muddy today. The desert highway became four lanes with a median: Main Street. This boulevard could be the main street of any American midsized city. There was a Sam's Club, a Target, nice and not-so-nice hotels and almost every fast food joint known to man. Other than the plastic sculptures of little green men on every corner, this could be Anywhere, America.

At the next light, the exit for the gothic walls of the New Mexico Military Institute, the ping on Denise's left temple grew worse. Nastia was in trouble. On cue, Denise heard the beep of a new text.

AT MUSEUM.

ALMOST THERE, Denise texted back.

Roswell had a surprisingly modern art museum right on Main Street, north of Roswell's downtown. Nastia must work on the janitorial staff and was cleaning up for the night. The museum itself was adobe and fit in more with chic Santa Fe than here in the heart of the "Little Texas" part of New Mexico.

Denise realized that this was also a crime scene, well the site of the other party's violations of a restraining order. She was wary that he would show up again.

Denise parked the Lexus and took her staff out of her gym bag. She screwed the halves together. It was time to watch for rattlesnakes.

An elderly woman answered Denise's knock on the museum door. Nastia was not what Denise had expected. The woman was stout and had high cheekbones, perhaps she was an Eskimo after all. She had a tattoo in Olde English Script on her arm—GROUNDLINGS. That was one she hadn't seen before.

Denise wasn't sure what it meant. Were they a gang or an improv group? Next to the script, small letters in plain English—BITCH GF.

On closer examination, she could see that the BITCH GF was crossed out. Presumably that meant someone didn't consider her a girlfriend or a bitch anymore.

"Nastia Kowalski?" Denise asked. "I'm Denise Song."

"You must be the legal ninja." The woman had a strange accent, a cross between Native American and Russian, mixed with the Texas twang of Roswell. Nastia's dark hair covered part of a skull tattoo—only the letters UT could be seen. This woman did not look like a Texas Longhorn fan.

Denise sensed a strange energy, a psychic energy, coming from Nastia. Denise could tell that this woman once had direct contact with her brother, but a long time ago in a town far away.

"It's *Laser Geisha Law*. How can we help you, Ms. Kowalski?" Denise asked, and then went with a lie. "My mother said good things about you."

"Then she doesn't know me. Or you're lying. That doesn't matter. This is like totally free, right?"

"Well, I'm also hoping you can help me find someone. Do you know a Denny Song?"

"Of course I do, I raised him for a while," she said. "Is he like your long-lost brother or something?"

"*Kinda.*"

Chapter 5

There was silence for a moment. Denise felt a vague electrical field even from outside the door. Nastia once had a spark to her, but years of abuse and drugs had dulled it. Denise couldn't read her, but felt *something*...

"I don't know about this," Nastia said. "You look pretty young."

This woman could be the last best chance to find Denny. Time to play lawyer, or at least a clinical law student pursuant to Rule 5-110.1. "There will be no charge for our services. Since you are employed, you might not qualify for the legal aid or the public defender. A different lawyer might charge you two-hundred dollars an hour for your case."

"And you're still free, no? No money down?"

"Everything is free. Just give me some information. You needed help with a restraining order?"

Nastia took another moment to judge. Cop cars raced down Main Street. Nastia shuddered reflexively. Denise knew that this woman had been in the back seat of more than a few cop cars. Those were prison tattoos on her arms and neck.

"Yeah, I need an extension of the restraining order against Fally," Nastia said. "My ex. He knows I'm alone here cleaning, and we can't turn the alarm on."

"Fally?"

"It's short for Falstaff or some funny old English name like that. People have weird names where he's from."

"Is he in a gang?"

"Yeah they're called the *Groundlings.* They're like all over the state, all over the *planet* maybe."

Nastia's electrical field spiked, indicating stress. Denise had to step back. She surmised that this man Falstaff aroused deep emotions in the poor woman, and it increased the charge in her spark. After a moment the charge dissipated, and Denise grew closer.

"What do the Groundlings want?"

"Fally doesn't want me to testify in court tomorrow at our restraining order hearing, because it makes him look weak or whatever. He used to work here with me, till he got fired."

On the other side of the door the museum was small and illuminated by the red safety lights. A Georgia O'Keeffe hung among paintings by artists she recognized from her one art history class in college. As for her client, Nastia had a tattoo of an iris on her neck that could have been inked by O'Keeffe herself. While Denise sensed danger, she figured she could handle a small-town museum and its janitor.

"I like your tattoo," Denise said.

Nastia smiled, but still hesitated, her field weakened some more. Denise moved closer. Without another word, Denise shook Nastia's hand. The contact cancelled much of the negative energy coming from the other woman. Nastia pulled her inside the threshold, then closed the door behind them.

"I can't lose this job," Nastia said. "I love this job. It took me forever to get back on track after I got paroled the last time. I can't let Fally mess up my life again."

"I won't let that happen," Denise said. She needed to keep this woman relaxed. "I like *your* place."

"Do you want to see *my* museum?"

"I'd love to."

Nastia gave Denise a quick tour of the museum and pointed to a small room in the back labeled WOMEN'S PRISON ART COLLECTIVE GALLERY. One painting showed a flying saucer hovering above a prison rec yard, with the women looking up with rapture. It was Diego Rivera meets the *X-Files.*

Just by looking at that painting in the gallery, Denise felt something. She then touched the frame. "You did this," she said.

"You like?"

"You've got talent," Denise said.

"I *did*."

Suddenly, they heard a loud knocking on the back door of the museum.

"That's him!" Nastia said. "And he knows the alarm code. He used to be a guard here till he got fired."

Denise nodded. "I'll handle this." She gestured to Nastia to remain behind her and then opened the back door to reveal Fally in the flesh. Fally was morbidly obese in his so-called "wife-beater" tank top, but still able to move like a Sumo wrestler. The museum floor literally shook under his feet, some sculptures vibrated on their perches.

Sure enough, he had the same GROUNDLINGS tattoo. The three bloody tear drops under his eyes showed that he must have earned his stripes. He was clearly not impressed by the petite young woman in charcoal with a pink streak in her hair who blocked his path.

"Where's my wife?" he yelled. "I got to see her!"

It was hard to describe what she sensed from Fally. It wasn't a distinct spark like hers or Nastia. It was more like *static*, as if he'd been rubbing his feet on a shag carpet before coming inside. She could literally feel his anger.

Then again, there might be nothing electrical about him. He could just be an asshole.

Instinctively, Denise went into her defensive posture, the wooden staff at ready. "She doesn't want to see you. Not until court."

Fally laughed and pushed the staff away with a flick of his wrist. "You better move it, girl." He then tried to use his size and barrel right through her. He outweighed Denise by two hundred pounds.

She wasn't a laser geisha, but she wasn't chopped liver either. Denise dodged left, swung her staff expertly and took him down with a single blow to the knee cap. He fell forward. She then used leverage to put the staff over his back, before switching hands and rotating the staff so it was at the base of the man's skull.

The museum sculptures wobbled, but none of them fell over.

"You were saying," Denise said to the man beneath her.

Nastia hurried over to the door, after steadying one or two sculptures.

"Oh my god, don't kill him," Nastia said, shocked. "How did you do that?"

"Practice," Denise said. She'd taken a week-long "women's self-defense course" from someone who claimed to have trained with the late women's MMA fighter Heidi Hawk. It might actually have been *the* Heidi Hawk in the flesh hiding her identity.

The instructor had told her to never take her eyes off an opponent, but Nastia now touched Denise on the arm. "Let him go," Nastia said.

"Are you sure?" Denise asked.

"I still love him," Nastia whimpered. "I don't want to see him anymore, but I don't want him locked up or dead."

Denise lifted the tip of the staff but did not lend a hand to help the man up.

Jumping up with surprising dexterity, he now tried to tackle Nastia. Denise spun her staff around one more time and tripped him. Fally fell so hard that a vase did fall off of its perch and landed on top of his chest. The vase didn't break.

Denise held her staff an inch from his eye. Fally whimpered, and gently put the vase on the floor.

"Who the hell are you?" Fally asked.

"*Laser Geisha Law*, it's what we do. I'm representing Nastia in court, tomorrow." Denise had been careful to say "law" and not "lawyer." She was a laser geisha not a lawyer after all. "Are we cool?"

"We're cool, geisha girl."

She let Fally up but kept the staff at the ready. "This isn't the last of this." Fally said as the door closed behind him. "See you in court. You better stay the hell out of our way, little girl."

"See you in court," Denise said to the closed door.

Nastia wiped away a tear. "Thank you. Sometimes I have mixed feelings about him, he provided for me for a while. But I know I should never have let him into my life. And I hate his damn family, they're worse than a gang."

That would explain the tattoo. Denise had a bad feeling

39

about these Groundlings, whoever or whatever they were.

"You're still going to testify in court, right? If you don't get that restraining order extended, he'll kill you. I can't be around all the time."

Nastia shivered. "I guess I have to."

Denise helped Nastia put the vase back on its pedestal. Hopefully no one else would notice the slight crack near the lip. She turned it so the crack faced the rear. Denise looked around. "Is this all on surveillance camera?"

"I shut them off during my shift. Let's just say this has happened before."

The two of them cleaned up the rest of the museum. Denise's skills with the staff helped her in wielding a mop. After they were done for the evening, they sat on a bench in front of Nastia's painting. Nastia's electric field had finally dissipated, she was finally relaxed. Even the painting lightened in color. Denise knew she had to tread lightly.

"You said you knew my family—my mom, and my brother?"

Nastia nodded. "I knew your mom like a million lifetimes ago. We were friends when you were born."

This time Nastia's painting vibrated on the wall. Was Nastia doing that, or Denise? "And you knew my brother? We were separated at birth. I didn't even know he was alive until a year ago."

"Denny?"

"He still goes by that name, good. You know him?"

"I was like his stepmother. I was the one who took him on the day he was born. On the day you *both* were born."

Chapter 6

Denise felt Nastia's field spiking up again, the painting growing darker again like a discount Dorian Gray. "Are you OK?" she asked.

"I'm starving," she said. "I can tell you over dinner. I've always wanted to go to the Oil Baron."

They got in the Lexus—Denise's first passenger ever—and Denise drove the woman to the *Oil Baron,* the nicest place in Roswell. On the outside, the building looked like an adobe palace designed by Frank Lloyd Wright. Inside, the marble bar with brass railing could pass for a private country club's bar in Dallas, not that she'd ever been to one.

It was late, but they could order food at a table near the bar. The middle-aged white men in bolo ties and cowboy hats were doing million-dollar deals over a whiskey sour or two or three. The hostess, who could pass for a young Dolly Parton, gave the two women a dirty look after she seated them. "Are you sure y'all will be umm... *comfortable* here?"

"I'm her lawyer," Denise said. "We're talking about a case."

Denise flashed the magic credit card.

"Of course," the hostess said. A Korean Swan Bank credit card explained everything. She left them with the dinner menus. "We got some surf and turf specials tonight in the insert."

Denise went with the salad bar. Nastia went for the surf and turf "deluxe" and had to ask the waitress what the "turf" meant.

Denise gave the poor woman a quick lesson in etiquette, to no avail. "There's like two different forks?" Nastia asked.

Nastia nearly choked on the surf portion of the meal,

the lobster, which she attempted to eat without cracking the shell. This woman had raised her brother?

Nastia kept waving away Denise's questions, until the meal was done. "So, what do you want to know?" Nastia asked.

"How did you know my family?"

Nastia spit out some lobster tail onto a napkin and then left it on the table next to her plate. Denise frowned. Wasn't there a scene in *Pretty Woman* like this? Nastia was no longer pretty of course.

"I had known your mother off and on until she ran off with that Dan Shepard lawyer guy and everyone thought she was dead. Then she was living with your Aunt Luna and Luna was representing her on all those charges. You know your mom was charged with murder?"

"My mom was innocent."

"The charges were just *dropped*," Nastia said. "As someone whose been through the system as many times as I have, there's a difference."

Denise said nothing. She had Googled her mother many times of course and knew that her Aunt Luna had won her mother's case and cleared Jen Song's name. Her mother had always told her that it was "no big deal," and Denise tried never to give it another thought.

Nastia cracked open another piece of lobster with her teeth. "I also knew your late father, Mr. Dellagio. He was a lawyer too. He died before you were born."

She didn't care much about the other side, her father's side, of the fractured family tree. They had abandoned her back then, so she had abandoned them.

Nastia was pouring back shots of expensive whiskey. She had one too many and lost her grip on the shot glass. It skittered off the table and broke on the floor.

"That should do it for you for now," the waitress said, not bothering to sweep up the broken glass.

"*Uno mas?* For the one that just spilled."

Denise nodded and pointed to her purse, indicating that she had this expense covered. The waitress complied and brought one more.

Nastia was red faced and smiling. Time to strike. "So how did you get involved with my brother?" Denise asked.

"I was the one who rode the bus with your mom down to the border to meet your grandfather when she was pregnant with you guys. I didn't want to risk going across the border those days, because I was a parolee and Border Patrol can be weird about that at the check point. I waited on the American side while your mom met up with your grandfather. Your mama went into labor on *this* side, just to make sure you'd both be like citizens."

Her mother had never mentioned this part of the story, but she knew a vague story of her birth. Her late grandfather, a doctor, had delivered her on the American side and Denny had died in birth. Or so everyone had thought.

"You were there, like *right there*, when I was born, when *we* were born?"

"Jen Song, I mean your mama, had left her phone on the Mexican side, and I was a contact. I guess your other aunt, what was her name... Selena, called me and said where they were going back to the American side, in El Paso. She wanted me to pick your mama up or whatever, just in case."

"Seriously? I never heard that."

"I found them in El Paso in a parking lot, found *you both* there, but it was crazy. There were cop cars everywhere and like I said, I had a warrant in Texas that I didn't tell your mom about. I watched your grandfather, the Mexican doctor, deliver both of you in the back of a station wagon. I heard your mama say Denny's name and then say your name Denise."

"I knew that much."

"Well here's where the story gets weird. It seemed like your baby brother was dead, but I held some water to his lips and then he came to life, and your mama nodded at me so I could keep him."

"*Keep* him?"

Denise stared at this strange old woman and the mangled lobster parts and broken glass. The story made no sense. A woman hiding in an alley witnessed her birth and that of her brother. Her brother supposedly didn't make it. That might be true. An ambulance was about to take a dead baby to the morgue, but this crazy Eskimo just snuck over and gave him a cup of dirty water while no one was looking? The baby came back to life, and her mother allowed this woman to take said miracle baby?

"He probably wasn't really dead, just like dehydrated or something," Nastia said.

"But then my mother told you that you could keep Denny when you found out that he was really alive?"

"Something like that. She just gave me like a nod as she drove away in an ambulance."

"Why did you keep my brother once he was alive?"

"He was reaching out to me, with his mind. He wanted to be rescued. And your mama nodded, so it was cool."

"My mom probably was in pain after labor and didn't know what she was doing," Denise said.

"She even signed away the rights. Here I still got the papers if you don't believe me."

Nastia handed her some documents she kept in a purse, as if she was waiting for this moment. One was an El Paso, Texas birth certificate listing the live birth of a baby named "Denephew Solzhenitzen," with a "Nastia Solzhenitzen" as the birth mother. They didn't do DNA tests back then. And apparently Nastia used the name of a Russian novelist. She had some literary appreciation at least.

The next document was some kind of termination of parental rights signed by her mother, and notarized, dated a few months after the birth. She recognized her mom's signature and it was witnessed by a lawyer, her Aunt Luna.

The form was filed in some county in Texas. Denise knew nothing about family law, especially not in Texas. Why would her mother agree to this?

"Let me see that. Denise touched the paper and sensed that it was *legitimate*, not quite the same thing as legal.

"You lied to my mother to get her to sign."

Nastia's field sparked up again. The TV flickered and for a moment the cable blacked out. The oil men swore at the screen.

"The game went off!" an oil man shouted.

The game came back on, and both women leaned back

from each other. Nastia wiped away a tear from her red cheeks.

"I couldn't have kids," she slurred her words. "And Denny was so beautiful back then. He needed me. He wanted me to take him. I saved him! And once your mama found out about it, she was cool. See right there, she signed over the rights."

Exasperated by the two women, the oil men now left the premises hopefully to close their deal somewhere else in the barony. Denise didn't even notice.

"So, what did you do once you got him?" she asked Nastia. "And it was legal, *allegedly*."

"I raised him. In Mexico at first, just to hide out. I had an old boyfriend over there. Then I made everything legal, sort of. When things settled down, we moved out to Roswell, then Las Cruces, then Deming and then finally to Lordsburg where he spent the rest of his time. I got a job at a truck stop there. That was when I hooked up with Fally."

She didn't have to say what she meant by working the truck stops.

"But I know you saw my mother after that, and you didn't let her know what happened?"

"I wanted to bring it up, but I sorta lost Denny too when I got sent up to prison the first time, and then I got paroled up to Albuquerque. First with Fally."

"With Fally's family? That guy who just tried to kill you?"

"I was headed back to prison. Fally was the closest thing to a father figure back then. He was there for your brother till he went back to prison himself."

Her brother was raised by that obese man Denise had just put on the floor. Her dinner stirred up inside her.

"What happened after that?"

"That was only for a while," Nastia said. "As part of my parole, I wasn't allowed to have no contact with him. Then he got raised by our neighbor Cordelia's family at the New Shakespeare Ranch. The Dunsinanes. They were rich folks back then. Well rich for Lordsburg. I had to leave him with them when I went to prison the last time. It was for the best."

Nastia was crying. The Oil Baron was now empty of oil and barons. "Can you forgive me?"

Denise didn't answer at first. Without Nastia, Denise would never learn about Denny. "What was he like? My brother?"

"Denny was gifted. He could do anything he put his mind to. He even wrote for the paper." Nastia listed Denny's accomplishments: school, athletics, joining the military etc. She even showed Denise a picture of Denny winning the middle school state championship in wrestling at eighty-eight pounds of pure muscle.

Denise smiled. God what they could have done together, supporting each other.

"Can you take me to him?" Denise asked.

Very long pause. "I can help you find him," Nastia said. "I think Old Man Dunsinane just died, but I know where their ranch is over in Lordsburg."

"Is his legal name Denny Song?"

"No, that's what's weird. All the paperwork got fucked up in the system and then they had that computer hack. I'm like part Russian and my real name is Solzhenitsyn like the writer, but none of them clerks knew how to spell it, and then the Dunsinanes came in, so his real name is like Denny Solzhenitsyn-Dunsinane. But like I said, no one knows how to spell it."

That explains why she could never find him when she tried to use Google or even combing through official state records.

Denise felt an incredible rush. This was finally going to happen.

Nastia put her hand on Denise's wrist and squeezed. "You have to win my case first."

"Can you at least give me his phone number?"

"But you said..."

Dan Shepard once said the three worst words a lawyer could hear from a client were "but," "you," and "said." There was a quid pro quo.

"OK. I'll help you first," Denise quickly said.

It was all catching up to Nastia, the stress, the spark and the alcohol. "Can you take me home so I can rest before court tomorrow?"

Some more well-heeled patrons entered the bar but turned around once they saw the weeping, wobbling Nastia. "Why don't you spend the night with me at the hotel?" Denise knew she had to say, "In double beds."

Denise touched the woman, and Nastia opened her eyes wide. "OK."

Denise paid the bill up front with the magic card and left a fifty percent tip. "Please don't come back here again," The hostess said.

"Are people complaining about my client?"

"No, they're complaining about *you*. You make people feel uncomfortable."

Maybe it was her spark, but Denise had heard this before. She could never grasp why people didn't feel comfortable around her.

As they walked outside, Denise helped Nastia keep her balance. In the Lexus, with Nastia sprawled on the back seat, Denise drove them up Main Street to one of the nice chain hotels—*Holiday Comfort*, or something like that.

The desk clerk looked at them strangely—was this a drug deal, some lesbian prostitution, or a kidnapping? He stared at Denise, puzzled. "*What* are you?"

Why do people keep asking her that? Denise gave him the magic credit card and flashed her law student ID.

"Are you *Attorney* Jen Song?" the clerk asked.

"I'm her *daughter*, I'm an authorized user of this card." Denise showed her clinical law student ID.

"OK, I have to run it through for one night. Do you mind if we take an extra deposit on the card, just in case?"

"Not at all."

The magic card came through. It always did. Thankfully, Room 333 had two queen beds. Denise assembled her staff and put it at the side of the bed, just in case. Nastia quickly retired to the bathroom and locked the door. Whatever drug Nastia had used behind closed doors was some kind of downer, she was groggy when she emerged.

"Can I see the photos of Denny?" Denise asked.

"Not now, too tired."

Nastia safely snoring, Denise picked up her staff. She did

five minutes of martial arts *katas* with her staff—a pantomime of combat taught by her women's self-defense teacher.

Nastia would sleep through anything. Denise rifled through Nastia's large purse, avoiding the zipped compartments. She noticed a flask poking out of one compartment. She unscrewed the cap and sniffed at the opening. It smelled terrible. Was it a precursor for meth? She really didn't want to know what this woman hid and zipped the flask back into its compartment.

She emptied out some of the items she presumed were related to Denny. They were the usual photos and even a small wrestling trophy from that junior high tournament. First, she held the piece of paper where her mother supposedly signed away her rights to Denny.

As she closed her eyes and concentrated, Denise could picture her mother getting the form in the mail. "It says here that I might have a claim to someone named 'Denephew Solzhenitsyn,'" Jen said out loud in the vision to Aunt Luna, the big-time lawyer.

"Just sign it so they can't come after you for money," Luna said in the vision. "It's probably a scam. Denny's dead."

Denise didn't know whether she was angrier at her mother or aunt. That was all she could get from the form. Denise had never made it to the Domestic Relations class in law school, so was unsure of the document's validity in American or International court. Still the document must have been authentic enough to allow Nastia to take care of the boy for the first few years of his life and then allow him to be taken in by this Dunsinane family over in Lordsburg as a foster child. Record keeping in the New Mexico outback didn't always make it online so that's why he was so hard to find.

Nastia chortled in her sleep. Denise put the forms back in the purse and picked up some pictures. One was a photo of Nastia with a fourteen-year old Denny, and a young cowgirl; the three of them standing by the ranch. Denise put the photo to her forehead and felt a slight vibration.

She instantly disliked the tall cowgirl in the picture. Cordelia was everything Denise was not—tall, confident, a woman who belonged.

Denise held the picture to her forehead again and could picture the scene. She visualized Nastia giving Denny a final hug before leaving him at Cordelia's ranch.

"Your mother is going away for a while," Nastia told Denny in the vision. "So's Fally. You'll live with these people."

"You were never my mother," Denny said to Nastia. "Will you finally tell me: who was she?"

"Your real mother was a woman named Jen Song," Nastia told Denny.

Denise could visualize what happened next. Denny took the name Denny Song and probably wrote to Jen. Jen was probably away in Asia at that time, and she either never received the letter or Aunt Luna handled it. Aunt Luna probably figured it was all part of the same scam and never responded.

"Do I have a sister?" Denny asked Nastia in the vision.

"Denise."

Denise dropped the photo as if it had cut her. She carefully put them back in the purse. Nastia gave another loud snore and tossed and turned some more.

Now what?

Denise hesitated for a moment, but realized it was time to dive in, so to speak. She took a deep breath and went to the other bedside.

"You can do this," she said to herself. She had used her touch on Marley's brick, why not try it on the live body of a stranger. After another moment of hesitation, she gently touched Nastia's forehead.

Denise wasn't like Freddy in *Nightmare on Elm Street* or even Leo in *Inception*. She couldn't influence dreams, and most times people didn't even notice her. She'd done it a few times with her cousin Dew when they were younger.

Invading Dew's dreams made her feel dirty. With Nastia, she knew it would get downright ugly.

Denise focused all of her energy and was soon inside Nastia's dream. The discussion must have triggered a memory and Nastia was reliving it in her mind. After her eyes adjusted, Denise recognized the El Paso skyline twenty-seven years ago, right across the border from Mexico. In revolving police and ambulance lights, she could see herself, her infant self, being cradled in her mother's arms. Damn, her mother was so young and even more beautiful back then.

In the dream, the infant Denny lay stillborn on a blanket. The small body was lifted carefully and taken to an ambulance by two EMTs. The ambulance door was not shut. The two EMTs, male and female were distracted, tired. They were smoking joints against the red ambulance doors before the final run to the morgue.

Denise could shift her point-of-view and could see that Nastia was indeed behind an abandoned car in the alley, just as she had said. Denise spied a shiny object on the ground in the distant revolving ambulance lights.

And then Denise noticed a silver cup on the ground.

Where had Denise seen that cup before? The cup was similar to the ones featured in the 24 Grails Contest. That was odd.

The object wasn't just a *cup*; it was heavy, like it was made of sterling silver. It was a *grail*.

Nastia had a flask and when she opened it there was a whiff of something terrible. It wasn't alcohol, it smelled like cleaning fluid and motor oil. Why would this woman keep that in her flask?

The ambulance door was still open, the EMTs were still smoking. They looked up for a moment, cognizant of the smell, but soon turned their attention to each other. Nastia was drawn to the grail, poured the liquid into the grail. The liquid bubbled. She hesitated for a moment, noticed that Denny was still on the gurney and the EMTs were still distracted. She hurried over to the gurney, then poured it from the grail directly on Denny's face.

Denny opened his mouth, and some of the liquid got into his mouth. He then took a breath and opened his eyes abruptly but didn't cry. He smiled at Nastia.

"Save me!" a voice said in the dream. Was the voice Denny's? How could an infant talk?

"I will save you," a voice replied. It was Nastia.

Meanwhile, the male EMT continued his embrace of the female EMT. It was almost as if Nastia was doing some Jedi mind trick to keep them occupied.

Denise could see her own mother, still cradling her infant self, look over at Nastia. Was there a nod? It was hard to tell. If anything, Jen was nodding at the young Denise in her arms.

Nastia nodded back. The coast clear, Nastia grabbed the infant Denny and took him away, right off the gurney. Nastia hailed a cab down the street and drove off with the baby. Denise was there in the cab with them. Suddenly Nastia noticed her.

"What are you doing in my dream, bitch?"

Who said that? Denise felt intense pain, she couldn't breathe, someone was choking her. No this wasn't the dream. She opened her eyes to the dark hotel room.

"Get the fuck out of my dream!" It was Nastia, now wide awake. Nastia's arms tightened around Denise's neck...

Denise gasped...

Chapter 7

They struggled for a moment, but Denise was younger and stronger than Nastia. Denise pushed the older woman back onto the bed. Before Nastia could charge her again, Denise grabbed her staff and assumed a fighting stance like a stick fighter from a martial arts movie.

Still intoxicated and half asleep, Nastia stumbled toward Denise but when she saw the staff, she held up her hands. "Don't ever go inside my brain again!"

"I'm sorry," Denise said. "You're like me?"

Nastia snarled at her. "I *used to be*. I don't like it when people like you get inside my brain."

"I promise I won't do it again. But I need to know, was that real? Did you see a silver cup or whatever it was? Was that a memory or a dream?"

"I don't know, kinda both."

"So how did you bring Denny back?"

"It wasn't me that brought him back, if he was ever really gone. It was the cup. What do they call those cups, like with King Arthur?"

"A grail?"

"Yeah a *grail*. Just like in that 24 Grails Contest. I never saw it before, never saw it again. It just appeared for a moment and I figured it had to be there for a reason. And I don't know why I always carry this flask with me. It's kinda funny, but Fally always told me it would bring good luck. And I can order this fluid online. Don't even ask me about that!"

Denise wanted to know more about the smelly liquid in the flask, and sensed it would be important, but she didn't want to change the subject. "So, what did you do with that liquid?"

"I poured the stuff from the flask into the grail and then poured it on Denny. And then the grail was gone."

"Gone?"

"But then again, maybe it was never there at all."

"So, you can't do things like that anymore?"

"I can *sense* things. I sensed your brother's pain and I just knew that the grail could save him. That's why I grabbed him. I was trying to save him."

"So why did you *really* call me here?"

"I want to make it right with you, right with Denny, right with your mom," Nastia said. "Maybe this is all happening for a reason. I know my ex, Fally, is involved in all of this. You got to help me. This restraining order is real. I am in real danger."

The room lights flickered on and off.

Denise was a sucker for tears. "So, what do you need from me?"

"Just promise me one thing, no matter how messed up it gets, even if I tell you to stop, you've got to protect me from Fally and his gang. And I will help you find your brother. I will make everything all right."

Nastia reached out to Denise with her left hand. Denise took it. The rumbling subsided.

"Promise," Denise said.

The two hugged. Denise did feel a slight electrical charge which faded rapidly. Moments later, Nastia was fast asleep again in her bed.

The grails, and the smelly liquid, clearly had something to do with her brother. What could this silly treasure hunt have to do with her brother's resurrection twenty-seven years ago?

Denise took an allergy pill, and then another and was finally out for the night.

Chapter 8
Thursday, July 9

Denise awoke Nastia at 6:30 in the morning, hitting her lightly with a pillow. Nastia awoke and after one moment of confusion, she nodded at Denise.

"We got to get to court," Denise said. "You're still coming with me?"

"Yes." Nastia rubbed her eyes. "We're cool, no? I told you that your mom signed the rights away. It's like what-do-you-call-it, *kosher.*"

"I think the statute of limitations has long since passed. We can work it all out later."

Thankfully Nastia didn't mention anything about the night before. Denise showered; Nastia did not. Nastia wore the same clothes as before. Denise had gone with her usual courthouse ninja style—all black.

Denise had a mobile printer and printed out some documents and case law for the morning. How hard could this hearing be?

Outside, Crazy Town Roswell felt sane so early in the morning, but that could change as the temperature and humidity began to rise. She could smell the dairy farms off in the distance. The tourists in UFO t-shirts looked for fresh alien wreckage up and down Main Street.

When they arrived at the courthouse, it was already hot and muggy. Roswell must be the most humid place in New Mexico from the farms and lawns irrigated by the brown waters of the nearby Pecos River. If this was Little Texas, it was more like the swamp of Houston than the desert of El Paso.

The town's district courthouse looked more medieval

than New Mexican. In the front, a majestic green dome float-ed over the brick walls, but the more modern back of the courthouse was now the entrance.

Denise parked the Lexus as far away from the court-house entrance as possible in the large parking lot, which was surprisingly full this early in the morning. They were next to a shiny black van that looked like it had a bicycle on the roof. Denise felt something electrical emanating from the van. Nastia looked at her, she clearly felt something too. Nas-tia pointed to the courthouse. "Are you sure about this?"

"I guess so."

Nastia pointed to a few beat up pick-up trucks in the parking lot.

"Those are Fally's people," Nastia said.

Denise wished that she could bring her staff. The two women ascended a steep flight of stairs to get to the main entrance. Nastia was winded by the third step and hesitated, especially when she saw a large group ahead, waiting to go past the metal detectors inside.

"I don't know about this." Nastia said. "Are you sure you can protect me?"

Fally, now dressed in a light suit, was already inside, on the left side of the atrium. He was soon joined by the rest of the Groundlings, ten strong, who were all waved through by security. They wore polyester suits that tended toward the brown and tan, reflecting the desert outside, and looked more like a church group than a street gang.

One of the ten, a man even larger than Fally, must have had Tourette's because he kept swearing as he talked on the phone which was against the rules. The man was completely dressed in purple but was certainly no prince. When a depu-ty approached, he showed her some kind of laminated green disability card. She sighed and let him keep the phone.

The Groundlings were of various races and ages, as if someone had plucked random people out of a crowd and gave them a bad attitude. But there was something about this bunch. Denise felt a wave of electricity pass through her like a solar flare. Upon closer inspection, the Groundlings had tattoos sneaking up under their sleeves and around their necks—tattoos of snakes and tentacles wrapped around virginal maidens. Were those neck tattoos moving?

Nastia was clearly agitated by the Groundlings. So was Denise. Nastia turned back to the door to flee but Denise grabbed her. The posse stayed there in the atrium, watching Denise and Nastia as they waited in line to pass security.

Denise and Nastia finally made it to the security checkpoint comprised of a heavy-set man and a large female deputy. The female deputy had a commanding presence—she looked like a mixed martial arts (MMA) competitor who was more martial than artistic.

Nastia made it through the checkpoint without issue. She was a frequent flier here after all.

With Denise it was another story. The male security officer grabbed Denise's phone when it went into the metal detector. "You can't have a phone in here unless you're a lawyer or you have a disability. ID?"

Denise flashed her clinical law student ID.

"Do you work for a lawyer?" the male guard asked. "Only lawyers are allowed to bring their phones in."

"I'm a clinical law student under Rule 5-110.1 of the New Mexico Rules of Criminal Procedure for the District Courts," Denise said by rote. "My *supervising* attorney is on her way. Look for a well-dressed Asian woman named Jen Song."

"I don't know her," the guard said.

Nastia signaled to the female deputy. "She's with me," Nastia said. "She's my *lawyer*."

The female MMA deputy gave her the benefit of the doubt. "Court is downstairs."

"I'll look for that other lawyer," the male deputy chimed in. "The *songbird,* if and when she gets here."

"We might be done before she gets here," Denise said.

The Groundlings hadn't moved. Their ears perked up. "She looks like Denny," the purple man said.

"Yeah, Prospero," Fally replied. "That's why we're here."

A guard announced that the air conditioning was out, but they were working on it. Denise took a moment to get her bearing, hoping the AC worked somewhere in the building.

From a guard she learned that the domestic violence/

restraining order hearing would be held in the basement, in one of the cramped magistrate courtrooms. The Groundlings clearly wanted to get ahead of Denise and Nastia, they had already crowded ten in a single elevator.

When Denise and Nastia found the courtroom in the basement, the Groundling were already seated inside. The courtroom air was even more fetid. The crowd made it even worse. Had the polyester ever been washed? Denise had suffered from occasional bouts of claustrophobia, but never like this. It was more of a coffin than a courtroom.

Down here, Denise had no phone reception whatsoever. Even worse, her spark reflected off the walls back at her, giving her a headache.

The MMA deputy came down to play courtroom bailiff. She directed them inside to the right side of the court room. The Groundlings were already on the left, in the two back rows.

"We're good to go. But you gotta fix the air conditioning down here, we're dying," she spoke into the radio. "The courtroom is really uncomfortable."

A door opened in the back of the courtroom. A burst of fresh air came from the back, and then stopped dead once the door closed.

"All rise!" the deputy said. "The honorable hearing officer, Jim Tucci, is presiding."

Tucci was short, bearded and wore a black bowtie. His deliberate manner in the way he arranged his desk indicated that he was by the book, and the book was a long one. He was only a hearing officer and not a judge, so he sported a red, white and blue plaid jacket instead of a robe. Not being a judge perhaps made him *more* judgmental. He did have a gavel, a small one.

Tucci stared directly at Denise and played with his gavel. "Have you entered your appearance, young lady? I've been informed that there was an issue at security."

Young lady? "My name is Denise Song. I'm a clinical law student practicing under Rule 5-110.1. My supervising attorney is Jen Song, NM bar number 66666."

Denise presented him with Form 9-902 of the criminal

forms for the New Mexico Magistrate courts.

The hearing officer put on a pair of reading glasses and scanned Form 9-902. Then he clicked on his keyboard, presumably looking her up on his computer.

"I've practiced all over New Mexico and there's never been an issue," she said.

The purple man really must have Tourette's. "Bullshit. Bullshit. Bullshit."

Tucci was engaged on the screen. "I don't know about this."

"I can send you references in a few minutes," Denise added. "But I don't have any internet reception down here."

She looked over at Nastia. The woman was shaking again from a mix of fear and drug withdrawal. Nastia took one more look at Fally, and then grabbed Denise's arm. "Help me!"

Denise remembered why she became a lawyer, or at least played one at the courthouse. "It's only a restraining order hearing to you, your honor. To my client, it's literally a matter of life and death. As I said, I am having trouble with the internet down here in the basement. I can send you further documentation later today, but the rules allow me to do hearings like this in magistrate court. Restraining order hearings are time sensitive and considered priority hearings that really shouldn't be delayed."

"Bullshit," Prospero said again. The other Groundlings repeated his words three times under their breaths.

Tucci checked his watch, scanned the crowded courtroom and took off his glasses. The last thing he wanted was a riot. He sure didn't want to come back tomorrow.

"I don't have a very good internet connection either, maybe the router has melted in this heat. I'm going to let it go. This time. You may proceed, ummm *counsel*, as a *friend* of the court."

Denise didn't like the way he said counsel, or friend. She knew that if she could get the restraining order granted, it would be valid all over New Mexico, all over the planet even. It wouldn't matter if she was a lawyer or not.

Fally was at the other table, playing lawyer in his sweaty

polyester. As he was *pro se*, he didn't even have to pretend to have a bar card. He waved to the Groundlings. They waved back, like a church group to their preacher.

"Counsel, we don't have all day," the hearing officer said. "You have three minutes for openings."

"Denise!" Nastia said. "You're on."

Denise nodded at her client and made a brief opening statement about Fally's pattern of abuse. She was back in her Team Turquoise days with Dew, Rayne and Hikaru when she had first played a lawyer. Team Turquoise was there for her in spirit at least. She finished her three minutes without notes and sat down at the table. Not bad for a young lady.

"Do you have witnesses?" Tucci asked.

Denise realized awkwardly that she wasn't done, not by a long shot. She called Nastia to the stand. It was all coming back to her. Just by touching the court documents from her briefcase, Denise knew what questions to ask to make even Nastia look sympathetic.

She had Nastia testify to every bad thing that happened to her at Fally's hands. When Fally erupted in anger every few minutes, she responded effortlessly with objections, as if parrying him with the wooden staff. The man in the back kept swearing under his breath.

"Does the respondent wish to question the witness?" Tucci asked Fally. "That means you, sir."

"With bells on, baby," Fally said. The crowd let off a cheer.

"Why are you lying?" He looked directly at Nastia. Did he whisper "bitch" under his breath?

Prospero said "bitch, bitch, bitch," out loud. If Nastia could shrink under the witness stand, she would have. She looked over at Denise for help. Denise didn't have to be a psychic to hear her unspoken plea.

"Objection argumentative!"

Tucci looked at Fally. "Please keep this polite, sir."

Fally asked some more questions of Nastia. Denise objected to everything, using every objection—argumentative, leading, improper question, etc.

If Tucci had any doubts that Denise was a real law student—maybe even a real lawyer—he was over it by the third objection. Fally was exasperated after the seventh question and sat down.

Denise wished it was all over, and that the other side wouldn't put on a case, but this was only a *hearing* and not a real criminal trial. Tucci looked over at Fally. "Does the respondent wish to present any evidence?"

Fally then took the stand himself. Going *pro se*, he asked himself the questions *and* gave the answers.

"Did you ever hit her?" he asked.

"No, I did not," he answered. "Well not when she didn't deserve it."

"Why is she lying that you hit her, sir?"

"Because she's a drug addict and a whore."

"Objection!" Denise said. "Assumes facts not in evidence."

"Sustained."

"That's all your honor," he said. "Can we dismiss this thing now?"

Denise rose. "May I question the witness?"

"Please," said Tucci. "Sir, you might think you're in *your* home, but you are in *my* courtroom."

Fally sat back down in the witness chair.

Denise cross-examined him. "Can't we agree that she's smaller than you?'

"Umm... yes."

"Isn't it true that she went to the hospital on three separate occasions?"

"She fell."

"Three times?"

Fally was sweating through his jacket and not because of the heat and humidity. If he had ever had a spark, it had long since shorted out in the dampness.

"I've had enough," he said to Tucci, as he wiped more sweat from his face. "I don't want to see the bitch again. That lawyer chick neither. Nastia can have the god damn restraining order extension!"

He walked back to his seat and slammed a law book. "Why did we have to come here?"

Tucci banged his gavel. "I've made my decision. I'm going to rule in favor of the *petitioner*."

"Who's the petitioner?" Nastia asked.

"We are and we just won!" Denise told Nastia.

"So that means he can't bother me anymore?"

"You're safe now."

"You're just like your brother," Nastia said, hugging Denise. "He would be so proud of you."

Before she could reply, some rustling came from the respondent's side of the courtroom, from the Groundlings in the back. The purple man had accidentally touched the deputy while muttering yet another obscenity.

"Order!" Tucci yelled. "I'm calling security."

Tucci must have pressed a silent alarm. More deputies came in, but the Groundlings were ready to rumble right there. Would Denise have to defend her client without her staff? Would she have to be the Laser Geisha for real?

Nastia, moving toward the fray, pushed Denise forward. Nastia might have lost most of her spark over the years, but Denise still felt electricity behind her with Nastia's rising stress. The hairs on Denise's arms were standing up.

The Groundlings were actually stomping their feet and pounding on the benches, performing their own version of "We will rock you."

The lights flickered, alternating between blinding light and total darkness. Denise grounded herself on the wooden floor and held Nastia back with her left arm. Denise could take on one man, maybe two, but she couldn't handle the whole crowd, especially without her wooden staff.

Fally was now using his friend's smart phone to capture this all on camera. "My cousin is disabled! You better not hit him, or we'll sue," he said.

Denise held her ground, blocking Nastia from joining the tumult by holding onto her arm. Still more and more electricity came from the woman behind her. Could Denise actually get electrocuted from her own client?

After a few more seconds of bedlam, Denise's heart was racing to the breaking point. She feared she would join the twenty-seven club of Jimi Hendrix, Janice Joplin, Jim Morrison and millions of others who died in their prime.

"Calm down," Denise said. Was she talking to Nastia or

herself?

"Let me go!" Nastia shouted.

"I'm protecting you," Denise reminded her.

The stomps grew louder. After five more armed deputies finally entered, Tucci resumed banging his small gavel. "If you don't calm down, I'll send all of you to jail on contempt."

The MMA deputy took her handcuffs out. "Raise your hand if you want to be cuffed!"

The Groundlings shrugged *en masse*. They'd made their point and sat down on the benches, nearly breaking them with the impact. Denise took a deep breath.

"Let go of my arm," Nastia said to Denise. "You're hurting me."

The situation was finally calm. Or was it?

"I'm posting this online!" Prospero yelled, looking at his phone.

"We're gonna sue everyone in the county!" Fally shouted.

Tucci banged his gavel again. "Everybody stay in place." Tucci signaled to the deputy. "Can you check on something for me?" He handed the deputy a note. Fally and the Groundlings stayed put.

Moments later, the deputy returned and nodded at the hearing officer.

"Ma'am, I'm sorry," Tucci said in a stern voice, pointing his gavel at Nastia. "But there's a warrant for your arrest for a failure to appear out of Hidalgo County. I'm afraid the deputy has to take you into custody."

"But I *won*..." Nastia said. "But you said..."

Before Denise could respond, the deputy dragged Nastia away through the back door of the courtroom. "*But you said*..." Nastia whined.

Tucci disappeared through that same door right behind them. Fally looked down at the playback on Prospero's phone and laughed.

"Got it," he said.

"You can edit it," Prospero said. "And then post the shit out of it."

"Hallelujah," Fally said. They walked out in triumph; church was done for the day.

Denise was now alone in the cramped courtroom, still gasping for breath. The lights flickered again. She heard the door lock and then unlock when someone noticed she was still inside. She had to get out of here, before she was locked in forever.

She heard laughter coming from the stairs. She hurried up to the big atrium on the first floor, where the laugher was echoing all through the courthouse. She looked up. The Groundlings, still in a tight group, were now on the mezzanine. The wireless reception was better up there. They were looking down at her and pointing.

"Wait till you see your expression on your face as you're squeezing that bitch Nastia half to death," Fally said. "Both of you are like blue in the face. You've gone viral!"

Viral? That was not meant as a compliment.

"You gotta see yourself." The male guard at the metal detector in front showed her the video which already had over a thousand hits on YouTube. In the video, Denise looked like she was a scared five-year old. In the edited video, Nastia was being led in chains while her "lawyer" gasped for breath.

"*But you said...*" Nastia's words now echoed in the atrium. "*But you said...*"

"Let me see," the MMA guard said, grabbing her fellow officer's phone and hitting play.

"Hey girl," Fally shouted down at her. "You might be safe inside a courthouse, but like I said, don't ever come to Lordsburg, bitch!"

"*But you said...*" The purple man mimicked Nastia's whine.

So much for winning, Denise hurried out of the courthouse and stopped at the top of the stairs, to gulp down a breath of somewhat fresh air. It wasn't much better—she could smell some dairies off in the distance.

At the bottom of the courthouse steps, she saw a man, who pointed at her.

"Denise Song?" he yelled.

She stared at the man down below. Was he there to arrest her? Or to rescue her? He was a dead ringer for Keanu Reeves in his black jacket, black jeans and long hair and stubble. Keanu was part Asian, but this man was Asian all the way. Tall, thin but muscular, this man could easily be the wrestler in Nastia's picture of the young Denny—if he'd had a growth spurt.

Could it be? She was definitely getting an electric signal from this man. She had clearly encountered him before, years before...

She ran down the steep concrete stairs, tripped on the bottom step and fell into the man's arms as he caught her.

"Denny!!!!!"

"Uh, no," the man said, taking her in his arms and then propping her up gently so she wouldn't fall. "But you have to find him. He's in jail. He needs your help!"

Could this get any worse? Denise backed up and took a good look at the handsome man in black in front of her. Perhaps him *not* being her brother could be a really good thing. Could this be love at first sight?

"Don't you remember me?"

"*Kinda,*" she said.

Chapter 9

"We did mock trial together," he said. "Go Team Turquoise! My name is Hikaru Yu. I thought I was hard to forget, right?"

Hikaru Freaking Yu. She was shocked. Hikaru Yu had been thirteen—he hadn't even hit puberty yet—when he skipped a grade to be on Team Turquoise. She had a crush on her fellow weirdo back then and now here he was *all grown up.*

She was hit with déjà vu. Team Turquoise was the first and only time she had ever been on a *team* or felt that she belonged. The four of them were teenagers but got to play lawyers, got to play *grown-ups.* And then the four of them had to go through three mock trial matchups that had bonded them even further. Both she and Hikaru had played witnesses rather than the attorneys, but they rehearsed together. She helped him with his stutter. He helped her overcome her silence. By the final round, as they faced that Native American team and that damn Jane Dark, they were a real team, a real family.

Too bad the whole tournament was fixed as part of some corporate game to appease their parents. They weren't a real team after all, they were just a bunch of kids whose parents had stock in a closely held corporation. By letting the kids win, the corporation hoped to influence their parents' share in a proxy vote. Hopefully Hikaru didn't know that, and she sure wouldn't tell him that now.

He hadn't stopped smiling. He stared a bit too much, but she liked that. The long hair and scraggly beard made him look both older and younger at the same time.

And then she noticed it as they awkwardly shook hands.

They had a connection, and not just a physical one. He clearly had a spark to him as well. That must have hit him after puberty. Even touching his hand she felt a slight vibration, a comfortable spark, like being in the world's best massage chair.

She blushed. It was indeed love at first sight or rather love at first tingle. She had better change the subject, before she embarrassed herself even further. She let go of his hand and stepped back to make sure she didn't feel anything more. "Where is my brother?"

"He's in Hidalgo County jail, over in Lordsburg. He's asked you to be his lawyer and I promised I would find you. You're hard to find ummm... Ms. Song."

"Call me Denise. I remember you of course. You told me that *Hikaru* was Mr. Sulu's first name on *Star Trek.*"

"I'm flattered you remember that. No one else gets why a Chinese man has a Japanese first name."

"I get it," she said. "What's Denny in jail for?"

"Attempted murder of a peace officer," he had an awkward smile. "Only in New Mexico is a cop called a 'peace officer.' Several counts. You know the old song, *I shot the sheriff?* Well here, he didn't shoot the sheriff, but..."

"He shot several deputies," Denise said, smiling in spite of herself. "Allegedly."

"And felony animal endangerment of a police dog. He has a detention hearing tomorrow. He really needs you to be there."

"Attempted murder? More than one count? That sounds way over my skill set."

"It is. And you might be in grave danger yourself," he said. "But I have faith. Can you come with me please? Let's talk over there."

He texted something into his gigantic phone, frowned and then put it away.

"Is everything all right?" she asked.

"It will be."

"Do you still work for your Dad?"

"I work for my father's *company*, but we got bought out by someone else, who then got bought out by someone else

66

in Asia, and we've been spun off. I can't keep track. But my big boss is local. I guess. We're a military contractor. Kinda. It's complicated."

His dad, the legendary Dr. Yu, had invented the "electronic thimble" back when he was at LANL, Los Alamos National Laboratory. The thimble was the ultimate smart phone that you could wear on your fingertip. It even had a "hologram app" to project three dimensional images into thin air. The app alone would have made his dad a billionaire, but Hikaru certainly didn't act like a rich kid.

Denise sensed a change in his vibration with the mention of his big boss. He frowned. "Like I said, it's complicated."

They walked out to the parking lot where they were met by a very large man, also dressed in black. Hikaru introduced him. "This is Brutus, my ummm... assistant. Brutus, this is Denise Song, a colleague of mine."

"Brutus?" Denise asked. "That's your real name?"

Hikaru smiled at her. "Yes, that's his real name. If you're a boy named Bru-tus, you have to be tough for real."

He looked more like a bodyguard than an assistant, but Brutus handed her a folder with a print-out from a court website. Denise opened it and gasped at the police report.

"Does Denny even know who I am?"

"He can sense you I guess," Hikaru said.

"Why does he want me to be his lawyer?"

"Because he trusts you."

"He doesn't even know me."

"That's why he trusts you," Hikaru said. "I think you need to see this too." He handed her a tablet with a news website on the screen. The website showed an officer's lapel cam video of a figure shooting at three cops, each of whom fell to the ground. The figure then crumpled even though there were no shots fired. Stunned by the violence on the screen, Denise handed the tablet back to Hikaru.

"That's my brother?" she asked. "The one that did the shooting?"

"He was the only one other than the cops," he said. "Do you still want to take the case?"

"I want to see my brother."

"You didn't answer my question."

"I know," she said. "I guess you know that I'm not really a lawyer."

"It's been dealt with." He smiled at her. "Let's just say we got the proper authorization for you to practice as a clinical law student under your mother's supervision."

"Did you want to become a real lawyer?"

"No, I'm good with audiences, not good with umm... *people*. I knew you wanted to be a lawyer back when we did mock trial together. You were shy too, but you've gotten over it."

"I don't know, but I'm still shy in everyday life. Yet, when I'm in court, even on the little things, I feel like I'm playing a part on stage. I feel powerful. I love it. Then I leave the courtroom and I'm back to being me."

"I saw it in you back then," he said. "How did court go?"

"Court itself went OK," she said. "Then everything went to hell... until I saw you."

"I was thinking the same thing."

Was he making a pass at her? They locked eyes again. His spark aligned perfectly with hers. Definite chemistry, well definite electricity. But both of them knew the situation was too awkward, too new.

His giant phone buzzed again, he half-jokingly clutched his heart. He was clearly trying to pretend that it wasn't serious, but she sensed that it was. "I'm going to call them back. To be continued," he said.

"Hope so."

She shook his hand again, the current passed back and forth between them. It was a real spark, a corner of the folder she was holding smoldered. He broke contact.

They both smiled at each other. "So, what are you going to do?" he asked.

"Let me meet with my brother in the jail and then I'll decide."

His phone buzzed again, indicating a text. He frowned. "I serve a harsh mistress," he said. "I've got to take care of this. You better get on your way. You can meet him in Hidalgo County jail. Lordsburg. Just go four hours due west, and you should make it by the end of visiting hours this afternoon. If you hit Arizona, you've gone too far."

"Are you sure you're all right?" she asked him.

The phone kept buzzing. "I *was*. I'll email you the rest of the paperwork this evening if you decide to take the case."

She walked over to the Lexus in the next spot over. Hikaru closed the back of the van and got in the front passenger seat. Brutus backed out of the parking spot and pulled up next to the Lexus. Hikaru waved at Denise and smiled. "Save your brother. Hopefully I will be able to come back for you."

"I'd like that."

Denise melted into his smile—Hikaru was a smart, successful young man who clearly was attracted to her ever since those hours practicing cross-examination answers. His shyness was somehow a turn-on. She wanted to protect him and speak for him, tell his boss to, "Take this job and shove it!" on Hikaru's behalf.

Even better, he had a spark to him, a real spark. There weren't many of them out there. He was like her, and he had made it on his own, despite his shyness. This might be the man to wander the earth with.

The van went north. Who did he work for and why did they keep calling? She got the impression from his reaction to the texts that whoever he was working for wasn't exactly pleased that he had approached her. Would they let him see her again?

Chapter 10

Denise drove westward as fast as she could. After leaving Roswell, the four lanes of US 70 floated up into the high plains before descending into a narrow mountain valley that followed the shallow brown waters of the Rio Hondo. The road followed the river all the way up to the tall pines of the tourist trap town of Ruidoso. She was so excited after meeting Hikaru, her heart was pounding the whole way. There were a few more HERRING FOR CONGRESS. GO BIG RED! billboards, each showing Rayne and Rita at their matriarch's side.

She tried to call Rayne, but there was no reception up here in the tall pines. She had a better look at Rita on one big billboard. It was odd that Denise had talked to Rayne and Rita almost every week but had never met up with Rita in the flesh. She hadn't seen Rayne since high school.

Denise thought again about poor Rayne, back in their Team Turquoise days. When her mom would pick her up from practice, Rayne looked like she was going off to boot-camp. Her mom invariably yelled at her for not having her shirt tucked in or having a single hair out of place.

After gassing up at the Casino Apache travel center, the highway descended into the Tularosa Valley, a gigantic desert valley sixty miles across. There was a "beltway" around Alamogordo, and she was back on 70 again. She soon passed the exits for the massive Holloman Air Force Base at the edge of the desert.

After the last Holloman exit, she passed a dirt turn-off with a stylized image of binoculars on a metal sign. She felt a vague spark from the turn-off but was dissuaded by the smell. She realized that she had to use the facilities and turned the

Lexus around, hoping the turn-off held a rest stop. This had to be the back entrance to White Sands National Park, right? There was a lake ahead and some people walking in the sand, so she looked for an outhouse.

Not even.

The dirt road was too narrow for her to turn around. She had to keep going till she got to the lake shore where it was sandy. The water was blue, maybe she could fill her thermos.

However when she got to where she could turn around right by the lakeshore, a sign indicated that this small body of water—well small body of *fluid*—was a "Toxic Waste Evaporation Pond," for the air force base. Did they dissolve alien bodies in the pond? It smelled like death.

It reminded her of the odor coming from Nastia's flask.

Desperate, she drove back to the main road and continued west. The entrance to White Sands National Park was only a mile away and had a public bathroom. After using the facilities, she bought some bottled water from a vending machine and put it in her thermos. She quickly got back on the road.

She sped up even further as she did a straight shot adjacent to the vast expanse of the White Sands National Monument on her right. The wind blew sand toward her windshield. One dune actually spilled out onto the shoulder of the highway.

She had to stop at a roadblock and a whole platoon of military police. An electronic sign flashed: WHITE SANDS MISSILE RANGE. ROAD CLOSED! MISSILE TEST IN PROGRESS!

She pulled over to the side of the road, tenth in a line of cars. Many of the drivers got out of the cars, some smoked cigarettes. This stop wasn't that unusual apparently.

"The second day in a row," one driver said.

"The fifth this summer," another said.

"Wait for it," the first said, and he pointed to a flash of light. Seconds later, they heard a distant explosion. The lights and sounds finally stopped, and after a few more minutes of waiting, a Military Policeman finally let her through the checkpoint. She wondered if the test had succeeded or failed.

The MP indicated with a hand gesture that she should keep it slow.

As she drove west through the barren wasteland, she realized that White Sands Missile Range was probably the size of Delaware, maybe even with Rhode Island added in. She knew the first atomic bomb was exploded at the Trinity Site, not sixty miles north of here.

Further west, the white sand turned brown as she passed various turn-offs to the missile testing sites. One had an ominous name of something like Hell-Staff. Deep in the heart of the desert was a turn off to *Syrinx Mission Control Experimental Drone Testing.* She could see a hangar, a large satellite disk, and some pavement graced by a large black helicopter.

Were there flying saucers way in the back? No, they looked more like spheres with tubes through them. Denise pegged the four or five objects as military drones, the type that would go out and greet the flying saucers to see if they were hostile.

This wasn't Area 51, but perhaps Area 51 *adjacent.*

A few miles down the 70, she passed the main entrance to the Missile Range at the far west end of the Tularosa valley. The main facility looked like a small town, a Mayberry of mayhem.

At a barren rest stop at the top of San Augustine Pass, she saw yet another billboard for Big Red Herring and the family, with the tag line about supporting military families. This billboard was next to another flashing sign that indicated another missile test was in progress, back in the valley below.

There was no turning back. There never was.

She tried Rayne, but there was still no reception. After passing over San Augustin Pass, she headed downhill into the Las Cruces suburbs. She passed fast food chains, Walmarts and subdivisions. She was back in America.

She had a sharp pang of memory as the road descended. Her cousin Marley had died near here, shot at his boarding school.

"You're on the right track!" a voice said as she passed the

exit for his former school. The lights flickered in her car.

"Marley?"

No response.

She took the freeway around the heart of Las Cruces, feeling sad there was no time to see her other cousin, Dew—the final Team Turquoise member. Dew lived off campus by the adobes of New Mexico State. She texted Dew but did not get a response. Her cousin must be busy.

On the other side of Cruces, Interstate 10—the Ten—took her through the hard-core desert.

Right before Deming, she saw a façade of a fake town at the Akela Flats Travel Center. There was even a façade of a courthouse. Next to the "courthouse," a sign advertised discount fireworks. Discount fireworks at a courthouse, talk about a metaphor for her life right now.

One hand on the wheel, she googled Lordsburg and learned it was famous for being the destination of John Wayne's "Ringo Kid" in the film *Stagecoach.*

She blinked after Deming, and her stagecoach had arrived in Lordsburg. There were two competing truck stops on the east side of town.

"Where's Denny?" She asked out loud. She had meant to ask the location of the Hidalgo County Detention Center, but her phone answered anyway.

TAKE NEXT EXIT, her phone replied.

She took the first exit and pulled into a truck stop parking lot. Had she found him? She got out of the vehicle and laughed when she saw the name of the truck stop's restaurant—*Denny's.*

She frowned as she got gas and then drove west on Lordsburg's main drag, Motel Drive. The static lessened with every mile, she was getting further away from her Denny, further away from her goal. Motel Drive was a few miles of broken-down motels and closed auto-repair stores. One business boasted "direct dial phones" and "ice cold air-conditioning." The Joad family of *Grapes of Wrath* fame could stay there on their way to the promised land and not noticed that the century had changed.

Other than a relatively nice bank, only a handful of businesses were open in the downtown area. She passed a store front for a closed newspaper called the *Lordsburg Liberal.*

Liberal? There was likely nothing liberal about this place.

She soon found herself at a crossroads with the north road leading to Silver City and the south road heading to Mexico. The railroad "station" on the corner was an open shelter that could barely hold the two people waiting for the midnight train to somewhere, anywhere.

She continued west. There were a few more closed motels on the west side of town, then there was only Arizona ahead. She really was in the corner of the state, west was Arizona, south was Mexico. This wasn't just the end of New Mexico, this was the end of America.

She made a U-turn over the dirt median, and headed back east into town. The sheriff's vehicle, the biggest vehicle she'd ever seen, had been parked behind a dumpster and flashed his lights. He wore sunglasses even though it was almost dark out.

Denise froze. After all this, she would be busted for an illegal U-turn? Thankfully, the sheriff's vehicle remained stationary. She made out the sheriff's face in her rear-view mirror, and those damn glasses. He smiled at her and mouthed the words, "I know who you are."

The trip back through town was even more depressing the second time around, especially since she drove one mile below the speed limit. Once she passed the Denny's restaurant and got on a frontage road, she finally came upon a small, brick building surrounded by barbed wire. In the twilight, she saw there was only one other civilian car, an old black jeep, in the main lot.

She checked her watch—5:55 in the evening, she still had time for a jail visit, right? She knew she'd have to leave her staff in the car.

The static in her brain was overwhelming. She hit a buzzer by the front door and spoke into an intercom.

"What do you want, girl?" a tinny voice responded. "Regular visiting hours end at six o'clock!"

Girl? This was getting old. "Attorney visit."

"Please show some ID." She flashed her law student's card at the black ball she perceived to be the surveillance camera.

"Do you have an active New Mexico bar card?" the voice asked. "You need a bar card for *attorney* visits."

Denise frowned. "I'm *family*, then. For Denny Song. I'm his sister, Denise Song. And it's 5:59."

"He's already got someone here, but we'll see."

After a few long moments, the door finally clicked open and she entered the building. They didn't believe she was a lawyer, but believed she was *family*. She didn't know what to think about that.

Inside the unlit room, a woman in high cowboy boots and western wear fumbled with her purse in the small, cramped lobby. There were no guards in sight. The only illumination came from the windows and a sign that said: "Emergency Exit Only."

Denise saw another intercom, and spoke into it. "Denise Song for Denny Song."

"So, you really exist?" the woman asked. "You're the world-famous Denise Song?"

This cowgirl from hell stepped in front of Denise. "I'm Cordelia. Denny's been talking about you for like his whole life. I thought you were just a figment of his imagination."

Denise tried to read this cowgirl in the fading light; but she couldn't. Cordelia's brain was wired differently.

"I'm real," Denise said. "Kinda."

"*You're* the one who is gonna save him?" Cordelia spit on the floor "We're better off with a *real* lawyer."

Denise took a step back, but Cordelia leaned down until her face was inches from Denise and said, "Don't fuck with my man. This is my town, bitch."

"I'm here to save him," Denise replied. "I don't want to take over your town. He's my brother, he's my blood. I will help him. You have my word."

"Give me your card," Cordelia said. Cordelia unzipped her purse to put Denise's law student card inside. Was there a gun in there? Cordelia turned to leave, but said over her shoulder, "Just meet with him and we'll see if he still wants to hire you."

Cordelia slammed the metal jail door behind her.

Denise was alone in the jail lobby for a moment. Nothing happened. The lights came on but blinked off then on again. Was it closing time?

"Go to visiting room C," a voice said from above. "He's waiting for you."

Denise entered the room and saw this was the family room, not the attorney visitation room. She didn't want to push that right now. She sat down and picked up the phone and looked on the other side of the bulletproof glass to see an empty chair.

The off-white room was empty for a moment and then the door opened. When she saw Denny, she nearly fainted from shock. This was her long-lost twin? She probably outweighed him, even if he was a few inches taller.

"I'm Denise," she said. "You *might* be my brother."

"I know who you are," he said. "Denise, I'm Denny. I know that we're related. Do you know the story about how we got our names?"

PART II

THE COMEDY OF ERRORS

Chapter 11

While Denny went through the *Denise and De-nephew* recitation, Denise smiled politely. "I've heard the same story from my mom," she said. "I guess we really are related."

They stared at each other for another moment. She couldn't sense anything directly from his mind, but they both emanated so much *spark,* so much psychic energy, one of the light bulbs actually burst. It was both blinding and deafening at the same time.

She had felt a slight charge with Nastia. The charge was stronger with Hikaru, but with Denny, the static caused tidal waves to rush through her veins. She wiped away the glass shards from the counter. The remaining lights flickered on and off for a moment, and there was crackling noise from the HVAC system. And then everything went out.

Did the two of them black out the power supply? She took a deep breath and made her mind blank. Denny apparently did the same.

The silence in the room grew more comfortable as the static slowly dissipated and their sparks adjusted to the other's presence. The current got in sync, like two drummers keeping the same beat. The lights came back on. The small hairs on her arm lay down of their own accord.

Unfortunately, they couldn't read each other if they kept their sparks in tune. Time to make brother-sister talk, before she got to the attorney-client questions.

"Denny, so how did you end up here in a place like Lordsburg?" she asked.

"It's home, as much as any place. I ended up with a foster family after my mom, well my stepmom, had to go to prison. Did you ever meet Nastia?"

"I've met her," Denise said, trying to gauge what to say. It was hard when she couldn't read him. "She seems ummm... *nice.*"

"She was never a *real* mom to me."

"Did you know her boyfriend, Fally?"

"Briefly," he said. "Let's just say we didn't hit it off."

Denny continued. "He was with her for a while when I was in middle school. Children Youth and Families was called in. That's why I had to move to a foster family."

She sensed that she'd hit a sensitive spot, as her spark kicked up again. Time to move on. "New Mexico is a small state, maybe we've crossed paths over the years and didn't know it."

"Once I settled down at the ranch, I went to high school here."

As they caught up for the next few minutes, Denise realized that they'd indeed had a few near misses. He'd gone to Shakespeare Community Academy, which despite its lofty name was an *alternative* school for kids with *issues.* He was able to play eight-man football there.

She'd gone to the best high school in the state, Albuquerque Academy. She'd done a cross country meet in Deming while his football team was playing on the next field over. She vaguely remembered feeling a sharp ping in her brain that day, halfway during her run. She didn't make it to the finish line and blamed it on a migraine. There'd been a few random power failures over the years while traveling. Could those have been caused by them being in close proximity?

Denise wanted to know about Denny and Cordelia. "So, you lived with Cordelia in high school and now you're dating..."

"I moved in with her *family* on the ranch. But she wasn't really family to me. I was the foster kid, and they treated me like a hired hand."

"I met Cordelia outside," Denise said. "Seems like a ummm... *nice* girl."

"I love her. She loves me. She would die for me. But enough about me, tell me about my family, our family."

"Your mother, *our* mother, is Jen Song."

Denise had an old family picture of her and Jen on her phone. She held it up to the glass for Denny.

"I want to meet her so much," Denny said. "What's she like? She's so beautiful."

"That's an old pic. She's in her late forties now and she's still beautiful. And very rich, and powerful."

"Like a millionaire? How did she get rich?"

"She won a lawsuit for Susie Song."

"Who's Susie Song?"

"You've never heard of Susie Song the golfer?" she asked.

"This is Lordsburg, we only have the local paper down here and we didn't even have a home computer or high broad speed-span or whatever they call it."

Denise had remembered reading about a deficit of connectivity in the rural parts of New Mexico. They were probably only on "one g" down here until very recently. The only newspaper, The Lordsburg Liberal, probably didn't have good national or even statewide coverage.

"She's my cousin. She's *our* cousin. You didn't know about that?"

"I don't follow golf. Wait, is she that tall Asian girl that does those ads for the insurance company?"

The ads were technically for a wealth management company. Susie Song—her long legs bursting through a short plaid skirt—chatted with old white men about protecting their retirements on a tropical golf course. "Swing for the stars," Susie told them and gave them a link to a website.

Swing for the stars? What did that even mean?

"I guess so. I haven't seen either of them *in person* for over a year. I wasn't really raised by my mother, I spent most of my time with my, *our*, grandmother for middle school, and then with Auntie Luna for high school. My mom—*our* mother—had... psychiatric issues. She was away for a while to deal with them. Then when she won all that money, she just went away to Asia for her career."

The lights flickered again, but only on her side. Denise wiped away a tear.

Denny wiped one as well. "If I could have been there, maybe we could have been a family."

Chapter 12

It was time to move to the attorney-client part of the conversation, well the *clinical law student*-client. "So, tell me what happened that night at the ranch. Why are you in jail?"

"We found that Omega Grail on Cordelia's property, it like appeared overnight. So, we went into town to use the internet at the library to verify it or whatever. Somehow the sheriff finds out that the grail was there, and they seize her property for back taxes or some bullshit. Still we were planning on just walking up and me touching the grail to win the prize. Didn't want to hurt anyone. And then when we're checking it out, all a sudden, this UFO comes and hits me with a laser. And I got no *recollection* after that."

"You don't remember shooting at three cops?"

"Not even."

"What's the last thing you remember?"

"I was still going to walk up to the grail, and I took a step forward just to check things out. It must have triggered the UFO. And like this drone or saucer or whatever it was comes out of the earth and hovers above me. It like shines a laser beam on me. Like I said, I don't have any *recollection* of what happened after that."

Recollection was a strange word for him to say. It had a few too many syllables.

"Were you armed?"

"Kinda," he said. "But I didn't want to shoot nobody."

"That's a bad fact."

"I didn't want to shoot anyone. It's like I lost control because of the UFO and the grail."

"Are the grails good or bad?"

"They're not either. They're just tools to find people

81

like us and sorta like *test* us and probe our powers to see if we're dangerous to them. That's what the whole contest was about, I guess."

"Are you sure about this?"

"Positive. And the military at White Sands Missile Range and over at Holloman, they're in on it with the grails. The aliens can only communicate through the worm holes with neutrinos or whatever. So, they got the half-aliens and also like real *human* people here to do their dirty work. We got time, maybe another hundred years before the big invasion, but they're setting things up right now."

Denise covered her eyes. Did her brother really believe this crap? "And the grails, do the aliens make them?"

"Not anymore. Somebody makes the grails overseas in Asia because that's where some of the rare earths are or whatever they use for them. And they can manufacture them with less oversight or whatever."

That almost made sense. "Have you actually been *abducted* by aliens?"

"Not yet, but I can get glimpses of them watching me from afar. Can you get glimpses of them?"

"No, I can't."

"I can see the aliens in my dreams. Ever since I started working with them grails in the military."

"What did you do with grails in the military?"

"That's classified. I can't tell anyone, or I could be busted for like treason. You wouldn't really understand it anyway."

"Were you like a test subject, like a guinea pig, with the grails?"

"I don't want to talk about it."

That weird electric current passed through her, like he was scanning her. She didn't like it. "Stop it."

"I guess we're like two charged people and we can't read each other," Denny said.

"Please don't do that again, and I promise I won't do it to you."

He touched his hand to the window. She touched hers to his on the glass. There was a brief current, but it stopped. "Deal," they both said.

"Jinx," she said. He stared at her. "That's something me and my cousin Dew would say if we both said the same thing at the same time."

"Jinx" he said. "Then it's just like jinx, the grail. Maybe we both have to touch the grail at the same time to get it to work for us."

"I don't really know much about the grails or jinxes," she said. "I think we need to concentrate on the case at hand, the attempted murders on the cops. You're facing some serious charges."

"Whatever. What I need you to do is like subpoena all the top-secret military records, if you get them, I can prove everything about the aliens."

"You want me to subpoena umm... *them* aliens?"

"Well, I guess so."

How would one serve a subpoena on Alpha Centuri? She looked over at her brother. He was breathing heavily; his bloodshot eyes were bulging. His eyes were similar to hers in their vague Asian influence, but his eyes were... *crazy*.

There was video of Denny shooting the cops that would come into evidence. The case could not be won at trial. She would have to raise competency, and given Denny's alien fixation, he would be found incompetent. She wasn't sure what happened after that.

"Maybe there's another way," she said. Denise knew a little bit about the mental health laws of New Mexico after her disastrous run-in with the infamous Professor Kang.

But Denise now had a very real reluctance to take this case. "Cordelia said it's up to you. So, Denny, do you want me to be your lawyer?" she asked.

No hesitation at all. "Of course. It's got to be you. You can touch the grail with me, and we can see the aliens. We're the twins, the *Gemini*, like Castor and Pollux."

Denise had spent her whole life waiting for this moment to meet her brother, to be part of a real family. Now she couldn't wait for it to end and be all alone again. "First I have to get you out of custody."

"It shouldn't be that hard. Just tell them the aliens made me do it."

There was a knock on the door behind her. A big correctional officer opened the door. His badge said "Horatio," and Denise wasn't sure whether that was a first or last name. "Visiting hours are over."

Denny had calmed down. "My detention hearing is tomorrow at nine. Will you be there for me?"

Horatio held the door open. "Miss?" She had a very simple choice to make. She could leave, get in the Lexus and drive away on the interstate and never see her brother again. Or she could stay here for the long run.

She looked at Denny one more time. Their currents were in sync. It was as if they'd known each other forever.

"I'll be there," she said. She was clicked out the front door.

But would she really be there? "Welcome to Lordsburg," she said to the end of America.

Chapter 13

Denise sped out of the jail parking lot, got on the freeway and headed west. She needed a place to stay other than the broken-down motels on the boulevard. Part of her wanted to keep going all the way to Arizona.

Still, a billboard advertised the ubiquitous chain hotel, the *Holiday Comfort*, at the next exit. She'd given her word to her brother after all. The place looked *comfortable*, and her *holiday* would be convenient to court and to the freeway to get out of town. When she exited, she noticed several transients were hitchhiking near the off ramp. They didn't look at her, they looked at her car. At least it had an alarm.

She went inside the hotel. The spacious beige lobby with pine accents doubled as a dining room. She could be in anywhere America. Fine by her.

"Should I park the car around the back?" she asked the concierge inside the bland hotel lobby that looked like every other bland hotel lobby. He was a big guy and his muscles barely fit into his white and tan hotel uniform. Then again, everyone was big compared to Denise. The concierge's name badge said CALIBAN.

"No, I can't see it if it's in the back when they try to break in," Caliban said.

He pointed to a boomerang hanging on the wall. "If someone breaks into the car in the front, I scare them off."

Denise nodded. "Sounds good."

She received a call from Cordelia the minute after she entered the nice room.

"Denny called and said he wants you to be his lawyer," Cordelia said. "I don't know why."

"I told him that I'll do it."

"You better get him out *tomorrow*. I know a lot of people here. We can pay you a lot of money if you can do it."

"I don't need your money," Denise said, the Swan bank card firmly back in her wallet. "This is my *family*. And you know there's no way I can guarantee anything."

"Just get him out," Cordelia said and hung up.

Cordelia didn't say "Or else." She didn't have to.

She noticed an email from Hikaru when she set up her laptop. He had prepared all the paperwork for the case, even prepared the entry of appearance forms for her with *docu-sign*. She signed them with her finger indicating that she was a clinical law student operating pursuant to Rule 5-110.1, under the supervision of Attorney Jen Song. There was an electronic signature that was marked "/JS/".

Denise didn't know if that meant that her mother had physically signed it or someone else had clicked a few keys on their computer. Did it matter?

She noticed that by signing with her finger she had somehow cut herself on her laptop's track pad. She dabbed the cut with a tissue until it stopped bleeding. She tried to calm herself down by practicing her martial arts kata with her staff again, and doing it slowly, as if doing *tai chi.*

She still almost broke the mirror with her staff.

Chapter 14

Bored and it was only seven at night, and she didn't want to risk breaking the mirror for real. She used the stationary bike in the hotel's gym to pedal away the anxiety. She assumed Hikaru too was on his bike catching the last hours of daylight so couldn't talk right now. She messaged him a "?"

He sent her some incredible pictures of his last cycling adventures—on the white pyramid of Sierra Blanca glowing in the moonlight. This man actually biked in the snow and at night.

Another picture, presumably an old one, showed the sun setting over some desert lake, the waters of the lake a bright fuchsia. Perhaps it was her spark, but there was a whiff of that dying smell that burst through the phone for an instant. She recognized the scene; it was the toxic pond she had passed earlier today.

"Love it!" she wrote. He did not text back but did send her an email regarding the case for tomorrow. But that could wait, right?

She got a salad for takeout from the nearby McDonalds and settled in for the duration. That night in the tan, spacious hotel room, Denise downloaded the "Petition for Pre-trial Detention" sent by Hikaru. The petition had been filed by "Special Counsel," indicating the New Mexico Attorney General was taking over this case, presumably because the local prosecutor didn't have the expertise or resources to handle a case of this magnitude.

As for the allegations contained within the petition itself, while Denny didn't have a felony criminal record, the four counts of attempted murder were by definition "violent." Thus, there was a presumption that he be held for pre-trial

87

detention for the duration. While Denny lived with Cordelia at a local address, he was not a property owner and was unemployed. Besides, Cordelia's family's property had been seized by the state, so technically she had no address either.

Denise recognized the name of the judge, Shahrazad Sanchez. Shahrazad had been a court reporter not too long ago and Denise had seen her listen and type cryptic notes onto her strange device. As a court reporter, Shahrazad often seemed distracted and looked at her phone as if she was reporting on the courts of other worlds. Denise shuddered to think how she'd be as a judge.

New Mexico had a small population spread out over a big state. Back when Denise did social media, they'd even been "friends" on Instagram because the court reporter was a "friend" of Dew's. Shahrazad had a short stint as an "alt-model" on Instagram, posting provocative pics showing her piercings and tattoos against ample helpings of skin. Denise's cousin, Dew, had posted a snarky comment, something about Shahrazad being a *slut reporter* instead of a court reporter. Denise had merely *liked* the comment. But that was enough.

Shahrazad had unleashed her Instagram fury on Denise. All her fellow mean-girl alt models followed suit. The attacks on Denise for merely "liking" a comment on Instagram were vicious—nerd girl, virgin, ugly bitch—were the ones she could remember before the postings got racist.

Denise quit *all* social media after that.

In the here and now in her Holiday Comfort room, she winced at the thought that the "slut reporter" was now a judge, her brother's judge. She felt utterly alone in the room as she unpacked her small suitcase. She had enough clothes for three days at most, even though all the clothes were black— well her *cheerful charcoal*. The hotel had a washer-dryer, so she could holiday here comfortably for the duration.

This was home? Denise threw away the plastic of the Mc-Donald's salad. A piece of lettuce was stuck to the floor. What had she got herself into? She did have her wooden staff, in case she needed to defend herself, but it was still dissembled in the gym bag in the Lexus's trunk.

Chapter 15
Friday, July 10

Denise awoke before dawn to Cordelia's phone call. "What's going to happen in court today?" Cordelia asked. She repeated the phrase "What's going to happen?" three more times before Denise had fully awoken.

"I don't know yet."

"I need him out! Now!"

"I know. I'll do my best."

"So, is he getting out?"

"I don't know."

Downstairs, Caliban the concierge had set up the hot breakfast. There was a waffle machine, and scrambled eggs. Other than a handful of wayward Oklahoma tourists who had taken the southern route to California, most guests sported tan uniforms marked simply "Federal Agent" without specifying the agency. A man in a blue polo shirt and khakis had the name of a chic sunglasses firm on his breast pocket. He was pitching his wares to one of the agents.

"Your troops should be wearing my glasses that protect against radioactivity," the pitchman said. The agent tried on a pair of stylish wraparound shades.

"We'll take four thousand," the agent said.

Everyone was staring at Denise. What in the world was this petite young part-Asian woman, traveling all alone, dressed all in black, doing at the Holiday Comfort hotel in Lordsburg, America?

At a far table, one Oklahoma tourist muttered that she must be a victim of human trafficking who had escaped and was on the run. His companion thought she was a spy for the North Koreans here to smuggle people across the border. The sunglasses salesman even took off his shades to check her out.

"Why are you here again?" Caliban asked as he cleared her cereal bowl.

"A case," she said. "At the courthouse. I *work* for a lawyer." She almost flashed her ID again, but he had moved onto bringing more coffee for an agent.

Denise noticed a very pregnant woman in a red power maternity suit enter the breakfast room. The woman waved at her, but Denise had to get to court and hurried back toward her room.

Did the woman in red say her name? Denise was already out the door.

Outside in the lot, the Lexus was untouched. Caliban had done his job as night guard. The car started right up, and she drove the few short blocks past abandoned buildings to "downtown" Lordsburg. It was down all right, but not much of a town.

The Hidalgo County Courthouse itself was a block off Main Street on Shakespeare Street. It was presumably named after the nearby ghost town and not the bard since there was nothing Shakespearean about the street—or this town. The architecture was out of the fifties and not the 1600s.

Unfortunately, there was no parking on Shakespeare Street today. It was lined with pick-up trucks and old Chevys. Denise had to drive around the block again on Main and then Motel Boulevard and back again. Court days must be a big deal around here.

She had taken an English class at Albuquerque Academy which focused on Shakespeare. She played with Shakespearean puns as she surveyed the streets filled with abandoned buildings. Laws' Labors Lost. A store, a store, my kingdom for an opened store. This was the avenue of our discontent. The quality of mercy was not strained here, there was no mercy.

After parking and walking past a few more deserted buildings, she finally arrived at the courthouse itself. It was a two-story building made of bricks that belonged in the Australian outback. Hopefully, this wasn't a kangaroo court.

Denise entered the courthouse and walked up the steep staircase to the lobby area. The elevator was for OFFICIAL USE ONLY. She walked right through the unmanned metal detector. She beeped even though the detector was unplugged. Everyone in town was crunched inside the courtroom itself. It was a full docket that day—divorces, child custody and even wrongful deaths. One court fits all.

"Is anyone here the counsel for the State in Denny Song's case?" she asked around. There were a few well-dressed people in the room who could be lawyers. Not one of them answered.

A team of power-suits entered. Denise recognized Jane Dark, her nemesis from mock trial days. Jane Dark was pregnant and dressed in a red suit. Jane Dark was the woman at the hotel.

Ms. Dark was Native American and had her long black hair tied back in the Navajo *tsai*, hairstyle. Dan Shepard had once called it the "power tsai."

Denise's heart skipped a beat and not for a good reason. She'd known this princess of darkness when Dark had prosecuted her late cousin Marley for a shoplifting case. Before that, Ms. Dark's mock trial team should have beaten Team Turquoise.

There was a rumor that Dark had had an affair with a Supreme Court Justice and was now pregnant with his child. Had she been exiled to the end of the earth in Lordsburg? Or worse, had Jane Dark deliberately asked for this assignment as a way to get back at Denise? She would know about Denny. She knew about everything.

"Ah, Ms. Song," Jane Dark said in a faux English accent that tried to mask a Western New Mexico drawl. "So good to see you again. We got your entry yesterday, but we've had some trouble verifying that you are indeed admitted to practice law in New Mexico. We've made a few calls and sent out a few emails to your mother, supposedly your 'law student supervisor,' but we haven't heard back yet."

Denise heart skipped another beat. "Why are you here?"

"*I was sent for*," she said in a sotto voice. Didn't Rosencrantz or Guildenstern say that in *Hamlet*?

Jane Dark had two big dossiers. One marked DENNY SONG and the other DENISE SONG. "Maybe we should call your old mentor, Professor Kang, to find out why you failed out of an *accredited* law school. You never went back there, did you?"

"I'm still admitted to an accredited online course and..."

"But since we're up against a deadline, we'll stipulate that you're an *attorney* for the purposes of today's hearing, even if we can't reach your *mommy*."

"Thanks, I guess."

"If you weren't here, we'd have to release him. I guess you might as well stay for the hanging, I mean the hearing."

Dark laughed at her own joke. Denise was confused, they wouldn't release Denny because he *didn't* have a lawyer? No, this was Jane Dark's way of stirring the pot, as Cordelia had overheard.

It worked. Cordelia had walked in and now wormed her way into the conversation. "So, if we fire her, Denny gets out?"

Dark stirred the pot even further. "No, young Miss Song has already entered her appearance as a clinical law student under the supervision of an *attorney*, so we'll have to go forward with the hearing, or it will be deemed *waived* and he remains in custody for the duration. You understand that because of budget cuts, the Public Defender Office can't always provide attorneys in certain remote parts of the state like this one, especially if the victims are law enforcement and everyone has a conflict. It could take months before he gets someone else. If ever."

Denise sat down; her eyes lowered.

"Quiet please, court is in session," a bailiff said. She recognized Caliban. He did everything in this town. He even had his boomerang with him.

A big man with a badge brought Denny in. Denise recognized him as the sheriff from their brief encounter on the west end of town. He was still wearing his sunglasses even indoors.

The sheriff wagged his finger at her. "Slow the hell down in my county," he said. He turned back to Denny. "Don't shoot any of my other troops, Denny!" the sheriff said before roughly pushing Denny down in the front row with some other inmates. The three cops—Antonio, Beatrice and Claudio—the alleged victims in the case, also sat in the front row. Each sported fresh bandages and crutches arranged over ill-fitting suits. They eyed Denise with anger.

"Where do I sit?" Denise asked Caliban. "Which is the defense side?"

There wasn't even enough room for a defense "side" in this cramped courtroom. The tables were actually perpendicular. While Roswell had been humid, a hot, dusty wind flowed through the opened windows in this courtroom. This was the outback all right.

"All rise."

The judge was indeed Shahrazad Sanchez, her tattooed arms showed through the openings in her robes. New Mexico needed judges so desperately in this part of the state, the Administrative Office of the Courts must have waived the requirement that she have five years of practice. The judge looked lost in her billowing robe.

"Let's do the pre-trial detention hearing first," she said, looking down at her phone for guidance. "Why don't you sit at counsel table, young lady?"

Young lady? She was the same age as the judge.

"Appearances please," the judge asked, eyes back on the phone.

"Jane Dark for the great state of New Mexico. Sheriff JC Diamond will be sitting at counsel table with me as the case agent."

"Your honor, Denise Song for the defense. I am a clinical law student practicing under the supervision of Attorney Jen Song pursuant to Rule 5-110.1 under the Rules of Criminal Procedure for the District Court. Here's Form 9-901 which shows the designation."

Denise handed the form to Caliban the bailiff. Jane Dark held up her hand, indicating Caliban should stop.

"Your honor," said Jane Dark. "There is some question about the legitimacy of her law student supervisor as we couldn't locate that person anywhere in *America*. But we will *stipulate* to her ability to practice under these circumstances, as all other attorneys under contract in this jurisdiction have excused themselves because they know the officers in question. Time is of the essence here."

Denise looked around. All the other people in nice clothing had suddenly cleared the courtroom.

"We've had a great deal of difficulty getting attorneys to come all the way out here since the budget cuts on travel," the judge said. "We might be forced to improvise and use Ms. Song, clinical law student or not."

She glanced back at the phone for guidance and then looked at Denny. "Mr. Denny Song, do you agree to let Ms. *Denise* Song represent you in her capacity as a law student under the supervision of this attorney, *Jen* Song. Pursuant to Rule 5-110.1?"

The lights flickered. "I do," said Denny.

"Then, Ms. Dark you may proceed with the hearing for your petition for pre-trial detention. Mr. Song you are charged with three counts of attempted murder, one count of aggravated assault on a peace officer."

"Your honor, I am raising competency in this case," Denise said.

"Now is not the time to raise competency," Jane Dark said. "This is only a question of pre-trial detention—whether he stays in custody during the pendency of the case. The issue of whether he's competent is immaterial at this point."

The judge scratched a nose stud as she looked out the window.

Dark pantomimed that the judge should bang the gavel and the judge complied. "We will address competency at another time," the judge said. "Ms. Dark, you may now proceed with the motion for pre-trial detention after that uncalled-for interruption."

Jane Dark approached the podium. "Your honor, we call Sheriff JC Diamond to the stand. And please remember that the burden of proof to detain someone during a pre-trial detention hearing is only clear and convincing evidence."

"Isn't it beyond a reasonable doubt?" Denny asked.

Denise said nothing. Basically, Jane Dark only needed to be *clear* to be *convincing* at this hearing.

The sheriff wore a suit and a turquoise bolo tie that matched his silver and turquoise star badge. He did take his sunglasses off, and it looked like he hadn't slept in days. With minimal prodding from Jane Dark, he went quickly through how he seized the property legally which made Denny a trespasser. He talked about Denny shooting the officers in cold blood.

Jane Dark smiled. "And your dog, what's his name and breed?"

"Earl. He's a German Shepherd."

Dark produced a blown-up picture of the dog. Everyone in the courtroom sighed and muttered "Good boy."

"Was Earl in danger?"

"Yes."

"That's a lie! I wouldn't shoot the dog! He wasn't an alien!" Denny shouted.

Jane Dark ignored him. "Pass the witness."

Denise would give it the old college try. "You said he had a blank stare on his face when he allegedly came at you?" Denise asked.

"He did."

"You're not a psychiatrist, are you?"

"No."

"You don't know if he was in a *psychotic* state, or maybe a fugue state, do you?"

"No. I don't even know about no fugues."

"You don't know if he indeed believes in aliens, do you?"

"No."

"If he believed in aliens, and was acting to protect himself, he might not be able to form specific intent, wouldn't he?"

"I have no idea."

"Competency is *not* an issue for the purposes of this hearing," Dark reminded the court.

Still looking out the window, the judge now played with one of her five ear studs on her right ear. "Move it along counsel."

Denise asked a few more questions and then sat down. After the state rested, Denny tapped her on the arm.

95

"Call Cordelia," Denny said. Denise hesitated, but she had to do something.

Cordelia didn't wait, she just got on the stand.

Denise went to the podium. "Ma'am, have you ever seen him be violent prior to this incident?"

"No, I have not."

"Where could he live if he was released?"

"Well, the sheriff seized our property, but I got another place in town, the Last Palm hotel, just down the road from here on Shakespeare Street and he could live with me."

"Do you consider him to be a threat to the community?"

"No, I do not. He loves Lordsburg. He just has issues with some of the umm... *authorities*. They didn't believe him back then; they don't believe him now."

"Could you describe his demeanor on the night of the incident?"

Cordelia stared.

"How was he *acting*?" Denise asked.

"He was normal at first, and then we heard this screeching sound and some lightning, and he went into a daze, like a zombie robot."

"So, Denny Song wasn't in his right mind?"

"Objection your honor," Jane Dark said. "The defendant's mental state is not at issue in this hearing. Only whether he should be detained."

The judge didn't even look over. "Sustained."

Denise ran out of gas. "Pass the witness."

Using a dossier marked "Girlfriend," Jane Dark hit all of Cordelia's past contacts with law enforcement and made Denise regret calling her.

"Any other witnesses?" the judge asked.

Denny rose. "Let me testify!"

"You should let him take the stand," Jane Dark said. "I'd love to cross-examine him."

Denise winced. "Your honor, my client will get to tell his side of the story, but now is not the time nor place. He has things that he needs to say to the court in private. Things of national, international and *interplanetary* importance."

"Your honor, that may be," Jane Dark. "But that is not relevant today. We've more than proven that there's no alternative to detention prior to trial."

The judge must have received guidance from her phone. "He will be held in custody pending the completion of his trial."

"For how long?" Denny shouted.

"I need him out!" Cordelia added. "Do something, Denise!"

"Your honor," Denise said. "According to case law we can submit a motion to reconsider pre-trial detention under Rule 5-401 as long as we bring in new information, unavailable to us now. There's considerable information that we don't have access to."

"What information?" The judge looked even more lost.

"We can get witnesses," Denise said. "I guess."

"Who are you going to subpoena, the aliens?" Jane Dark said. "I don't think our subpoenas are good outside the solar system."

Dark walked right up to the bench. "Your honor, we're taking this case to grand jury next Friday. They will determine whether the case moves forward with a 'true bill.'"

"So, we can do the arraignment on Monday, July 20th?" the judge asked. "That's the next time I'm scheduled to be here."

"That should work," Jane Dark said.

"Assuming the grand jury returns a true bill," Denise said. Both Jane Dark and the judge rolled their eyes. Of course, the grand jury was going to return a true bill and indict Denny on all the charges.

"Anything else, counsel?" the judge said. "I mean counsel and clinical law *student.*"

"Your honor, we need to clear up the issue of Ms. Song's ability to practice in this matter," Jane Dark said.

The judge nodded at her phone. "Then Ms. Song, you have till arraignment on the 20th to clear up your admission status and we can reconsider conditions of release at that time."

"And one more thing your honor," Jane Dark added. "There's the possible *felony* offense of Ms. Denise Song prac-

97

ticing law without a license. Not to mention fraud. My investigator will be researching her conduct over the last year to potentially charge Ms. Song, *personally*, with numerous violations of law. We might be doing two criminal arraignments on the 20th and not just one."

The judge stood. "All rise!" Jane Dark said, sensing that no one else was going to do it. The judge closed the door behind her.

"What just happened?" Denny said.

Jane Dark looked at Denise. "It's such a small jail, perhaps you two can share a cell together, just like old times."

The sheriff was holding up Denny from behind, like a prize buck he'd just shot. "Can't you see the resemblance? They're twins all right. Especially the eyes."

Denny squirmed a bit and stared at Denise. "The judge knows you! The prosecutor knows you. It's like they're trying to get back at you. The whole case is rigged!"

"Welcome to Lordsburg," the sheriff said, before yanking him away. Denny could be right; the whole system was rigged. But who or *what* was rigging it?

Chapter 16

Outside on Shakespeare Street, Cordelia was nowhere to be seen. Denise scanned the area for a possible ambush, just in case. Other than a few zombies over on Main Street, the coast was clear.

This truly was the summer of her discontent. She got into the Lexus and cranked on the air conditioning, turned on the Wi-Fi hot spot and opened her laptop.

Denise took a deep breath; she couldn't do this alone. Her mom might be able to help out, she had signed the form after all, so was presumably aware of the hearing, right? Denise called the five possible American and international phone numbers for Jen Song, Attorney at Law. Instead of getting the usual endless ring and then a transfer, she learned that each number was no longer in service.

Who else could she call? Team Turquoise had beaten Jane Dark before, perhaps they could do it again.

She called Hikaru first, but he didn't pick up. She texted him to call her. He texted her back a picture of the entrance to a military check point in the desert, with a big red circle with a white line through it. It could be Alamogordo; it could be Afghanistan. She knew enough to realize he couldn't talk right now. One down.

She called Dew next. "I need some help on Denny's case."

"I've got a group project due this week," her cousin snapped at her. "My friends are counting on me."

Denise could feel a cold wind blow all the way from Las Cruces.

"I'm counting on you," Denise said. "I'm *family*. Denny is family. You have like a supercomputer. You can help your family out."

Playing the family card must have worked. "Is there anything I can do from here?" Dew asked at last.

"They're checking my credentials," Denise said, panicked. "They might even charge me with a crime of practicing law without a license, like every time I picked up the phone could be a new felony."

"They *can* do that."

"I still haven't heard from my mom, maybe you'll have better luck."

Someone else was in the room with Dew, Denise could hear heavy footprints. "I'll try. All your mom has got to do is renew a form or maybe call the judge. Something like that."

"I don't think that is all they want. They will check my mom's signature on the forms. Remember Jane Dark? She's back and she is that much of a bitch. And my mom won't even return my phone calls. The only way I know she's alive is that she keeps paying my bills."

"I'll do what I can," Dew said. Had Dew hung up on her? The train whistled again. Two down, one to go.

Denise tried Rayne Herring. Unlike Dew, Rayne picked up on the first ring. She was liking her friend better than family.

"I was expecting your call," Rayne said.

"You're good with that," Denise said. "You are always monitoring all the news."

"I grew up with an Air Force colonel who did military intelligence, it's in my blood. And she might be our next congresswoman."

"I'll vote for her," Denise lied. "You're still a private investigator, right?"

"Barely," Rayne replied. "I'm supposed to be helping the Big Red campaign, but I'll look for any excuse to get out of it."

With Rayne, Denise needed to play the team card. "Remember Team Turquoise."

"Those were good times."

"I need you to look up some things for me," Denise said. "Do you know anything about Lordsburg? I think I'll need some help with this case."

"I've only been there once, like ten years ago. I don't have a good memory of the experience. What happens in Lordsburg doesn't always stay in Lordsburg."

Denise heard a voice say "Mommy, can I come play detective too?" and then "please, please, please" on the other end of the phone.

Denise asked, "Is that you, lovely Rita, meter maid?"

"It's me Auntie Denise!"

"I'm home schooling her," Rayne said. "I wish I could put her in detention right now."

"Auntie Denise is in Lordsburg, right?" Denise heard Rita say. "I'm going on the Upbound Train this weekend to Lordsburg with grandma. I can meet my Auntie Denise then. You promised!"

"Let me think about it," Rayne said. It was unclear who she was talking to, Denise or Rayne. "There might be a conflict in me handling this case, now that I think of it."

"Mom you really should help Auntie Denise out with her case," Rita said.

"Let me think about it," Rayne said again. "I'll have some time this weekend while Rita is away. And Rita's going to be passing through Lordsburg with her grandmother on that damn whistle stop tour. The girl really wants to meet you."

"I can tell," Denise said. "I want to meet her too."

"I told her that back in high school on Team Turquoise, you were like a psychic. She's kinda psychic too."

"You weren't supposed to tell anyone about me," Denise said.

"She's my daughter." Rayne paused, then said, "Well, I can get a lot more done for you, if she's out of my hair..."

Was this a quid pro quo? Rayne was the only investigator she knew. "OK," Denise said. "I will try to meet Rita at the Upbound Train tour when it comes to Lordsburg. I'll show her the sights if I find any. And hopefully you can help me out with the case."

"It's a deal."

They hung up.

She noticed that she'd missed a text from Hikaru.

"I'm alive, barely" was the text. He included a pic of him sitting in his cycling outfit in a rustic cabin by a fireplace, under a blanket, nursing a cup of a steaming hot liquid.

She called him immediately. "What happened?"

"I can't say too much, but let's just say not everyone is happy that I reached out to you."

"I'm sorry."

"My father, the world-famous Dr. Yu is still a big wheel and he called in a lot of favors with the powers that be, so I'm keeping my job for now."

"Who are the powers that be?" she asked.

"You don't want to know," he said. "You don't want to mess with them."

"OK, but I do need some information. Can you help me get some information about Denny? I understand you know about his military experiences."

"Give me a few weeks. I'm sorta on probation. But I promise I will do whatever I can to help. I promise you that I had no idea that any of this would happen to your brother. Or to you."

"I hope we are on the same side."

She could hear his heartbeat through the phone. "We *will* be. I can't talk right now." He hung up.

A spark came through the phone. Hikaru was blowing her an electronic kiss. He texted a new pic of a snowcapped peak, Sierra Blanca, through his cabin window.

It was getting hot inside the car, straining the air conditioning. She'd better get back to her hotel room.

Inside the Holiday Comfort, her key card took a moment to work on the 4th floor room, but she finally got into her room on the third try. The bed had not been made up yet.

She turned on some K-pop music on her computer and opened a browser to surf the web. Unfortunately, the web was down for the whole hotel.

It was Friday night in Lordsburg. Thank God It's Friday?

She did her katas over and over again until she collapsed into the bed.

Chapter 17

Saturday, July 11

When Denise entered the hotel lobby at dawn for coffee, she was surprised to see Jane Dark.

"Don't worry," Jane Dark said, getting herself coffee from the front desk. "This is the demilitarized zone. You should know about demilitarized zones."

Was that an off-handed remark about her Korean heritage? Denise shrugged.

"I want you to know that I'm just doing my job. Like I said, I was sent for."

"By whom?"

"The government. That's all I can say. We can be pals outside of court since we both have to stay here at the Holiday Comfort. I have a lot of respect for you."

"Thanks."

The lobby muzak played a version of the old Loverboy song "Working for the Weekend." God, she really hated old white man music. Some weekend.

No one else came down for breakfast. They might be the only two guests in the hotel for the weekend. The Oklahoma tourists must have gone on to California, a long day's journey into night. The Federal agents had been deployed to the border of the Federation for the night.

There was a "weekend brunch" buffet at least. Caliban had prepared a spread with omelets containing mystery meat. Looking at his boomerang, Denise hoped the meat wasn't Kangaroo. She wouldn't mind ostrich, however.

"Is it a boy or girl?" she asked Jane Dark.

"It's going to be a girl," Dark said. "I'm going to name her

Jean Dark because it sounds like the French for Joan of Ark."

"*Jean Dark, Jean Dark*," Denise said, savoring an exaggerated French pronunciation of the name. "I like it."

"I predict she's going to save the world someday, just like her namesake. *Jean Dark, Jean Dark* indeed."

"That's a lot of pressure on your child. My cousin Dew was supposed to rule the world but that didn't happen... yet."

"Maybe they can rule it together. You don't have kids, do you?"

"I don't think that's in the cards for me," Denise said. "Let's just say I've never even had a boyfriend."

"What was the name of that boy on your mock trial team? He was adorable in an Asperger's sort of way."

"Hikaru Yu," Denise replied.

"The scientist?"

"You've heard of him?"

"Yeah. I hadn't realized that he did mock trial with you. He was in middle school then, so I didn't make the connection with the tall, handsome scientist. Have you seen him?"

"Yeah. We just met again a few days ago."

Jane Dark could read Denise easily. "Do you like him? I mean *like him*, like him?"

"*Kinda.*"

The two finished their coffees and left.

The internet was still down at the hotel, and the bars on her phone were weak. She saw a new Big Red Herring congressional billboard out the window. It must have sprouted over breakfast. At least the Upbound Train Whistle Stop tour was passing through town for its final stop on Sunday evening, and she'd made that deal with Rayne to see Rita. Lordsburg was literally the end of the line.

She drove to the jail to visit Denny, but apparently there were no visiting hours on weekends without an appointment. She returned to the hotel and sat in her room. The internet fluctuated in and out, so she tried to research the case. There wasn't much to look up yet, just a one-page criminal complaint.

She finished all the research she could do. Now what? It was too hot to go outside, so she did katas for a while, first slow and then fast. She looked at herself in the mirror, she was actually getting in shape.

She even flexed. Feeling confident, she sat on her bed and Face Timed Hikaru, they talked about old times, and then school days. But whenever she wanted to talk about his interactions with her brother, he politely changed the subject.

"Give me some time," he said. "I don't know what I'm allowed to say yet."

"Take all the time you need," she lied. She saw he had his big screen TV on pause. "What are you watching?"

"An old movie called *The Player*," he said. "It's about Hollywood. My dad suggested it. He said that the military industrial complex is remarkably similar to show business. Everybody's pitching something."

"So is the justice system," she said. "But I remember that movie, there was some line in that movie, I think it was said by Bruce Willis at the end. I can't remember the line, but both Dan and Luna told me that it's been in every story that our family has."

"That's very *meta*," he said. "I haven't seen Willis in the film yet, but I'll keep that in mind when he says that line."

"It's a weird coincidence that you're watching that film when it's been so important to our family."

He smiled. "There are no coincidences."

She didn't ask him to explain and they hung up. She didn't have Netflix on her hotel TV, but thankfully, there were infinite channels so she could binge watch Korean soap operas the rest of the afternoon. Denise was hooked by the second episode. How Korean was she? She might say she was half on her mother's side, but her mother was really half Korean and Half Latina. That would make her only a quarter Korean if she took a DNA test. Still, she could relate to the trials and tribulation. "My life is a Korean soap opera."

At six o'clock, utterly restless, she ate dinner at Denny's at the travel center, which at least had decent Wi-Fi for her laptop. She watched the video of her brother's incident over and over again. Some soap opera. What was that damn line in *The Player*?

105

Chapter 18
Sunday, July 12

She could have closed down the Denny's restaurant in Lordsburg, with coffee after coffee but Denny's never closed of course, even here. She surfed the web and only reluctantly went back to her room after midnight and went to sleep.

Absolutely nothing happened on Sunday morning. She wasn't allowed to visit Denny, and she couldn't think of anything else to do. She wasn't particularly religious, so church was out of the question. Her plan to research the case was thwarted because the internet was off and on again. A quick update on her phone warned of interrupted service because of "sunspot activity."

Apparently, sunspots were affecting the internet all over the world, yet for some reason the sunspots affected Lordsburg worst of all that weekend.

She talked to Hikaru again and somehow the conversation switched to their favorite movies. They both favored science fiction; he liked the science and she preferred the fiction.

"We have a lot in common," he said.

"*Kinda.*"

She was smiling when she hung up. Could she be falling for this mysterious stranger? It's not like she had anyone else, ever. He was a weird scientist who was always traveling and preferred sending pictures to talking. He probably never had a girlfriend either. On her phone's home screen, she now saw a pic of two figures cycling together through the desert. Seconds later the image was gone.

She sighed. Was there anything else to do in this town on a Sunday while she killed time waiting to see Rita? There was no local shopping of course, the Walmart in Deming was sixty miles away. She wasn't going to drive an hour for a Walmart. It was over a hundred and five degrees, so hiking was out of the question. There was a nearby state park called City of Rocks, but that sounded well... rocky.

She briefly considered crossing the border in Palomas and shopping at the legendary Pink Store. She was the daughter of Laser Geisha Pink after all. Still, she didn't want to risk Border Patrol, especially since there were Federal agents everywhere.

The Holiday Comfort's pool was closed for maintenance so she couldn't swim. She hadn't packed any books and the hyped-up K-pop beats made her nervous. She soon tired of the Korean soap operas on TV.

Restless again, she rode a stationary bike in the hotel's gym. After an hour, she was exhausted but hadn't gotten anywhere. She was sure that was a metaphor for something. She practiced a few moves with her staff, but quit when she almost broke the mirror.

The waiting was unbearable. She almost thought of riding the stationary bike again to pass the time. She even missed Jane Dark who must have escaped town for the day.

At five o'clock on that endless Sunday afternoon, it seemed even hotter and even brighter. Denise wondered if this day would ever end. She tried Hikaru again and they talked, mostly focusing on their respective childhoods. He'd grown up in Los Alamos where his father was a rock star in the lab's universe. Even though Hikaru was brilliant and skipped grades, he'd lived his whole life in his father's shadow. Dr. Yu had invented the electronic thimble, basically *Star Trek* technology, and was usually off on lab tours.

"I get it," Denise said. "My mom wasn't always there for me after she won that massive verdict. We're the same in that respect."

"*Kinda*," they both said at the same time.

His phone beeped. "I've got to take this," he said.

She knew she couldn't call him back. It was twenty after five, at least she could head over to the Whistle Stop event which was supposed to start at six.

She didn't want to park the Lexus out in the open by a crowded train station. It was less than half a mile walk north to the railroad "station," that small shelter, and the sun had gone behind the single cloud in the sky. She might as well walk.

The sun came back out and it was still over a hundred degrees. So much for the dry heat. As she walked toward the small shelter where the passengers were supposed to wait, she was surprised that there was a sizeable crowd already there. This was a big deal out here in the outback—a congressional candidate on a train! It might as well have been FDR back in the forties.

It was a largely Hispanic crowd with a few Anglo cowboys. Everyone mixed together. This town sure wasn't racist. She stopped at the back of the crowd so she could be alone.

And yet she felt strangely at home here. She shouldn't be such a snob; these were good people, and while she was a quarter Korean, she was also a quarter Latinx. She noticed that a few people smiled at her. One nice grandmother offered her a clear plastic glass of cold *horchata* that was beyond refreshing.

"You look like someone from around here," the grandmother said, surrounded by a pack of adorable kids.

"I have some *kin*," Denise said, but didn't say anything more.

"Are you moving here?" the grandmother asked.

"We'll see."

The station shelter had a few people cramped inside next to the shade of one wall to escape the heat. On the tracks, there was Amtrak train headed to LA that was being searched by Federal agents.

Two young Asian men were taken off the train in handcuffs, while another officer carried a suitcase with an evidence tag on it.

"We didn't know anything about what was in the suitcase," one young man said.

The other young man was crying.

Not a good day to be Asian in Lordsburg. The crying man caught her eye. She nodded with empathy. He nodded back.

The unmarked car with Fed plates drove away, the two men in the back, apparently in custody. The coast clear, so to speak, a crowd now gathered around the tracks. Right at the edge of the crowd, an overweight young man sat on a picnic blanket on the rocky dirt. The man wore a big pink sombrero that was so big and so pink that it was clearly worn ironically. The man and his sombrero took up most of the blanket; the remaining corner held a keg, which he had already tapped. Was he going to drink it all himself?

The man pointed at Denise as she walked by. She gave him a wide berth.

"Hey baby *que paso?*" he said to her. Then, she realized that he had on headphones and was humming a popular tune. "I thought I was your only *vato.*"

There was something about the man in the pink sombrero. He now danced like a baby elephant, singing the song out loud between gulps from the keg. Despite the surging crowd, no one stepped on his blanket as if it had a forcefield.

"It's just Pedro being Pedro," someone said, walking by, but the way they said his name it sounded more like *Petro.* Nearby people actually clapped in rhythm for him, and while the man had his headphones on under the pink sombrero, Denise swore she could hear the late Freddy Fender.

The crowd was growing impatient. The Upbound Train was already parked behind the Amtrak to LA and would have to wait for the first train to leave. The Amtrak was delayed because the authorities were still searching the train for contraband.

Behind the Amtrak train, the Upbound Train looked like one of those Shinkansen bullet trains from Japan. It could go into orbit if it wasn't stuck on the tracks. On the side were the words: UPWARD BOUND GO BIG RED!

"Big Red's around back!" someone muttered, as if the colonel was a rock star. A few people headed toward the caboose. Denise followed them, looking forward to meeting Rita.

Sheriff Diamond was personally handling security at the caboose. He looked at her with daggers, especially after she was pushed forward by the crunch of people behind her.

109

Denise grew uncomfortable. Perhaps she'd just wave at Rita and then sneak out, but the crowd made that impossible.

Moments later, Big Red Herring herself came out and waved to the crowd. Big Red was indeed bigger and redder in person—well over six feet, maybe six three in her rattle-snake cowboy boots. Her hair might as well be on fire, her face sunburnt.

"Go Big Red! Go Big Red!" The crowd was in a rhythmic chant. Denise couldn't get a read on this ginger force of nature; there was too much going on in the crowd. She grew more uneasy with every chant.

Big Red called for her granddaughter to come out and join her. Time for a photo op for Big Red Instagram. Unfortunately, the poor girl was clearly shy and kept her head down.

While Denise was short and awkward, Rita was *tall* and awkward. She had red hair like her grandmother and mother, but there was something about the girl that was *different*. She was far darker than her grandmother, but not Latinx. Rayne had never said who the girl's father was. Denise didn't want to guess; people were always wrong about her ethnicity and she didn't want to make the same mistake with this girl.

Denise was only a few feet away and made eye contact with the tall girl. *"Lovely Rita, Meter Maid?"*

"Auntie Denise!" the girl yelled. "You're here, you're *really* here."

Suddenly Big Red pulled the girl back into the train as if Denise was a shooter. Denise sensed a sudden influx of bad energy as the crowd pushed forward even more. What was happening? The winds were blowing in constantly shifting directions, almost at random. The crowd pushed Denise right up to the caboose.

"She's over there!" She turned and recognized Fally and the rest of the Groundlings. She shouldn't have been surprised. This was their hometown, and this was the biggest party in years.

They were no longer in suits but sported dirty white tank tops in the heat. Maybe their tattoos of snakes and demons were moving, or perhaps it was just the light. She

110

swore there was a flying saucer above her, but it was the pink sombrero of the dancing man that had been caught in the wind.

"By the caboose," Fally said. "She's over there."

Denise looked around for the Sheriff, he should protect her, right? But he had gone inside the caboose to protect the candidate.

Denise thought of escaping by sliding under the train, but if the train jerked, she could die instantly. She ducked down and pushed her way through the crowd to the far side of the caboose. Through the right-side caboose window, Rita saw her. Denise froze, and gave a guilty wave.

Thankfully, Rita waved. Her window was open. "Auntie Denise?"

"Just call me Denise," she replied. "Glad to finally meet you in the flesh after all these years. I knew you before you were born."

"You always say that. Do I look different than you expected?"

"Kinda," Denise said with a smile. "You're much taller than me."

"Who's that dear?" Big Red said from the other side of the train.

"Just an old friend," Rita said, as if covering for Denise.

"I didn't know you had old friends," Big Red said. "Stay here, I better go back out."

There definitely was some jostling from the crowd behind the caboose, and the crowd was getting rowdy with the "Go Big Red!" chant.

"You really better come out here," the sheriff said to Big Red. "They'll listen to you."

Big Red left Rita alone, and returned out to the rear of the caboose with the sheriff. Denise heard footsteps on the other side of the caboose. She bent over and saw the feet of a group of people walking slowly along the caboose around the rear of the crowd. Were the Groundlings coming after her anyway?

After nodding at Rita, Denise ran around the train and then cut between the gap of the Amtrak train. She heard more footsteps.

She was sure someone had seen her from behind the train, but before she could look, she heard a voice in her head. It sounded like Rita's. "Run, Auntie!"

"Next time, Rita," Denise thought back. She started running south away from the train through the outskirts of the crowd.

"She's getting away," Fally shouted.

"They're coming from your right," a voice said. It took Denise a moment to realize it really was Rita, and the voice was in her head. "You should go down that alley."

Denise ran towards the bank and saw and alley. She ducked down the alley. "The newspaper building door is unlocked," the voice said.

Denise cut across and saw a broken door to the newspaper building, the Lordsburg Liberal. She opened the door and ducked inside. She pushed the door back into place, so it appeared to be closed.

"Be quiet, they're coming," the voice said.

Denise sat in silence for a few moments. She heard some heavy footsteps race by her.

She waited a full minute; she could hear her heartbeat. "Coast is clear," the voice said. "For now."

She glanced out the broken door, whoever was chasing her wasn't visible. "Go around the back side of the courthouse just to be sure," the voice said.

She did a long lap around the courthouse and then got back on Shakespeare street. She then cut over to the hotel. Just as she made it to the Holiday Comfort door, she heard the train whistle blow. The whistle stop tour was apparently over.

"You should be safe now, Auntie," the voice said. "They're driving out of town. Wish we had more time to talk. But the train is moving away, and I lose my range."

"I really wish we could talk," Denise thought back.

There was no answer. Denise heard the rumbling on the train tracks even though she was far away. Denise looked toward the tracks. The crowd was coming clearing from the train station, so she would have safety in numbers.

She walked briskly to the hotel and was pleasantly surprised that Jane Dark pulled up in a white state car holding some dry cleaning in plastic wraps. Where did one have to go to have a blazer dry-cleaned in this neck of the woods?

Jane Dark looked over at the panting Denise. "Can you give me a hand with my dry-cleaning?"

Denise smiled. Nothing was going to happen to her now. "Gladly."

Chapter 19
Monday, July 13 through Friday, July 17

It was Monday, time for the work week. She had a week to kill before the arraignment, assuming the Grand Jury indicted Denny on Friday. Over the next few days, Denise got into what she called the Hidalgo groove after the name of the county. Since there was nothing more to do at Holiday Comfort after breakfast—the holiday was over, and it was no longer comfortable—Denise spent each morning visiting Denny at Hidalgo County Detention Center.

The small jail was now packed with detainees on immigration holds so Denise had to wait for a while for a visiting room to open up. Even worse, the visiting room now had a large video apparatus the size of a gas pump, with the screen itself barely the size of a computer screen. It was taller than she was. There wasn't enough room for her to sit down, so she had to stand.

On Monday, Denise convinced Denny not to testify at Friday's grand jury. "I want to tell my side of the story," he said. "About them aliens."

"I can't protect you at the grand jury," she said. "It's an exceptionally low standard of proof and you can't have a lawyer with you when you testify. But we will try to get you out at arraignment next week."

"You better promise that you will get me out at arraignment."

"I promise. I guess."

But had she made a promise she couldn't keep?

She learned more about her brother to help fight harder for him. While he was vague about his earliest years with

Nastia, he was more forthcoming when they talked about middle and high school which he'd spent in Lordsburg. They had a lively discussion about small town sports, class elections and the big controversy over the yearbook photo where he appeared to be holding a beer. He also told her that he was a frequent letter writer to the local paper.

"I'll check those out sometime," she said.

"Wish we all knew each other. We could have been a family," he said repeatedly. That became his mantra.

"I would have liked that," she replied by rote.

Maybe they did have a lot in common. They liked the same music and computer games, and even the Laser Geisha TV show.

"I love that Laser Geisha Pink the best," he told her. "She's a bad ass."

She didn't tell him that during a psychotic break, their mother had once actually claimed to be Laser Geisha Pink *for real.*

On Tuesday, the discussion took a detour to fill in the blanks of his youth. He had spent most of his life as a foster child. First, with Nastia and the occasional sojourn with Fally. After Nastia cut him loose as she got locked, he became the ward of the Dunsinane's, Cordelia's family, at New Shakespeare Ranch.

Denise had been part of the family (kinda) when she had lived with her grandmother, and then Luna. Denny was more of a hired hand with the Dunsinanes. He knew how to shoe a horse and castrate a bull. Denise could picture the forbidden romance between him and Cordelia—she would watch him work and then sneak into his converted bedroom in the barn.

"How about you, did you have a boyfriend in high school?" Denny asked Denise.

"Not even."

Then things took a darker turn as they continued talking about his Lordsburg days. She could sense his growing unease talking about his childhood. Clearly, he had been physically abused, both by Fally and Cordelia's father. She didn't want to ask if it got worse than that.

The big video apparatus behind vibrated, turning on by

itself. She feared that it would crush her against the glass. She wasn't sure if Denny was doing this inadvertently, or she was causing the vibrations from her own pain at hearing his story. It was probably her imagination, but she cut the meeting off early that day.

On Wednesday, it was time to turn the page and discuss life after graduation. They talked about his military service starting at eighteen. "Did you go overseas?" she asked him.

"I never left New Mexico. After basic, I worked at White Sands Missile Range."

"Who did you work for?"

He was vague on which service he actually served with. There were Air Force bases nearby, but the Army operated White Sands. Denny described almost washing out on a Section 8—being declared mentally unfit for duty—but somehow ended up at something called the "Syrinx launch site" within the vastness of White Sands Missile Range.

Denise had trouble following him after that. His talk about the grails made utterly no sense. First, they were a mental portal to another dimension where the aliens lived. The next minute, the grails were created here on earth by the Chinese to find psychics or something like that.

When he talked about life after the military (still not clear which branch), he was a regular small-town vet with PTSD who got into drugs. He never had a chance for rehab. He did love Cordelia and hoped to marry her. He talked about getting off drugs and hopefully getting into a treatment program.

"With the right meds, I could be normal again," he said.

"I think so too."

By the end of every visit, he would talk about meeting his "real mom," and he might as well be five years old. He wiped a tear away and actually said the word "mommy."

When Thursday came, she tried to focus again on the case at hand. "Are you sure you don't remember what happened?"

"I have no *recollection* of anything," he said again and again. He pronounced it like a foreign word that he was trying to learn phonetically.

He did say one thing that disturbed her. "I was really angry before it started. I was angry at the town; angry at the cops, and I was angry that Cordelia said you didn't exist. But I don't *recollect* anything after that."

Anger was not a good thing as it showed he might have been in his right mind when this all went down.

"Hopefully nothing will happen, because the grand jury won't give me a true bill or whatever," he said.

"Hopefully."

* * *

In the afternoons that week, she traded calls with Rayne Herring. Rayne was glad that Denise had met Rita, even briefly. Apparently meeting the poor girl was indeed a quid pro quo. "She was so happy to see you," Rayne said. "I didn't even have to put her in detention this week."

Rayne didn't mention that Rita had said anything about the chase and their psychic conversations. Denise figured it was best not to bring that up, especially now that Rayne was more than happy to dig through Denny's past, free of charge. "I don't think the conflict I had is that important anymore."

Denise wasn't sure what conflict Rayne was talking about, she was concerned with the legality of Denny's adoption. According to Rayne, Nastia had indeed sent the paperwork to their mother who had indeed signed away all rights to Denny, thinking that Denny was dead, and this was some attempt to scam some money if Denny got into trouble that would make Jen Song responsible. When he was finally adopted by the Dunsinanes, notice had been published in the *Lordsburg Liberal*, which wasn't ever online. Jen probably never knew that her son was really alive.

"It's sad," Rayne said.

"I wish I had known him growing up," Denise said. "I could have saved him."

* * *

Denise spent that Friday outside the courthouse, waiting to see what the grand jury would do with Denny's case. She waited patiently on a bench in the shade to see whether they would true bill or not true bill.

As she waited for the answer, she tried again to resolve her status to practice law. Hikaru had told her that everything was in order, but via text he revealed that he hadn't actually spoken to an actual human; he had only received an electronic signature via email from a Korean corporate email address. Denise tried that email, but it bounced back—NO LONGER IN SERVICE

Denise called all of her mom's numbers again, but they were still disconnected. She shoved the phone back in her pocket. It rang. She recognized a Korean prefix on the number. Could it be her mom? There was no one on the other end when she picked up.

What was going on?

She checked every number she had of other Korean contacts, but none matched. She did have a number for her cousin Susie Song the famous golfer.

She tried Susie, but someone else answered the phone and said a few words in Korean before hanging up.

She tried her cousin Dew. "Now that I finally have a brother, I want him to be able to meet my mom. Can you work your computer magic?"

"That's funny," Dew said. "I spend every minute trying to avoid my mom and now you're trying to find yours. I'll see what I can do over the weekend."

After she hung up with Dew, Denise took a few deep breaths. She sat in silence for almost an hour until Caliban came out of the courthouse. "What happened?" Denise asked.

"Not allowed to say until it's filed," he said, fingering the boomerang lodged under his belt. "See you back at the hotel."

* * *

Back at the hotel, Caliban was playing a different kind of bailiff. Apparently, the Oklahoma tourists didn't like California and were heading home. They were bringing some relatives with them and the whole clan was there for dinner. Caliban looked the other way when they brought in a few six-packs but indicated they had to drink out by the empty pool. They were celebrating like it was Thanksgiving, Christmas and the Fourth of July all at once.

Denise and Jane Dark had to share a table.

"Good news," Jane Dark said.

"You're dropping the charges?" Denise asked.

"Well good news for *me*. The grand jury indicted Denny on all counts, plus one count of felony animal endangerment. He's now facing life in prison. But don't worry, I won't hold your brother against you."

"Thanks," Denise said.

"By the way, we still haven't heard from your mom about all she's doing to supervise your work as a clinical law student. You might want to check into that."

Alone in the Holiday Comfort that night, she tried all the Korean numbers one more time, but no one answered. She felt a strange tingling in her wallet, the magic card gave her slight shock. It must be static electricity, right?

Chapter 20
Saturday, July 18 and Sunday, July 19

It cooled down a bit on Saturday, so she drove to the City of Rocks State Park about an hour away. Stonehenge on steroids, there were acres and acres of boulders the size of cars. There was even another outcropping of boulders a few hundred yards away (the *Suburb* of Rocks?). At least she got some fresh air and exercise. She even practiced with her staff, fighting off imaginary enemies coming out of the earth.

On Sunday, the day before Denny's arraignment, the jail staff allowed her to spend all day in the jail interview room talking to him. After some awkward moments, they each vowed to talk about anything, but the case.

"Do you like Lordsburg?" she asked.

"I call it the *City of God* sometimes, the *Cidade de Deus*. That's from this Brazilian film about this *favela* in Rio. My Spanish teacher, Ms. Castaneda, showed it to us in class."

Their cousin, Marley, had a teacher named Yvette Castaneda over in Las Cruces. It could have been a coincidence.

"So, will I get out?" Denny asked.

"I don't know."

"Suppose my *real* mom comes to take custody?"

She didn't know how to respond. "That would be a nice surprise."

At dinner that night in the hotel, Jane Dark was nowhere to be found. Had the queen of darkness been taken off the case? The Okies were long gone, and it was even lonelier than usual. Caliban brought her some leftovers as the kitchen was closed. "You're the only one here," he said.

* * *

Denise received a call from Dew after she took the leftovers up to the room. "Anything about my mom?" Denise asked. "I'm getting worried for real."

"I did some digging," her cousin said. "Your mom has been in and out of hospitals in Asia for the last few years. Even when you lived with us."

"So, the reason she left me and had Luna take care of me was medical?"

"Again, I'm not a doctor and don't speak Korean, but it seemed like your mom was dealing with some serious health shit."

Denise spit out her food into a napkin. "And I thought it was because she didn't love me."

"I don't know what to say when you say things like that," Dew said.

"I just have a lot of mixed emotions about my mom. Where is she now?"

"She was discharged from the hospital in Seoul. One notation that I could translate with Google said something about a *hospice* in some place in Japan. *Aokigahara.*"

Dew spelled it out for her. Denise had heard of that place somewhere. Still on the phone, she Googled "Aokigahara" on her laptop.

"Aokigahara is like the famous suicide forest of Japan." Denise was really worried now. "Is she dying? Or dead already?"

"I don't know," Dew said. While hospitals over there have records in English, *hospices* don't. Like I said, I can't read Korean or Japanese."

After hanging up, Denise tried to locate her mother via the weak internet connection, searching both Korean and Japan websites based on the info Dew had given her. Her mother had been in hospitals in Korea, Hong Kong and Tokyo but the records were sealed so tightly in English as well as the native languages, she had no way to get to them. The hospice did have an English speaker, but the person didn't understand Denise's questions and would neither confirm nor deny whether her mother was there.

Her spark was sensitive to her mother's distress, and she actually developed a splitting headache. Would her mother stay in the hospice to die, or go out into the forest to save everyone the trouble?

Her phone rang. She jumped. Cordelia had set up a three-way call with Denny.

"They're finally letting me use the phone! I'm not in Seg anymore. I can call you through Cordelia."

"That's good," Denise said weakly. "Hello Cordelia."

"Hello," Cordelia said.

Denny sensed her distress. "What's wrong Denise?"

"My mother, *our* mother is very ill. They think she's in hospice over in Asia."

"I know," Denny said.

"You can reach her? On the phone?"

"In my *mind*. I felt her reach out to me, in my mind. She was in a forest somewhere."

"Did she..."

"I don't know. I was in the forest with her, but everything went black."

"What do you think that means?"

"I don't know," he said.

"Does that mean she might already be dead?" Denise asked.

There was silence on the other end and then a click. "I think they're back in lockdown," Cordelia said.

* * *

Just before bedtime, Dew texted a working phone number for Susie Song. On her third attempt, Denise finally got through to an assistant who answered, "Cygnus Moon, special affairs."

"I'm trying to reach Susie Song," Denise said. "It's her cousin Denise, I'm calling about my mother, Jen Song."

"One moment, please."

The moment lasted a full five minutes until Denise finally heard the voice of the woman who had once been her idol and role model, the woman who had told the whole world to

"Swing for the Stars."

"Denise?" Susie asked.

"How's my mom?"

"I don't know what I'm allowed to say," Susie said.

"Did she commit suicide in the Aokigahara forest?"

"I don't know what I'm allowed to say," Susie said. "There's a lot going on and the situation is in flux. Don't call me, I'll call you."

Susie abruptly hung up. That sure didn't sound good. Denise touched the Swan card that night, but it felt ice cold. She looked at the logo again, Korean Swan Bank. Hmmm... Cygnus meant swan, right? Did the Swan bank have a connection to Cygnus Moon? And why would a corporation have special affairs?

Curious, Denise decided to investigate with her laptop. Originally, a company called Cygnus Aerospace merged with her mother's former employer, Dragon Moon. And then Dragon Moon became *Cygnus* Moon. Cygnus Moon had entered into massive contracts with various national governments and then started the 24 Grails Contest.

Denise clicked on a link for the Cygnus Moon Corporation website, but the site was "under construction." She Googled the Greek mythology for Cygnus, thinking it might be a clue.

In the myth, Zeus took the form of a swan, Cygnus, and that swan somehow impregnated a maiden named Leda. She didn't want to imagine how. Leda then gave birth to the Gemini twins—Castor and Pollux.

Huh?

Was the fact that she had a twin have anything to do with the myth of Cygnus?

Her own father had supposedly been a lawyer; her mother was his legal secretary. He had died before her mother gave birth and his family had essentially disowned Jen. He wasn't on the birth certificate and that's why Denise's last name was Song.

But suppose that the man she had thought was her father wasn't just a dude, and her father was really ummm... *Zeus*?

Before she could laugh that off, she thought about Zeus being a metaphor. She had read the Erich Von Daniken book, *Chariots of the Gods* and seen that stupid show *Ancient Aliens* with the premise that all mythology was a retelling of alien settlement on the earth.

If that show's mythology had any basis in fact, perhaps she was part alien. That might explain her powers.

A Korean corporation took a name based on a Greek myth about a god impersonating a swan impregnating a woman. That woman then had twins. According to one version of the myth, Leda died of shame.

So what?

Greek mythology had nothing to do with her or her brother, right? It certainly couldn't have anything to do with her mom, dead or alive.

Denise touched the credit card again and ran her finger along the sharp metallic edge. She jerked her finger away. The card had given her a slight cut. She sucked on her finger until the bleeding stopped.

She didn't sleep that night.

Chapter 21
Monday, July 20

The day of the district court arraignment finally came. In the hotel shower, Denise put shampoo in her hair but suddenly the water stopped, and then the bathroom light went out.

The shampoo still in her hair, she carefully stepped out of the shower, wrapped herself in a towel and picked up the room phone to call the front desk. The phone didn't have a dial tone. Her phone had been hooked to the charger, but the battery display said zero percent. She got dressed and put her hair in a tight bun, hoping no one would notice her accidental dreadlocks.

* * *

Downstairs, Caliban the desk clerk/bailiff frowned. "Ms. Song, I'm sorry, but your card, your *mommy's* credit card, has been declined."

"Declined?"

His boomerang was on the desk so he could grab it if need be. "It's frozen, retroactively. You now owe us for the one week's stay, at two hundred a night, over a thousand bucks. If it was up to me, I'd let it go. But..."

"Did you just turn off the power to my room?"

"That's company policy," he said. "When there's evidence of *fraud.*"

"But you said..." She was sounding like her clients.

"Do you have another credit card?"

"Not with me." Her purse felt heavier. Why hadn't she bothered to ever get another credit card, just in case? Maybe that was why Susie couldn't tell her anything, because of potential litigation against Denise for various felonies.

"Hold on for one moment," Caliban said. He nodded at a maid. Moments later, the maid came down with all of Denise's earthly possessions in the unzipped suitcase and the gym and computer bags. Worse the laptop was about to fall out, along with her underwear. She didn't know which was worse.

"Do we have to call security?" Caliban said.

Denise grabbed the laptop before it fell out, and then packed her underwear quickly. She then shuffled out of the lobby, hoping to beat Jane Dark out the door. The coast clear, she hit another obstacle—her fob didn't work on the Lexus. Thankfully she was able to open the door manually with a spare key.

Once connected to the car charger, her phone jumped to life in mid-ring. She picked it up before it rang again. Sure enough, the car rental company from the airport was sending her an automated message that the card had been declined. She needed to return the car or face possible criminal charges.

Denise had a disturbing thought. Each transaction made with the Swan bank card could be considered a separate count of fraud. She had used the card every single day for the last year. Even if the allegedly fraudulent card charges were considered mere misdemeanors because the amounts were under the two-hundred and fifty-dollar felony threshold, she knew she faced at least 365 years in prison and would certainly never be admitted to the bar to be a real lawyer.

In addition, her mother's lawyers could potentially argue that since the Korean Swan bank card was from an overseas bank, the fraud was *international.* Korea was not known for having nice jails, especially for Americans.

Hell, Denny could sue her as well for stealing money that he would potentially inherit. She really wished that she had taken a banking law class so she would know for sure.

She jerked the Lexus out of the parking lot. Should she go hide somewhere? Aokigahara? It wasn't that bad yet, maybe she should go west to California or run to Mexico? What was that resort on the gulf Rayne had mentioned? Puerto Penasco? It couldn't be that far from here; she was so close to the border.

At the entrance to the freeway, sheriff's department vehicles blocked the east bound and west bound entrances. Denise turned around and parked by the courthouse on the west side of Shakespeare street, trying to figure out what to do next.

There in the car, she jumped to the worst conclusion. Perhaps her mother had really died or had been declared incompetent. Why couldn't Susie tell her? The executor or conservator was tying up all the loose ends. The Swan bank card was one of those loose ends.

Denise was one of those loose ends. She wouldn't be able to afford to go to her mother's funeral if it was overseas, not that the family would want her. She would be too humiliated to go to any ceremony if it was here in New Mexico. Poor Denny would meet his mother right before she was dropped six feet under.

Still on Shakespeare Street, she tried to concentrate on happy memories of her mom, but still couldn't see her mother's face.

Another car, a white state car, pulled alongside her, it was Jane Dark. They both opened their windows. "See you in court, *counselor.*" Jane Dark said.

Denise didn't reply as she looked at Jane Dark in the other vehicle. If there was a DMZ, it did not extend to this side of Shakespeare Street. "By the way, we're flying Professor Kang out to testify that you failed out of law school and are not really a law student. She's on our witness list for Denny's case and *yours.*"

Jane Dark did an illegal U-turn and found an open space right in front of the courthouse.

Still in the car, scared to leave, Denise checked for her own name on the court website on her phone. Sure enough, there was a "*Mis* hearing" with her name on it this morning, and worse, her nemesis the dreaded Professor Kang was indeed on the witness list as an expert witness in mental health law.

Mis hearing? Did that stand for miscellaneous or mistake? Or Misdemeanor?

Denise thought of trying Korea one more time, the land of the morning calm. But what was the point?

Denise got out of the car and saw a crowd pouring into the courthouse from Shakespeare Street. The whole town was here to see the show in this Globe Theater from Hell. Denise was playing Ophelia, Juliet, and Desdemona. All of them dead girls.

What did Ophelia say before she died? *"There's rue for you and some for me."*

She waited outside for another moment. A man who could pass for a Hispanic James Bond in a stylish black suit and black tie approached her. He flashed a badge for the U.S. Marshals.

"Ms. Song, the judge needs you in the courtroom right now!"

"Am I in trouble?" she asked.

"I don't know yet."

Chapter 22

The tiny courtroom was even more crowded for arraignment day. Judges usually only came once a week so all legal business for the county would be done over the next few hours. There were criminals, ranchers, traffic cops, a few people getting divorced and even a couple getting married by the judge.

The windows let in that hot dusty breeze. Denny sat in the front row, next to the three other inmates. He wore orange. They wore yellow. Four jail guards sat behind them, one for each inmate. A half-dozen lawyers sat one row behind the guards. They wore black suits despite the desert heat, like the hit men in *Reservoir Dogs* but with laptops.

The rest of the courtroom presumably held family members of the usual suspects on the docket. Fally and three of the Groundlings were in the back. They were in their courthouse best at least, but their tattoos were brighter, fresher in this light. Fally's snake tattoo hissed at her.

She hoped that was only her imagination. She avoided eye contact with the back of the court room and focused on the inmates instead.

One inmate looked like Gollum from *Lord of the Rings*. She was sure she'd seen him before. He kept muttering something about aliens and flying saucers as he talked with Denny. They were arguing about Alpha Centuri versus Cygnus X-1 and flying saucers versus flying spheres.

She recognized the two young Asian men who had been picked up on the Amtrak train. Denise figured them to be Chinese. They were stupid enough to be talking out loud about how they shouldn't have transported the suitcase from Colorado for one of their uncles in California.

"Your *nai nai* better be coming from Hong Kong to bail us out," one said to the other. "Is that her at the doorway?"

"Is this the courtroom?" a soft voice asked from the doorway.

Denise looked back as an ancient Asian woman entered the narrow courtroom door, hobbling on a walker. Could that be Professor Kang? The professor had been in her fifties, but this woman looked much older. Could anyone really age that much in two years?

The other Asian defendant frowned. "I've not seen my grandma since I was two years old. I don't know what she looks like, just that she's old."

The old woman frowned at them.

"I don't like that look," the first defendant said. The other didn't get a chance to reply.

"All rise," the James Bond bailiff announced. Judge Shahrazad Sanchez entered. She wore long sleeves even in this heat and had taken out her nose stud. The hole hadn't healed yet.

"Are we going to do the *miscellaneous* hearing about Ms. Song first?" Jane Dark asked.

"I think we have a resolution to that," the judge said. "Could the parties approach?"

Denise stumbled on the way to the bench. Was the judge going to lock her up before court even started? The judge hadn't gone totally mainstream, she had a fresh tattoo of an avenging angel on her hand that held the gavel.

The judge turned on a white noise machine so no one could hear them except for the new bailiff who was now behind them. This bailiff had a pair of handcuffs instead of a boomerang.

"Bad news," the judge said. Denise put her hands behind her back, ready for them to be cuffed.

"So, you're granting my motion, your honor?" Jane Dark asked. "Can we remand Ms. Song right here in the courtroom?"

Remand meant locking her up. The judge then smiled at Jane Dark. "The bad news is for *you*, Ms. Dark. Ms. Song, I apologize to you. All *your* paperwork is in order. We have a signed affidavit allowing you to practice signed by your mother's power of attorney, Susie Song, whose name I recognize from her golf days and that insurance commercial. Another attorney, a Luna Cruz, will be responsible for your supervision right now. I'm certainly aware of Ms. Cruz, she's one of the finest attorneys in the state."

Why would her mother have a *power* of attorney unless she was at death's door? Or already dead. The fact that her official supervisor would be her *aunt* rather than her mother really made her nervous.

"We will be vacating the miscellaneous hearing regarding Ms. Denise Song's ability to practice in this jurisdiction," the judge continued, rubbing her tattooed hand. "She's good to go. Let's get this one over with. You may proceed with the arraignment for Mr. *Denny* Song."

"But you said," Jane Dark began.

"That's all Ms. Dark," the judge cut her off. "The affidavit signed by the power of attorney, Susie Song, has been approved by the New Mexico Supreme Court. Luna Cruz signed off on the clinical law student form. All is in accordance with the local court rules here in Hidalgo County. You have friends in high places, *Denise* Song."

Denise and Jane went back to their respective tables. The woman on the walker clearly wanted to say something to the judge, but the bailiff signaled for the old woman not to disrupt the courtroom.

"Are you really sure that's not your *Nai Nai* from Hong Kong?" the first Asian defendant said. "She's really trying to get the judge's attention!"

"All *Nai Nais* from Hong Kong look the same," the second replied. "That could be her. I don't know."

"Your damn family is so messed up," said the first.

"You were the one who thought we should bring weed on the train through the asshole of America."

"Order in the court!" the judge yelled. "Denny Song, please come up to the podium for arraignment with your umm... *representative*."

One of the guards dragged Denny up to the podium.

"Appearances?" the judge asked.

"Jane Dark of the Attorney General's Office for the Great State of New Mexico."

"Denise Song, a clinical law student operating pursuant to Rule 5-110.1 of the New Mexico Rules of Criminal Procedure for the District Court under the auspices of supervising attorney Jen Song, I mean under the supervision of supervising attorney, Luna Cruz. I'm appearing for the defendant, Denny Song, who is present and in custody."

She heard some mumbling from the back of the court and turned around. The old woman was still trying to get everyone's attention by shuffling her walker.

The judge banged her gavel. "Ms. Denise Song, I'm up here. Look at me. Do you waive a reading of the defendant's charges?"

"We waive reading and enter a plea of not guilty on all of them!" She knew she was supposed to do something more right now but froze in the heat of the moment.

"The waiver is noted. Next case! *State v. Shifman!*"

Gollum rose up. "My turn. I'm getting out!"

"I got to get out of here!" Denny said. "Tell the judge! I think someone can take third party release for me."

"Can we address conditions of release?" Denise asked, still at the podium next to her twin. Third party release? To whom?

The judge frowned. "There's a *no bond* hold on the defendant after the pre-trial detention hearing. Counsel you were supposed to get us new information regarding conditions of release. Have you done so?"

Denise turned and scanned the courtroom, praying that Cordelia had come so she could at least argue that Denny had someone to be a third-party custodian.

Unfortunately, Cordelia was nowhere to be found. Worse, Fally was there. "Keep him in, keep him in," he had the Groundlings chant. "Keep him in!"

"You in the back," the judge asked. "Do you wish to address the court?"

"You heard us," Fally said. "He's a little liar. Keep him in. Denny's a menace, he was my stepson for a while and he's no damn good. Neither is his sister."

"Thank you," the judge said. "Anyone else wish to address the court?"

"Back there!" Denny said, hitting Denise in the side with his handcuffs as he turned to look at the old woman.

The judge pointed to the old woman on the walker. She had now propped herself up on her tippy toes, leaning toward the judge.

"Ma'am, you in the back," the judge said. "You've wanted to say something about the case of *State versus Denny Song?*"

The old woman moved to the aisle, so she was clearly visible to everyone in the courtroom. "I can take custody of Denny Song," she said in a wavering voice.

The two college kids looked back at her. "That's definitely not my *Nai Nai*," the second Asian student said to the first. "I know my *Nai Nai's* voice and that's not her. I have no idea who that is."

Denise wiped her eyes and finally got a good look at the old woman. No, it wasn't Professor Kang. The woman clearly had a spark about her, indicating some familiarity, but it was weak as if the woman was at death's door. But who could it be?

The judge pounded her gavel. "Your name, please, and your relation to the defendant?"

"My name is Jen Song, I'm his *mother.*"

Denise nearly fainted. It was Jen Song all right, but something terrible had happened to her in the intervening year. This forty-something woman could pass for eighty. Cancer? Radiation poisoning? A broken heart for abandoning her daughter?

Jen Song fumbled with her walker as she got into the aisle and tried to walk forward, but then she stopped. Before Denise could say anything, her mom, *their* mom, stumbled and dropped to the floor.

"Is she dead?" Denny asked.

No one answered.

PART III

THE TEMPEST

Chapter 23

In a town without an emergency room, it was unclear where Jen Song might spend her final minutes on earth. A dust storm to the west precluded a trip to Tucson, so Jen was transported by ambulance east to Las Cruces, about two hours away. She would end up at Centennial Hospital, across the freeway from New Mexico State University.

Once she knew the location on her maps app, Denise drove the Lexus at its maximum velocity on I-10.

Her phone rang as she passed the Lordsburg City Limits. It was Rita. "Auntie Denise, your mom made the news. There was even an alert on the news and everything. I hope she's all right. I didn't realize what a big deal she was. They had a link to the story when she had a big case with your Auntie Susie the golfer."

"Susie Song is my first cousin, once *removed*," Denise said. "*Not* my auntie."

"Anyway, Auntie Denise, I hope your mama's all right!"

"Rita!" Rayne picked up the phone. "Stop bothering your auntie! Sorry about that, Denise. I heard. Is your mom OK?"

"We don't know yet. I'm on my way right now to the hospital in Cruces."

"We're in Cruces. It's where my mother's campaign office is. If there's anything you need, we are here for you. *Anything at all.*"

"I'll keep that in mind," Denise said. "You're a good friend, Rayne. You too Rita." She could hear Rita crying softly. Why was the poor girl taking this so hard? Curious about the story, Denise searched for it on her own phone. While a story did appear, it had the ominous word "developing story."

Rita couldn't possibly have read it yet. There was so

much about the girl she didn't understand.

* * *

Centennial Hospital was a large white building, lined by palm trees, across from a Hilton Garden Inn. They could have been in a new Phoenix suburb with all the xeriscaping.

Denise parked in the lot in the heat of a 105-degree day, but, inside, the hospital had the air-conditioning cranked so high she felt goosebumps. Her spark didn't work here in the lobby; there was too much sickness coming through the air.

Denise approached the front desk to ask about her mother. Portia—an elderly lady in a pink vest—responded that she couldn't give out that information without a HIPAA waiver from the patient. Denise sat down in the lobby to consider her options.

She was soon joined by her cousin, Dew, who lived just down University Boulevard, right off the NMSU campus. Dew wore a Pokémon t-shirt and shorts and stank of stale coffee and foreign cigarettes. Her brownish hair was tortured into faux dreadlocks dyed blue. They hugged and then sat in silence.

Denise approached the concierge at the desk again. Portia reiterated her original statement. Denise sat down and swore.

"I've never seen you like this," Dew said, playing with a dreadlock.

"I've never been like this," Denise said. "I don't know what to feel."

"My mom's on the way," Dew said. "Get ready for Hurricane Luna."

* * *

By the late afternoon, the next members of Team Song arrived. Jen's half-sister Selena and her wife hurried into the hospital. Selena was totally Latinx and had married a Native American woman named Heidietta, the sister of the famed MMA fighter Heidi Hawk. Denise definitely saw a resemblance between Heidietta and her self-defense *sensei* up in Albuquerque. Could it have been Heidi herself?

An hour later, the one and only Hurricane Luna made landfall. Everyone rose out of reflex. Luna Cruz had once been a judge, a district attorney and a CEO; she commanded every room. Luna wore her usual black with discrete but shiny turquoise earrings. Luna hugged her daughter, Dew.

"Hey Luna," Dew said. She joked that she only called her mom "Mother" when she deserved it or was trying to get something.

"My little *Sacka-dacka-dew*," Luna replied to her daughter, a childish term of endearment.

Luna merely touched Denise's shoulder with a cursory squeeze. "Denise."

"*Aunt* Luna," Denise replied.

Luna must be back with Dan Shepard, Marley's father. Dan walked a few yards behind the hurricane in his own eye of the storm.

Denise could still read Dan like an open book. He had dated Jen Song before he met Luna. The complicated relationships were creating a bit of conflict between him and Luna.

"Why don't you just go back to the hotel, Dan? I'll rent a car," Luna said.

"You aren't even in this story," Dew added, twisting the knife in.

Shepard checked his phone after it let out a tone of an old song of some raspy voice singing that he believed in a "Promised Land." Denise couldn't tell if it was Bob Dylan, Bob Singer or one of those old white guy singers whose first names started with a "b."

"I've got to be somewhere else, anyway. Mitch Garry needs help with some client named Sage Cage whose accused of killing a woman at a nursing home. This could be the big case. I just hope that author in Albuquerque doesn't write about this one."

Denise vaguely recalled something called the *Rattlesnake Lawyer* series by some unknown attorney-author up in Albuquerque that supposedly dealt with Shepard's adventures. She hadn't read them of course. Nobody did. She also sensed something about a funeral, a *rattlesnake* funeral, but that would be a story for another time.

"No one cares about an underachieving middle-aged lawyer with white male privilege," Dew added, biting down on one of her blue dreadlocks. "I doubt anyone will ever write about you again."

Shepard asked the security guard about something, and then hung his head and left. "We'll see about that," he whispered to the wind.

Shepard gone; Hurricane Luna had now hit the front desk. "What's happening with my sister?" she demanded.

"Sister?" Portia was confused. Luna Cruz was Latinx, and Jen Song was marked down as Asian.

"She's my *half*-sister," Luna said. "The good half."

It took Portia a while to find the patient, which made Luna even more impatient. Portia signaled to the small but wiry security guard to escort the Song clan to a neutral corner of the lobby until a doctor could come out. His name badge read Perea, but he looked more like a Piranha. Small, but tightly muscled; his skin was mottled from faded acne. He must have been aware of the resemblance because a sticker under his name badge advised people to CALL ME PIRANHA. The sticker had a picture of a cartoon fish. If it was supposed to put people at ease, it failed.

Denise could see why Centennial needed a Piranha to guard its doors. There were several prison facilities nearby, in this border area—both Federal and State. Several times, Denise saw EMTs coming in, dragging gurneys with people hand-cuffed to the sides. Law enforcement scrambled to keep up with the gurneys, and family members followed behind them.

Piranha kept track of every police officer, every patient, and every prisoner coming and going. He took away several weapons from the family members who might be there to finish the job on a rival. He might not be a doctor, but it was *his* hospital.

Finally, around six in the evening, two doctors came out to the lobby. The younger doctor introduced himself as Dr. Schwartz. His hair was already receding but was curly around the sides. He looked like he should be doing stand-up comedy as opposed to emergency medicine. He was Denise's age, and was accompanied by an older, female doctor, Dr. Patel. Dr. Patel stood behind Dr. Schwartz, holding an iPad, as if grading him.

"She's in a coma," Dr. Schwartz said. "At least she's stable. We have no idea what caused her illness but suspect a link to radiation poisoning. There's not much we can do except keep her well."

"Is she going to die?" Denise asked.

"Her long-term prognosis is *not* good." Dr. Schwartz looked back at Dr. Patel, who nodded. "Six weeks max perhaps. But we'll keep her comfortable. We'll observe her here before deciding whether to move her to hospice."

"*Hospice here?*" Dying in the desert sounded much more depressing than dying in the misty pines of the suicide forest of Aokigahara. "Will she ever regain consciousness? I want to say good-bye."

"I can't make a prediction on that at this time," Dr. Schwartz said.

As the two doctors walked away, the older woman gave pointers to her student. "So, what should I have said instead?" he asked.

Denise didn't listen. Her mother's death should not be part of a medical school class.

"Are you OK, Denise?" Luna asked.

"I don't know yet."

* * *

Around eight that evening, young Dr. Schwartz—under the supervision of his mentor—let Team Song visit Jen in a private room. The room had a view of the Organ Mountains to the east, with the full moon rising over the granite formations resembling organ pipes.

The private "suite" was barely big enough for all of them, especially with all the modern medical equipment crowding the petite woman in the bed. Denise still had difficulty grasping that this wizened figure was her once-glamorous mother. Jen Song had been the original Laser Geisha Pink back when Luna, Jen and Selena had billed themselves the Laser Geishas. Her hospital gown was pink at least, but Denise could see faded bloodstains.

Denise could feel an energy emanating from her mother, an energy so strong that Denise couldn't focus on it, couldn't read it. Why hadn't she ever felt this before? Had her mom stifled her own spark?

"Don't get too close to her!" Dr. Patel ordered. "Not everybody in the room at the same time."

After rotating in and out of the room for a few minutes, Luna and the others went back downstairs. Luna mentioned an arrival of someone else who they'd meet in the lobby.

"I'm staying here till they kick me out," Denise said. She had nowhere else to go anyway—nothing in Albuquerque and a brother in jail in Lordsburg. She wasn't comfortable with this instant family after being all alone for so long.

Alone with her mother, the coast relatively clear, she pulled up a chair close to the bed.

Denise struggled to keep her eyes open for the next few hours. At midnight, a very tall, middle-aged Asian woman with a cane entered the room. This woman was younger than her mother and shared her unhealthy skin. This poor woman was also bent over like a question mark.

Denise stared at her. What was wrong with her spark today? She could read nothing from the figure. The woman held out her hand stiffly. Denise shook.

"Don't you recognize me, Denise?" the woman asked. "I knew you when you were little. I'm a little disappointed, I used to be famous."

This was clearly a biological relative on her mother's side, although Denise couldn't place the gray business suit and severe coke bottle glasses.

"Umm..." Denise said. She was getting a residual spark from the handshake. She knew this person.

The woman flashed her magical smile. Even with a few missing teeth, Dew saw her former idol, at one time the most famous female golfer in the world.

"Susie?"

Susie Song had the billion-dollar smile that had once sold golf-clubs and yoga pants when she was only a teenager.

Had that only been fifteen years ago? This woman once hit a golf ball three hundred yards when she swung for the stars but now could barely swing her cane much less a golf club.

"I guess I'm not so famous anymore, even to family."

"You'll always be famous to me," Denise said.

"I don't really believe you. Your mom looks stable at least," Susie said.

"No change," Denise said.

Susie did a careful inspection of the room. Once everything passed inspection, she nodded at Denise.

"Come downstairs with me," Susie said. "I need to meet with all of you."

Outside in the parking lot, the desert night air was crisp and dry. Denise, Dew and Luna sat on cold metal benches. Denise half-expected to hear ominous music coming from the massive granite pipes of the Organ Mountains. The Lexus and its visible dent were parked right in front of them.

"What's going on with Jen?" Luna asked. "You know what's going on, Susie. We have a right to know."

"It's a long story, but I'll start from the beginning. I now work with Cygnus Moon in 'special affairs.' Cygnus Swan Bank was a financial consulting company in Korea that merged with the Wagatsuma corporation of Japan. They formed a joint venture with Zhang corporation of China which eventually bought out Dragon Moon here in America to form Cygnus Moon. A few years ago, I got Jen a job at the company. Jen was supposed to 'manage me' when I did appearances all over Asia. It was the least I could do."

A manager? What did that mean? It could either mean that Jen worked for Susie or Susie worked for Jen. And why was that the *least* she could do?

"I think we know all that," Luna said.

Denise didn't really know the difference between Cygnus Moon and Dragon Moon. She had lost track of the various corporate entanglements. All she knew is that when she started high school, her mom had moved to Asia. Since Luna was her godmother, Luna raised her.

"Does this have something to do with why my mom gave legal custody of me to Aunt Luna?" Denise asked.

141

"Jen accompanied me on my Asian tour that summer before you began high school at Albuquerque Academy," Susie said. "You were still at the group home getting home schooled because of your *issues*."

"I know about that," Denise said.

"We were touring a nuclear facility to promote the corporate health plan or whatever. We did a lot of corporate promotions for Cygnus Moon."

"Nuclear?" It was all starting to make sense to Denise.

"While we were there, there was an accident, an industrial *nuclear* accident. Your mother was exposed to radiation. I was exposed. At first, they thought it was radiation poisoning, it was a new type of radiation—gamma rays, omega rays, whatever it was—and no one knew its effects, and they feared that it might be contagious. She didn't want to be around you and possibly infect you. But no one really knew the extent of her... illness."

"She was good a year ago," Denise said.

"She *was* fine, or so we thought," Susie said. "Her doctors called it remission, but there was another relapse a few weeks ago. A bad one. She hasn't been the same since. I was infected along with her back then, and I haven't been the same since."

A cloud slowly eclipsed the moon while Team Song sat in silence, absorbing Susie's dark story.

"Is there anything I can do for my sister?" Luna asked. Jen apparently was a full sister and not a *half*-sister now.

"Is there anything I can do for my *mother*?" Denise asked, simultaneously.

"Not right yet," Susie said. "She needs her *sisters*."

"We'll be there," Luna said.

"I know you will."

Denise winced when Susie said the word "sisters" instead of something more inclusive like the word "family" which would have included Denise. Luna gave Susie a hug.

"Can you two excuse us?" Susie continued. "I need to talk to Denise alone."

Luna and Dew left. Susie rose, but indicated to Denise that she should remain seated. Even stooped over, Susie towered over her.

"I'm sorry that it has come to this, but you've left us no choice," Susie said. "That's your mother's rental car with the dent in it, right?"

"Are you pressing charges against me for keeping the rental car and the credit card?"

"Not *yet*. Neither your mother nor the corporation is pressing *felony* fraud charges against you for taking the rental car for over a year and using a *corporate* credit card for your own purposes. All you had to do is ask, and we would have helped you out."

"But I *did* ask. You didn't return my calls."

"Your mother had a relapse when she returned to Korea," Susie said. "She couldn't call."

"I had no idea," Denise said.

"Then you stopped calling and that hurt your mother very deeply. Right now everything is in flux, while we're waiting to see..."

"To see if she *dies*?"

"We'll see. However, once she learned of her son, your mother recognized that he would need our help, need *your* help."

"Thanks for the vote of confidence."

"You can continue working the case, under Luna's supervision, but you will be on a strict financial diet. We will give you another credit card to live on during the trial. All major financial and legal decisions have to be run by *me*."

"You're not my mom, Susie," Denise said. "You're not even an attorney."

"From now on, I might as well be. I'm your mother's power of attorney. You can't practice law without my say so. Or your aunt's."

A power of attorney was more powerful than a real one; they controlled the purse. Susie sat back down and they both sat still. The moon was now totally hidden behind the cloud. Another ambulance pulled into the hospital and EMTs came out with a body which they put in a hearse.

"How will I be able to still practice as a clinical law *student*?"

"Your Aunt Luna will be signing off as your attorney-mentor through that barely legal online law school you allegedly attend. All legal documents will be signed by her. You will be able to handle the other hearings solo in Hidalgo county only, short of going to jury trial."

"Where will I live? The case will take months."

"You'll probably need to live in Lordsburg for the duration. A room will be available for you there. I'm sure you can stay with your cousin here on weekends."

"What about my mom? What happens if she umm... dies?"

"There is a trust set up for you, and one for your brother, fifty-fifty. There are some ummm... *issues* that still need to be resolved that could affect the final distribution. Let's just say that Cygnus Moon can certainly review all their civil and *criminal* options regarding your behavior over the last year, so I wouldn't necessarily count on inheriting *anything*."

"This isn't about money."

"Everything's about money," Susie said. Denise looked at the Lexus and sighed. She knew what was coming next.

"One more thing," Susie said. "Give me your car keys."

Chapter 24
Tuesday, July 21

It was well into the wee hours, and Dr. Patel wouldn't let Denise spend the rest of the night with her mom. After some humiliating begging, Dew reluctantly came back to pick her up. Dew drove the world's dirtiest Mercedes sedan. The black exterior was caked with desert sand. Inside, it smelled liked Dew used the car to transport tigers, or their prey. There were bloodstains on the floor.

"I forgot how much I hate your car," Denise said. "I probably should have taken an Uber or something."

"Desperate much?" Dew asked.

Dew's off-campus neighborhood was not just a student ghetto, but a real one. The students were just part of the mix. Dew lived in a two-story Spanish-styled apartment building called *Vista de Estrella*, aka the Star View.

A few young people were partying in the parking lot, drinking beer and smoking pot around a fire in a trash barrel. One man looked like a Hispanic John Belushi from *Animal House* and wore a New Mexico State University football t-shirt that failed to cover his vast gut. His "outie" belly button was pierced with a giant rhinestone. It looked like an alien about to erupt from his gut. To top off the look, he had on a pair of plaid shorts and rattlesnake cowboy boots. He also sported a pink sombrero.

Was this the same pink sombrero man she had seen over in Lordsburg? It was too dark to tell.

"That was odd," Denise said as they went up the stairs to the second floor of the *Vista*. "I felt something weird just now from that group, but maybe it was the heat from the fire."

"They're harmless," Dew told Denise. "Well, *mostly* harmless."

That was a private joke between them, a line from *The Hitchhiker's Guide to the Galaxy*.

Inside the apartment, Denise collapsed on the couch. There was a squeal, and Denise jumped. She had disturbed the nap of Dew's two cats—a white cat named Sahar and a black cat called Suri. The cats must have stunk up the Mercedes, and the apartment was little better. For some reason, Dew *always* had cats named Sahar and Suri, so Denise called them the *Star Cats, the Next Generation*. Sahar was always white, and Suri was always black. Dew often explained that Sahar and Suri would be the names of her real children someday.

"In the future, my kids will probably have the Star Cat DNA mixed in," Dew had always joked. Sahar the white cat had sunk her teeth into a *Star Wars* plush toy, a laser pistol shaped like a mouse. She pointed the laser's barrel right at Denise, marking her territory.

Near the couch, Dew had two framed pictures on an end table. One was a picture of a seven-year-old Dew and her father, the late Sam Marlow, flexing in tandem on top of Acoma Pueblo. Another showed a teenaged Dew, her mother Luna, Dan Shepard and an infant Marley (who had been named after Marlow—yes, the family history was complicated). Denise had been in that picture, but she had been cropped out, so Dew was in the center of the square frame.

Denise reached for the pictures, but Sahar jumped up on the end table, the Star Wars toy still in her mount and pointed at Denise, ready to pounce.

"I'm *family*, Sahar," Denise said.

That worked. Sahar dropped the laser toy and snuggled against her.

"We're good, Sahar?" Denise asked. Denise saw a chewed pen cap on the floor and handed it to the cat.

The cat purred and then bit the pen cap. All good.

* * *

A few hours later, a sleepless Denise went out to the balcony of the Vista to get a breath of fresh air. Denise turned her eyes down to the parking lot where the last of the partiers lifted up their cans and bottles to toast the dawn.

"Hope we didn't keep you up all night," the drunken man in the pink sombrero slurred to Denise.

"No, it's cool," Denise lied.

"Hey Dew!" he shouted when Dew came out behind Denise. Dew was wearing an oversized t-shirt for Laser Geisha Blue, but Blue was crossed out and TURQUOISE was written in. Denise recognized that that was Aunt Luna's old shirt from back in the day. Had Dew stolen it from her mom? Was Dew wearing anything under the shirt?

"Who's your new girlfriend?" the man yelled, slurring his speech.

"Hey Petro!" Dew responded. "This is my cousin, Denise Song. She's a lawyer."

"Kinda," Denise said sheepishly.

Petro smiled. "Any friend of Dew is a friend of ours. I always need legal help."

"You were at the rally in Lordsburg," Denise said. "You were the guy on the picnic blanket."

"Guilty as charged."

"I'm going to call the cops," yelled a resident from a window.

"*We're not going anywhere,*" Petro said three times, his eyes closed. For some reason, his words—his rhythmic chant—had *gravity.* Denise had to brace herself to keep from falling over the railing. Did this drunk have psychic powers?

"*We're not going anywhere; we're not going anywhere!*" he kept chanting. The others joined in.

"*We're not going anywhere!*" Denise was surprised that Dew had joined in, chanting along.

Denise didn't know how a drunken chant from an overweight college dropout in a pink sombrero gave him control over the earth below; but it definitely did something. It was like he had become one with the planet, and had roots that extended all the way down to the core.

After five more chants of *"We're not going anywhere,"* the cop-calling resident slammed their window shut.

Petro opened his eyes and then leapt up as if on a

trampoline. He did a clumsy victory dance around his grounded sombrero, a cross between the git-up dance and the macarena.

"You're *never* going anywhere, Petro!" Dew said with a smile.

"I still got it," he shouted, and took another chug directly from the keg.

Dew and Denise hurried back inside. "What was that all about? The *'We're not going anywhere'* chant?"

Dew shrugged. "That was something Leo said when he was playing the disabled kid in the film, *What's Eating Gilbert Grape?*"

"I don't understand."

"*We're not going anywhere!*" Dew chanted. "Petro says *'We're not going anywhere'* and they all join in and sure enough no one can ever make them go *anywhere*. Ever."

"How do you know that? You dated that fat slob? Alcoholic much?"

"He's not all bad. And I only dated him very, very briefly. And I wouldn't call it dating. He's really smart when he's sober."

"Was he actually enrolled in school?"

"He was into astrophysics before he became an alcoholic."

"His name is Petro?" Denise asked. "Like p*etroleum*?"

"It's short for *something*, I don't know. He's got a funny name. Or maybe he was a petroleum engineer in addition to him being a rocket scientist."

"But is he a psychic or something?" Denise asked.

"He might have been. Now he's just an alcoholic. But his heart's in the right place."

* * *

Dew left for class and Denise spent the rest of the morning alone in Dew's cramped, smelly apartment at the Vista, getting judged by the star cats.

"I won't take your toy away, Sahar," Denise said. "Ever."

Sahar finally agreed and sat on Denise's lap. Suri was lurking somewhere, coughing up the occasional furball. After a few anxious calls to the hospital, Dr. Patel got back to her. "It's touch and go," the doctor said. "I'll call you if there's a change."

Denise and Sahar fielded hourly jail calls from Denny. "How's my mom?"

"I don't know."

* * *

Dew finally returned from her morning computer lab and expressed disappointment that Denise was still there. "You couldn't get in to see your mom?"

"I'm waiting to hear something, anything."

On cue, Luna called Denise. "You're still at Dew's place, Denise?"

"Yes, *Aunt* Luna."

"Put this on speaker." Denise did. "Girls, we need to meet in Dew's apartment this afternoon."

"Shouldn't we meet at your hotel, *Luna*?" Dew asked her mother nervously. "Aren't you staying at the *Encanto*?" The Hotel Encanto was the nicest place in Las Cruces.

"I think I want to see how my little *Sacka-Dacka-Dew* actually lives," Luna said. Denise stifled a laugh. "I'm paying for it."

"Hey *Luna*," Dew said. "I can always come home, move back with you, and go to a community college."

"Moving on," Luna said. "Denise, you're going to need help with this, and I can't do everything for you. Your brother was discharged from the military. He was stationed over at Holloman and then at White Sands. Do you know any private investigators or paralegals? I need someone with a security clearance."

It all came together in a flash. "Yes, my friends, *Aunt* Luna," Denise said. "I'm pretty sure that Rayne Herring has a clearance because of her mom, the colonel. Hikaru Yu probably has one because he works for a military contractor."

"They were on your mock trial team, right?" Luna asked. "Team Terror?"

"Turquoise. We can put the band back together," Dew added.

Denise looked over at Dew, who nodded. "*Team Tur-*

quoise!" they both said at the same time. They were about to say "Jinx" but thought better of it.

"Well let's see if you can have your band together by six tonight," Luna said. "My little *Sacka-Dacka-Dew*, please clean your room before I get there. I don't want to get infected from all the radioactive cat shit."

Chapter 25

With the star cats scrambling to stay out of the way, Dew and Denise did a mild cleaning of the apartment, but it was a lost cause as Dew and the cats quickly grew distracted. She played film maker and made a video of Sahar and Suri playing with the plush laser pistol toy. After frantically directing the cats, she edited the final product to depict Sahar firing a laser with Suri rolling over, playing dead. Dew fiddled with her phone to add special effects and uploaded it with a smile.

"Three hundred likes on Instagram," Dew said, checking her phone, moments later as Denise emptied a final load of trash. "You're famous, Star Cats, Next Generation. We can finish cleaning later. Now you see why I haven't taken over the world yet."

A few hours later, with Petro's parking lot party back in full swing, there was a knock on the door. Rayne Herring and her daughter Rita had arrived. Rayne wore a red shirt underneath a red Texas Tech blazer. After a successful sports career at Clovis High, Rayne had actually been recruited to be a power forward on the school's well-regarded women's basketball team. Unfortunately, she had to bow out after she got pregnant in high school with Rita.

Rayne had a "Big Red Herring" campaign button with her mom's picture. "I'm contractually obligated to wear this."

Rita also wore red, with the obligatory campaign button, but it was pinned upside down over a t-shirt for BTS. BTS was Denise's favorite K-pop band. Rita's awkwardness was even more apparent this close up. She resembled her mother in height and hair color, but her face lacked the symmetry of her mothers. Everything was a little off, and Denise could empathize with the poor girl.

Rayne nearly hit her head on a low-hanging light fixture and caught Rita before the girl did the same.

"Howdy Auntie Denise," Rita said, bending down to embrace the smaller Denise.

"*Lovely Rita Meter Maid,*" Denise sang. "I knew you before you were born."

The four of them sang all the verses of the song. After laughing at the end, there was an uncomfortable silence.

"You live like this?" Rita asked Dew when she sat on a couch and nearly cut herself from some mystery item that the cats must have gnawed all the flesh off. Beef jerky? "Aren't you supposed to be like really smart?"

Denise was liking Rita even more. Although they often talked by phone, this was the first time they'd all been together in the flesh since high school. Denise could sense that both Herrings had sparks to them. Rayne hid hers away in embarrassment, and clearly wanted Rita to do the same.

"Be careful, Rita," Rayne said. "This place is dangerous."

"I'm sure you've been in worse," Dew said. "Didn't your mom take you to Iraq when she was with the *Luftwaffe?*"

"She wasn't in the Luftwaffe," said Rayne, a step slow. "That's the Nazis, right?"

"Iraq was safer than here," Rita chimed in. "They cleaned up after the camels."

Dew laughed. "Your daughter is clearly the brains in the family, Rayne"

From the interaction between Rayne and Dew, it was clear that they had some unfinished business from mock-trial days. "You really should have cleaned up the place," Rayne said, her military upbringing apparent.

"I'm not going to clean it for you guys," Dew replied.

"I almost didn't want to come to see you, Dew," Rayne said. "But my daughter was quite persuasive. She says her Auntie Denise needs us."

Denise smiled when her phone beeped and broke the silence. "I just got a text, Hikaru Yu is on his way."

She didn't show them the text as it was merely a pic of his van with the Organs in the background as he came down Route 70. He was a few minutes away.

"Team Tur..."

Dew stopped her. "We should wait till he gets here."

"Hopefully, he can sing with us next time," Denise said. "He's got a nice baritone."

A short time later, there was a knock on the door.

"Hikaru?" Denise asked.

"No, it's me." Denise and the cats looked for cover when Hurricane Luna made landfall in Room 237. The light fixtures shook. The cats scurried under the couch.

Dew was unaffected. "Hey *Luna.*"

"*Sacka-Dacka-Dew,*" Luna replied.

"How is my mom, *Aunt* Luna?" Denise asked.

"Had to pull a few strings but I got in to see your mother and she's... *stable.*"

"Thank God," Denise said. "What does stable mean?"

"She's not getting *worse.* But no one can see her for a few days which might be just as well," Luna said. "I literally had to walk over some fat guy in a pink sombrero who had passed out on your stairway. Some *Vista de Estrella.*"

"Petro and his gang are harmless," Dew replied. "Well mostly harmless."

"I hope you lock your door," Luna said. "Is this your so-called supercomputer? The one I gave you all the money to buy after you left your last one in your unlocked car."

Dew shrugged. "I think spies took it. Or aliens."

Luna introduced herself to Rayne and Rita. "I know Big Red Herring, the colonel. We were on a corporate board together."

"We've heard of you," Rita said. "You're like the best lawyer on the planet. My grandma said so."

"I try. Is anyone else coming?" Luna said.

"My friend, Hikaru," Denise said. "He's almost here."

Hikaru arrived moments later, in jeans and a cycling jersey sans blazer that showed off his lean, but muscular arms. His French *equipe* jersey was turquoise, worn to show Team spirit. His cologne took the edge off the feline smell of the apartment.

"Like old times," Hikaru said. As Rita sat on the couch looking with longing, the four teammates formed a circle like

153

athletes before a big game. "Team Turquoise!"

In that instant, the Rayne-Dew feud was over at least for a moment. "Well Team Turquoise," Luna said, "let's get on with it. Do you have case notes, Denise?"

"Right here, Aunt Luna." Denise handed some notes to Dew who scanned them onto her big computer screen.

Luna frowned. "Denny's saying he was *abducted* by aliens?"

"No, Aunt Luna, he's saying that the grails warped his mind as they are really conduits to the aliens in another dimension," Denise said.

"I stand corrected," Luna said. "And he was first exposed to the grails when he was in the military?"

"I guess so," Denise said. "It doesn't really make sense."

"How bad was the shooting of the cops?" Luna asked. "Do they have lapel cam videos?"

"It's pretty bad," Denise said. "Dew, can you play the lapel cam videos from Channel 8's website?"

The grainy video showed an anorexic man, walking like a well-disciplined zombie, firing away at the cops.

"He looks innocent to me," young Rita said. She was strangely entranced by the video on the screen. "I mean he looks like he doesn't know what he's doing. And he looks just like you Auntie Denise."

"Quiet Rita!" Rayne said. "Hopefully you didn't take that the wrong way, Denise."

"I'm all good. He says the aliens made him do it."

"Well, maybe we can subpoena the aliens," Rita said before Rayne could shush her. "That sounds like a dirty word, *subpoena*."

"Our strategy is obvious," Luna said, banging a gavel down with her voice. "We are raising competency and raising his inability to form specific intent. I already drafted the motion to determine competency and we can e-file it tonight. I will contact Dr. Maryann Romero. She's been the expert in this stuff ever since I was a rookie lawyer. She will do the forensic evaluation on Denny while he's in custody."

"That's what I was thinking," Denise said. Luna didn't acknowledge her.

"Rayne, like I said, I knew your mom, the colonel," Luna said. "She was a big deal on all the bases. Do you have a security clearance of your own?"

"My mom made me get one so I could babysit my daughter on base if need be."

"I have one too," Rita said. Rayne clamped down on her daughter's shoulder.

Luna nodded. "Find out who we have to serve our *subpoena duces tecum* to get all Denny's military records. It's my experience that if he worked with any classified materials you might have to go on site to get them, and it always helps if someone has a clearance."

"I'll check with my mom," Rayne said. "She can help us get on base. At least I hope she can help, if she's not too busy campaigning in the asteroids or whatever."

"My grandma doesn't like to help anybody with anything when she's campaigning," Rita added.

"Hikaru, I knew your dad," Luna said, ignoring Rita. "Can you help get the records of the civilian contractors who dealt with Denny on base? We don't even know where to begin."

"Well, it's not as hard as you think," Hikaru said. "A lot of them are stored on site at the Syrinx facility, but it will take another subpoena to get to them."

"We'll exchange emails tomorrow," Luna said. She turned to Dew. "*Sacka-Dacka-Dew*, my lovely daughter, I want you to help Rayne and Hikaru with the computer files after they get them from the base."

"Love to, *Luna*," Dew said.

Denise looked around. "What do I do, Aunt Luna?" Denise asked.

"You're going to be doing client control," Luna said. "You're Denny's twin sister, he trusts you. You're going to be our point person in Lordsburg, starting tomorrow."

Denise shuddered.

Luna nodded. "That's all then. Hikaru, is something wrong?"

Hikaru frowned. "I didn't realize you all would be here. I thought I was coming here to see Denise."

Denise smiled. Was he hoping for a date?

Chapter 26

Hikaru nodded at everyone in the room, took a deep breath and then looked directly at Denise. "Denise, can I talk to you, outside?"

Luna interrupted. "You don't have much time; she needs to get back to Lordsburg *tonight*."

"Lordsburg isn't going anywhere," Rita said. "Let her have her moment."

Luna looked at her watch. "You've got an hour. I have dinner plans of my own at six."

Denise blushed for a moment, and then nodded to Hikaru. They didn't say a word, but the two of them walked out to the balcony.

Outside, the party in the parking lot was still going strong. It seems like there was a whole new supporting cast, but Petro was still the star.

"You guys want to join us?" Petro asked. He wore a white cowboy hat and white boots this time, but the same shirt and the same shorts. His belly button ring was now a turquoise nugget.

Hikaru went down the rickety stairs to the lot, took a beer cup from Petro and chugged it, much to the crowd's delight. They offered Denise a beer when she joined them, but Hikaru pushed them away.

"I want her to have a clear head," he said, "and avoid the appearance of impropriety."

Once they walked out of the lot and were around the corner from the party, Hikaru turned to Denise and smiled, suds around his mouth. She wiped them away.

They walked across the four lanes of University Boulevard and onto the "pueblo revival" structures area of the

NMSU campus. "It's like an adobe Amherst," he said.

"Cornell with cactus," she added. "Or Cal Tech with cactus if that's where you went."

"MIT by the way, so it would be MIT on the mesa."

"Of course, you did," she said with a smile. "I failed out of Harvard Law, kinda."

They passed the massive NMSU Performing Arts Center, where an electronic billboard proclaimed that famed New Mexico singer Anna Maria Arias would be performing with her daughter Jaylah. As a promotion, the duo's *musica romantica* blared from the building's loudspeakers, and the mother-daughter team harmonized their greatest hits.

"Follow me." Hikaru and Denise kept pace to the lilting beat as they walked over a barren field to a large puddle underneath some windmills. He pointed downward; the still water perfectly reflected the windmills in the pink of the sunset. The last notes of the *musica romantica* reflected off the windmills and onto the waters.

"What is this place?" Denise asked, leaning closer to him.

"The Zuhl museum grounds. I wonder if it was named after the demon in the first *Ghostbusters*." Hikaru smiled.

"I loved that movie, but I think *Zuul* was spelled differently. That's the first movie I've seen about people like me. People who have umm... powers."

"People like *us*," he said.

"*Kinda*," she said.

"How did you know this puddle was here and that there would be reflections of windmills and sunsets and soft romantic music?" she asked.

"I googled romantic places in Las Cruces, and it identified Zuhl museum after a rainstorm. I heard the music when I was driving in."

She tried to reach out to him with her mind, like a current passing between them. Perhaps it was a matter of charge, or frequency, they couldn't quite read each other's thoughts, but colors came through, like images of sunsets and sunrises.

"I like this," he said. He touched her shoulder. "I really, really like this."

"I do too," she replied.

Their combined charge must have been what was making the metal windmills turn even faster. He looked around, making sure that no one was looking and took her hand. "You don't mind, do you?"

"Not at all," she said. "So why are we here? Are we tilting at windmills? Am I your Sancho Panza or your Dulcinea?"

To her disappointment, he released her hand. "You're not Sancho Panza. I'm still on double secret probation at work," he said. "I'm not even supposed to be talking to you."

"Probation with whom?"

"My big boss," he said. "All the way to the top."

"I thought you worked for your dad."

"I thought I did too," he said. "But it turns out he works for someone else."

"So, you can't help us at all?"

"I can't help you *yet*," he said. "But I'll find a way."

"You were there when Denny got in trouble," she said.

"I was and I didn't mean for any of this to happen," he said. "The drone made him go crazy."

"So, it wasn't a UFO?"

"Just a drone, a terrestrial drone," he said. "Probably made in Asia at some cut-rate factory and sent to New Mexico for a test flight or two. There are a lot of these drones hidden around this area. That's all I can say right now. But I will try to get you all the information on how the drones affect people, despite what my bosses say."

"I was actually hoping it was a UFO. I was just in Roswell and all the alien stuff was so tacky. I want to go to the real site someday."

"Maybe I can take you there."

"*Romance in Roswell*," she said. "Sounds like a Hallmark movie."

"Never seen one."

"Have you ever seen a Korean soap opera?"

"I'm Chinese."

They looked at each other. She felt enveloped in a protective cocoon. "I've never felt like this before," he said.

"We're like Romeo and Juliet," she said. "Kinda."

"I'm still hoping for a happy ending," he said, blushing.

"Kinda. Oh wait, that doesn't sound right."

His awkwardness was endearing. He touched her hand again, and the current was even stronger. For one brief moment, she thought they would kiss, but then one of the windmills turned faster, and even faster. He released his hand before the blades flew off.

He got another text again, spoiling the moment. She got one from Luna about getting back and getting on the road which made it worse.

"We better go back," he said.

* * *

They held hands tightly while crossing University Boulevard, and once they adjusted their energies, they found that the current was comfortable, like a vibrating bed that relaxed the muscles. The *musica* was still *romantica.*

If she strained her neck, she could see the top of the hospital tower. "I wish my mom and I could sing together like Anna Maria and Jaylah," Denise said. "We might never get the chance."

"I have a feeling you will. Kinda."

She couldn't tell if he could foresee the future or was being hopeful. She didn't want to know; she was happy with either. He walked her back to Dew's apartment. Petro's party was being busted by the cops.

Petro somehow managed to convince the cops to leave without incident, without even turning down the stereo or hiding his bag of marijuana, which was visible in plain sight.

Petro waved at Denise and Hikaru as the cops drove away, their signals off. "I'm not going anywhere."

"How did you do that?" she asked him, amazed.

"You just gotta have faith," he said. "You've got to put every ounce of energy into staying put, into creating your own *gravity* so that nothing can move you. I was an Astrophysics major."

Denise nodded. Before she could say anything more, Petro belched. The air smelled like petroleum.

* * *

Everyone stopped talking the minute Denise and Hikaru went back up the stairs and entered Dew's apartment, the door still open to let the air in. Hurricane Luna had left the building to spread havoc somewhere else.

"We were starting to wonder about you two," Dew said. "We were about to get Colonel Herring to order the 101st Airborne to pick you up."

"The Airborne is Army, my mother was in the *Air Force*," Rayne said. "Well, she was in *Space* Force at the end. She always pointed that out to us."

Denise ignored them, kept smiling.

"You're glowing, Auntie Denise," Rita said.

"You're actually smiling," Dew said. "I didn't know you were capable of that."

"I'm capable of a lot of things you don't know about," Denise said.

Hikaru was the one who blushed this time. "I've got to get going," he said.

"Call me," Denise said to him.

He smiled, clasped her hand one more time in front of everyone, but didn't kiss her. Self-conscious he hurried out onto the balcony of Room 237 but left the door open. Denise followed him outside for a second.

He lifted a hand to wave, and hurried down the stairs to the van. He looked up at Denise. "Didn't someone write a scene about a guy looking up at a girl on a balcony?" he asked as he opened the van door.

"Unfortunately, they named a ghost town after him," she said.

"Got to go to Los Alamos tonight," he said. Hikaru drove the van away, very slowly.

Denise let out a sigh and leaned against the stairway for a moment. She had almost forgotten about the case, about her mom. Her phone vibrated and her idyll was over. It was a text from Susie.

"We've booked your room in Lordsburg, you need to get back there tonight."

She remembered that Susie had repoed her Lexus. How was she going to get back to Lordsburg?

Chapter 27

Denise reluctantly went back inside Dew's apartment from hell. Had it become more littered in the few minutes she had been gone? The Star Cats had sure done a number *near* the litter box, but not *in* the litter box.

Rayne and Rita were still talking to Dew. Rita playing peacemaker between the two sides. Rita was playing the YouTube video of the great mock trial tournament and was literally lip-synching along.

"She does you better than you," Dew said to Rayne. Rayne wasn't able to sense that was an insult.

Denise's phone beeped with another text from her aunt. "Do you need an Uber to get back to Lordsburg?" Luna texted.

Denise frowned, then spoke to the room at large. "I never thought I'd say this, but can someone take me back umm... home?"

"Where's home?" Rita asked.

"Lordsburg right now."

"Don't look at me," Dew said. "I've got a project due tomorrow."

"We can take you," Rita said.

Denise couldn't tell if Rita was kidding. Rita pulled on her mother's sleeve to convince her.

"That's like two hours out of our way. OK, but you've got to promise that you'll make it up to us some day," Rayne said.

Denise didn't have a car anymore, so she doubted that Rayne would hold her to it. "I promise."

Denise followed Rayne and Rita to a red Buick Regal. The Regal sedan suited Rayne to a T—it was solid, a bit oversized and not too flashy. The inside of the car was immaculate and smelled of strawberries. A relief after the catshit of Dew's

Mercedes. Rita got in the back seat and put on the seatbelt without complaint.

"Girl's night out!" Rita said. "Lordsburg baby Lordsburg."

Outside, Petro's party had resumed again as two new people had joined him and opened bottles of beer. It was now pitch-black out, but they had lit fires in some old trash cans.

Petro and a friend were actually playing frisbee with that pink sombrero, doing diving catches all without spilling their beers. The sombrero hovered directly above his head for a full thirty seconds, before it descended, and he caught it. Must be the wind.

"Don't you ever leave?" Rita asked him through the window.

"We're not going anywhere," he said.

"*We're not going anywhere*," the other two members of the posse sang drunkenly.

"Creating our own *gravity*," Petro said with a smile, as he threw the sombrero back to the friend. Did the sombrero actually curve in midair? That couldn't be the wind. "You should try it sometime."

At that moment, Denise felt *something*. It really did feel like the earth was reaching up and holding the Regal down. Rayne had her foot on the gas, but the vehicle didn't move. Perhaps they really weren't going anywhere.

The ground stopped pulling the minute Petro chugged another beer. He caught and released the sombrero again, not spilling a drop. Rayne's car jerked forward and then stalled.

"There's something weird about that guy," Rita said. "Did you see that sombrero? Like it hovered in the air. He can control gravity."

"It's just a coincidence," Rayne said. "There have been earthquakes around here. There are all kinds of freaky wind gusts here in the desert. You can actually major in windmills out here, right Denise?"

"Kinda."

Vista de Estrella behind them, they grabbed some take-out for dinner and then Rayne gunned the gas and they were on Interstate 10 westbound to Lordsburg. If they hit Arizona, they'd gone too far.

"So, how's the private investigation company coming along, Rayne?" Denise asked.

"So far, you're our only client. Here's our new business cards," Rayne handed one to Denise. The cards were red of course.

"I am the junior investigator," young Rita said. "I get academic credit for this."

"How's that?" Denise asked.

"Home school," Rita said. "Well *home on the range* school."

"Don't sing for us, dear," Rayne said. "Please don't."

"Auntie Denise, I know you're a fan of ninjas, geishas and ronins," Rita said. "I'm like the samurai. I want to marry a samurai or just be one on my own someday."

"I'm part Korean, not Japanese," Denise said. "There's a difference."

"Stop jumping to conclusions, Rita," her mom said. "Just sit quietly for a change."

"Yes, mom."

* * *

Deeper into the desert, it was now totally dark, and they could see the stars.

They passed the Akela Flats travel center with its façade of a western town. The travel center looked weird in the floodlights, like a movie set about to have a gunfight.

"Is that a real courthouse?" Rita asked. "Have you ever done a trial there Denise?"

"It's a *façade*," Rayne said. "It's a fake courthouse. The whole town at this travel center is fake. It's there to get people to stop at the convenience store in the middle. There's nothing behind the set."

"I'm a fake lawyer," Denise said. "Maybe I can do a trial there."

"You're not a fake lawyer, auntie," Rita said. "Well, you'll be a real one soon."

After Akela Flats, they drove an hour west. Rayne followed the speed limit, even going one mile under. Every few miles they passed signs warning: GUSTY WINDS MAY EXIST.

163

"Does that mean the winds can exist here, or anywhere?" Rita asked after the third sign, clearly not paying attention to whatever homework she was allegedly doing on her tablet.

"I don't know dear," Rayne replied.

The gusty winds were definitely existing here on this stretch of interstate, and the Regal wobbled in the turbulence.

"Look mom!" Rita pointed to an electronic sign that warned about an approaching dust storm. The sign told them to pull off the road and turn off the lights if they were caught in the dust storm.

Just past Deming, they could make out a lightning storm headed right toward them.

The storm had lightning, but the lightning was in different colors and seemed to be sending a message in Morse Code as if the storm had consciousness, or perhaps was being controlled by something inside it.

Denise had heard these storms called *haboobs* after the sandstorms in the middle eastern deserts. This was the mother of all *haboobs.*

Rayne pulled off the road and turned off her lights.

"Mom, why did you do that?" Rita asked.

"Didn't you see the sign about what to do in a dust storm?" Rayne replied. "You're supposed to pull over and turn off your lights, right?"

"But suppose someone hits us in the dark?" Rita asked. Her mom said nothing. Moments later the Regal was totally engulfed in dust.

"They're here!" Rita said, sounding exactly like that young girl in *Poltergeist.* She pointed above at the blinking lights that were rotating around them in the haboob. No that wasn't a helicopter in the storm. It might be a drone, but in any event, the object was unidentified and flying. "They're *really* here!"

The storm howled around them. For a moment, Denise feared that even this solid car would be blown away in the winds. Although the light configuration was ambiguous at best. Rayne reached back and held her daughter's shoulder.

"No, they aren't dear," Rayne said. "Your grandma was a

colonel and worked on base. They're probably just surveillance drones, storm-chasers."

"Why would drones care about us?" Rita asked.

"They're probably taking measurements of wind speeds and electricity, or that sort of thing, to establish a baseline," Rayne said. "That's really important information when you're launching missiles."

"What do you think, Auntie Denise?" Rita asked.

Denise didn't know what to believe. The military drones—or whatever they were—hovered directly above them. The vehicle began to vibrate. "I don't know."

It was hard to tell what was happening above them in the dust and the darkness of the haboob. The lights stayed above them as the eye of the storm passed.

Whatever was above them was definitely probing them with some kind of invisible electrical beam. Denise felt a wave of electricity start at her head and go down to her toes and then back up again. She could be going through a fax machine and the pixels were being sent back to Pluto.

How could she protect them? Denise closed her eyes and tried to think happy thoughts, thoughts of staying tethered to the earth. What did Petro say—create your own gravity?

How does one do that?

She felt another surge of electricity, a ray from above as if the drone was still sending out a message to someone or *something* before deciding what to do.

The Regal continued to vibrate.

"I'm starting to get scared, mom," Rita said. "Really, really scared. Auntie Denise, is there anything you can do? What did that weird fat man in the parking lot say about creating your own gravity? What were they all chanting? It seemed to work…"

The lights revolved faster and faster with all the colors of the rainbow from infrared to ultraviolet. And then something really odd happened. Perhaps it was the flashing light, but Rayne phased in and out of sight.

Rita screamed. "Mom! Help her Auntie Denise!"

Denise grabbed Rayne's hand, hoping that would double their spark, and after one brief moment, Rayne solidified.

"We're not going anywhere!" Denise said out loud. Why did the words from a forgotten film echoed by a drunken lout have any power?

The car's vibrations abated slightly. The car felt heavier, clinging to the earth.

"We're not going anywhere!" Rayne echoed, still holding Dew's hand. She now seemed anchored to the car seat, anchored to reality.

Still, it might not be enough. Was the car now levitating off the ground? Was Rayne fading out again?

Leaning over from the back, Rita then clasped the others' hands. *"We're not going anywhere!"*

Denise felt a surge through her body that went through the others and then into the car itself. The car grew heavier and the earth's gravity, their gravity, grew stronger. Rayne nodded.

"We're not going anywhere!"

The car buckled for a moment, and it looked like the roof was coming off. Suddenly, the lights of the object disappeared, and the air grew calm. Too calm.

Denise looked around. Rayne looked around. Rita finally opened her eyes. "Are we OK?"

"I guess so," said Denise. "See it's gone!"

"What just happened?" Rita asked. "They were here. They were *really* here."

Rayne opened the car door, got out and threw up.

"Are you OK, mom?" Rita jumped out of the car and hurried over to her mom.

"If that happens again, it could kill me," Rayne said, wiping her mouth. "I just know it. I think I'm OK, now."

"Are you sure you're OK, Rayne?" Denise asked, also getting out of the car.

Rayne stood up, clutching her belly. "I guess so. I can't go through that again. Ever! I didn't exist for a moment. It affected me the worst."

They stood there in the starlight, taking deep breaths and recovering from the excitement of the last few minutes. A car passed in each direction. No one noticed them.

They stood in silence for another minute, and then they

got back into the car. Rayne took a few more minutes to settle down before turning the engine back on.

"Was that a UFO, Auntie?" Rita asked.

Denise knew she had to calm the poor girl. "Technically *everything* unidentified and flying is a UFO. Probably those were just weather drones. Or the new drones used by the border patrol. The military also has drones to check out microclimate."

"What just happened, Auntie?" Rita asked.

Denise had felt like she was being put through a fax machine before; now she felt like she was a smart phone, and something remote was deleting some files and doing a reboot.

For a moment, everything went dark again, and then she felt like she had flashed back. Unfortunately, she felt like something was missing, but she wasn't sure what it was.

She did what lepers call a visual surveillance of extremities. No, she had all her fingers and toes, but something was gone. Rita and Rayne were doing the same thing.

What had just happened? Denise's brain felt like dust.

Rayne and Denise looked at each other. "I have no *recollection* of anything," they both said in unison. They had forgotten the last two minutes. In fact, Denise didn't remember anything since the fake courthouse façade at Akela Flats.

"What does 'recollection' mean?" Rita asked.

They all shrugged. What had happened? Why were they on the side of the road. Must not have been a big deal, right?

"Might as well keep going," Rayne said. "Why did we pull off the road again?"

"I don't have any recollection," Denise said. Her companions smiled as if that was a joke.

"I feel like I should thank you, Auntie Denise," Rita said. "I'm not sure why though."

They drove in silence. For perhaps the first time in her life, Rayne was speeding.

* * *

The remaining hour drive on the interstate sped by, the

skies now dark and quiet. The moon was behind clouds, so the highway felt especially lonely.

Denise checked her watch and thought back for an instant. She knew she was heading to Lordsburg for Denny's case and that she'd met with Hikaru and she was with her two friends. However, she remembered nothing after she had passed Akela Flats, about an hour ago. How'd she get all the way out here so quickly?

She tried to concentrate and felt extreme pain. Must be from the bad takeout food they'd eaten at the start of the trip. Where was that again?

Oh well, might as well keep going? Nothing could happen to them all the way out here in the middle of the desert, right?

Chapter 28

It's not that they didn't remember the rest of the drive, there was nothing to remember. Denise rubbed her head from her headache. As they approached Lordsburg, they passed the detention center. "Mom, can we see Denise's client at jail?" Rita asked, strangely excited.

"No, that's a terrible idea," Rayne said, a little too harshly. She took the first Lordsburg exit, and made a point of making a hard turn away from the road to the jail. If Denise and Rita hadn't been wearing seatbelts, they might have been thrown into the side of the car. No one said anything as they passed the Denny's restaurant.

"Have you ever been here before?" Denise asked Rayne.

"Just once," Rayne said with a cryptic smile. "Now, where are you staying, Denise?"

"I'm not sure." Denise almost directed them back down Motel Boulevard to the Holiday Comfort and then remembered that she didn't live there anymore.

Her phone beeped. She noticed a text from Luna with a link and clicked on it. Her phone now directed them to the *Last Palm Motel*, which was behind the Holiday Comfort, even sharing the rear parking lot. It looked like the servants' quarters for the big house.

Rayne almost missed the entrance for the Last Palm, since most of the lights were out. A compact rental car, a Kia, sat in the parking lot. She knew that the Kia would be hers, and the keys would be at the front desk.

Another aunt, Mia, once drove a Kia. Mia had gone insane and was currently a fugitive. She disliked the Kia for that reason alone.

"Lordsburg feels different now," Denise said.

"Well this doesn't really feel like America," Rita said. "This feels like the surface of the moon. Just look at the stars."

Denise looked out the car window at the clear outline of the Milky Way. She didn't want to leave Rayne's car.

Rayne put her hand on Denise's shoulder. "Do you want us to come inside with you?"

Denise took a deep breath. "That might be best. Just in case."

Inside the lobby, Denise recognized Cordelia taking a coke out of a community fridge. Cordelia wore her usual cowgirl from hell outfit with new rips in her pants and a fresh scar across her forehead. Cordelia saw them and frowned. She opened her coke and put something into it from a flask. The smell reminded Denise of Nastia for some reason. After a slug from the flask, Cordelia went out the back door without a word.

"Ms. Song?" the desk clerk asked her. "We've been expecting you."

Denise nodded. "That's me, I guess."

"I got your room right here. Everything's been paid in advance! You even get a free breakfast across the street at the Holiday Comfort."

That meant she'd have to face Jane Dark each morning over the waffle machine, before facing her again at court.

Something else was bothering her, but she had no recollection of part of the drive over. That weird word again. She tried to recollect back to the last few hours of the night and felt an intense spasm of pain, like she was eating a liquid nitrogen popsicle too fast. Why couldn't she remember?

"Hold on a second," Denise said. "Rayne, what do you think?"

Rayne looked around the lobby like a detective. "Are you sure you want to stay here, Denise? Are you even sure you want to keep doing this? We can drive you wherever you want. I want to keep going west. Or south even. Hell, I've got relatives who run a bed and breakfast over in *Puerto Penasco* a few hours across the border in Mexico if you want to hide out where no one can find you. I ran away from it all when I was on a high school field trip. I hid there over Spring Break till my mom sent out the Air Force to get me."

Denise knew vaguely that Puerto Penasco was where Rayne had conceived Rita with some mysterious stranger. Rayne had a wistful look in her eye, maybe she was thinking of a lost love.

"What's a *Puerto Penasco*?" Rita asked.

"It's a resort town on the Gulf of California and it's like only five hours from here. It's, ummm, where I *met up* with your father."

Rita smiled, but said nothing.

"What would I do there?" Denise asked.

"Denise, they're always hiring at the resorts. You can get a job as a waitress, as a lifeguard, as anything."

Working at a beach resort as a tour guide or even as a waitress sure sounded better than being stuck in Lordsburg as a clinical law student trying to get her brother out of jail. There was enough sand here for a beach, but no ocean. Denise blinked and felt a cool ocean breeze blow across her face. She didn't really drink, but she could almost taste the Pina Coladas. Being a bar tender at a tiki bar would pull her out of her shell. Maybe Hikaru could even come down to join her...

Someone pulled her hand, yanking her away from the beach. "Auntie Denise," Rita said. "I mean just *Denise*. You have court tomorrow morning. Your brother needs you. Your mother needs you. *Denise*, you don't want to be a fake lawyer forever."

Denise stared into Rita's eyes. She was on the edge of tears. This girl actually looked up to her and no one had ever done that before. If Denise got in that car and left Lordsburg with them, Rita's heart would be broken.

"I'll do it for you, Rita," Denise said. "And you can call me Auntie again."

"Are you sure you want to stay here?" Rayne asked. "Last chance at freedom."

"I'm going to stay," Denise said.

"Can we go now?" Rita turned and asked her mom. "I'm glad Auntie is staying, but this place creeps me out."

"You're in room thirteen," Titus said, placing the key in

171

Denise's hands. They hadn't realized that he had still been standing there the whole time.

It was a regular key; magnetic key cards hadn't arrived at the Last Palm. The new century hadn't arrived here either.

Denise took a deep breath and looked around the Last Palm. She somehow knew that Denny was dead without her. Somehow, her mother would be dead too, if she didn't help Denny.

"I'm good," she said. "Room 13?"

After a round of hugs, Rayne and Rita hit the freeway back to Las Cruces. Denise was now all alone in her room at the Last Palm motel. The TV was color at least.

She checked the nmcourts.gov site. Luna had indeed entered her appearance as counsel of record for the status hearing tomorrow. Denise was still listed as a clinical law student. What was a *status* hearing anyhow?

Chapter 29
Wednesday, July 22

Feeling groggy the next morning, Denise crossed the parking lot and faced Jane Dark at the Holiday Comfort breakfast buffet. A sign in the lobby said: WELCOME HIDAL-GO COUNTY ROTARY. Denise had to show a free buffet ticket. Caliban pretended that he didn't recognize her.

Standing in line behind the Rotary members, Denise slipped and nearly fell. Catching herself on the counter, she noticed the waffle batter dispenser had exploded and the batter was flowing out of the faucet like lava. The batter had already attached itself to her black shoes.

"How much batter is in that thing?" a man asked, pointing at the batter flow. Denise recognized the famous attorney-author who was sidestepping the batter flood. "It keeps coming!"

Caliban hurried over to staunch the flow. "Please be careful, sir," he said. "That stuff has a mind of its own."

"Invasion of the batter snatchers," the man said. "I think there's a book there." The attorney-author hurried back to his room leaving specks of batter on the carpet with his waffle soles. Caliban quickly produced a mop and bucket and cleaned up the flow of batter before it reached any of the other tables.

Denise grabbed a hard-boiled egg and some fruit on the far side of the buffet, then turned around to see a smiling Jane Dark.

"Please join me." Jane Dark wore green Dartmouth University sweats, rubbing her swollen belly. "I sure hope your mom is OK. She was a role model to me."

"My mom? *Jen Song* was a role model to you?"

"That big-dollar verdict inspired me to pursue law. And now look at me, barefoot and pregnant in Lordsburg."

"You have nice shoes on your bare feet, at least," Denise said. "I have dried waffle batter on mine."

"This is just my job, there's nothing personal. I have to win this case if I ever hope to get back to civilization and provide for my daughter. Let's just say Lordsburg is a detour."

"What happened?"

"I signed a non-disclosure agreement about that, but let's say I'm in Lordsburg for my sins. I'm practically wearing a scarlet letter."

Was it a judge's child, a supervisor's, the Governor's?

"I think I'm here for my sins as well," Denise said.

"What sins do you have?" Jane Dark asked. "I bet you're a virgin."

Denise frowned. "I'll take the fifth on that. See you in court, counselor."

She crossed the parking lot back to her room at the Last Palm Motel to get ready for the day. Why did Jane Dark's assumption draw blood? After freshening up and grabbing the last of her files, Rayne called via FaceTime.

"Good news?" Denise asked.

"Good news and bad news. Hikaru was right. All the records involving Denny are in one place. At the Syrinx facility on the missile range. I've got the name of the contact to serve, someone named Maldonado or something like that."

"They should be easy to get then."

"That's the bad news. They won't let us anywhere near the missile range without some kind of *super* subpoena. And I have to be there personally because I have the right clearance."

Denise realized she had never filed a subpoena duces tecum. She would have to ask her aunt how to proceed. "Luna will handle it I suppose," Denise said. "Email her the name of your contact."

"I'll do it, but that Maldonado person gave me some more bad news. As some of the records are medical, you'll need your brother to sign a HIPAA release."

Denise frowned. "He'll freak."

God, she hoped Luna had this all under control.

* * *

Denise drove the Kia to the district courthouse for the status hearing. When she arrived, Shakespeare Street was already packed. She parked two blocks down from the courthouse. While the town's population doubled on docket days, on jury trial days, it would go up by another twelve, with two alternates.

Inside the cramped courtroom, the Asian students were sitting in the front row this time. Out of custody, they were dressed in the latest fashions. Denise didn't recognize the conspicuous labels on their polo shirts.

She heard them muttering about being stuck in Hidalgo County, and not being allowed to cross the county line for any reason. As she passed, they recognized her from court the last time.

"One of us," the first student said to her. "*Ni hao,*" he greeted her in Chinese.

"*Anyoung haseyo,*" Denise replied in Korean, correcting them on her ancestry.

"We're all the same out here," the second student said. He was actually quite handsome and looked like a young Bruce Lee.

"Denise come here!" Hurricane Luna had already made landfall at the defense table. Luna was talking to Denny. He was in his orange jump suit, still a little unsure of who this well-dressed woman was and why she was taking over his case. "So, you're my lawyer *and* my auntie?"

"Haven't you heard the story? I named you guys before you were born," Luna was saying to Denny when Denise joined them. "*De-niece* and *De-nephew*. I'm glad you went with *Denny.*"

"I am too," he said.

"I see the resemblance between you and your sister, my niece."

"Thanks," Denny said. "But I still want my sister, *Denise,* on my case."

175

"She will be, but she's working *under* me."

"I told her I'm not crazy."

"Crazy isn't the legal term," Luna said. "*Competency* is. Just think, if you're found incompetent to stand trial, the case *might* be dismissed."

"Will I be able to get out then?" Denny said. "I really got to get out."

"I hope so."

"Is there anything you need me to do, Aunt Luna?" Denise asked. Denise could only read Luna when Luna let down her defenses. Now was not one of those times.

"I'm *Ms. Cruz* when I'm in the courtroom," Luna said.

Denise felt even shorter than usual next to Luna in her towering heels made of a barracuda's scales.

"Let me work my Luna Law magic," Luna said. She went over to Jane Dark at the State's counsel table. After a moment with Hurricane Luna, Jane Dark stipulated to Luna and Denise continuing as counsel for the defendant.

"Oh by the way," Denise said when Luna returned to the table, "Rayne said the records are all at the Syrinx facility, but we'll only be able to get the records with a subpoena duces tecum and someone with a security clearance has to pick them up. And we'll need a HIPAA release from Denny."

"Way ahead of you," Luna said. "She already sent me the name of the person we need to serve to get the records, we only need to get it drafted."

"All rise." Caliban was bailiff again. He didn't feel the need for a boomerang today. "Judge Shahrazad Sanchez presiding."

"State v. Song," the judge said. "Appearances please?"

Luna stood up. "Luna Cruz for the defendant. Denise Song will be appearing as a clinical law student under my direct tutelage and we will be raising competency on *our* client's case."

Denise noticed that her aunt had shifted her accent, so it was more of a down home New Mexico lilt. Luna had spent her formative years in Crater County, New Mexico, so she could lilt with the best of them.

"Thank you, *your honor*," the judge said to Luna. "I mean

thank you *counsel.*"

"Umm... Jane Dark for the great State of New Mexico." Normally the state was supposed to go first.

"When can the forensic evaluation report be completed?" the judge asked.

"I've already contacted Dr. Mary Ann Romero," Luna said. "She can be here on Monday to begin the evaluation."

"Monday?" the judge asked. "That was quick."

"I'm on top of this case," Luna said.

"We will have another status hearing in thirty days," the judge said.

"Can I get out on my own recognition or whatever it is?" Denny asked the judge. "My mom is in the hospital."

"Let's see what happens with the competency evaluation which will start on Monday," the judge said, "and whether you're considered *dangerous.* Your lawyer can file a motion for a furlough for you to visit your mother in the meantime. Anything else?"

Luna shoved several HIPAA release forms in front of Denny. "What are these for?" he asked.

"We can't issue subpoenas for records without a medical release. You need to sign these forms so we can get the medical records from the military," Luna said, ignoring the judge and everyone else in the courtroom.

"Your honor, we are opposed to the release of any military records," Jane Dark said. "They might be classified."

"I'll only sign the forms if you get me out of jail," Denny said.

Luna was prepared. "Your honor, my *assistant* here, Ms. Song, I mean my clinical law *student,* will be drafting a motion for a furlough for the young man and will draft a brief in support of getting his military records via subpoena duces tecum. We do have people on our team with security clearances. Ms. Song will be preparing them both *forthwith.*"

"*Forthwith*?" Denise asked.

"I'll reserve ruling until I see the motion and the brief," the judge said.

"See, Denise is filing the motion to get you out, sign the damn release so we can get your records," Luna said to Denny. Denny looked over at Denise who nodded. He signed it. Luna handed the release form to Denise.

"Get them both done, Denise," Luna said. "*Forthwith.*"

"Forthwith it shall be," Denise said. "Ms. Cruz."

"You're on your own in Lordsburg for a while," Luna said, her back already turned. "Have fun. I'm late for court in Truth or Consequences."

"Is her hearing in Truth or is it in Consequences?" one of the Asian students asked, not aware of the New Mexico town named after the old game show.

Denise watched as Hurricane Luna, with her long stride, was quickly out the door and halfway to T or C.

Chapter 30

So much for forthwith. Denise sat in her motel room for the rest of the day with a bad case of writer's block. Hikaru, Rayne, Rita and even Dew all told her that these motions couldn't be that hard. She wanted to believe them.

Denise hadn't written any substantive briefs or motions in her time as a clinical law student. She had failed out of law school before enrolling in those classes. She might as well be writing a novel.

She talked to Hikaru before she went to bed. After she told him that her mom had been in Korea, she'd asked if he'd ever been there.

He had. "Sometimes I feel like I'm going into the future when I'm in Seoul or Tokyo."

"That's cool," she said. "When I'm in Lordsburg, I feel like I need to turn back the clocks. Back to 1950."

"I was born in Los Alamos and it can be the same way once you leave the labs and go into town. The main street is named after the Trinity site and Trinity happened back in 1945. The town sometimes seems stuck in a time warp. I wonder if all the radiation in the water made everyone so crazy."

"That's an interesting theory," she said. "Did you ever get bitten by a radioactive spider?"

"I was stung by a bee once, but I just got hives."

"I was only in Los Alamos once, that time we went for a mock trial competition, and everybody acted smart there."

"There are a lot of dumb people in Los Alamos. I've sure worked for a few."

"I haven't gone to as many places as you, I'm sure."

"If you could go anywhere on Earth, where would you

go?"

She thought for a moment, she noticed that her Nastia files were sprawled on the bed mixed with her brother's files. "Would it have to be on Planet Earth?"

"For now."

"Then Roswell, the actual alien landing site. After seeing all the hype in the town, I'd like to see what the hype is about."

"I'll keep that in mind," he said. "Did you know the actual landing took place closer to a town called Corona. The aliens crashed there, it wasn't supposed to be their final destination."

Chapter 31
Thursday, July 23

Denise woke at the crack of dawn on Thursday and made another attempt at writing the briefs. She hit writer's block again. Well, it hit her, right in the forehead. She had a splitting headache.

She saw a text from Rita. AUNTIE I TRIED TO LOOK UP YOUR BROTHER BUT NONE OF THE OLD STUFF IS ONLINE!

Rita was right. None of the local media companies had websites. Then she remembered the abandoned Lordsburg Liberal building. Where did people go to find old news stories before there was an internet? She took her laptop along with her to the car. They would have wifi there, right?

The Lordsburg public library opened early. She was the only patron there at nine, and the ancient librarian was scanning her every move. "You're representing Denny, no?" the librarian asked.

"Kinda."

The librarian smiled. She looked like the cliched librarian with her glasses and hair tied in a bun and an outfit that was right out of the fifties. She was happy to talk as Denise might be the only person who she would see today. "He came here to this library a lot when he was in school. He was odd, but his heart was in the right place. You're his lawyer, no? The twin sister?"

Denise didn't know what to say. Was this librarian for him or against him?

The librarian smiled at her. "He came here a lot in a town where people don't read," she said. "How can I help you?"

Denise remembered the film *Desperado*, where a young

Salma Hayek ran a bookstore in a tough town. This sixty-year old librarian could have been Salma Hayek, if she ended up in Lordsburg and never escaped with Antonio Banderas.

"Did Denny ever make the local papers?"

The librarian laughed. "His letters to the editor ran every Tuesday in the *Lordsburg Liberal* Speak Up column starting when he was in eighth grade."

She directed Denise to old newspaper clippings around the year when Denny would have moved here. "Is there like an index or something?" Denise asked.

"In my head. You'll have to go through them one by one in that particular year's volume, about halfway through."

Denise went through every Tuesday letters page in the dusty book that hadn't been opened in years. Denny's first letter described the adoption process. He talked about missing his birth mother and his experiences with Nastia and how he was glad that he was finally being placed with a decent foster family. He mentioned Fally as well and how the town never dealt with the man's domestic violence issues toward Nastia and toward him. Denny ended his letter by vowing that he would find his birth mother someday.

The letter was well-written for an eighth grader. She smiled; his desire to meet his birth mother might help out in her motion for furlough. Denise copied the clippings on the library's old copy machine.

She went back to the bound newspaper volumes. Denny was silent for the next few months, but then he began a streak of writing letters every week.

In Denny's next letter, he wrote that his foster-father with the unlikely name of Dogberry Dunsinane (Cordelia's dad) was unqualified and that the entire family was strange except for Cordelia. Denise now understood the Denny-Cordelia relationship a bit better; he was the foster kid and Cordelia was the only one who was nice to him.

As to Cordelia, she probably liked him to piss off her parents at first and then found out that there was more to him than meets the eye.

The next letter was far more heated in its prose—the Dunsinane family (except for Cordelia) was all mentally ill and conducted weird rituals behind closed doors.

By the fifth letter, Denny had gone full-fledged alien-conspiracy theorist, going on about how Dogberry and the rest of his family (except for Cordelia) was part of an alien cult.

In the sixth letter, Denny named names of local dignitaries, including Nastia's ex, Fally, and Sheriff JC Diamond himself. Denny mentioned something about a "Shakespeare Incident" in 1947 that happened out by the Shakespeare ghost town. This incident had some connection with the Roswell crash and both Dogberry Dunsinane and the sheriff knew about it.

There wasn't a seventh letter.

Denise looked around at the librarian. "What was the Shakespeare Incident?"

The librarian took her to the 1947 volume of the Liberal and opened right to a dog-eared page. A local rancher reported a UFO on July 7, 1947, the same day as the Roswell crash.

The article itself wasn't that helpful. The rancher was riding on horseback near the Shakespeare ghost town and saw some flashing lights. A flying saucer landed, let some "people" out and then the saucer disappeared. By the time the cowboy got to the landing site, the people were gone and there were no traces of the flying saucer. For some reason the article reminded her of something, but she couldn't place what it was.

"Where was this?"

"Well, the cowboy would have been on top of the hill where the cylindrical water tower is now. The so-called landing would have taken place on the other side of that hill. There's a rumor that the flying saucer is still buried under the water tower, but there's no proof of that."

"How come no one's heard of this?"

"Roswell got all the press. And his story makes no sense. The flying saucer lands, people come out and then both the people and the UFO disappear without a trace. There's no proof of any of that. Let's just say the cowboy wasn't the most reliable witness."

"So Denny believes the cowboy, he thinks the aliens are still here?"

"Or the *descendants* from the original aliens who married local folks." The librarian came closer as if scared she was disturbing the invisible patrons of the library. "Here's my theory. He probably got beaten by Fally. No one believes Denny or his mom about the physical abuse. Then Denny gets adopted by the Dunsinanes. Things go from bad to worse—his foster father, the late Mr. Dogberry Dunsinane abused him, sexually maybe. Denny tried to tell some people, and no one believed him again. He writes about it in the *Liberal*, but they stopped printing his letters after that. Denny's projecting all his anger on his abuser, on his foster father, and on the authorities onto these quote-unquote *aliens*."

Denise stared at a map of the county posted on the library's wall. "Wait a second, did the so-called landing take place on Dunsinane Ranch and that's right by the Shakespeare ghost town?"

"It's a big ranch," the librarian said. "It's just a coincidence. Well, it's not a coincidence that Denny blamed his issues on something that happened fifty years before he was born on the property he was living. I'm no therapist, but it's narcissism."

Part of Denise believed the librarian's theory. Denny had deep abandonment issues that might have stemmed from abuse—physical and perhaps sexual abuse. He was projecting all of his trauma not on an *abuser*, but on the quote-unquote *aliens* as way as if proving that he was somehow important in an unforgiving world.

"I don't know the details about the boy's case," the librarian said. "But he's not all there. He used to sit right where you're sitting, and write his letters."

"Thanks for your help." Time for round one. Denise used the old law books in the library to draft the motion for a furlough on her laptop. She included the newspaper clipping as evidence to show how much he missed her. Maybe by sitting at a table where her brother sat helped her understand him better. She was able to knock out a draft in fifteen minutes.

"Round 2," she said to herself. Next, she thought of how crucial it would be to find the military records, especially the psychiatric ones if they existed. Her bother had had a Section 8 discharge, right? And then he was reinstated for experiments by military contractors?

She found some good case law on point and composed a draft of the motion for a lawyer see the military records without a security clearance. She included the clippings from the *Liberal* to show his attitudes before he started in the military. She also found some case law about how the interests of *justice* could override secrecy, override national and perhaps *planetary* security.

Once she had a decent draft of each motion done on her laptop, she sent them over to Luna. The wifi did work, thank god. Before she could leave the library, Luna texted that she would get back to her. Denise spent the next few hours in the library reading up on the town. She was starting to like this place in spite of herself.

No one else came that day. At five, the librarian told her that it was closing time. As she closed the door behind her, the librarian gave her a stern warning. "Whatever you do, don't go visit the ranch to check on any UFOs. It's very dangerous over there for outsiders."

"But you said," Denise said.

"Just because your brother is crazy, doesn't mean he isn't telling the truth. A lot of people have gone over to the water tower to check things out, not all of them have come back."

This woman didn't have a spark, but Denise knew the woman might as well be reading her mind. "I don't think I'm the type who goes to a haunted ranch to find alien ruins," Denise replied.

"I hope not. I'm sure your motions will do just fine on their own."

Denise couldn't decide whether the old woman was warning her or inviting her to check out the ranch. She spent another night at the Last Palm stuck in her motel room, which had a microwave in the room at least. There'd been a slim selection of frozen dinners at the local Family Dollar.

One of the TV stations was showing an *X-Files* marathon. Was she Mulder or Scully? She knew that either one of them would want to check out the ranch, despite what the librarian had said. Just because her brother was crazy, didn't mean he wasn't telling the truth.

185

Chapter 32

Friday, July 24

On Friday, Denise awoke in the Last Palm to a text from Luna. Denise could feel the negativity of the current. Something had come up with Luna's big case, but she'd had enough time to review the first drafts of her motions and hated them. REMOVE THE NEWSPAPER CLIPPINGS!

At the rickety motel desk, Denise took out the clippings, made some minor adjustments reflecting the lack of exhibits in the briefs and sent them back to Luna.

While waiting for Luna to respond, she texted all of her friends and told them about the original Shakespeare Incident.

WHAT SHOULD I DO TO PREPARE FOR THE CASE?

They all answered back, nearly word for word, that she should visit the crime scene at the Dunsinane Ranch or Shakespeare ranch whatever it was called, despite the warnings of the librarian.

WAS SHAKESPEARE AN ALIEN? Hikaru texted back. I LOVED "MERCHANT OF VENUS."

I LIKED "ROMEO AND JUPITER" MYSELF, she texted back.

After a few more exchanges of bad puns with Hikaru, she got in her car, crossed the freeway and headed south toward the site. Main Street curved past a few restaurants and a small park with an old army tank at the entrance, next to a big flag. The grass in the park needed watering.

Above the park, she could see a hill with a cylindrical water tower on it. The tower had LORDSBURG written on its circumference in bold letters.

That must be the place.

On the drive toward the hill, she saw a sign for the Shakespeare Ghost Town and couldn't help but check it out. She turned and drove a mile down the dirt road. She might as well see what the whole Shakespeare thing was all about. To be or not to be.

She had been expecting a recreation of Stratford-on-Avon with a full-scale replica of the Globe theater. When she arrived at the end of the road, the ghost town had nothing Shakespearean about it, not much ghostly either. It looked like an old western town that had voted for *not to be*.

Disappointed, she drove back to the intersection with the main road. A car heading in the direction of the ranch turned out to be the Sheriff's vehicle. He didn't recognize her in her new car and drove right by her.

The ranch was over the hill, so Denise parked by the old army tank at the entrance to the city park. The tank blended in with its desert camouflage as if guarding it from the aliens.

She thought again about the librarian's warning. Armed only with her staff, she wasn't going in with heavy artillery, that was for sure.

She hiked a half mile up to the cylindrical water tower on top of the hill. She walked around the curve of the cylinder and looked down at the ranch below.

The New Shakespeare Ranch was smaller than expected, barely the size of a football field with some barbed wire around it. Inside the wire were a residence, a stable and a barn or two. An arroyo around back that dipped under the fence.

Down below at the ranch, Sheriff JC Diamond had already parked his vehicle, and was smoking a cigar. His deputies were there as back-up. Meanwhile, a CSI team of four figures in hazmat suits was bending over the ground taking some soil samples with long poles. Two others were wielding radiation detectors and doing a lap around a big boulder that seemed to guard the back of the ranch.

She could see the Omega Grail, still there on top of the boulder like Excalibur, daring anybody to remove it. The grail was smaller than she expected. It looked more like a country club's tennis tournament trophy.

And yet, there at the water tower, maybe a few hundred yards away, pulses of electricity passed through her every second like clockwork.

She noticed that if she clung close to the metal of the cylinder, she was grounded from the pulses. If she leaned closer toward the grail, away from the water, those pulses grew stronger.

Then again, it could all be in her imagination.

Another car came to the gate, a black Escalade. All of the people at the ranch—the hazmat workers, the deputies—were drawn to the car, as if it had a magnetic pull. The sheriff stayed put, however.

Moments later, the crowd descending on the Escalade dispersed. The people seemed to adjust to the magnetic field and went back to their duties.

Two people exited the vehicle. She didn't recognize the non-descript people in work clothes carrying assault rifles. Another car came to the gate moments later and the same ritual repeated. Everyone, including the new people came forward, surrounded the car and then dispersed. Two more people got out of the second vehicle.

She walked a few yards toward the ranch. She could see an image of Denny standing in front of her, about two paces ahead. This must be where he was possessed by the drone or whatever it was.

If she took those two steps, she knew that the drone would appear, and she would go into the same fugue state as Denny. She wasn't powerful enough to fight it, she could already hear something incredibly strong in the ground beneath her. Was the drone—or whatever it was—below her under the water tower?

She went back to the water tower and hid behind the curve. Her stomach settled. She was *grounded* again.

No, now was not the time to go after the grail. She certainly wouldn't get any closer than Denny had.

A third vehicle came to the gate, a big red pick-up truck and the ritual was repeated a third time. This time a large figure emerged from the truck and strode to the grail, appearing to inspect it. The people in the hazmat suits, the workers with guns—everyone except the Sheriff—leaned toward the figure. It looked to Denise like they were *bowing* to the figure.

If this group had a leader, this person was definitely the one. The pulses coming from down below grew stronger. She sensed something familiar about the figure, maybe they'd cross paths sometime during her life. But the figure was too far away for her to recognize by sight or by spark.

Denise suddenly felt nauseous. Could the figure sense her all the way up here? She pushed back even further behind the curve of the cylinder until she could barely see down below. She could tell the water inside the tower was rushing back and forth, a maelstrom going on inside.

She worried that the tank would burst, and thousands of gallons of water would pour down on top of her. Would the cylinder open up and an alien emerge?

Despite her curiosity about this big boss, Denise didn't want to risk discovery. Maybe it didn't matter if she stood where Denny stood. She crawled around the cylinder until she was as far away that she could be from the ranch.

Had it helped? The ground rumbled, the cylinder shook from the rushing waters within. She had better get the hell out of there before she triggered whatever was swimming inside the waters.

She cautiously inched away from the cylinder, back toward the park below which she hoped was a safe distance from the ranch. She wanted to hide behind the army tank just in case.

By the time she was halfway down the slope, away from the ranch, the rumbling had lessened. Once she made it all the way to the park, the ground was finally still, but her phone was beeping indicating some kind of alert.

She got in the Kia and drove like hell out of there.

Once she was on the other side of the freeway, she cautiously checked her phone. There'd been an earthquake reported along something called the Rio Grande Rift and the epicenter was a short distance away, west of Socorro, NM. It had all been a coincidence that it hit at the same time as her stint at the cylinder, right?

Back at Room 13 of the Last Palm Motel, still shell-shocked, she called Hikaru again and told him about her experiences at the ranch.

"I felt nauseous and paranoid," she said. "But the memory seems to be fading. Online, they're saying it was an earthquake along the Rio Grande rift, but I think it was me getting close to the grail and triggering *something*. I'm sure the person in the red car had something to do with it. Do you know who the guy was?"

"They don't tell me anything."

"But why did I feel nauseous?"

"The grails affect different people in different ways."

"Maybe there's a rocket in an underground silo beneath the water tank and it was starting to launch. That's what it felt like."

"Those drones can be anywhere," Hikaru said. "Not all UFOs come from outer space. Trust me on that."

After she hung up, Denise checked her emails on her laptop. Sure enough, Luna now demanded that she put the newspaper clippings *back* in the motions and make the appropriate corrections in the exhibit numbers. She also needed to specify that Rayne Herring had a clearance to get into Syrinx, as well as a *designee*, whatever that meant.

Denise did not have time to digest the incident on the ranch. Was the recollection of that fading? She wrote it down on a pad and that seemed to help her remember it.

After making the revision, Denise sent the motions off again. Moments later Luna offered more corrections and Denise spent another hour addressing them. Apparently, Denise had put the wrong name as the custodian of records who wasn't quite named Maldonado.

Denise made revisions two more times before Luna was satisfied.

God, she hated people editing her stuff.

Once Denise saw that everything had been successfully e-filed on the New Mexico Courts website, she breathed a sigh of relief. Once the order was signed by the judge, it couldn't be that difficult to get some military records, right?

Chapter 33
Sunday, July 26

There was absolutely nothing to do in Lordsburg on a weekend. There was no hotel dinner buffet Sunday night, so she decided to cruise Motel Boulevard to see if anything was open that served edible food.

After cruising up and down the five mile stretch of Motel Boulevard, twice, Denise finally found a nice Chinese buffet at the western edge of town, with the improbable name of *Shiprock Wok*. The sign indicated that they also had locations up in the Navajo reservation.

She had a rule, no Asian restaurants in towns smaller than 10,000, but she was starving, and would make an exception for this converted Pizza Hut building. The dining room had a mural of the great land bridge between Asia and Alaska, with people in traditional costumes crossing back and forth. Denise noticed an interesting young couple in the back—an attractive Asian woman holding hands with a young Native American man sporting a turquoise bolo and matching turquoise pony-tail holder. He was on the phone.

"Yeah, it's *Romeo and Juliet on the rez*," the man said. "Her dad was on the run from the Chinese mob and he took over a restaurant from his cousin in Shiprock to hide out. Then she fell in love with me. But like the triads found out and tried to take him out, then like our whole chapterhouse fought off the Chinese mob right there in Shiprock. Talk about multi-cultural—Asians and Indians. I see it on Netflix or maybe Hulu. It can even be a series."

The man listened to the response on the other end. "No, we're not out in Hollywood, we got married and started another restaurant in Lordsburg. We named it after her dad's restaurant on the Rez, *Shiprock Wok*. Hello? Hello?"

Whoever was on the other line wasn't interested in *Romeo and Juliet* on or off the Rez. Still, *Shiprock Wok* could indeed be the name of a multi-cultural thriller that the attorney-author might write if he ever had the time.

The man dialed someone else and did the same pitch. Too bad no one in Hollywood would ever care about a story about a UFO legal thriller with a female protagonist of color.

Denise scanned the room for an empty table and was shocked to see her former mock trial coach, Bebe Tran was slurping some *pho* with green chile. Tran was there with an extended family group, sitting next to a handsome Asian man. Denise couldn't tell if it was her brother or her husband.

"Denise Song, is that you?" Coach Tran said. "Where's the time gone? What's it been, nine years? Please come join us."

Denise walked over to their table. "What are you doing out here?" she asked.

"The green chile chicken *pho* is to die for. We are moving my daughter out to Tucson to start at the U of A. She got a full ride on a soccer scholarship. This was on the way to campus."

Denise didn't know Coach Bebe Tran had a daughter. The petite, but muscular looking young woman was texting someone.

"Congratulations," Denise said to the young girl. "Good luck with soccer."

The girl ignored her.

"And you?" Tran asked. "You went off to Harvard Law School or something, right?"

"Kinda."

Denise looked toward the buffet and saw a kindly Chinese woman, who must be the owner, smiling at her. The woman wore an exquisite traditional red outfit fit for an imperial empress. "Please sit," she said. "We'll cook you some *real* food."

Denise sat in an empty chair at Tran's table and the owner brought her a cup of hot jasmine tea. As the other diners hit the buffet, with its chicken fried steak and spareribs mixed in with *moo goo gai pan*, a handsome young man came out of the kitchen bringing her a plate of specially prepared food.

Denise recognized the waiter; he was the second student from the courthouse. He introduced himself as Wu as he set down the plate of food in front of her. "I'm stuck in this damn county. This is the only job I could get, but the food is really good. The chef had a place in Chinatown, back in LA, and another restaurant in 'LA town,' back in China."

Denise smiled at Wu. "I'll eat here from now on," Denise said. "Do you deliver?"

* * *

Back in her motel room, she received a text from Dr. Maryann Romero, the woman who would evaluate Denny. COMING TO LORDSBURG TOMORROW. YOU STILL THERE?

WHERE ELSE WOULD I BE? Denise responded. I LIVE HERE NOW.

Chapter 34

Monday, July 27

Monday morning, Dr. Maryann Romero called at dawn, waking Denise. The doctor had been involved with the extended family's cases ever since the Rattlesnake Lawyer, Dan Shepard, had begun his career in the Aguilar County Public Defender's office. Dr. Romero would probably keep doing their family cases long into the future.

"Should I just meet you at your hotel?" the doctor asked.

Denise looked around the Last Palm. "Let's meet at Denny's. The *restaurant.*"

* * *

As Denise was walked by the host to a back booth at the diner, several people from around town had given her polite nods.

"I'm starting to fit in here," Denise thought.

A few minutes later, a tall woman arrived in a business suit and walked back to the booth. Everyone was tall to Denise.

"You must be Denise all grown up," she said, sitting down. "So good to work with you at last. I knew your mother. And your aunt. And the guy who married your aunt for a while. And..."

"I know. I know."

"How are *you* doing, Denise? This must be hard on you."

They talked for a few minutes, catching up on the family. Dr. Romero had diagnosed her mother back in the day.

"I do know that my mom once thought that she was an anime character or something like that," Denise said.

"Your mom is not as crazy as you think," Dr. Romero said.

"Of course, that would be confidential. Perhaps your brother isn't that crazy either."

"I don't know if that's a good thing. If he's incompetent, maybe we can get the charges dropped."

Denise definitely wanted an hour's therapy of her own with this nice doctor, but Dr. Romero was all business when she took out a tablet. "So, Denny is your twin? Isn't that a conflict, you representing your brother?"

"He said he wanted me to be his lawyer," Denise said. She explained the case and Denny's issues—and the librarian's theory that Denny was projecting his own abuse onto the aliens.

"I should be able to make my own conclusions after I talk with him." Dr. Romero smiled. "And then I'll see if he's telling the truth when I see the military psychiatric records."

"The judge should be ruling on that any day now." Denise checked the NM Courts website on her phone. She wilted when she saw that Jane Dark had objected to the subpoena of the records and filed a reply brief.

Jane Dark was asking for restrictions on the defense access to classified records and whether a state court judge had the authority to order a Federal military entity to release them in the first place. That was way over her pay grade.

There would have to be another hearing, Tuesday morning. And Luna was still at the trial in Truth or Consequences, right? Denise might have to do it herself.

"Is everything OK?" the doctor asked. "You look like you're in distress. Should I wait before I see your brother?"

"I'll know more tomorrow about the records, but you might as well see Denny today."

"Without those records, I'm writing my report blind."

* * *

Denise spent the rest of the day back at the Last Palm, prepping for the hearing on the subpoena and the furlough. Luna called and explained that she had faith in Denise to handle it alone.

"Put on your big girl panties," Luna said and hung up.

She called Hikaru who gave her a pep talk. "It's a motion hearing, just regurgitate your brief back to the judge," he said.

"I'm not that good at regurgitating. Even though I'm getting lots of practice lately if I keep eating junk food."

They talked about movies. He wasn't sure exactly what line she'd been referring to in *The Player*. "I suppose it's not that important," she said.

After they hung up, he texted her a video of a young Bruce Willis carrying a young Julia Roberts out of the gas chamber, very much alive. Willis clearly quipped something, but Denise couldn't get the audio to work. Oh well, it would come to her sometime.

Before she went to bed, Denise checked in with Dr. Romero. "I'm not done with my analysis yet," the doctor said.

"We have a hearing tomorrow," Denise replied.

"I know. I'm subpoenaed to be there," Dr. Romero said.

"I didn't file that."

"The State lawyer Jane Dark did."

The doctor hung up. Why would Jane Dark call her doctor as a witness?

Chapter 35

Tuesday, July 28

When Denise arrived in court the next morning, the judge wasn't in her robe and was already hearing some neighborhood dispute over a trespassing goat. The courtroom was otherwise empty.

"Your client is in the holding cell with the shrink," the sheriff said.

Denise found the cramped holding cell and walked in to hear Denny going on a tirade to Dr. Romero.

"The army did *experiments* on me," Denny said. "I've told you that a million times already."

"And what were the experiments about again?"

"To see if I could communicate directly with them aliens. Why don't you believe me?"

Dr. Romero finally looked over at Denise and cocked an eyebrow. "I don't know about this," she said to Denise. "He might be *malingering*."

Malingering? Denise had to recollect exactly what that meant. Malingering meant faking symptoms to get out of something, right? She knew she had to win this simple hearing and get those records if she had any chance to save her brother.

Moments later, the sheriff—still in his damn sunglasses—walked into the holding cell and roughly jerked Denny up out of his chair. Denise and the doctor followed them, like an entourage, into the courtroom.

The judge scratched a fresh neck tattoo of the flaming scales of justice. Apparently, the scale tipped in favor of the plaintiff on the goat case. Jane Dark now sat at the State's table and had three people in dark suits standing behind her. They reminded Denise of *Men in Black.*

Dr. Romero joined Jane Dark at the State's counsel table. "I have to testify by phone in Federal court in an hour. Don't take too long."

"Don't worry," Jane Dark replied.

"Are the parties ready?" the judge asked, rubbing the ink on her neck.

It was time to do a hearing without training wheels. It was technically a defense motion, she expected to go first.

"Your honor, Denise Song, clinical law student appearing under the auspices of Attorney Luna Cruz."

"Your honor, Jane Dark for the great State of New Mexico. Since our witness is in a bit of a time crunch, may the State proceed with its argument first?"

Jane Dark didn't bother to wait for the judge to decide. "Your honor, we call Dr. Maryann Romero."

Jane Dark had another one of those dossiers marked DR. ROMERO. After the doctor was sworn and gave her qualifications, Jane Dark got into it. "Have you completed your evaluation of Mr. Song?"

"I interviewed him yesterday and today," the doctor replied. "But I haven't finished my report yet."

"How many of these reports have you done?"

"Hundreds."

"Isn't it true that you testified in the case of *State v. Jesus V*, a juvenile case?"

"I did. That was twenty years ago, but I remember it like it was yesterday."

"And who was the defense attorney?"

"Dan Shepard."

"In the case of *State v. Jeremy Jones*, did you testify on behalf of the state?"

"Yes."

"Who called you in that case?"

"The prosecutor, Luna Cruz herself."

"The same Luna Cruz who is now the defense lawyer in this case?"

"Yes. I guess she's changed sides."

"Are you familiar with Jen Song?"

"I interviewed her for a case."

"Were you involved in the case of *State v. Sam Marlow*?"

"I was. I interviewed the alleged victim, for her attorney, Luna Cruz."

"And a juvenile, Marley *Cruz*? Excused me, *Marley C.*"

"Yes."

Denise winced. Why did Jane Dark bring her dead cousin Marley into this?

"Relevance, your honor?" Denise said, rising. Was this an attempt to rattle her? Every single name the doctor mentioned had some connection to her family.

"I'm getting there your honor." Jane Dark put the dossier down and didn't wait for the judge. "And in *any* of those cases, did you need top-secret, classified military psychiatric documents to complete your evaluation?"

"No. Not in *any* of them."

"Pass the witness."

"Proceed Ms. Song," the judge said. "By the way, apparently your umm... *mentor*, Ms. Cruz filed the appropriate paperwork with the Federal District Court up in Albuquerque to allow the base to release the records under certain circumstance and got the issue of the records custodian settled. But the base is deferring to my judgment whether to allow it at all. So why should I let you get classified records from our military?"

"Dr. Romero," Denise asked. "None of those people that you interviewed had any military service?"

"Not to my knowledge."

"None of those people you interviewed had been the *subject* of experiments in the military?"

"Not to my knowledge."

"Do you stipulate that Denny was in the military, *our* military, and claims to be the subject of experiments in the military?"

"Yes."

"Do you think Denny might be telling the truth regarding these experiments?"

"He might be. Or he might be malingering."

"And wouldn't the presence of these military records, be helpful in making a final determination regarding competency or whether he is just umm... *malingering?*"

"I guess they would be."

Jane Dark consulted with the men in the suits—who appeared to feed her questions—before striding to the podium. When it was her turn at the podium, she was her brutal self again. "You said he might be malingering, and *not* actually the subject of experiments?"

"Yes, but I have no way of knowing."

"He might be malingering and not be totally truthful about the experiments even existing?"

"He might be, I don't know."

"If he's merely a liar, that would require conscious thought on his part?"

"It would."

"That might mean that he is competent to stand trial." That was phrased as a statement, not as a question.

"I won't know without those records."

"So, if the military simply confirms or denies that he was the subject of some tests, wouldn't that be enough?"

"No, it would not."

"They did tests on me!" Denny yelled. "Put me on the stand."

Jane Dark smiled. "Pass the witness."

Denise was ready to go to the podium and gestured to Denny to be quiet. "You've received classified documents before, haven't you, doctor?"

"Yes."

"And how is that arranged?"

"Usually there's a way to let you look at them onsite with someone who has a clearance who looks at them first under custodian of records' supervision."

The judge's phone rang. Her ring tone was a K-pop song that Denise recognized and hoped that was a good sign. The judge abruptly left before the bailiff could tell them to rise.

The judge returned a few moments later frowning. "That was the base commander. I'm going to take the discovery issue under advisement. Just wanted to check on one thing, you do have someone with a military clearance on your umm... team, correct?"

"Yes, your honor," Denise said. "Rayne Herring."

"Anyone else with a clearance?"

She didn't want to bring Hikaru in just yet to risk getting him in trouble at work. "Not at this time."

"OK, that's what I was afraid of," the judge said, she was leaning in, looking at her computer as if learning the law on the fly. "I'll take this under advisement and get back to you."

Denise looked at Denny and Dr. Romero. "At least she didn't deny us outright," Denise said, hoping for the best.

"Even if they give you the records, they won't let you see the good stuff, the stuff about the UFOs," Denny said.

Denise shrugged. She was pretty sure that any good UFO material was not going to be released, if it existed at all. She would be happy if they could get Denny's records of misconduct and a diagnosis for PTSD. If they could show that Denny scored highly on one of those psychic card reading tests that couldn't hurt. But even with Luna's Federal filings, a state judge wouldn't be able to force a military base to release the good stuff.

"We'll see," Denise said to Denny.

"Anything else?" the judge asked.

Denise drew a blank, before Denny tapped her in the arm. "The furlough to see my mom."

"Your honor, we have a pending motion for a furlough for my client to visit his mother in the hospital."

The furlough motion hearing was much easier, and no witnesses were called. Denise was well-prepared. She recited the facts about how her mom's diagnosis might be fatal, and Denny still had the presumption of innocence, as he hadn't been convicted of anything. The furlough would only be for a few hours, and the hospital was less than a two-hour drive away.

Jane Dark didn't even rise from her table for her say. She merely recited that she would defer to the court, but insisted that Denise Song be present in the hospital room as a third-party custodian.

"What does that mean?" the judge asked.

201

Jane Dark smiled. "Ms. Denise Song would be the third-party custodian of her brother during the hospital visit. She would literally be her brother's keeper."

"Are you willing to do that, Ms. Song?" the judge asked.

"Of course, your honor," Denise replied.

"It has to be tomorrow," the judge said, looking back at the computer instead of the courtroom.

"So I'll pick him up and take him there?" Denise asked.

"That's not what we're proposing," Jane Dark said. "The Sheriff's office will be transporting Mr. Denny Song to the hospital room and be present at all times. We are asking that Ms. *Denise* Song be in the room and be responsible for his actions during the actual visit."

"So ordered," said the judge.

"You're the greatest," Denny said, as the guard took him away. The sheriff remained in the courtroom.

Once he was gone, Jane Dark turned to the sheriff. "If he takes one second too long in the bathroom, that's escape. If he trips over her cord, charge his ass with resisting arrest or whatever," she said, loud enough for Denise to hear. "And it's all going to be on her watch."

Denise now worried that Denny was being set up. That she herself was being set up. Denny would have to be on his best behavior. Seeing his long-lost mother might be a bridge too far for Denny. There was a whole litany of charges that Denny could pick up in the hospital. Even the slightest slip-up could make the issue of the medical records a moot point.

And if anything happened on her watch, as the third-party custodian, she would be subject to contempt of court. She could actually go to jail if Denny acted up.

"I'm going to see my mommy!" Denise heard Denny yell from out in the hallway.

Maybe this furlough wasn't such a good idea after all.

Chapter 36
Wednesday, July 29

The judge still hadn't ruled on the discovery issue regarding the military records, but Denny's furlough to the hospital to visit his mother was scheduled for a brief window on Wednesday. Denny had to be at the hospital promptly at four in the afternoon and out the door by five at the latest. Denny was supposed to make up for an entire lost lifetime in only an hour.

On the drive over to Cruces that afternoon, Denise stayed on the phone with Hikaru. He was an only child and had a tortured relationship with his overachieving father. "My dad would always say, why don't you have any friends?"

"My mom would say that to me too," Denise replied.

"By the way," Hikaru said. "I have access to the corporate helicopter. And a pilot on Friday... if you just happen to be free..."

"Are you asking me on a date?"

"I'm asking you on an *adventure.*"

"Of course."

"And bring ummm... *athletic* gear. We'll be outside."

He texted her an image of two figures cycling in the desert at sunset. Because of the filtering of the image, she couldn't tell if it was a picture or a painting. She didn't care.

As she passed the Akela Flats courthouse facade, she received a call from Rita, asking her about Denny's case and Jen's condition.

"I don't know about my mom," Denise said. "I just hope she's still alive when he gets there. Actually, I hope she's still alive when he leaves."

"You must be a pretty good lawyer if you can get your brother out, even for an hour, Auntie Denise."

"Thanks, Rita."

"If there's anything I can do to help," Rita said.

"I'll keep that in mind."

"Just don't tell my mom I'm calling you. I think she wants to get off the case..."

Rita hung up, before Denise could inquire further. Still looking at her phone, she noticed a text from the sheriff. Denny would be running late.

If Denny missed visiting hours, he would freak. He might pick up a new charge if he tried to escape.

* * *

Denise arrived at the hospital by three and sat with "Piranha," the wiry guard. "What are you doing here?" she asked Piranha.

"Just keeping my eye on you," he said.

"Don't you mean my brother?"

He just smiled. "Both of you then."

She watched her mother lie there, only her eyes moving under their lids. What was she dreaming about?

Would she ever get to talk to her mother again? She texted Hikaru a few more times and he offered his support. At least she had him.

FRIDAY? he texted.

FRIDAY! She texted back.

Her phone rang. It was Rita again. "Auntie Denise, how's it going?"

"I'm sure everything will be fine." Denise couldn't help but be a little impatient with the young girl. "Don't you have any friends to play with, Rita?"

"No, I don't." Rita hung up. It was now after four.

"He's got to get here by five," Piranha said.

"I know," Denise replied.

It was 4:55 when Sheriff JC Diamond himself finally arrived in the room with Denny. Denny wore high-risk red prisoner garb with leg and ankle shackles. Denny was fidgety, even more so than usual. The shackles were rattling.

The sheriff gave Denny a wide berth once they entered the hospital room.

Denny nodded at Denise, who nodded back. One glance from the Piranha indicated that they should not get too close. In his excitement, Denny tripped, but managed to regain his balance. Piranha stepped between Denny and his mother, just in case. "Doctor!" he yelled.

"That's as far as you go!" Dr. Patel said to Denny, appearing from nowhere. "No physical contact!"

Denny stood still. He closed his eyes, trying to contact his mother psychically. The lights in the room flickered on and off, the hospital machinery beeped, but nothing happened.

Denny frowned, opened his eyes and wiped away a tear with a shackled hand.

"I wish we could have known each other, mom," Denny said. "I wouldn't be wearing handcuffs if you could have been there for me growing up."

Over on the bed, their mother took a deep breath. Her eyes remained firmly closed.

Mother, oh mother. Denise knew that if her mother had been there for her, things might be different for her as well. Maybe she wouldn't be a clinical law student, but a real *lawyer* right now. If only the three of them could have been a family...

Suddenly, the steady rhythm of the monitors suddenly began beeping at the rate of the fastest K-pop songs. Denise felt a pulse of electricity racing in a circle from her to her mother to Denny and back to her again. Lights blinked off and on, and then the fire alarm went off.

Would this be too much for Jen Song?

"Oh my god!" Dr. Patel ran over to the monitors, clearly alarmed. "Everybody out!"

"But I just got here!" Denny shouted. "This is the first time I've seen my real mother! I've waited for this my whole life!"

The sheriff grabbed Denny roughly.

"Her too!" Dr. Patel ordered. Piranha grabbed Denise and dragged her outside.

Denny lost his balance and fell to the floor. "I can take

you out on the elevator or take you out the window," the sheriff said.

"I didn't do anything!" Denny yelled.

The fire alarm stopped. "He's cooperating with you!" Denise yelled, still being held by Piranha.

Denise worried that the sheriff would testify that Denny caused the disruption. If Denny couldn't even handle being with his sick mother in a safe setting, he sure couldn't handle being out in society. It was a trap after all.

"Let go of me!" Denise yelled.

Piranha released his hold and checked his watch. It was five after five. His shift was over and he was losing interest.

Denise walked to just outside her mother's doorway. Her mother's vitals apparently were back to normal.

Dr. Patel was at her mother's bed, along with Dr. Schwartz.

"Is she all right?" Denise asked, remaining in the corridor.

"Everything's fine now," Dr. Schwartz said. Dr. Patel double-checked and nodded. Her mother now looked positively serene. "I won't let the son see her again," Dr. Patel turned to face Denise. "Just to be on the safe side."

"What about me?" Denise asked. "She was fine with me for the last few hours. And she seems better now."

Dr. Patel waited a full minute, eying the monitors. Jen Song was back in a groove, all signs normal. Before the doctor could give an answer, she looked down at her beeping pager. "I've got to take this page." Dr. Patel left at a fast clip.

Dr. Schwartz was still in the room. He did an experiment—he gestured for Denise to come closer. If anything, Jen's monitors improved with every inch. "You seem to check out just fine."

With another gesture by the doctor, Denise inched forward. He smiled. "You might even be good for her."

Denise took another step into the room. "Can I stay here with my mother?"

All was serene in the room. "I guess so," Dr. Schwartz said.

Piranha was still in the room, and he looked disappointed that he would have to work overtime. "I've got my eye on you," he said to Denise.

Denise sat by her mother's bed. Dr. Schwartz watched the beepers for a few more moments and then nodded.

"Good luck," the doctor said. "Mr. Perea, you could give her some space."

"That bitch is crazy," Piranha said as he left the room, glad to be out of here after all. "That whole family is."

Chapter 37

Denise sat alone with her mother for the next few hours. All the staff looking in would assume that they were a normal mother and daughter bonding, perhaps for the last time.

"I know you know I'm here," Denise said.

Her mom blinked once. Denise assumed it was one blink for yes, two blinks for no.

After checking in one more time, Dr. Patel left. Dr. Schwartz checked the monitors a few minutes later. "Your mother does seem to be doing well with you in the room, Ms. Song."

"I really need to spend time alone with my mom. I just want to spend the night in her room if that's OK."

"I've got to check with my attending," he said and hurried down the hall.

When he returned, he gave her a form and a temporary pass just to be sure. The door to her mother's room had to remain open.

It was after midnight and the night nurse had finished her hourly rounds. The coast was clear. Jen Song's eyes were still moving under her lids, she was in REM sleep. Perfect timing.

Denise rose from her chair and arranged herself so she would be invisible to people passing by the room—unless they actually poked their heads in. She touched her mom's hand. Thankfully the skin was still warm, the pulse strong.

Holding her mother's hand, Denise closed her eyes and concentrated. Nothing happened, it was like staring into a blank wall. Denise opened her eyes took a deep breath and this time made her mind go utterly blank... and she seemed to melt into the air.

There was a flash, a burst of electricity through her brain and then darkness. She was now falling down a hole in the hospital floor. She hit solid ground, but it was totally dark.

"Please let me in, mom," Denise said.

Denise felt an electronic pulse, hopefully that meant yes or that her mother was too weak to resist. After a moment, her eyes and lungs adjusted, she was there inside her mother's dream. It wasn't like a simulation; she could feel and even smell this corner of this universe. Still everything was a bit off, like watching a blurry TV whose cable connection needed to be tightened. Denise concentrated and when things finally came into focus, she realized that this was Jen's memory—and not necessarily a perfect rendition of the past.

Denise looked around. Behind her, she saw a large figure in a military uniform leaving the podium of an outdoor concrete amphitheater, beneath a modern skyline. The audience were Asian workers in hazmat suits, their helmets off. The camouflage of the uniformed speaker sure looked American, but the details were vague.

No one noticed her as of yet. She was in the dream, but not *of* the dream. She had been in Nastia's mind and that hadn't ended well. She'd get out of her mother's mind way before it got to that point, right?

Denise now recognized a young, *healthy*, Susie Song come up to the podium to address the workers. Susie gave a speech in halting Korean, reading the words in English phonetically on a teleprompter. Apparently, she was trying to convince the workers about enrolling in a corporate health plan or against unionizing. Or both.

Susie then thanked the American military for the big contract. The American military person had entered a tunnel leading out of the amphitheater and gave a wave from the darkness.

A hazmat worker in the back looked in Denise's direction. Denise knew from her experience of entering Nastia's dream that Jen could sense that something was out of place in her mind. Denise didn't have much time.

Denise noticed a figure at the back of the stage, dressed in a pink blazer and khakis. It was indeed Jen Song—maybe in her thirties—looking as beautiful as Denise remembered. What did she once call her mom? A half-Korean Jackie Kennedy.

Her mom wasn't paying attention to Susie at all. With a wink of an eye, the POV shifted. Denise looked over her mom's shoulder to see that she was texting in English about the next stop on the insurance plan tour on one phone, while simultaneously texting someone about something else on another phone. It was to a number in the 505, the Albuquerque area code.

The texts were MISS YOU BABY, MISS YOU TOO. That sort of thing, back and forth. Jen and her correspondent really missed each other, that was for sure.

And finally, I'M COMING BACK TO AMERICA. WE CAN LIVE TOGETHER.

THAT WOULD BE WONDERFUL was the reply.

Did her mom have a boyfriend that Denise never knew about?

Her mom texted the person in the 505 one more time. THE LAWYERS SAID WE CAN FINALLY BE TOGETHER!

Why did those words sound familiar? Denise realized where she had heard those words before and why that number in the 505 was so familiar…

Her mom finally got the Skype to work and the image of the other party came on the screen. Denise recognized the young girl on the screen as herself. She would have been in 8th grade, living with her grandmother. The video was frozen, so they had to keep on texting.

Denise now remembered those texts clearly. Those texts were the last time she and her mom communicated like mother and daughter. Back then she had hopes that they would be reunited for real, be a family for real.

GOT TO TAKE THIS. Dream Jen shifted to the work phone.

Her mom wiped away a tear and then texted someone about Susie's lodging in Hong Kong for the next corporate trip. Susie's contract specifically mandated that she had separate rooms for her and her handler, *each* room with a double bed.

I LOVE YOU DENISE! Dream Jen texted back on the personal phone.

I LOVE YOU MOMMY! Young Denise texted back.

Her mom then looked up from the phone. Jen looked right at Denise, but stared through her.

"Denise?" Was Jen talking to young Denise or the current Denise? Jen was clearly confused and hung up. The colors of the dream faded a bit. That couldn't be a good thing.

Susie ended her speech with "*Gam-sa-ham-ni-da*," which Denise knew meant "Thank you" in Korean. There was only polite applause. While the workers weren't that impressed with Susie or the plan, the short heavy-set manager, was awed by the former celebrity. He brought Susie back over to Jen's chair, all the while talking rapidly.

The colors were getting vivid again in the dream. Jen's memories were sharper now. Something important was imminent.

"Jen," Susie said in English, "Mr. Choi's going to give us a tour of the nukes!"

Denise felt a thumping, like a rapid heartbeat. She wasn't sure if Jen's heart was beating faster in the dream or in real life. Her own heartbeat sped up to sound like dueling drummers.

In the dream, Jen looked around for a moment but didn't notice anything. Jen rose and followed Susie and Mr. Choi through the tunnel and then through an airlock. Denise went along behind them.

They went through another airlock and then another as Mr. Choi gave the two women a tour of the massive plant. Still, Denise could sense the tension in her mother's dream. Denise jumped after every airlock door clanged shut.

Many of the workers were in "bunny suits," but Mr. Choi, Jen and Susie were unprotected. The workers displayed tangential awareness of Denise and avoided her.

Both Jen and Susie feigned interest in Mr. Choi and his excited patter about the wonders of the atom. Susie pestered Jen in English about the double queen bed situation at their next destination in Hong Kong, as she preferred a second queen bed for her luggage and that Jen get a room with double beds of her own, one bed which would hold Susie's golf clubs.

Jen assured her that it would be taken care of, but was looking around, clearly perturbed by something. Mr. Choi then glanced in Denise's direction, but still didn't notice her.

"Something's wrong," Jen said in the dream.

Everyone else ignored her. Deep inside the plant, down a long hallway the plant's warning lights came on illuminating the walls like a strobe light. Jen looked concerned, but Mr. Choi kept smiling, assuring them in faulty English that there was nothing to worry about.

In the dream, Jen grabbed her stomach and Denise felt the pain in her own gut, as though she was a discount voodoo doll. While the hazmat workers in their suits were unaffected, her mother suddenly bent over and threw up, then threw up again. Susie also wobbled and fell over. Denise felt intense pain all over her own body. It felt like the radiation was probing every inch of skin with a needle, looking for entrance into her bloodstream.

Mr. Choi helped pick Jen up, but nearly dropped her when a worker shouted at him in Korean. Choi shouted some orders and the workers rushed away. The only words Denise could understand were centrifuge and core. How do you say meltdown in Korean?

Jen wiped her mouth the best she could and stood up under her own power. She looked through the thick glass and pointed at something glowing...

And that's when Denise noticed what was on the other side...

"OMG, it's a grail!" Denise said out loud. This was a big grail, maybe as big as the Stanley Cup, the hockey trophy.

Instinctively, Denise ran toward her mother to try to help her. Jen finally saw her.

"Denise?" It was her mother asking her the question within the dream. "You look different, all grown up. Why are you here at the plant with me? You've got to get out of here!"

Get out of the plant or get out of the dream? Her mother reached for her in the dream. The shock waves emanating from the grail cracked the bulletproof glass. Those shards pierced her mother's skin, drew blood from a thousand different holes.

"Denise, what's happening?" her mother asked.

"I don't know mom."

Denise looked down at her own body in the dream, she was bleeding all over every inch of exposed skin as well. She had to get out of the dream, or it could kill them both. Could Denise die in the dream? Could Jen?

The dueling heartbeats were deafening. Her mother moaned in agony and it looked like the nuclear plant walls were collapsing around her.

Denise winced in pain both in and out of the dream. The winds got worse. The heat got worse. The shards got worse.

"Denise, save me!!!" Her mother's face was now directly in front of her. The whole plant exploded in the dream.

Denise let go of her mother's hand. Was the explosion real or some psychic reaction?

Denise next saw a blinding light and then darkness with the afterimage of a mushroom cloud. She felt a burning sensation in her hands, as if her blood itself was crystalizing. Was she stuck in her mother's dream?

There was another flash and then darkness with that damn mushroom after-image. Was she shooting back to reality or shooting straight up to heaven?

"Denise come back!!!" her mom yelled. "Save me!!!"

It stayed dark. The last sounds of Jen's words faded. There was a thud.

What caused that thud?

After an eternity later, Denise finally opened her eyes. She was flat on the floor of the hospital room. It hadn't changed at all. Her mom was still asleep in the bed a few feet away. She looked down at her own hand, while she wasn't bleeding, it was actually red as if the blood, the glass or whatever it was had pushed her skin out from the inside.

Dr. Schwartz hurried in from down the hall. "Why are you on the floor?" He helped her up. She winced when he touched her hand.

"What happened to your hand?" he asked.

This was real?

But by the time the young doctor had finished examining her hand more closely, the swelling and scarring in Denise's hand was gone.

"It must have been the light," the doctor said. "You seem Okay."

Jen snorted for a second.

Dr. Patel had now arrived, dressed in sweats as if she'd slept here. Piranha the guard returned. Did he sleep here too? He looked groggy and worse for wear.

Without even looking at the doctor, Piranha grabbed Denise by the shoulder. "If I see you again, you will be admitted here as a *patient*," he said. He steered her to the elevator and pressed the button.

"Hold her there," Dr. Patel shouted, before coming over. "Miss Song, I think it might be best if you find somewhere else to stay and kindly refrain from visiting your mother for the immediate future."

"But she said she wanted me to save her."

Dr. Patel shook her head. "And Dr. Schwartz, we will have to discuss your conduct regarding this patient and her family in private!"

She didn't quite rip his ID badge off, but she might as well have. "Now take Ms. Song away and don't let her back in the building without my express authorization."

His hand still on her shoulder, Piranha escorted Denise out the door all the way to the Kia. He remained outside until Denise drove out of the parking lot.

Denise pulled into a gigantic parking lot near NMSU's athletic facilities, which were empty this time of night. There had to be a connection between the grail in her mother's dream and the grail that made Denny go insane. There had been an American military officer at the plant in the dream. Perhaps the officer's trip to the Asian grail factory had some connection to Denny and the experiments back here.

Denise was too tired to ponder it anymore, and her entire body was still recovering. She couldn't drive back to Lordsburg this late. She called Dew who was up despite it being nearly one in the morning, working on that class project. "Can I spend the night with you?"

Chapter 38
Thursday, July 30

"It all has to do with the grails," Denise repeated to herself before going to sleep on Dew's couch, well after midnight. Sahar purred.

When Denise put her head down, she was in pain, like something was stabbing her through the back of her neck. She hoped that it was a small grail, something that would help her with the case, but when she turned over, she found that it was only a plush cat toy shaped like a laser blaster. It was supposed to be a cat-friendly version of one of the weapons the laser geishas used in their anime series, but there was some hard plastic on the tip that must have splintered.

Out of nowhere, Sahar grabbed the toy and drowned it in her water dish.

"Sorry," Denise said to Sahar. Denise petted the cat who purred back in satisfaction.

"Glad you're finally up," Dew said. Dew had given up the dreadlocked look for straight hair, and now was wearing a t-shirt that depicted the anime team of Laser Geishas engaged in a life or death battle with some alien invaders.

Had Dew created it herself? The lettering on the shirt was in Japanese in sloppy handmade kanji. Dew even munched on a seaweed snack to complete the cultural appropriation. Her class project would never be done at this rate.

Denise didn't want to tell Dew about her mother's dream yet. She noticed a text from Hikaru confirming their date. "I have a date with Hikaru on Friday, we're supposed to meet at White Sands Missile Range, at the headquarters."

"You guys are so perfect for each other," Dew said. "The

215

two weirdos on Team Turquoise."

"Hey," Denise replied. "That's not fair."

"I'm saying that with love. For both of you."

While checking her phone, Denise noticed an update from the nmcourts.gov site. "The judge finally granted our motion for a subpoena duces tecum."

Denise called Rayne and told her the good news and reminded her that she needed to be there. Rayne was less than enthusiastic. "I don't love going on base," Rayne said. "It reminds me of growing up with the colonel."

"It must have been tough for you," Denise said. "My mom was just crazy, she wasn't a colonel."

"Do you really need me for this?" Rayne asked again.

"We can't do it without you, Rayne," Denise said. "We had to use your name on the subpoena just to get on base in the first place."

"Let me check on something," Rayne said. "I'll get back to you." She hung up.

"Why is this visit to the missile range so important?" Dew asked.

Denise thought back to the grail in her mother's dream and the military man walking down the tunnel. There was a connection to this case somehow. "Denny says he was the subject of *experiments.* Let's just say I know the military was using some technology—the grail technology—that does indeed cause adverse reactions in people, and maybe that technology caused an adverse reaction in Denny causing him to go insane. That would make him innocent."

"I think the term is *not guilty,*" Dew said. "No one is ever innocent. So, you believe him now?"

"Well, I think one of those grails affected my mom—don't ask me how I know that—and maybe these grails that were used on Denny while he was in the military. Maybe there really were experiments. He says that the technology is extraterrestrial, but they might just be coming from Korea. I don't know which is worse."

"Do you have to go on site to get those records?"

"Yeah," Denise said. "The judge is requiring Rayne Herring to be there as she's the one with the security clearance.

There's even a temporary badge that can be downloaded with her name on it. And one that says DESIGNEE.

Denise had Dew print the badges. Denise frowned. "The visit time would be the same time as the date. I'll have to cancel with Hikaru."

"You'll do no such thing," Dew said. Sahar purred in agreement, rubbing up on Denise's leg. "You haven't had a date, like *ever*. And Rayne? She's not the sharpest saw in the shed. I think she hit her head on the rim when dunking a basketball. Right here, it says that a *designee* can accompany Rayne."

"So?"

Dew pointed at herself with two thumbs. "I got your designee right here."

"I don't know, Dew," Denise said.

Dew was practically hyperventilating with excitement; she spilled her seaweed snacks on the dirty carpet. "Denise, do you have to be the one to *personally* check the records? You're not exactly a computer whiz. And you didn't do so well in the mental health classes in law school. And besides, I'd hate to see you cancel your first date this *century*... this millennium."

Denise magnified the order onscreen. Denny's attorney or *designees* could be the one to review the records. Rayne had to be there with the custodian of records, but could anyone else accompany her?

"Rayne has to go," Denise said, "but won't you need a clearance yourself?"

"Want to see a magic trick?" Dew asked. She got on a video chat with Luna, putting the call onscreen.

"*Mother*," she said to Luna. Denise remembered that Dew only called Luna mother when it was important. "Can you get me on base with Rayne when she looks at the files for the case?"

"We'll see," Luna replied.

They could almost feel the wind inside the apartment as Hurricane Luna got to work somewhere in New Mexico. Moments later, Dew's email clicked. Dew pressed a button. As if by magic, Dew picked up a temporary badge printed with her name on it and showed it to Denise.

Dew smiled. "Now call and confirm that date with your fellow weirdo."

Denise went outside and called Hikaru via FaceTime. He wore a white lab coat, but she could see his cycling jersey underneath. "My probation at work seems to be over," he said.

"Hopefully, I won't get you in trouble again."

"Don't worry about it," he said with a smile. "I heard that they're letting you onto Syrinx."

"How did you hear that?"

"I spend half my time over there."

"I know you wanted to meet at the main White Sands base, but can you pick me up over at Syrinx and drive me back to your helicopter?"

There was a pause. Denise heard some clicks over the phone.

"That might even be better," he said. "I can meet you there and take you anywhere in the helicopter. Remember to bring *exploring* clothes."

They firmed up a few more details and ended the call. When she went back into the apartment, Denise had on the biggest smile of her life.

"You're blushing, Denise," Dew said.

Denise felt fantastic for the first time since this all began. She had a date with a boy she could really love. Dew and Rayne were going to get the records that would hopefully free Denny.

What could possibly go wrong?

Her phone rang. It was Rayne. "I don't know if I can do this," she said. "I will need a babysitter."

Chapter 39
Friday, July 31

After an hour of solving logistical challenges with Rayne and Dew, Denise didn't bother going all the way back to Lordsburg. She planned the excursion from Dew's apartment, while dodging the star cats. Dew and Rayne would access the military records on base while Denise did the air tour with Hikaru. Hikaru would fly her back to wherever she needed on his magic carpet, well his magic corporate helicopter.

As for little Rita, she would be spending her time with Big Red Herring on the campaign trail at a "whistle stop" up at Spaceport America. The Upbound train didn't really go to the spaceport of course, but the caboose would be transported by truck for the photo op. Big Red was passing through Cruces and would take her granddaughter up to the spaceport and presumably bring her back.

Rita wasn't happy about being stuck with grandma. Despite her military precision, Big Red always ran late. "She's always taking a long-distance phone call from someone important and she makes me wait like ten feet away because the call is so secret. Maybe she's calling Mars or something. I don't want to go with her."

"You don't get a vote," Rayne reminded her daughter while talking on the phone with Denise.

"Glad you were able to work it out, Rayne," Denise said to her friend.

"I'm doing it for you," Rayne said. "You know how I hate these bases."

* * *

Denise spent another night on the couch from hell in Dew's apartment. She awoke in the middle of the night with Sahar on her chest.

"Are you OK?" Denise asked the cat.

Sahar purred, all good and licked her fur.

When Denise woke up for good the next morning, Dew was already on the computer, five windows open on her screen. Dew must have given herself a crew cut in the night and was wearing army fatigues, but they were deliberately ripped.

"Did you enlist?" Denise asked.

"I'm wearing them *ironically*," Dew said. She stared at the screen again.

"Everything OK?"

"There will be a delay," Dew said. "I guess Rayne's mom is firing missiles again."

"She doesn't do that anymore now that she's running for Congress," said Denise. "As far as I know."

Dew rolled her eyes. When did she become a pacifist? Suri the black star cat had coughed up a hair ball and Denise stepped in it by accident. "I've got a bad feeling about this."

Moments later, there was a knock on the door. It was Rita and Rayne. "We're supposed to meet my mom here," Rayne said. "She's supposed to take Rita out on the campaign trail."

"My grandma uses me as a prop."

Both Rayne and Rita wore red polo shirts with the campaign logo and buttons. "I don't know which of us has it worse," Rayne said.

"I do, mom," Rita said. "At least you can be with your friends while I have to be with grandma for that stupid campaign ad with a train that you're supposed to be able to take non-stop to Neptune."

"I don't know if she's going to be with *friends*," Dew said. "We were just teammates."

"So, you've become an ensign in *Star Fleet*?" Rayne asked, glancing at Dew's rumpled fatigues.

"At least I could get in," Dew replied. "You have to be a college *grad* to be an officer."

"What's she like?" Denise asked Rita, trying to break the

tension. "Your grandma? Colonel Big Red seems like a tough cookie."

"She was supposed to be an astronaut," Rayne said. "But she was too big for a spacesuit, male or female. She took it personally."

"If they had let me fly to the moon, we would have free interplanetary trade right now," Rita imitated her grandmother. "We can't let them aliens from Andromeda take American jobs!"

As if on cue, Rayne got a text from Big Red and showed it to the group. There would be a lengthy delay as the logistics of the whistle stop tour grew more complex. A soon-to-beformer aide had forgotten to secure an oversized load escort for the truck carrying the caboose. Big Red would now be picking up Rita here at the apartment at high noon.

"Now what?" Rita asked. "We have a morning to kill."

As Petro and his posse were back and already out in full force, the smell of high-grade marijuana wafted in through the windows. Rayne took a sniff, shook her head and suggested a girl's morning out, preferably with a different vista than the *Vista de Estrella*.

Rita checked out Denise's usual "cheerful charcoal" outfit. "Is that what you're going to wear for your big date, Auntie Denise?"

"I told her she looks like an Amish assassin," Dew said.

"No, she looks like Wednesday from the *Addams Family*," said Rita.

"Or a Ninja school drop-out," said Rayne.

Denise knew she had to play along. "Someone told me I looked like Darth Vader's intern." She looked down at her phone, there was that pic of two figures hiking up a ridge toward the desert sunset. "Oh damn, he told me to wear *exploring* clothing. I assume we're going hiking or maybe cycling. What would an explorer wear?"

Dew brought up an image of the film *Out of Africa*. While Robert Redford's character looked dashing, Meryl Streep was in a long dress.

"Not that," Denise said.

Dew next brought up an image of Marion Ravenwood

from *Raiders of the Lost Ark.* "I like that a little better," Denise said.

Dew then went with a still with Lara Croft Tomb Raider with Angelina Jolie.

"That's way too much," Denise said.

"We have some time," Rita said. "And this room is kinda gross, can we go to the outlet mall and give the Amish Assassin a makeover?"

Rayne checked her watch. "It will take half hour to get there and half hour back. We can do it with time to spare. You need a makeover too, Dew. They might not let you on base dressed like a Section 8."

Dew shrugged. The smell from the outside got worse, and the cats sure weren't helping with the smell inside. "Let's do it," Denise said, checking Google Maps on her phone and doing math in her head. "Maybe I should drive. I can get us there quickest. We never have enough time as we think."

With Denise driving her Kia, they made the thirty-mile drive over the Texas state line in less than twenty minutes and soon parked at the massive outlet mall off Transmountain Road. At least the tension between Rayne and Dew had simmered down.

Rita apparently knew her way around the outlet mall. With her help, Denise found the Banana Republic knockoff with a clearance sale and bought some exploring clothes—some kind of breathable khaki that would move well in the heat. She even found a nice hat to protect her from the sun.

"You look like a sexy Indiana Jones," the young clerk said. She looked like she had come back from a cocktail party on the Nile.

"I can live with that," Denise said.

"My little cousin is all grown up and ready to go on a safari date," Dew said.

"I feel like Indiana Jones *herself*," Denise said. "He found the grail in one of his movies, right?"

"Do you want to wear them out?" the clerk asked. "You looked great."

Denise felt empowered, all her workouts in the motel rooms had paid off. In this breathable khaki, she could conquer any temple, from reform to orthodox.

Rita found the same outfit in her sizes. "I'm like your Mini-me, Auntie Denise," Rita said. "Except that I'm taller."

"Thanks for reminding me," Denise said.

"I can put your old clothes in a bag," the clerk said. "I'll meet you up front."

Still in the exploring outfit up front, Denise was about to use her remaining credit card and pray that it went through. Luckily, the clerk told them that they could get twenty-five percent off if they opened a store credit card and would be billed later.

"No payments for sixty days," the clerk said. Meanwhile, Rayne was fiddling with her own wallet, frowning. Rita was still in her matching outfit. Rayne was supposedly a private investigator, but Denise was her only client and Denise hadn't paid her yet. Denise figured that Big Red probably monitored every purchase Rayne made.

"Don't worry, Rayne, I've got Rita's stuff," Denise opened the account. Hopefully, she'd be in a position to pay the bill in full when it came due.

"Thanks, Auntie Denise."

"Thank you, Denise," Rayne said.

As they walked back to the car, Denise felt a spark, and the hairs on the back of her neck literally stood up. It wasn't a sensing of danger; it was something else. She was close to the location of where something important in her life had happened. It took her a moment to realize what it was.

She smiled when she checked her watch. "We have a little extra time. I want to see something."

The passengers were surprised to see Denise take charge like that and said nothing. Rita was smiling.

Denise took the Kia back onto I-10, but drove in the opposite direction, a few miles south into the heart of El Paso and exited downtown. "Where are we going, Auntie Denise?" Rita asked.

"I want to see where I was born," Denise said. "Where this whole Denny and Denise saga began."

She could see signs directing them to Juarez but knew if she hit Mexico she'd gone too far. She tried to rely on her memories from Nastia's dream for directions. After a few wrong turns, she neared the spot but found that the one-way street to her birthplace was blocked because of new construction. She had to pull over for an ambulance and wondered if it was headed for the birth of another pair of twins.

"Do you know where you're going, Auntie Denise?"

"I think it's over there on the other side of that construction," Denise said.

"You can't get there from here," Rayne said.

"Maybe you should just let it go," Dew added.

"Let it go?" Rita belted out the song, "*Let it go*," from *Frozen*. The three of them joined in, Dew surprising with a nice Falsetto. Hikaru called as the women had launched into a reprise, Denise put him on speaker, and he harmonized with an impressive baritone.

"*Team Turquoise!*" They all said after reminding the world that the cold never bothered them anyway per the song.

"I love you guys," Denise said.

"We love you, Denise," they all said at the same time. Denise wiped away a tear.

"I hope we can do this again," Hikaru said. "Just letting you know that I'm ready for you guys when you get here."

He hung up. Denise smiled.

"Am I officially part of Team Turquoise, Auntie Denise?" Rita asked.

"You are now, Rita," Denise said.

Even Dew was smiling, and she gave Rayne a friendly poke on the shoulder. "That was fun," Dew said to Rayne. "We used to sing together in practice, I missed that."

"Missed that too. We're cool?" Rayne asked her.

"Cool," Dew replied. "So, have you let it go, Denise?"

"For the moment." She was at peace. She was with her friends and it felt great. Let it go had become let it *went*. Her pain was in the past now, just a few blocks from her birthplace. Denise wondered how long it would last.

It didn't even last till she made it to the freeway. There was more construction and she was almost grazed by some truckers at the feeder road. It was only one lane northbound on the interstate toward New Mexico. It didn't take a psychic to figure that the van ahead of them that was going under the speed limit probably held contraband, people or both.

So much for letting it go.

Rayne frowned while looking at her phone. "We got to get back, my mother the colonel got out early after all and is already waiting to pick up Rita. Apparently, the missile situation cleared up and the caboose has arrived at the spaceport. The campaign ad is ready to shoot to make up for lost time and they're waiting for Rita."

The construction ended; Denise now had the Kia break the speed of sound. They arrived at Dew's in a matter of minutes. Petro and the posse had been out in full force, an early morning party in the parking lot. This one involved deck chairs and a keg that poured out pink beer. Unfortunately, the party was coming to an abrupt end.

Petro had finally met his match. The colonel interrogating the gang, as if reviewing the plebes at the Air Force Academy. Petro had no powers over Big Red, and his party crew actually dispersed, for perhaps the first time in recorded history. So much for *we're not going anywhere.*

The party over, the colonel turned to her granddaughter who was cowering in the back seat. "Rita, get in my car this instant. That's an order!"

"Yes, *sir!*" Rita said and even saluted before she hurried into the official campaign vehicle, a Jeep. Without another word, they sped away.

"I only saw the colonel when she came to pick you up from practice," Denise said. "And even then, she intimidated the hell out of me. I always thought she was going to make me do KP or whatever they call cleaning the toilet with a toothbrush."

"Me too," Dew said.

"Think how I feel," Rayne replied. "Are you sure you ladies still want to go through with this?"

Denise didn't hesitate. "This is about my brother; I need your help. I'm almost tempted to come myself."

"No, you're going on your date today," Rayne said. "Dew

and I can handle the base."

"I'll drive," Dew offered. Rayne was skeptical until she saw that the Mercedes had been washed for a change. The interior smelled of lemons.

"I hope Hikaru can take me back here," Denise said.

"Hopefully he does it *tomorrow*," Dew said.

Rayne nodded. "Be careful or you'll have a Rita of your own."

Dew drove her Mercedes quickly, and the car maneuvered through traffic like a race car. Rayne clenched her fists. "You drive like a maniac. Denise at least had control."

"Jealous much?" Dew asked.

Denise frowned. "Hikaru texted again," she said. "No need to rush. There's more testing on the other side of the pass."

"What's up with all the missile testing these days?" Dew asked.

"Are you sure it's safe?" Rayne asked.

"They won't let us through if it's not safe, right?" Denise asked.

Sure enough, they had to stop on the top of San Augustine Pass—at the rest stop off the highway—and wait for the missile test or tests to be finished. Nothing was happening down in the valley below at any of the various launch sites. Was it a stealth launch or something?

"It's going to be another half-hour," an MP announced via loudspeaker to the line of cars.

Waiting there in the San Augustin Pass parking lot, they grew more uneasy by the minute, especially when the MPs kept frowning.

"Why are you so nervous, Rayne?" Denise asked. "Is it going back to a base that triggers something?"

"Not just me, I'm scared that Rita will do something stupid in front of Big Red," Rayne said. "I'm terrified of my mother, but Rita has no fear."

"That's a good thing," Denise said. "If I had a daughter, I'd hope she'd be like Rita."

"Be careful *tonight* or you might have a daughter of your own someday," Dew said. "We'll be fine on base."

"I'll be fine if Dew over here doesn't act up," Rayne said. "They got rules on base."

"Aye aye, captain," Dew said mockingly.

Even with the air-conditioning it was getting stuffy in the car. Rayne and Dew were giving each other dirty looks, their temporary truce about to explode.

Suddenly, an explosion rocked the valley and echoed off the Organ Mountains. An officer's radio announced a successful launch and ummm... *landing* down at the missile range.

"All clear!" A burly military policeman indicated that they were free to go down the hill to the range. Dew gunned the Mercedes downhill.

When they finally arrived at the Syrinx gate a few miles down the road, it was late afternoon and the dry heat was straining the car's air-conditioning. Dew slowed to a stop at the check point station. They were met by an even burlier MP.

The guard scanned every inch of the Mercedes with some kind of wand that glowed suspiciously when it neared Dew.

The MP finally lifted up the wand, checked with someone inside and then came out again, nodding.

"You guys can park by the hangar," the MP said.

Beyond the gate, the Syrinx facility was Spartan. It contained a small hangar building, a heliport with a shiny black helicopter and a radio telescope that looked like it could pick up signals from Saturn's TV. This site did no actual missile launches, just some kind of monitoring.

"They could fit a flying saucer in there," Dew said, pointing to the big hangar. It opened, and they all stepped back expecting a saucer or two to fly out and greet them.

Thankfully, only Hikaru emerged. He was back in black, even in the heat, with his usual cycling jersey top. He was flanked by a uniformed airman and the large bodyguard, Brutus, who'd been with him in the van. He smiled at Denise's new look.

"Ladies, so good to see you," he said.

He looked at Rayne, whose brightly colored shirt stood out in the military desert drab. "That is one red shirt, Rayne,"

Hikaru said. "You know the significance of red shirts in the original *Star Trek*?"

"Isn't a 'red shirt' like the expendable character that's going to die?" Dew asked.

Suddenly self-conscious, Rayne played with the red fabric of her shirt. "I just like the color, in spite of my mom."

Inside, the hangar was indeed big enough to hold a flying saucer. A female soldier now approached the party. Hikaru introduced her to them. "Sergeant Malvolio will be your liaison."

Denise realized her mistake in drafting the subpoena. She had confused the Spanish name of Maldonado with the Italian name of Malvolio. Did Malvolio know about the mistake? She sure acted like it.

"Who are Rayne and Dew?" Malvolio asked. "Rayne has the clearance and Dew is the *designee*. That makes Rayne the leader today."

"Should we wait for you, Denise?" Dew asked, before following inside.

Denise wasn't sure, but Hikaru put his arm on her shoulder.

"I can take her back to Cruces or even Lordsburg," Hikaru said to Dew. He pointed outside to the helicopter. "We're good to go."

"You can take me *anywhere*," Denise said. "Well, *kinda* anywhere."

Chapter 40

The door to the file room closed after Dew and Rayne, and now the hangar was empty. Hikaru took Denise out to the shiny black helicopter. The helicopter had the corporate insignia for Cygnus Moon, as opposed to a military logo. She hoped that was a good thing.

He pointed. "Ready to ride?" Sure enough, two bicycles sat in storage in the back. His pilot was Brutus, the man she'd met before. Brutus was already inside the helicopter, strapped in and ready for takeoff.

They fastened their seatbelts. The helicopter ascended quickly, too quickly. Denise cramped up from g-force. Once they were safely above the vast desert, the helicopter leveled off and Denise took in the view. Her cramps magically vanished.

"Brutus is used to flying paratroopers around Afghanistan," Hikaru said. "He's not used to taking it easy"

The ride now smooth, Hikaru pointed out various launch sites on the missile range. Thankfully, no missiles were launching this minute.

Hikaru directed Brutus to take them north. Denise started enjoying herself. Soon the white sands of the national park gave way to harsh tan desert and then the earth beneath them became a field of black rock.

"Is that the Trinity site?" Denise asked.

"No, that's the Valley of Fires," Hikaru said. "It's a national *recreation area,* whatever that mean as it isn't national and there's not much recreation. That's dried lava that is thousands of years old. The Trinity Site is like forty miles east of here and not worth the trip. It's just a pile of rocks in the desert with some broken radioactive glass pebbles."

Hikaru nodded at Brutus, who changed course. "Where to next?" she asked.

"It's a surprise," he responded.

The helicopter now headed northeast. The white pyramid of Sierra Blanca was to her right. The *sierra* was still *blanca* from a recent freak snow despite it being summer in the desert. On the other side of the forested hills, she could see Roswell in the plains and Alamogordo to the south.

Her stomach calmed, her pulse lowered. She felt safe with Hikaru.

Above an unremarkable patch of hilly desert, Brutus nodded at Hikaru. "This must be the place," Hikaru said.

They landed on a makeshift landing site, an intersection of some dirt roads that had been leveled off and widened for the occasional helicopter. Once the rotors had stopped, she noticed that they weren't alone. Some people trudged around with metal detectors. The people didn't give the helicopter a second thought.

"Now what?" Denise asked.

"We're going to have a picnic," he said.

"Why here?" Denise asked.

"Guess?"

Before she could guess, Brutus opened a lock box in the back of the helicopter and produced a picnic basket. Denise noticed a second basket waiting. Was Hikaru planning another picnic for later tonight? He then produced some folding directors' chairs and placed them on some level ground in the middle of the dirt road.

"Do you know where we are?" Hikaru asked her. "This is one of the most famous places in New Mexico, one of the most famous places on *Planet Earth*. Maybe the most famous place in the solar system."

She did the math. They were eighty miles from Roswell. "*The* Roswell site?"

"You got it. Even though we're eighty miles from Roswell. The truth is *in* here or *at* here. *Kinda.*"

"So, what's the truth about what really happened here?" Denise asked.

"They don't tell me. It's still classified."

"In any event, I'm starving. It's like three o'clock. Let's eat before the aliens come back. What do you have in there?"

"I heard you like *Shiprock Wok*, and, well, they cater," Hikaru said.

Denise didn't know if there was another branch on base, or if he had the meal flown in by rocket ship, because the food was still warm. They had a delicious lunch of Korean *bibimbap* with New Mexico chorizo.

"Amazing," she said.

After lunch, they wandered around the barren site, and the conversation shifted to fictional aliens and the debate of Star Wars versus Star Trek. "I'm *Star Wars*, because of the force, I guess," she said. "And Baby Yoda in *The Mandalorian*."

"I'm *Star Trek*, because I was named after Sulu of course. John Cho played him in the reboot."

"I love John Cho," she said.

"He was in the teen comedy *American Pie*," Hikaru added. "But he was just like the token Asian. And he was Harold in *Harold and Kumar*."

"I liked him best as the bad boy in *Better Luck Tomorrow*. An old film and he was like my age then."

"I'm not a bad boy, that's for sure, but I play one at work."

She wasn't sure how to take that. "Now what?"

"Ready to explore?" After taking off his blazer, he pulled down his pants. Before Denise could say anything, she realized he was wearing cycling shorts under his pants. Seeing her expression, he said, "Don't worry, I wouldn't take my pants off in front of you unless I have something underneath."

Her safari outfit really was able to move in the heat, and her sweat melted away without the humidity. They did a few laps around the crash site on the mountain bikes. Hikaru went slow for her, and soon even their breathing was in sync. Denise tried to use her spark on the site itself, but any evidence of aliens was long gone. Something *had* happened here. The government was hiding something, but she would never know the truth.

By the third lap, none of that mattered anymore. She was having such a good time breathing in the clean air with this handsome young man. They stopped on top of the ridge and looked at the incredible desert panorama.

"Do you believe in UFOs?" she asked him.

"I believe in *something*," he said. "How about you?"

"I don't know what I believe. You're hiding something. Why did you really bring me here?"

He smiled that million-dollar smile. "There's one theory, that this wasn't the only crash site, that one also happened in Lordsburg, and there were a bunch all over the world."

"I read the article in the *Lordsburg Liberal*."

"Your brother was obsessed with it. He had this theory that some of the flying saucers had people in them as passengers—either genetically created in a lab or ones that had been snatched before and then returned to earth as an experiment for future colonization."

"Do you believe that?"

"That's above my paygrade," he said. "I hate that expression, I guess I got that from all the work I do on bases."

"And the grails?"

"Well, here's where it gets complicated. According to one scientist, there are humans who are capable of either joining with the aliens or using the power of the grails to fight the alien colonization."

"So are the grails good or bad?"

"Depends on who's using them. They're like the sword in the stone, they're supposed to attract certain people. How those people interact with the grails is up to them or up to the grails. Same with the drones. But my own theory is that the grails intensify whatever emotion a person might be feeling."

"So, if Denny was feeling hate when he approached the grail that night?"

"Then the hate would be intensified. Beyond his control."

"What about love?"

"Then that feeling of love would be intensified."

"So do the aliens or whoever want Denny to actually touch the grail?"

"They wanted him to *try*, to reveal himself. Now, that they know about him, they don't want him anywhere near it. I bet they hope he sits in a cell or a mental hospital for the rest of his life."

It was getting hot. A creepy man was approaching them with a metal detector, hoping they were standing on top of the mothership. They got out of his way.

"Where to next?" Denise said.

"Another surprise," he said. "And you'll like this one even better."

Brutus launched the helicopter slower this time. They flew over the blue waters of Elephant Butte reservoir, and then back to the tall dark pines of New Mexico's Sacramento Mountains.

Hikaru pointed to a break in the pines with a small meadow, a cabin and a pond. He nodded at Brutus who landed the helicopter, scaring away a few deer into the pines. They could be in the Swiss Alps.

"Where are we?" Denise asked. "It's beautiful."

"This is my family's cabin," Hikaru said as they departed the helicopter.

The cabin sported a big satellite disk on the roof but was otherwise rustic and cozy. The deer had returned.

The sun was setting through the pines, and there was an unobstructed view of Sierra Blanca which was now becoming Sierra *Rosa*—the pink mountain—in the sunset. The pink summit reflected perfectly off the still blue waters of the pond.

"I love it!" she said.

Hikaru took her hand, but before he could say anything Brutus came over to them. "Do you need anything else, sir?"

Hikaru hesitated for another moment, looking at Denise, then at the cabin.

Denise checked her phone. There was a text from Dew.

EVERYTHING GOING GREAT. WE ARE COMING BACK AGAIN TOMORROW. YOU DON'T NEED TO COME HOME!

Denise smiled. She didn't need to come home. It was all going to work out perfectly.

"You can go now," Denise said to Brutus, touching Hikaru's arm.

Brutus looked at Hikaru. Hikaru looked at Denise. "Are you sure?"

"*Kinda,*" Denise said with a smile. "I'd like to stay here

with you."

Moments later, the helicopter took off, and the deer scattered again. Denise and Hikaru were alone in this alpine wonderland. A rabbit hurried past them without a care in the world.

A series of concentric waves now emanated from the center of the pond. Were they doing that with their spark?

Hikaru took a deep breath and then Denise kissed him.

Chapter 41

Saturday, August 1

When they woke up the next morning, Denise could not stop smiling. It was even better than she expected. Unfortunately, before she could revel in the bliss, she received a phone call. She didn't answer it.

The phone rang again, and then again. It was Rita. "Auntie Denise, can you pick me up? I haven't heard from my mom. I'm still over at the spaceport, but my grandma is really busy and can't watch me. She says I've got to go soon, something big is about to happen and she has to stay here."

That was odd. She looked over to Hikaru who was looking at his own phone, frowning.

"I can have Brutus fly you over to the spaceport and get you a car there," Hikaru said. "I'll stay here. Something's come up at work."

He pointed to the big computer screen on the far side of the cabin. She could see the shadow of the satellite dish on the ground as if it had eclipsed the sun. "They can find me anywhere," he said.

She didn't want to leave the cabin. She didn't want to leave Hikaru. They stared at each other for a long moment. "How about breakfast?" he said. "While we're waiting."

"Perfect," she replied. She put on her safari clothes, which were only slightly worse for wear after that magic night.

They had a delicious brunch at a picnic table overlooking the pond. The high-altitude air was extremely clear up here, but thin and cool. She smiled at the deer looking at them through the pines.

Brutus and the noisy helicopter soon arrived. After a final kiss, Denise took one last deep breath of mountain air and then climbed inside the black helicopter. She waved to Hikaru, and then Brutus flew her away. He was back to playing the bad-ass pilot and was flying too fast. They were rocked by turbulence. She hoped it was the wind and not a missile launch.

She texted Rita that she was on her way. Still no texts from Dew or Rayne, and she didn't know why that bothered her. She told herself that if there was an emergency on base, someone would have texted her, right?

"I've got to take the long way around, they're firing missiles again," Brutus said. "Something's definitely up. I've never seen so many tests in one week."

He pointed to down in the valley. Denise now saw a few blasts off in the distance at the missile range. She couldn't tell if they were launches or impacts.

"We're perfectly safe," he said. But were they?

A gust of wind suddenly blew them in the same direction as the tests.

"Are you sure?"

"Well, we better go south, and go the *really long way* around, just in case," he said, checking the radar.

The *really long way* indeed. After a grand tour of all of southern New Mexico, and then up the Rio Grande, Brutus landed at the spaceport. Spaceport America was more port than space. Most of the stubby rockets were launched by plane. The terminal itself looked like a gigantic turtle shell, fit for *Gamera,* the monster turtle of Japanese cinema.

As she disembarked, she saw her car, the Kia, being loaded off a tow truck. They had thought of everything.

Rita was still in her matching safari clothes, but hers were stained as if her grandma had fed her too much ice cream. Rita hurried over to Denise and gave her a hug. Denise's phone beeped, indicating a text from Dew. The phone said: MEET ME ON TOP OF PASS.

Rita shivered. "Wouldn't the text say meet *us?*"

"I don't know. I'm sure it's fine. Dew and your mom don't always seem to get along."

They got back into the Kia. "You seem different somehow, Auntie Denise," Rita said. "Glowing."

Could this girl sense what had happened? "I'm still me," Denise said. But was she?

They took a back road from the spaceport through the desert. Denise's glow faded with every mile. She tried to call Rayne, as did Rita, but there was no answer.

Dew texted MEET ME AT THE PASS again, with no explanation. Denise dialed Dew, but the line was busy.

"Once I meet my mom on top of the Pass, we can all relax," Rita said, biting her nails. "I just hope Dew didn't screw everything up for my mom."

Denise knew she'd have to distract the poor girl before she bit her fingers off. Once they hit Interstate 25, they passed a small elementary school. Denise saw a chance to distract the girl. "Do you like being home-schooled by your mom?"

"My mom's a really good teacher. Well, even when she isn't, I get to go and see exciting things. It's like one big adventure."

"I wish I'd had one big adventure with my mom," Denise said. "You're lucky in that respect."

"I wouldn't call it lucky. I miss hanging with kids my age. Auntie Denise, do you ever want to be a mom?" Rita asked.

Denise thought for a moment, and nearly missed the exit to get on US 70 East to head up to the pass. Denise turned the car sharply and made the turn.

"That's a long way off," Denise said. Or was it?

"That boy, Mr. Hikaru, really likes you. I can tell."

Now on Highway 70, Denise looked over at Rita again, to make sure the girl's seatbelt was still fastened. She must have somehow produced more stains on her outfit without moving.

This was a good kid, and Denise couldn't help but feel for her. Her maternal instincts were engaged for some reason.

"I told the team if I had a daughter, I hoped she'd be like you," Denise said. "I really mean that."

"Thanks. I feel a connection to you, Auntie," Rita said. Rita reached out to touch Denise. "I love my mom, but you and me, we seem to have more in common."

"Thanks."

Denise sensed something odd emanating from Rita through the touch on her shoulder. The girl was trying to tell her something but didn't want to say it out loud. "Do you ever hear anything about your dad?" Denise asked.

"I don't know my dad. It sounds kinda icky, but my mom told me that she didn't really know the guy either. You heard what she's always told me. That she was on a school trip and then they went over to Mexico, to that *Puerto* place."

"Wait, where was the high school trip to? I mean, the trip didn't go straight to Mexico, she had to start on the American side, right?"

"She didn't say."

They both looked at each other. Didn't Rayne say she'd been to Lordsburg once? "Who was he?" Denise asked.

"I don't know, my mom just said that she got all drunk at a party back when she was on the high school basketball team at this tournament down south, and then since there was a snowstorm back up north and the roads were closed, her and the local boy from Lordsburg went over to Mexico. Didn't my mom tell you the story, *Auntie* Denise?"

Denise looked at the innocent, gangly girl sitting next to her, she sure didn't want to tell her about the birds and the bees. Rita's hand was still on her shoulder, and Denise now concentrated on the touch.

Denise sped up, almost hitting the car in front of her before she realized what was going on. She pulled off the road to catch her breath.

"What's wrong, Auntie Denise?"

And then it hit her why this girl was so obsessed with her, with *Auntie Denise*, and so obsessed with the case involving her brother. Even obsessed with her mother, Jen Song.

They had pulled off the road near something called the Space Murals Museum which had a wooden imitation of a space shuttle, twenty feet high next to a cylindrical water tower with murals of outer space.

"Your mom went to Clovis High, right? And you're saying she played basketball, right?"

"Yeah. She was all-state and got recruited at Texas Tech.

She met this guy at a tournament down south."

"What's your birthday again?"

Rita told her. Denise now held her hand tightly. Denise went deeper with her mind, trying to get down to Rita's cellular level.

It wasn't exact science, but still holding Rita's hand, Denise subtracted nine months. With her other hand, she used her phone and checked out the schedule for the Clovis High Basketball team, and then cross-checked against a big snowstorm that would have closed the roads back to Clovis that year.

Sure enough, the basketball team had been at a tournament in Lordsburg. It was a Boys and Girls tournament for a variety of sports and the Shakespeare Classical Academy was there as well.

It didn't take Denise long to put together the rest of the pieces as she continued to hold Rita's hand in hers. A bunch of high school girls stranded at a motel for a couple of days. They get some food over at McDonald's. They meet up with some local boys. One of them is a cute "bad boy" at the time and says something about Puerto Penasco, Mexico and lies that it "is just over the border." He says he can get her back in time before her basketball team leaves for Clovis the next morning. Or maybe even the morning after that if the roads stay closed.

This tall, awkward, girls' basketball player jumps at a chance to rebel against her controlling mom and accompanies the bad boy across the border. She spends one extra day at a Mexican resort and probably drinks too much tequila.

"And your mom never said who the boy was?" Denise asked. Denise could tell from the current between them that Rita knew the truth too. "Even after you got involved with this case?"

They looked at each other and clasped their hands tightly.

"Did you know?"

"Duh, *Auntie* Denise," Rita said, and wiped a tear from her eye. "You really are my auntie."

"I love you, *Lovely Rita Meter Maid*," Denise said. "The

niece of Denise."

"I love you too. Now, where's my mom?"

Denise looked at her phone. Yet another MEET ME AT THE PASS.

But there was something new at least. I'M ALMOST THERE.

Why "I" and not "*we?*"

Denise got back on the highway and headed the last few miles to the top of the pass. While it was sunny on this side of the Organs, clouds had rolled in over the top of the mountains. Before they knew it, Denise and Rita had made it to the summit of San Augustine Pass with its expansive view of the entire Tularosa basin, but it was now totally cloudy, and they could barely see in front of them.

Dew and Rayne hadn't arrived yet. Unfortunately, an MP directed them to the rest stop with the rest of the vehicles on the road. The road was closed for testing yet again.

"Why is there so much testing?" Rita asked. "I hope my mom didn't get caught up in it."

"I wouldn't know," the MP said.

Denise and Rita parked there at the crowded San Augustine Pass rest stop. They were under the billboard of Big Red posing with her daughter and granddaughter. "That's me and my mom up there!" Rita said to a few passersby who nodded politely.

"If they're testing, aren't they stopping my mom and Dew from going out?" Rita asked. "Did they have to stay overnight and that's why they didn't call?"

"They would have to, right?" Denise replied.

But was that true? And why did Dew keep using "I" instead of "we?"

Down below, a dust storm existed all right. Because the sand was white, it almost looked like a snowstorm.

More apprehensive by the minute, Denise texted Dew a few times, but no response. Rita leaned closer to Denise, like a kitten curling against its mother. It was hard to tell where the khaki of one outfit ended and the other began. Denise patted Rita's head. They calmed each other in the storm. They were blood after all.

Another boom out in the valley. Why were they still firing missiles in a storm like this?

"Are you sure they're OK?" Rita asked. "It sounded like they just shot off a missile. They would have stopped my mom and Dew if they were going into the middle of it, right?"

"I'm sure they're fine."

"You're lying, Auntie. I can tell you're worried too."

The dust storm glowed in the setting sun. The phone rang. Both Denise and Rita jumped.

"Almost there," Dew said through the phone.

"Can I talk to my mom?" Rita said.

The phone cut out before Dew could promise anything. Why hadn't Rayne said anything just now? She was in the car, right?

"Do you think my mom's OK, Auntie Denise?"

Denise didn't know what to say.

Rita dialed her grandma, Big Red, a few more times to see if Rayne had called her, but Big Red didn't pick up.

The sun had now set totally behind the pass to the west, and it grew dark quickly. Denise and Rita could feel the dust blowing against the car.

More flashes of lights burst over the valley. Could those be drones? Missiles? Flying saucers?

Rita looked disturbed. "They're over there," she said pointing at some lights in the sky. "They're really over there!"

Hadn't Rita said that the last time they encountered weird lights in the sky? Denise couldn't remember. They held hands, but instead of comforting each other, they now shivered. She felt nauseous and dizzy at the same time, she opened the car door to vomit, but nothing came out.

Rita pointed to another explosion down in the valley that lit up the dust storm like a rogue firework. "That's where my mom is!"

Denise tried to call the colonel, but no one answered.

Suddenly it was quiet and dark. Even the winds stopped howling. Denise and Rita got out of the car and they could now see a line of cars coming up the road from the valley below.

The MP took a call and after checking a few more times,

finally moved the orange barrels. "All clear!" he said.

Denise and Rita stood there. Car after car passed them heading in the other direction. "Where's my mom?" Rita asked repeatedly.

Finally, the Mercedes pulled into the rest stop parking lot. Rita was excited until she realized that there was only one person in the car, Dew. Her mother was nowhere to be seen.

Dew had a black eye. Someone or something had punched her. She also had some scratch marks on her face.

"Where's my mom?" Rita asked. "Is she dead or something?"

"Your mom?" Dew had a blank look.

"She was with you!" Rita said.

Denise jumped in. "You told me that you *both* went back to the base today."

Dew exited the car, dazed. There was a charred space where Rayne should be sitting. There were some melted computer disks and burnt papers where the evidence records should have been sitting. Dew looked blank. "I have no *recollection* of any of that."

PART IV

TO BE OR NOT TO BE

Chapter 42

Sunday, August 2

For the next twenty-four hours it sure looked like Team Turquoise was down for the count. Rayne was missing, Hikaru was incommunicado and Dew was hospitalized for "stress." Honorary member Rita was holed up with her grandmother the colonel and might as well be in Leavenworth.

Even worse, Jen Song was having some "complications" and Centennial Hospital wouldn't let Denise inside. When Denise drove back to Lordsburg to visit Denny, a handwritten sign on the door indicated the jail was on quarantine.

Denise walked back to the Kia. It looked worse for wear after the miles of live sand and dead bugs. The beaches of Puerto Penasco sure sounded good right now.

After a takeout order of *won ton tamales* from Shiprock Wok, she reluctantly drove back to the Last Palm. She locked herself in, bolted the door and practiced her katas as if they would protect her from invisible enemies. That night, she had the same dream over and over. Rayne was reaching out to her. Her friend was struggling in quicksand and was sinking fast.

"Save me!" Rayne said.

"Where are you?"

"I don't know. I don't know if I'm even on earth."

What planets in the solar system had toxic quicksand? Venus or Mars?

* * *

When Denise woke up the next morning, she skipped breakfast and hit the road immediately. She brought her staff with her just in case. She knew of only one place to find help.

The drive to Albuquerque must have taken four hours, maybe five, but she had no recollection of the journey.

Encantado Gardens cemetery was empty when she passed through the half-opened brass gate. Her spark was picking up, she sensed something. Hotspur—the same guard as the last time—was rousting some sleeping drunks from the far side of the cemetery. Or maybe they were actual zombies, it was hard to tell from this far away. She had a minute, maybe two.

She parked and hurried over to Marley's brick on the memorial wall. She got on her tippy-toes and touched the brick. Maybe it was all the death around her, but she was nervous. Had Rayne passed over? Or had she been abducted and taken to another planet?

"Can you connect me with Rayne?" she asked the brick.

Her spark was rattled by the distant sound of a leaf blower.

Nothing.

Hotspur shoved the zombie drunks out the front gate, turned and now noticed her from across the way. He was coming over.

"Can you connect me with Rayne?" she asked again.

Still nothing.

Had she ever really been able to talk to Marley at all, or was it all her imagination?

She released her grip on the brick and walked back to the car. Maybe she was wrong about Rayne being alive. Where would Rayne be buried? Or would the colonel scatter the poor girl's ashes from orbit?

Denise thought for a second, on the last bit of pavement connected to the memorial wall. For some reason, she thought of Petro and the "We're not going anywhere," crowd. They had managed to stay put, by letting go and creating their own gravity, by somehow merging with the earth itself.

She did that, right there in the cemetery. It felt like she was connected to everything that had ever happened on the surface of the planet that had to do with Rayne. As she thought about her friend, she could suddenly recall what had happened with the three of them on I-10 hundreds of miles away. They had almost been abducted, but somehow fought it away.

She now had a *recollection* of that lost time and it was clear as day. Her mind kept probing and she felt the helpful energy of Marley, and perhaps all the others on the wall, all the others in the graves around her. She suddenly had more "reach" than ever before.

The dead knew things... They knew that Rayne was not among them.

Suddenly, Denise had an image of a small muddy lake surrounded by white sand, but most of all she was bombarded by an incredibly harsh smell. She could see Rayne in the middle of lake, alive but sinking. She still wasn't sure whether this was on earth. Titan, a moon of Saturn had methane lakes, right?

In the vision, something whizzed overhead causing a sonic boom and waves in the shallow waters. By concentrating she was able to get an image of the markings on the object's tail.

She couldn't tell if it was Marley sending the vision, or Rayne. Or maybe one of the hundreds of other souls in the cemetery. It didn't matter. She knew this place. She had been there. Hikaru had been there. She touched her phone. The photo Hikaru had sent her of this place appeared for a moment, and then disappeared. The aroma from the toxic waste lingered, however.

Rayne wasn't dead... yet.

"It's you again?" Hotspur yelled, breaking her reverie. "What the hell are you doing here?"

"I have to find my *friend* this time."

Why was Hotspur so angry? There was something more going on here. His antipathy towards her was visceral. She didn't want to stay to find out why. Denise hurried to the Kia and got inside.

"Next time you're here you better be here for a *funeral*," Hotspur yelled. "Either as a pallbearer or in the box yourself."

"I'll keep that in mind," Denise said from behind the window.

She drove the Kia south, very, very quickly. Should she

call Rita and let her know about her mom? Not till Denise knew if she would be calling an ambulance or a hearse.

After three hours through the high desert, Denise finally arrived at Lake Holloman, the "wastewater evaporation pond" that took the waste and the water from the nearby Holloman Air Force Base. The place where she'd gagged on the stench of chemical death. In the setting sun, the white sands had turned blood red. The revolving searchlight from the air force base and subsequent fighter jet launches made it feel like Mars.

When the searchlight revolved again, she spotted the white binoculars icon on a brown sign. She was less than a hundred yards away from the water, well whatever the liquid actually was. She opened her windows and took in the chemical stench. Did she hear a scream?

Unfortunately, the gate across the dirt road that led to the lake was closed. She hesitated for only a moment, exited the Kia and ducked under the gate. She took her staff with her. She had some bottled water and put it in her thermos, in case Rayne was dehydrated. There was a big pocket in her pants that was able to hold the thermos. The lake was only a few yards up the road. She heard another scream.

"Rayne!" Denise yelled. The searchlight made another revolution.

She heard nothing and kept running for the water.

"Rayne!"

"Help me!" a voice said.

When she hit the banks, Denise saw something in the water, a few yards from the shore. "Rayne!"

"Over here!" the figure said.

Denise used her phone as a flashlight and hurried into the pond, it was only a few inches deep, and she sank a bit in the muck. The water burned her skin like acid.

"Over here!" the figure said again.

The searchlight went around again. Denise saw Rayne laying prone on a boulder, her head barely above water. Despite her weight, the boulder had not sunk further into the muck. She had an object in her hand and she was putting it to her mouth.

Was it a gun? Was she going to blow her brains out? The searchlight swung away, and it was dark again.

"I'm coming!" Denise shouted, but she couldn't see Rayne in the darkness even with the help of her phone light.

When the searchlight revolved again, she quickly waded the rest of the way through the muck and acidic water to Rayne. Rayne grabbed the staff with her free hand, and it seemed to steady her.

The object in Rayne's hand wasn't a gun. By the smell Denise knew it was a thermos filled with lake water and was now putting to her lips. Was that better or worse?

"Don't drink that!" Denise said.

Rayne chugged it anyway. "The lake water saved my life."

Standing on the boulder, Denise helped Rayne up, but the big woman outweighed her and the two sunk a bit when they walked out into the quicksand. Denise was able to steady herself with the staff.

Finally, by sheer force of will, and the help of the staff, the two women made it out of the lake and onto the rocky shore. Rayne took another chug from the thermos.

What was in the water? Denise smelled it and nearly retched.

"Get more of the lake water," Rayne said. "Just in case."

Denise filled up her own thermos.

She handed it to Rayne, but Rayne pushed it away. "That water's for you."

Denise shook her head, but kept the thermos just in case. "Not even. Come on, I'm parked over here."

Denise had to help the big girl under the gate. Rayne collapsed into the passenger side of the Kia.

Inside the car, with the interior light on, Denise could see that Rayne was sunburnt but otherwise healthy. Her mother's campaign button was conspicuously absent.

"Where am I?" Rayne asked.

"You're safe. Let me guess, you have no *recollection* of anything."

Chapter 43

Denise wanted to take Rayne to a hospital, even though Rayne actually looked healthy—despite her sunburn and smelling like alien wastewater.

"I'm fine," Rayne said. "I'm really fine."

"You need to go to the hospital."

"You're not my mother," Rayne said. "She's gonna kill me."

"I'm sure that isn't true."

Denise took Rayne back to Centennial Hospital in Las Cruces, less than an hour away. The drive through the white sands was like driving through the Milky Way as it glowed in the starlight. She saw several shooting stars above and prayed that they weren't aiming at her.

Thankfully, Piranha wasn't on duty in the front, but Denise didn't want to risk going past the lobby and be with Rayne. A sheriff brought some small children in "just for a checkup." He mentioned to the receptionist that they were found in the desert just in time. Denise couldn't help but be relieved until she noticed two Border Patrol officers following behind, handcuffs out.

Feeling slightly paranoid, Denise moved to some chairs at the back of the lobby. Right as she was about to fall asleep, it felt like an earthquake jolted her awake. Colonel (retired) Regan "Big Red" Herring arrived in the lobby an hour later, Rita in tow. The colonel wore her blood red power suit and elephant cowboy boots. Denise hurried to meet her, but the Colonel lifted up her hand as if ordering her to attention. Was she blaming Denise?

Big Red was even more intimidating in person. To Denise she might have been seven feet tall and built like an upright

B-52. Denise couldn't read her, probably because of the colonel's military demeanor. This was General Patton in drag.

"We'll take it from here," Big Red said, and hurried to the elevator.

Rita waited till her grandma was out of earshot. "Thank you for saving my mom, Auntie Denise!"

"Does Big Red know that we're ummm... related?" Denise asked Rita.

"She knows *everything!*"

"Rita catch up!" the colonel ordered.

Was that Piranha coming in for the graveyard shift from a side entrance? Denise hurried out to her car, just in case, and was thankful the doors locked automatically.

Was Rayne abducted by aliens? Or God forbid *probed* by them? Who dropped her off at the lake? And why did the lake's toxic wastewater save Rayne's life? Denise remembered that she had first noticed that stench in Nastia's flask.

The Kia reeked from the fluid in her thermos, but she hesitated to throw it out. Denise was about to drive somewhere, but she was too tired to move and passed out in the driver's seat.

Chapter 44
Monday, August 3

It was just after dawn when Denise returned inside to the hospital, but Rayne was no longer in her room according to the receptionist.

"You can probably catch her in the cafeteria," the elderly woman said. Was she the same one as last night?

Rayne was indeed inside the small cafeteria, sharing a tiny booth with Rita. Through the window, Denise could see Big Red in the parking lot, barking orders into her phone.

"Are you sure you're OK?" Denise asked Rayne.

Over the last piece of bacon, Rayne sighed. "I don't really have any recollection of what happened, and don't want to talk about it. I need some time for me."

Denise chugged down a cup of coffee. Rita touched her on the hand. "Isn't there something you need to tell my mom, Auntie Denise?"

Denise took a deep breath. "We figured out the identity of Rita's father. It's Denny, my brother and client. Rita is my niece."

"Duh." Rayne took a swig of coffee. "You think I didn't already know that? That was the potential conflict."

"Does that affect our friendship now that we're *family*?"

"That isn't my call," Rayne said. "As for the case, I'm *done*."

"Why?"

"*She* wants me off it from now on."

Denise didn't have to ask who *she* was. Big Red materialized and squeezed into the booth, pushing Denise to one side. The three tall people towered over her.

"I want to thank you for saving my daughter," Big Red

said. She didn't look thankful.

"She would do the same for me."

"One thing I don't understand," Big Red said. "How did you know where to find her?"

"I had a... hunch."

"I was in the Air Force for twenty years. When we selected our targets, we didn't rely on hunches."

"I guess I got lucky."

"Is there anything else?" Big Red asked. "I think it's best for you to be on your way."

"But grandma," Rita asked. "She saved Rayne."

"Back when I was active duty, we never let people come on base to do wild goose chases for lawyers."

Denise wasn't sure why the colonel was so angry. "I didn't think I would put Rayne in any danger."

"Syrinx is by its very nature dangerous," the colonel explained

"My *father* needs our help. My *auntie* needs our help," Rita piped in.

"Some cop-killing case out in Lordsburg is not our concern." Big Red stood up, opening a narrow passageway for Denise to leave. Denise wanted to say attempted cop-killing, but was too intimidated to say anything.

"Ms. Song," the colonel continued. "I don't want you, or anyone else in your crazy little family to have any contact with us, whatsoever. That's an order!"

Denise shuffled away.

"Auntie Denise, give your best to my grandmother," Rita called after her. "My *other* grandmother."

Chapter 45

Denise wanted to take Rita up on her suggestion and tell Jen Song that she had a granddaughter, but Piranha intercepted her at the elevator, his teeth bared.

"I'm sorry Ms. Song, but you can't see your mother."

"How is she doing?"

"You're not on the list that we can authorize that information."

"I'm not on the list for my own mother?"

Piranha shrugged. "I don't make the rules, I just enforce them."

Denise went back to the parking lot and got in the Kia and sat in the car figuring out what to do.

First, she texted Hikaru and sent a pic of the hospital. "Rayne OK, Mom stable?"

He texted a pic of the Syrinx gate with a sign that said CLOSED UNTIL FURTHER NOTICE. That couldn't be good. She tried him again, but he did not text back.

Before she could feel totally defeated, she reminded herself, she still had one teammate left, didn't she?

When she arrived at Dew's apartment at the Vista de Estrella, the party was over. Petro and his gang were gone.

The parking lot was empty except for Dew who was thanking an animal control officer closing the back door to a veterinary ambulance. Denise had never seen a veterinary ambulance. She noticed a small plastic bag inside.

"Suri's dead," Dew said after the ambulance sped away. "At least Sahar's still alive." Dew, all in black, sported a t-shirt for something called SEVERE TIRE DAMAGE. Denise didn't know if it was for a band, a game, an apparel line, or the current condition of her soul.

"I'm sorry," Denise said.

They walked upstairs into the apartment and Denise noticed several opened pill bottles labeled Crotaladone. Was Crotaladone legal in America? The markings on the bottles sure looked suspicious and seemed to be in both Spanish and Korean. She couldn't read the name on the bottle, but it had way too many letters to spell out Dew Cruz.

Before Denise could ask the details about the drug, a sleepy star cat rubbed against Denise's leg. Had the cat taken the pills too?

"I'm sorry, kitty," Denise staring at the cat's piercing green eyes. "Good girl, *Suri.*"

"Suri's the one that died," Dew said. "That's Sahar."

Sahar kept rubbing against her, regardless. Could a cat have a spark?

"Are you all right, Dew?"

"No, I'm not all right," Dew said, popping two more Crotaladone and threw down the empty bottle, missing the trash. "Rayne was probably abducted by aliens and blames me, and I have no recollection of shit. Plus, my cat died. It was probably the aliens who killed my cat."

"I'm sure the two aren't related," Denise said. "I really need your help to try to figure out what happened."

"I don't want to see you for a while," Dew said. "I'm sorry about your brother, sorry about your mother, but ever since you came into my life here, you've been nothing but bad luck for me and my cats."

Dew was now looking up "treatment centers" online. Some glossy videos ran on the screen. Lots of beaches and mountains and smiling, sober faces illuminated the dankness of this crappy apartment.

"Do you have any recollection of anything?"

"It's worse than that. If I even think about it, I feel intense pain," Dew said.

"Do you mind if I umm... try to find out what happened?"

"I know what you're talking about," Dew said. "I know you can do the Vulcan mind meld shit or whatever, but I think it would be better if you got the hell out of here."

Sahar purred as if defending Denise, but then looked

startled. There were footsteps. Denise was nervous as well and didn't know whether to be relieved when it was only Petro who entered, without knocking.

"Hey Petro," Dew said.

"Hey Dew, hey cousin," he said to Denise. "Dr. Petro is here to save the day."

Denise now had some idea how Dew got the Crotaladone. But still she was curious about the man. "How did you get your name, *Petro*?"

"It's short for Petruchio, from *Taming of the Shrew*, which was like a play. Where I come from, near the Shakespeare ghost town, a lot of us get these names from the old plays."

Denise looked at this strange man and his shorts, cowboy boots, beer belly and pink sombrero. Sahar was now rubbing against him like an old friend.

He was holding a glossy brochure in his hand. "I got accepted into that good rehab center *Rancho Carrizozo*! Wanna join me, Dew?"

"I'm not really an addict," Dew replied. "But thanks for your last few crotaladones."

"You don't really have to be as long as you got *issues*."

"I've got issues all right," Dew said. She glanced at the brochure, brought up the "*Rancho Carrizozo*" website on her computer screen and then picked up her phone. "Oh, *mother*, I've got this really good idea for treating my PTSD…"

After stepping on a hair ball on the way out the door, Denise knew she shouldn't judge her cousin. If anyone needed treatment, it was Dew. Hell, perhaps she should go to *Rancho Carrizozo* herself. Did they treat mommy issues?

She was on the freeway headed to Lordsburg when a pic came from Hikaru: an ID badge falling into the trash.

She called him immediately. "I've been fired!" he said.

"Because of me?"

"No, well not *just* you. My big boss is pissed after the judge let you guys in. All hell is breaking loose. Even my dad can't save me. I might be taking a permanent vacation from America. From Earth even."

The phone went dead. So much for Team Turquoise.

255

Chapter 46

Tuesday, August 4

First thing Tuesday morning, Denise received an email with Dr. Romero's four-page "Forensic Evaluation of Denny Song." Four pages for a whole life? The doctor concluded her report by saying her prognosis regarding Denny was *inconclusive* as to his competency to stand trial because of the lack of secondary documentation. She didn't bother to discuss his ability to form specific intent as he didn't provide enough information to make a determination on that point. She wrote that Mr. Song was not a reliable narrator, and perhaps even a *malingerer*.

Being a malingerer was apparently worse than being an attempted murderer. Denise had barely finished reading the report when Luna called.

"I've got the report," Luna said. Hurricane Luna had become an ice storm. "What the hell happened? You were supposed to get his psych records on base."

"What did Dew tell you?"

"She doesn't have any *recollection* of anything. And now she's locked down in *Rancho Carrizozo* for twenty-eight days! What happened?"

"Everything went wrong on base," Denise said. "When are you coming down for the hearing?"

"Denise, I have a case up in Clayton, New Mexico. The prison wrongful deaths thing. It's like a multi-million-dollar lawsuit against a private jail company with two dozen plaintiffs."

"Where's Clayton?"

"It's on the Oklahoma border."

"I didn't know we had an Oklahoma border."

"I have to interview every inmate and every guard, so I'm going to let you handle the competency hearing yourself."

"What do I do?"

"Frankly Denise, I don't give a damn. Either he's competent to stand trial and he will be convicted—I saw the video—or he's incompetent to stand trial and because of the nature of the charges he will be considered *dangerous* and spend the rest of his life in a secure facility."

"But suppose he *isn't* dangerous?"

"Good luck with that."

"By the way, I tried to find out about my mom at the hospital, but apparently I'm not on the list of authorized..."

Luna had already hung up.

Dejected, Denise didn't bother to go to breakfast over at the Holiday Comfort. She had a vending machine chocolate bar from the Last Palm lobby and washed it down with a Diet Coke.

She picked up her briefcase and drove down Motel Boulevard to meet with Denny. She noticed the skin beneath his tattoos was bursting with newfound muscle tone.

"I'm ready to fight them aliens," he said. "You with me?"

"Kinda."

He talked about his workout regimen in his cell, and even challenged her to try some isometric exercises. Leaning hard against the wall while squatting was apparently effective for your glutes. She tried it to humor him.

"There's something I need to tell you," she said, her back against the wall.

"What's wrong?"

Denise mentioned Rayne and her so-called abduction and told him about saving her life. "Why didn't you tell me that you knew her?"

"That was a long time ago. I was on a break from Cordelia and I hear about this party at the motel with this girls' basketball team. I forgot her name. This beautiful girl, really tall, hooked up with me, but I guess she was *slumming*."

"Then what?"

"And I say, let's go to Puerto Penasco. We can make it by

midnight, sleep on the beach and wake up to see the sunrise. And she does. Whenever I try to think of her, it's like there's a forcefield inside my brain cutting off the thoughts. I get in physical pain."

"There's something I really need to tell you," Denise said. "Something else must have happened on that beach. She had a daughter, *your* daughter."

The whole building shook. Denise put her hand to the glass and that calmed him down. "I get this weird shaking lately, so I knew something was up, but I had no idea it was from her. What's her name?"

"Rita Herring, and I know her. I've been hanging out with her the last few weeks. We just figured it out ourselves."

He touched his head. "She's been reaching out to me, with her mind, but I didn't let her in. I didn't trust her. What's she like?"

"You would be proud of her," Denise said, getting up from against the wall and sitting back down again.

"Put your hand against the glass again," Denny said.

She put her hand against the glass, he put his hand against it as well. She knew what to do. She concentrated on Rita and let the image pass through her hand, through the glass and over to Denny.

"She's so beautiful," he said. "And so tall. I'm so proud of her. If I could have been there for her, she would have saved me."

"Saved you?"

"I would have been there for her," he said. "She would have been there for me."

A warm current passed between them. He was right. Denny and Rita would have been stronger together.

"It seems like too much of a coincidence, that everything, everyone is umm... *related*," Denise said.

"Don't you see, there are no coincidences. That was all part of a plan somehow."

Denny went on for fifteen minutes about how the aliens sometimes bred people for this or that. "Even that team you were on," he said. "Team Turquoise? I bet that is part of the plan too."

"I don't think anyone would set up a silly mock trial team as part of an alien conspiracy."

"A team where everyone on it is a psychic?"

"Dew isn't a psychic."

"But she's very smart, right?"

"Just a coincidence," she said. But as she left the jail, she wasn't so sure...

* * *

After leaving Denny, Denise spent the next few days doing her best to fit into Lordsburg. She spent her days at the small library reading up on New Mexico's standards on mental health law, and the librarian helped her learn more about the local history. She visited Denny at the jail each day right before closing, to tell him about his daughter. Every afternoon, she would burn off steam doing her katas with the staff. Every night, she ate at the Shiprock Wok and tried Wu's incredible fusions like the *kim chi chalupas*. She would end the night with another installment of a Korean soap opera on her room TV before she fell asleep.

Every morning, Hikaru texted her a picture. He was mountain biking all over New Mexico—she saw Sierra Blanca, White Sands, even Carlsbad Caverns. Given the lighting on the last pic, he must have been inside one of the caverns.

She texted pics back of Lordsburg's sunsets. The town did have nice sunsets, especially after a dust storm. She didn't love it, but she was adapting.

Still, it was a lonely life. She might as well be stuck down in the darkness of the Caverns. Team Turquoise was broken. Could she ever put it back together again?

The competency hearing was coming up. She was wondering if she would be competent enough to handle it.

Chapter 47

Monday, August 10

At dawn on the morning of the competency hearing, Denise wore one of her charcoal outfits—she didn't want to be too flashy—and arrived at the courthouse early.

There was plenty of parking on Shakespeare street. Too much parking. Wasn't Jane Dark going to call a bunch of witnesses? There weren't even any vehicles from the Sheriff's Department here, not even the Sheriff's.

Inside, the courtroom was empty. Denise sat at the defense table and spread out all her exhibits for the hearing. Moments later, Denny was brought into the courtroom by jail staff rather than the Sheriff's Department.

"What's going to happen today?" Denny asked. "When are they going to let me out?"

He must still be working out, doing his isometric exercises in his solitary cell over the last week. He looked bigger, or maybe he was just sitting up straight.

Jane Dark entered next. She had dressed down today in a casual maternity outfit. She was empty handed except for a pen bearing the logo of a big Arizona law firm with a matching travel mug. Was the firm name Nasty, Brutish & Short? Denise couldn't make it out.

Judge Shahrazad Sanchez came in without a robe and signaled that they didn't even have to rise. The judge had a new piercing, over her eye. "Let's get this over with."

Jane Dark rose. "The State of New Mexico stipulates that the defendant, Denny Song, is *incompetent* to stand trial."

"Counsel?" the judge asked Denise.

"Well, I stipulate to him being incompetent as well,"

260

Denise said.

"So, can I get out now?" Denny asked.

The judge looked over at Jane Dark, momentarily confused. "Does he get to be released?"

"Your honor, *both* parties can stipulate to *dangerousness* right here, right now," Jane Dark said. "That saves us the expense of having what's called a '1.5 hearing.' And this matter will be resolved immediately."

"If we stipulate or whatever can I get out now?" Denny's excitement was tinged with panic. "We stipulate! I don't want to have a 1.5 hearing whatever that is. What does stipulate mean?"

"As attempted murder, and most three counts of attempted murder on police officers are considered the crimes of *violence* under the statute," Jane Dark said, "Not to mention the felony endangerment of the police dog. He would *remain* in custody at the behavioral health unit for the duration of the maximum possible sentence of his charges."

"The duration?" Denny asked.

Jane Dark had to rub it in. "With the firearm enhancements, and aggravating circumstances, it could be seventy years."

"Seventy years? That's when the alien invasion will happen! I wanna get out of here right now."

"Like I said, Ms. Song could always stipulate to dangerousness," Jane Dark said. "As attempted murder is one of the enumerated crimes, there's a *presumption* of dangerousness. That way we don't have to have a hearing, and they send him up to the locked unit of the behavioral health institute up north and they can keep him, *indefinitely*. Your honor, I know you are supposed to start that new cabinet job up in Santa Fe and I will be moving to Phoenix after my maternity leave. I'm sure Ms. Song has places she would rather be as well."

Denise pictured biking on the beach on Puerto Penasco with Hikaru.

"I say we resolve this today," Jane Dark said.

"I want to see my daughter!" Denny said, pulling Denise back from the beach.

"No, your honor," Denise said. "We will *not* stipulate that

261

my client is dangerous. We will have a full hearing on danger-ousness under Rule 1.5."

"Can you be ready on Wednesday?" the judge asked.

"I can have my witnesses here," Jane Dark said.

"Does the defense have any witnesses?" the judge asked.

Denise looked down. "None that I know of, your honor."

Chapter 48

Denise didn't bother to call Luna; she knew she would have to do this by herself. She re-read the 1.5 statute at the library. Under the 31-9-1.5, the state merely had to prove by clear and convincing evidence that Denny had done the crime and that the crime was violent. Jane Dark could do that without a file. It would be a hearing with a judge and not a jury. With a violent crime like attempted murder, the presumption was dangerousness. Denise had her work cut out for her to overcome that presumption.

Denise had dinner that night at Shiprock Wok and talked with the handsome Mr. Wu. They were the only ones there. She learned that Wu and his buddy had purchased marijuana legally in Colorado and were transporting it to California where it was also legal. Unfortunately, recreational marijuana was *illegal* in New Mexico, and the amount they held made it a fourth-degree felony.

Wu had been placed on something called Pre-Prosecution Diversion or PPD. If he completed the program, PPD canceled the felony conviction and it came off his record.

Without asking, he prepared some *bulgogi fry bread* in honor of her mixed heritage. Since the place was empty, he joined her at the table.

"Do you also have some pasta and some bagels for the other parts of my DNA?" she asked.

"I've never met someone with that mix," he said.

"My twin brother," she said.

He took a deep breath. "Do you have a boyfriend?"

She glanced at her phone. Hikaru's latest pic was of him biking out of Carlsbad Caverns. The bats were following him out.

"Kinda," she said. He didn't say another word and hurried back to the kitchen. Did he like her too?

* * *

When she returned to the room that night, she stared at her blank TV screen for an hour. She was part of a team, right? She tried Dew. Dew's message indicated that she was unavailable for the next 28 days. She tried *Rancho Carrizozo*, but they wouldn't connect her to their "guest."

Rayne didn't pick up, so she couldn't talk to Rita. Hikaru didn't return her texts. Perhaps he had returned to the caverns. She had missed his last pic—one of darkness. So much for her kinda having a boyfriend.

She received a call from Dr. Romero just before bed. "The state has subpoenaed me to testify at the dangerousness hearing," the doctor told her. "In person."

"Are you going to say he's dangerous?"

"He shot three people and threatened a sheriff and his dog without any explanation or provocation. He blames the military for doing *experiments* on him and yet there is no evidence whatsoever of any of that and that there's an imminent alien invasion. What do you think I'm going to say?"

"But what about what happened to my friends? They can prove that these drones do affect behavior."

"Your friends? What relevance would your friends have to your brother's mental health?"

Denise was about to tell Dr. Romero that her friends had also had a similar experience to Denny, but she stopped. Her friends had never even met Denny, how could they help?

And yet, Denise knew that she had to put something on in her part of the case. If only Rayne and Dew could testify about their experience, that would be something at least. If only Hikaru could confirm that these experiments did occur, that too would be helpful.

After Dr. Romero hung up, Denise noticed a message from Dr. Schwartz that her mother could receive visitors in a few days; but would be moved soon to hospice. She called him back and didn't bother with pleasantries.

"Hospice?"

"You might want to see her when she's available next week. Before it's too late."

"Does that mean..."

There was no answer on the other end. There didn't have to be...

Chapter 49

Tuesday, August 11

Denise drove to the jail to meet with Denny again the next morning. The thermos in her car smelled even worse today. For a moment, she pondered throwing away the whole thermos, but relented. The contents had saved Rayne after all. Did the nasty fluid have some connection to saving Denny back when he was born?

In the jail meeting room, she told her brother the bad news about their mother, stressing the ominous words "before it's too late."

"I wish I'd gotten to know my mom," he said.

"I'm her daughter and I still don't know her," Denise said.

"I feel she's reaching out to us," he said. "We can save her."

"How?"

"By winning the case and getting me out," he said.

They touched their hands through the glass until the current increased so much that they had to break it off. "We can use the grail to save her," he said.

"Let's see what happens at the hearing."

"You gotta tell them that the aliens made me do it. That would mean I'm not dangerous."

"I don't know what happened when Rayne was with Dew. So why did it affect you and make you violent?"

"Those drones affect people differently depending on brain waves or some shit like that. But Rayne and Dew together might be a whole different combination."

"But you're the only one who became *homicidal* after contact with a drone, or grail or whatever. Why was that?"

"Was I the only one on earth who did that? There have been grails all over the world, and people acting strangely, and no one makes the connection. Maybe some of those mass shooters got affected by the grails or the drones. It's like a big experiment the aliens are doing for the government on how to like control minds."

"The aliens are doing this?"

"No, probably just the government on behalf of the aliens. What do they call it, the military industrial *matrix*?"

"Military industrial complex."

"Well, they're like doing the beta testing for them aliens. Like I did beta testing for a video game once."

He was shaking worse now. Denise worried that she was losing her brother for good. The drugs, the paranoia, the madness had all taken their toll on him.

"Are the aliens here in town?"

"They've always been here. They look like us. There had been like a flying saucer crash near the Shakespeare ghost town like seventy years ago. But nobody knows about it. Maybe them aliens mated with locals. Since the place was called Shakespeare, they took up Shakespearean names to like fit in."

"Like Cordelia? That's from *King Lear*."

"As I said, some of them don't know because they're only like *half-blood* aliens. They're like regular people. They're just as messed up as we are. They drink, they do drugs. Hell, they're probably more susceptible because they came here with pure blood on one side and got no immunity to all our shit. And when they're near someone with a spark, weird things happen. It's like fifth dimensional consciousness shit."

"Thanks for letting me know," she said. "See you in court tomorrow."

"Just remember, the cops, all of them are aliens, well at least they're half-breeds. They all got them funny Shakespeare names too."

Denise walked to the parking lot. Shakespearean names? Wow. Denny was right. There sure had been a lot of them over the last few weeks.

She was greeted at the Last Palm by Titus that was the

main character from the *Titus Andronicus*, right? Not that she'd ever seen that play, no one had. There had been a Caliban at the Holiday Comfort, who was also a bailiff. That was from the Tempest. Titus was at his desk at the Last Palm, spitting tobacco in a cup while playing with his boomerang. Is that the best the aliens could do?

Still, the way he looked at her made her nervous. She hurried back to her room.

That night after some more Shiprock Wok take-out, bulgogi tacos, Denise tried to call all her friends yet again. Dew's 28-day unavailability at *Rancho Carrizozo* had turned into six months. Rayne didn't pick up. If the latest texted pics were to be believed, Hikaru was now biking in a white void. She hoped that it was White Sands and not heaven.

Chapter 50
Wednesday, August 12

There was no new info about her mother when she woke up the next morning. She looked at her wardrobe with its dark contents. At least she wouldn't have to buy clothes for the funeral.

She wasn't sure if the funeral would be for her mother, for Denny, or perhaps herself at the rate she was going.

Today was the 1.5 dangerousness hearing. Her mom was holding on, day by day, and had made it to hump day without hospice at least. Susie had sent out a text with the same update: NO CHANGE.

She tried Rayne, Dew, and Hikaru one last time.

She typed a message on her phone and prepared to text. I NEED YOU GUYS. That was too needy. She erased that. THE FUTURE OF EARTH DEPENDS ON YOU! She erased that too, then typed a well-reasoned message on her phone about what was going on with Denny's case and why their presence would be so crucial. Luna herself would be proud of her reasoning. Instead of hitting send, she closed her eyes and issued a psychic subpoena. When she opened her eyes, there was a notation on her phone under a blank space.

MESSAGE SENT.

The effort of sending this psychic subpoena totally drained her. Nausea hit her hard. She didn't make it to the toilet. She began projectile vomiting into the sink and some of it splattered on to the mirror. She finally made it to the toilet and held her hair back with her left hand.

This would be a very short hearing—the state would put on their witnesses to dangerousness, she would have nothing to counter and the judge would rule against them.

She cleaned up after herself, and prayed she wouldn't vomit again.

* * *

When she arrived at the courthouse, she was surprised to see the Groundlings walking outside holding picket signs. There must have been fifty of them, all dressed in their Sunday best. Unlike the tans and browns they'd worn in Roswell that made them look like a Church group, this time they'd gone with more somber colors as if attending a funeral for a gang leader.

WATER IS LIFE! NMCOURTS TAKE WATER RIGHTS WITHOUT DUE PROCESS!

The purple man was there, wearing the same suit. He must not have gotten the memo about wearing black. His sign merely said JUSTICE!!! and he kept bringing the justice sign up and down like a hammer.

Inside the courtroom, Judge Shahrazad Sanchez was finishing up Wu's case.

"The review is over and I'm formally placing you on the diversion program," the judge said to the young man who was in his chef's outfit. "You will now be on *unsupervised* probation. I understand you wish to remain in town. In *Lordsburg?*"

"Your honor, I'm taking over as executive chef at Shiprock Wok, and we're being featured in a reality series on Netflix— *Wok the West!*"

After the judge left, Wu gave Denise a hug. "We need a waitress at the place," he said. "You get to keep your tips."

"I'll think about it," Denise said. If Hikaru stayed missing...

"We've got to do the water law case first," Caliban said to the crowded courtroom. "We got some *real lawyers* here in town."

The "real lawyers" were dressed in Santa Fe chic— thousand-dollar glen plaid suits and turquoise bolo ties and pony-tail holders. They sat on the plaintiff's side; the side usually reserved for the state. On the other side, Denise was surprised to see Fally and the Groundlings appearing *pro se* in the water rights case.

"Don't steal our water!" Fally yelled at the Santa Fe crew. "Locals only!"

"Locals only!" the rest of Groundlings chimed in.

How long could a water case go? They were in the desert after all.

Denise resent her psychic subpoena every hour. No responses.

The water case finally ended at 4:15. "We got home-towned," one of the Santa Fe lawyers said in the hallway, head held low. "First time I've ever lost when the other side went *pro se.*"

"One down, one to go," Fally said under his breath. "We own this courthouse."

The judge took a five-minute recess. The three sheriff's deputies followed Jane Dark into the courtroom and sat in the front row; they were the alleged victims. Dr. Romero came in behind the deputies and looked like a WNBA basketball coach—tall and lanky and ready to take off her suit, put on a jersey and get on the court.

Denny was brought in by the jail guard who practically threw him down into the seat next to Denise. He scanned the empty rows of seats on their side. "What happened to *our* witnesses?"

Denise looked downward then back up. She noticed a gigantic Mondo Pad set up in the far corner of the courtroom. A Mondo Pad looked like Darth Vader's TV set with a 72 inch screen. There was a map of the state of New Mexico. The water lawyers must have brought it in and had forgotten about it in their haste to get the hell out of Lordsburg.

"Order in the court," the judge said. They hadn't noticed her come in.

"If the parties are ready," the judge said. "I will let the State begin on the 1.5 hearing for *State v. Song.* Madam Dark, you look like you are about to explode. Are you sure you want to go forward?"

"I talked to my daughter," Jane Dark said, pointing down to her belly. "She said she would wait till this hearing is done."

The judge smiled. "We'll get this done as expeditiously as possible."

Jane Dark called Dr. Romero first to the witness stand. The doctor gave a weak smile to Denise. She might have said that she was inconclusive about Denny's competence, but she had sure come to a definite conclusion on his dangerousness.

Fally and the boys were still in the back murmuring amongst themselves. "Glad I gave him up!" Fally said.

Jane Dark began her questioning of the witness. "Your report didn't make a conclusion regarding dangerousness, what is your expert opinion?" she asked the doctor.

"Even a single count of attempted murder is by definition *dangerous*," Dr. Romero said.

"Can he be treated in the New Mexico Behavioral Health Unit so that he is not dangerous?"

Dr. Romero didn't hesitate. "No. Considering that he is an unreliable narrator, and a malingerer, it is unlikely that he would ever be amenable to any treatment."

"So, doctor, what is your recommendation?"

"That the defendant be held in the locked facility of the Maximum-Security Unit of the Forensic Division at the New Mexico Behavior Health Unit for the extent of his possible sentence."

"Even if it's fifty years? *Seventy* years if the court imposes additional time because of the aggravating circumstances?"

"Yes. That is my understanding of the current state of the law."

"Pass the witness."

Denise rose. "Your report was only four pages, double-spaced, counting a title page."

"It was."

"How long did you spend on interviews?"

"Probably an hour."

"An hour each or an hour total?"

"An hour *total*."

"You only interviewed my client, not anyone else?"

"Yes."

"You did some standard tests, correct?"

The doctor listed some basic testing that she had performed on Denny.

"You didn't have access to all his military psychiatric records, did you?"

"No. Ms. Song, *you* were unable to provide them for me."

"So, you don't know if some external factor caused him to act the way he did?"

"What do you mean?"

"You don't know if he was the subject of scientific experiments while he was in the military? It says here on the first page of your report that the defendant recounted that he was the subject of military experiments."

"He said he was, but I couldn't confirm that. I am sure that he is delusional."

"So, if these experiments did happen, could that have affected his mental state?"

"I have no way of knowing."

"Could those experiments have affected his supposed delusions?"

"I have no way of knowing."

"So, if those experiments did happen, he might not be delusional?"

"I have no way of knowing."

"So, if he's not *delusional*, he might not be dangerous?"

"He is charged with several counts of attempted murder. That's dangerous by definition."

"Denny told you that he encountered the so-called Omega Grail that was part of the 24 Grails Contest, correct?"

"He did."

"Do you know how he could be affected by radiation coming from a grail?"

"I have no way of knowing."

"You're a psychiatrist not a physicist, correct."

"That's correct."

"Various police incident reports have stated that there was some kind of surveillance drone present at the incident."

"That's what the reports say."

"Do you know how he could be affected by a drone?"

"I have no way of knowing."

"Do you know how he could be affected by radiation from an extraterrestrial object, commonly known as a UFO?"

"Objection!" Jane Dark said. "Calls for speculation!"

The judge nodded. "That's it, Ms. Song. You're done with this witness. Keep your cross-examinations here on earth."

Denise stopped, unsure of what to do next. The judge banged her gavel. "Madam Dark, please call your next witness."

Denise walked back to the defense table, wondering about the next witness. The map of New Mexico on the Mondo Pad had gone black. One of the Santa Fe lawyers was muttering to Caliban about the Mondo Pad by the door.

"We'll just ship it to you in Santa Fe," Caliban said. "When we have time."

Jane Dark was checking her own files, touched a few keys on her phone and nodded. "We call his mother to the stand," Jane Dark said.

Mother?

Chapter 51

Before Denise could regain her breath, Nastia entered the courtroom. Her flesh-colored makeup covered her neck tattoos. She was dressed in a gray flannel business suit, like a manager of a small-town bank.

"She's not my mother!" Denny shouted.

"I'm sorry, Denny," she said. "They made me come."

"Tell the truth!" Fally shouted.

"Tell the truth!" the others echoed.

Denise now understood why the Groundlings had stayed for the second case. They were here to intimidate Nastia, to make sure she testified *against* Denny.

"Your honor, there's a conflict," Denise objected. "I represented this witness in a recent matter, a restraining order in Roswell. And besides, we didn't get notice of this witness appearing today."

Jane Dark didn't bat an eye. She handed Denise a copy of a form and gave another copy to the bailiff. "Your honor, this witness signed a waiver of the attorney-client privilege and, as she is the holder of the privilege, she can testify if she wishes. And notice of witnesses is *not* required for dangerousness hearings because of the *relaxed* standards of the rule of evidence."

"Your honor," Denise said. "I don't believe her testimony would be relevant. She was not present during the incident."

"Your honor," Jane Dark said, not missing a beat, "this witness will testify about the defendant's history of violence."

"I'll allow the testimony of this witness for that purpose," the judge said.

Jane Dark questioned Nastia about taking Denny at his birth but didn't mention the presence of the grail. Denise cer-

275

tainly couldn't bring that up since she had found out about that incident by entering the woman's brain while she was sleeping.

Nastia then related Denny's lengthy juvenile history over Denise's objections, which the judge shot down. Denny had a history of "acting up" and had numerous disciplinary write-ups between the ages of twelve and fourteen.

"Your honor, these weren't provided to me by counsel," Denise said.

"Then I won't take his juvenile adjudications into account," the judge said. Her smile as she wrote down notes, indicted that she most certainly would.

"One more thing," Jane Dark said. Nastia even produced a letter signed by Denny's teacher, Yvette Castaneda, indicating that he put a tack under a classmate's seat in a seventh grade English class.

"Objection!"

Jane Dark was ready. "The classmate developed tetanus. While not a crime per se, it does indicate that he does not care about other people."

Jane Dark continued. "So, madam, this defendant can 'act up' even when he isn't in the vicinity of a so-called grail or a UFO?"

"I'm sorry, but yes. I had to relinquish my parental rights, as I couldn't control him."

"So he's dangerous?"

"Tell the truth!" Fally shouted again.

"Tell the *real* truth!" Denny followed.

"Yes, he *is* dangerous to the community," Nastia said.

"Pass the witness."

Denise rose. "Isn't it true that I represented you and won your case in a restraining order matter?"

"Yes."

"But you're here to tell the truth, aren't you?"

"Yes."

"While Denny had a history of 'acting up,' he didn't act up after you gave custody to the Dunsinane family?"

"Not as far as I know."

"So, once he was in high school, here in Lordsburg, he

settled down?"

"I don't know."

"You are aware that he wrote letters critical of you, critical of the town? And those letters were published in the local paper, *The Lordsburg Liberal*."

"I am."

The Groundlings murmured at the back of court.

"Do you know if he was ever abused, physically?"

"He might have been."

"Sexually?"

"I don't know about that."

"But no one was ever arrested on any of those charges?"

"Not as far as I know."

"Might that have caused to him be angry towards law enforcement in this town?"

"It might."

"And that anger could be affected by a drone or the grail?"

"Objection, lack of personal knowledge!" Jane Dark said. "Calls for speculation."

"Sustained!"

Denise knew she had teed it up. All she needed was another witness to testify that the drones did intensify existing emotions toward law enforcement, and thus Denny wouldn't be dangerous. But without either Rayne or Dew, she couldn't take her swing. "Pass the witness."

Jane Dark saw the opening. "So, the defendant had deep seated anger toward law enforcement in this county?"

"He did."

"Wouldn't that make him dangerous?"

"It would."

"Anything else counsel?" the judge asked. "The clock is ticking."

"Your honor," Jane Dark said, glancing at her notes. "I want to put the victims on the stand, very briefly."

"*Alleged* victims," Denny shouted.

"Please control your client," the judge said.

Jane Dark called Antonio first. She had gone up to the Mondo Pad with Caliban and he told her how to get it in synch with her own laptop.

"That's the name of one of them Shakespeare characters," Denny said to Denise. "Antonio, *Merchant of Venice*."

Antonio the former football player wore a letter jacket over a western shirt and silver bolo shaped liked a bucking bronco. Jane Dark played Antonio's lapel cam of the incident on the Mondo Pad.

He testified about being shot by Denny. Under Jane Dark's direction, he took off his letter jacket and unbuttoned his western shirt to show the scar. This guy was supposedly a tough cop, but he cried like a baby when he touched the wound.

"I was hoping to coach the boys' pee wee football team this year, but I can't even show them how to throw a spiral," he said.

"I didn't mean to," Denny yelled.

When Denise tried to question Antonio about the drone, he said he didn't know anything about any drone. "I was too busy looking at his gun. But remember one thing, I was just doing my job, doing my sworn duty."

"Pass the witness."

"We call Claudio to the stand," Jane Dark said.

Claudio wore a cowboy shirt and a corduroy blazer.

"*Much Ado About Nothing*, Claudio!" Denny said. It took a moment for Denise to realize that he was referring to a character in the play rather than diminishing the man's obvious pain.

Jane Dark played Claudio's video on the Mondo Pad. The perspective was slightly different. Claudio described his injuries and then testified about how he couldn't fire a rifle anymore. He was a proud man, confessed the embarrassment of no longer having a job and living off the damn government.

Denise couldn't make him budge. "Was Mr. Song affected by the drone?"

"I couldn't tell. My eyes were on his gun. We were just standing there when he came right at us."

"But you did try to stop him, didn't you?"

"Only after he shot my two best friends."

Denny looked downward when Denise returned to the

table. "I'm sorry, I'm sorry, I'm sorry," he said. "I didn't mean to. I didn't mean to. I didn't mean to."

"We call Beatrice Baca to the stand," Jane Dark said. Beatrice was in a dress uniform, but she had a lanyard with pictures of two young girls hanging around her neck.

"More *Much Ado About Nothing*," Denny said, still not looking up.

Beatrice was petite, and Denise couldn't help but think of the Latinx side of her family. This could be a cleaned-up Dew in a uniform. Hell, Beatrice could be a distant cousin to Denise, even if she was an alien according to Denny.

The deputy's lapel cam and testimony mirrored the other officers. There was one difference, Beatrice didn't cry as she talked about her injuries. "I wanted to prove myself," she said. "Even though I still have my injuries, and I could claim disability, I am still on the force, protecting the county, protecting the community that I love."

"Did you see a drone or anything like what counsel is suggesting?" Jane Dark asked.

"My focus was on the defendant's gun. And when Mr. Song pointed that gun at me, I thought I would never see my kids again. I have twins too."

Jane Dark had Beatrice show the picture on the lanyard of her newborn twins, the two adorable girls. "I promised them I wouldn't cry when I took the stand."

Jane Dark signaled to the bailiff who stood by the door. On cue, Caliban opened it to reveal an elderly woman sitting on a bench with twin toddlers. Denise guessed they were around four. Both had pink bows in their hair and yellow ribbons tied around their wrists. They sported oversized toy gold badges with their mom's picture pasted on as necklaces.

"Your honor, I kept them out of the courtroom, so they wouldn't have to see their mother be cross-examined." Jane Dark said. "But I wanted them to see how proud they could be of their mother."

Beatrice held back her tears. She was tough. Denise had empathy for this poor woman. She sure looked human to Denise. Even the judge had wiped her eyes under that new piercing.

Denny was the one doing the crying for all of them. "I'm sorry," he mumbled under his breath.

"Pass the witness," Jane Dark said, but the bailiff kept the door opened so the little girls could see their mother on the stand if Denise dared to cross her.

How do you follow that? If there was a moment when you knew you were going to lose, this was that moment. "No questions, your honor," Denise said.

Beatrice bounded off the stand, and hurried over to hug the little girls.

"Mommy, we're so proud of you," they said in unison.

The judge glanced at her watch. "Any more witnesses, counsel? I think we've heard more than enough."

"We call the final alleged victim, Sheriff JC Diamond to the stand." Jane Dark said.

If Denise thought Jane Dark couldn't top that, she was wrong...

Chapter 52

Sheriff JC Diamond strode forward in his dress khaki uniform like he was General Rommel of the *Afrika Korps.* "Can I keep my hat on?" he asked the judge, who nodded. "And keep my firearm? Just in case *someone* acts up."

"Of course, Sheriff," the judge said. He didn't bother to ask about his shades, he assumed he had permission for that.

"One more thing," Jane Dark said. She looked over at Caliban who went out into the lobby and returned with Earl the police dog. "He needs a *comfort* animal after these traumatic events. While Earl is a victim, excuse me an *alleged* victim, he will not be testifying."

"That's not fair," Denny said.

"I'll allow it," the judge said.

This big and macho sheriff now pretended to be vulnerable, he even slouched in his seat. He acted as though he would have been too scared to be here in court if it wasn't for Earl. While petting the dog, Sheriff JC Diamond talked about his family and how the incident scarred him and gave him PTSD and he could no longer sleep.

Even Denise now believed it. He talked about how he had to be there for Earl, as Earl suffered stress from the incident as well. As the boss, he had to remain on duty at all times and couldn't get counseling all the way out here. He even wiped away a crocodile tear.

All eyes in the courtroom were on Earl who was nuzzling against the sheriff for the occasional Scooby-snack. Jane Dark didn't even bother to play his lapel cam video.

"Pass the witness," Jane Dark said. "Good boy."

Denise knew she had to do something. Anything.

Earl growled as Denise stood to cross the sheriff. After

some preliminary questions, Denise got to the money questions. "Do you know if it's possible that an outside factor—drone, or the grail—might have affected his mental state?"

"You're saying that some UFO made your boy shoot at my men?" he asked.

"I'm asking the questions here, sir," Denise said. "And Denny Song is not *my boy*."

"Denny was crazy and violent already," the sheriff said. "UFO or drone. Grail or no grail. We were standing there, minding our own business, doing our duty, when he came at us like a bat outta hell. Your brother is a menace to this town, to this state, and to this *planet*."

Denny gestured to her and whispered in her ear. Denise said, "One more question, Sheriff. Your name is JC Diamond, what do the J and C stand for?"

"*Julius* and *Caesar*," he replied.

"Isn't there a play *Julius Caesar* by William Shakespeare?"

"*Et tu*, JC?" Denny asked.

There was some grumbling from the Groundlings, but the bailiff silenced them. Did this gang in the back with their Shakespearean names have ties to law enforcement? What was really going on here?

"Move to strike on grounds of relevance!" Jane Dark said.

"Your honor, I don't know the relevance," Denise responded. "Yet."

The Groundlings let out a taunting "whoop."

"If the defense has no more questions, does the state wish to do any follow-up?" the judge asked.

Jane Dark went over and petted Earl one more time. "And the Defendant shot several times in the vicinity of Earl, putting your dog, putting your pet, your comfort animal companion in danger?"

Earl took this one and gave a single bark in response.

"That means yes," the sheriff said with a smile.

"The state rests."

"When I'm locked up forever, will I be able to get a furlough to see my mom's funeral at least?" Denny asked.

The judge ignored Denny and took a minute to check her phone. She texted someone back, smiling the whole time.

Her attention back on the court, she said, "Do you have any witnesses, Ms. Song?"

Denise froze. It was the end of the line. Denny was going to be ruled dangerous and he was going to be sent up for the rest of his life. After she lost her mom, she would lose her brother.

She looked at her phone, no messages. She could hear the Groundlings laughing at her. "But you said, but you said," they chanted.

Even worse, dangerous defendants certainly wouldn't get to go to their mother's funeral.

"Do we have *anybody?*" Denny asked. "I wouldn't have hurt anybody except for the grail and the drone!"

"It's almost five," the judge said. "I need to be in Santa Fe by tonight to meet with the Governor at her event tomorrow. I'd like to get there before midnight, so I got to get on the road like five minutes ago. If nothing further, I am ready to make a ruling in this case."

Earl the dog barked once.

Denise closed her eyes, took a deep breath and said a silent prayer. The judge packed her desk of all personal items into a carryon bag while still on the bench. It was all over but the gaveling.

Denise looked at her brother one more time. She had let him down. She never had a chance and maybe that was for the best. She had sent out her psychic subpoenas to no avail. She held her phone, closed her eyes and sent a final follow up. Dew, Rayne, Rita, Hikaru where are you?

She opened her eyes.

MESSAGE SENT.

His hands still bound; Denny touched her on the shoulder. "Have faith," he said, not moving his lips. "We can do this."

He took her hand. Together they created so much psychic power that she believed the subpoena would go back in time. The lights flickered for a moment.

MESSAGE SENT.

"We're here..." a voice said. Denise opened her eyes. Rita walked in the courtroom door, followed by Rayne and Dew. "We're *really* here."

Chapter 53

"Team Turquoise in the house!" Rita shouted before Caliban the bailiff silenced her with his hand on the boomerang.

Denise smiled and looked back at Team Turquoise. There was still a chance to turn this thing around. Or was there?

"The defense *will* be putting on a case," Denise said. "If I can have a minute to confer with my witnesses."

"We didn't get notice of these witnesses," Jane Dark said.

"Notice of witnesses is not required for dangerousness hearings because of the *relaxed* standards of the rule of evidence," Denise said.

"It's too late in the afternoon to begin the defense part of the case," the judge said banging her gavel while glancing at her phone. "I told you I'm in Santa Fe tomorrow for a meeting with the governor."

"Your honor," Jane Dark added, putting her hand on the table to maintain balance. "I'm due at any minute. I don't know if we really need to hear some irrelevant information."

The judge had already stood up. Denise knew this could be her last chance. "Your honor, counsel has said that my client is dangerous. We have several witnesses who can testify that they have direct knowledge of what might have caused my client, caused my *brother* to act in a dangerous fashion. I believe it's highly relevant."

The judge paused. "OK, that's relevant. Well relevant enough."

Jane Dark was turning red. "Perhaps we should just reset this case when ummm... things settle down."

"Your honor," Denise said. "My client has been in custody for quite some time. There's a chance that the evidence we will present will lead to his freedom. Jane Dark might be the best prosecutor in New Mexico, but if this case is so *automatic* as she suggests, she can be replaced by someone with less skill. She's not irreplaceable. There are several attorneys in her office who could handle the matter. Can we come back after your meeting with the governor, first thing next week?"

The judge looked down at her phone and exchanged texts like a teenager. "We will resume the defense case next Tuesday. Ms. Dark, if you are unable to continue, you will find replacement counsel from your office."

Jane Dark looked down at her belly. "Oh, *we* will be here in the flesh, your honor. Both of us!"

"And counsel, your witnesses had better testify to something relevant or I will hold you in contempt. Do you know what they're going to say? Can you give us a sneak preview?"

Denise looked at Dew, Rayne and Rita. "No, your honor."

Hooting and hollering came from the Groundlings like a Greek chorus drunk on ouzo.

"See you next Tuesday." The judge said. She then looked down. "Excuse me, I start my new position next week on Monday, you better all be here this *Friday*. Can you get all your ducks in a row by then, counsel?"

"I can try once I know how my ducks are going to testify," Denise said. The judge was out the door. Denise had made a promise that she didn't know if she could keep.

Denny was still at the table, the guards right behind him. He stared at Rayne.

"Denny, this is our daughter, Rita," Rayne said. "Rita, this is your father, Denny."

"Hey Dad!"

Denny and Rita stared at each other. If it wasn't for the guard, they would have hugged. The guard took Denny away before they could say another word.

Rita looked at Denise. "How can we help him? My mother doesn't have any *recollection* of anything!"

Denise looked at her friends. She didn't have much time. "I've got an idea of how to jog your memory. Road trip."

"One car or three?" Rayne asked. "We came separately."

"We better take three," Dew said. "No offense, Rayne."

"None taken."

Chapter 54

Denise knew they only had a few hours of daylight left as she followed Rayne and Rita, with Rayne going her usual one mile under the speed limit. Dew followed them both in the Mercedes. They arrived at the Syrinx turn-off with the last rays of sunset illuminating the white sands. Pink Sands Missile Range certainly didn't sound like a macho military site, but it was more appropriate right now.

"This is the last place I remember," Rayne said after pulling off the highway to a dirt clearing. Denise pulled behind her in the Kia, and Dew brought up the rear in the Mercedes.

"This is where it happened," Rayne said as they all exited their vehicles. "Last thing I remember, Dew and I had finished up and drove away from Syrinx. The Military Police had blocked off the highway because of those missile tests. A guy in a jeep told us to pull over and then he disappeared. We just waited for an hour and then there was like a sandstorm."

Dew pointed to a blackened spot on the sand. "Right here."

"What are we going to do?" Rayne asked.

Denise looked around at the others. Denny had told her to have faith.

"I've got an idea," Denise said. "Let's make a circle. Close your eyes. Let's concentrate on Rayne."

With the sun now totally behind the Organ mountains to the west of here, the sky was dark, the road devoid of headlights.

"I don't get it," Dew said. While she held Denise's hand, she hesitated to hold Rayne's. Rayne certainly didn't want to hold Dew's.

"Concentrate on Rayne everyone!" Denise said, closing

her eyes. "You too Dew. Make your mind go blank."

Denise opened her eyes, embarrassed. No one had closed their eyes. "Guys, we can do this. For my brother. And for both of you, we need to find out what happened."

"I don't know about this," Rayne and Dew said at the same time.

Denise had an idea. "Rita, why don't you get between Dew and your mom to complete the circuit, I mean complete the circle."

"We can do this," Rita said. Rita got between Rayne and Dew and gripped their hands. Rayne now closed the circle with Denise who held Dew's hand.

"Now make your mind go blank," Denise said. She felt an electric current go around the four of them. Everything slowly came into focus as Denise guided them inside Rayne's mind. With multiple parties appearing in this "dream," they were ghostly, like avatars from one of those virtual reality games. Denise could see avatars of Rita, Rayne and even Dew herself as ghostly figures hovering over the images of Dew and Rayne in the past, parked in the Mercedes in this exact place.

There was a big box of computer disks and notebooks in the front seat.

"I'm confused," the avatar of Rayne said out loud and the Rayne below looked up for a second. At that moment, the sandstorm grew in intensity. Lightning crashed all around the Dew and Rayne from the past.

"Just concentrate on being an *observer*," Denise said. "You have entered your own dream."

It took a moment for things to calm down, the images of Dew and Rayne down below were squabbling.

"Why did you have to take all that extra stuff?" the image of Rayne asked the Dew below. "We can get in serious shit if they find out."

"Do you want to win this case or not?" that Dew replied. "I wonder if you've ever wanted to win *anything* in your whole life."

Rayne was definitely peeved at that, but then the sandstorm grew in intensity again. "This isn't me doing this," the avatar of Rayne said. "This is what happened. I have a *recollection* of it now."

In the intense sandstorm, a drone appeared above the Mercedes. There were more flashes of lightning. One of the bolts hit the car. Suddenly the box of evidence vaporized.

"What the hell?" Dew said down below. Or did the avatar of Dew from above say it?

Another lightning bolt hit the Mercedes dead on, the current flowed over the car like the rinse cycle of a car wash. Down below, Rayne went into some sort of fugue state and attacked Dew. Scratched her, punched her, even kicked her. And yet her eyes were blank, like a zombie.

The avatar of Rayne floating above nodded. "It was like every ounce of rage that I had ever felt toward you suddenly erupted in that instant. I had no control."

There was a momentary flux in the storm, and the avatars resumed their focus on what was happening below...

Rayne had stopped attacking Dew and had exited the Mercedes, her eyes still blank. She slammed the door behind her, but Dew didn't move. Rayne seemed to be greeting the drone. The drone then disappeared over the sand dune, and Rayne collapsed. Dew remained in the car, dazed.

Lights approached out of the darkness to reveal another vehicle, a black van with a bike rack. Someone emerged from the van, opened the door and lifted Rayne and put her in another vehicle. Dew was still out cold in the Mercedes.

The image down below grew less focused as Rayne was being driven away from this spot in the second vehicle. Denise worried that they were about to lose the image totally, as everything was dim, as if Rayne had only the vaguest recollection of this part as she was semi-conscious.

There was a moment of darkness, but then the image down below reappeared. They could now see that whoever picked up Rayne was turning off the highway and parking by the lake. The figure took Rayne out to the lake and handed her a thermos that the figure had filled with water from the lake.

"Drink this," the voice said.

There in the dream, Rayne's eyes opened, and they could

all see the stars and lights of the base reflected in Lake Holloman.

"Stay here," the figure said to the image of Rayne. "Someone will come for you. This liquid will heal you for the next twenty-four hours. Keep drinking it."

Denise tried to focus on the figure who picked up Rayne. She couldn't make out the figure's face. "Concentrate," she said to Rayne.

"That's all I remember."

A military truck roared by them in the real world, and it honked as if in spite. That broke their reverie. The scene faded to black.

"I think that's enough," Denise said. They opened their eyes. They were back in the desert, back in the present. They looked around at each other and nodded.

"It's past Rita's bedtime," Rayne said.

"Oh mom," Rita said.

"You guys go home," Denise said. "I can take it from here."

"Where are you going?" Dew asked. "Who rescued Rayne?"

As if on cue, Denise's phone buzz indicating she'd received a text. A click revealed a full moon shining on Sierra Blanca off in the distance, reflecting on a lake. Moments later the text disappeared.

"I'm about to find out."

Chapter 55

After driving due east through the blackness of the desert, Denise began her ascent into the mountains. The air thinned, the stars shined brighter, closer, with every mile. She received a few texts showing which turns to make.

How thoughtful.

She finally found Hikaru's cabin and was surprised to find him waiting by the pond, seated on a log in front of a campfire that reflected off the water. He was in his cycling outfit and his mountain bike was parked against the side of the log; an extra-large backpack was awkwardly attached to the bike. A second bike, her bike from their "Roswell incident," leaned against the other side of the log.

"I was expecting you," he said. "I don't have much time."

She sat down on the log and held his hand. "So, tell me what is really going on here?"

He opened a picnic basket to reveal a silver grail.

"The *alpha* grail." He filled it with pond water. This one was a bit smaller than the Omega. It even had some dents on the sides.

"Stand back." He then held the grail over the fire, the water bubbled, and he sprinkled in some powder with his free hand. A steam cloud formed above them, Denise half-expected him to pull a rabbit out of the grail.

Instead, there was something even more amazing. There was a projection in the steam. Wait, was that a moving image of young Hikaru picking up this very grail? The image repeated a few times like an internet meme. The cloud disappeared leaving only darkness.

"Let me guess, you were the first winner of the 24 Grails Contest?" she asked.

"Guilty as charged," he said. "This one was up at Los Alamos on the edge of the mesa. I had just graduated from college, a little unsure of what I was doing with my life. I was going to stay home and write a fan-fiction *Star Trek* spec screenplay—Mr. Sulu infiltrates the Klingons—but then I found this in my backyard."

"The people were the prize not the grails," Denise said. "They were supposed to be a beacon for people with psychic abilities. Something like that?"

"That's part of what they do, the grails are a *beacon* and even a portal. Technically they would be called a BCI for *brain-computer interface*."

"They also intensify emotions in people with psychic powers, no?"

"Now you're getting it. Unfortunately. a machine that amplifies human emotions might have some military applications. And not just *our* military."

"Did the US military make them? Is there really a Cygnus Moon or is it a front for someone or *something* else?"

"Cygnus Moon is a real corporation here on earth if that's what you're asking. The people who work for them are very much human. They do work for our military and also for the Chinese, Russians, Israelis, you name it. And they sometimes enter into what we would call joint ventures with *unidentified* parties."

"Unidentified *flying* object parties?" Denise asked.

"That's above my paygrade," he said. "Way *above* my pay grade."

"But what does that have to do with Denny? What do they have to do with me?"

"I'll show you," he took her hand.

Denise was a little leery. "Ummm... can't you put the information on a thumb drive? I can download it later onto my umm... hard drive."

He shook his head. "I don't think you understand. What I'm about to give you is highly classified. I had hoped that Rayne and Dew would have been able to obtain this material legally and it wouldn't be an issue. Unfortunately, you saw what happened. I guess Dew got more information than anyone bargained for. They must have triggered someone or *something* and that pissed off the people or parties *above*. I had no idea that any of that would happen. I couldn't let anyone know that I rescued Rayne."

"Are you still a part of... *whatever* it is?"

"Not even. But for your safety it's got to be this way that I give you the information, so no one knows about it. I don't want what happened to your friends to happen to you."

She stared at the grail as he put it in front of her. "Is it safe?"

"It is when you are with me. You don't want to kill me, do you? Because that could be an issue. As we know, the grails can intensify emotions."

"*Should* I want to kill you?"

"No, I'm on your side, or I *will be*."

She hesitated, and then nodded. "What do I do?"

"Grab one handle and I'll grab the other. This will be more information than a simple gif."

Before reaching over, a reassuring current enveloped her entire being, almost as if she was sitting in the world's most relaxing vibrating chair. She could trust him completely.

Denise now noticed a narrow beam of light between the grail and the pond. Hikaru indicated that she should touch the handle.

"You promise me that this is safe?" she asked.

"As safe as touching a mysterious object that utilizes unproved and possibly *alien* technology can be. There might be a slight shock," he said.

The shock was slightly more intense than she expected, but not unpleasant. Again, it reminded her of a massage chair in a nail salon where her mother once took her to a mani-pedi on a rare mother-daughter outing. She almost didn't want to let go, but then the vibration stopped, and the grail fell to the ground.

"What just happened?"

"It was the interface. I transferred a few gigabytes of information to the grail which then transferred them to you. Did it hurt?"

"Not at all, it actually felt good, but I feel like I have some kind of clot or something in my head."

"Close your eyes and count from ten to one backward."

Denise closed her eyes and counted. When she reached one, the clot released and she realized that she did have access to considerable information, as if a zip drive had been implanted into her brain.

"What just happened? I suddenly have all this data. She thought of the Keanu Reeves film, *Johnny Mnemonic*. She next thought of Keanu in *The Matrix*. In both films, her idol was able to retain all this new information in his brain, permanently.

"You've seen it in a million bad science fiction movies," Hikaru said. "Brain-computer interface. I was able to store information in a section of my brain and then transfer it to your brain. It's not really psychic, it's electronic. The grail just facilitates the transfer by removing the static and extraneous stuff."

"Is it permanent?"

"It's like your regular memory—you can forget—unless you get an implant in your cerebellum like I've done. But you'll be able to retrieve it over the next twenty-four hours. You'll be able to retain the broad strokes forever. You might want to close your eyes and try to retrieve it."

"What will I retrieve?"

"These are the records that you guys were trying to access. They consist of recordings of meetings and archived videos of Denny while he was on duty."

"So, these aren't dreams?"

"They're real. I made them myself from real data and then *uploaded* them using the alpha grail. Let's try it now to make sure it works."

Once her mind adjusted to the mental image of the data download, she could picture various icons arranged like a tic-tac-toe board. Each square held an image of a white carboard banker's box. She "opened" a "box" labeled as number one in the upper left-hand corner. The box opened to reveal some footage of Denny working with Hikaru at the White Sands Missile Range. She recognized the WSMR logo on badges for both of them, but there was another logo for something called Syrinx Mission Control. The logo had the nearby Organ Mountains somehow incorporating cartoon organ pipes. Denny wasn't in uniform, indicating he was a civilian employee of the WSMR. The video showed a warm relation between the two.

She then focused on the second box. She saw a meeting of military brass in an unmarked boardroom with a view out onto White Sands. The military was having some issues with their guidance systems in flight and several missiles had crashed or exploded. Someone had suspected that China or Russia was using weaponized psychics to hack into the guidance systems created by an American company.

Box three was in the upper right corner. At a subsequent military meeting, a video showed the parties voting to authorize funding for addressing the issue and setting up the grail system as a way of finding people with psychic abilities who could be recruited—or identified as potential risks.

Box four was back on the left side, in the middle. It was a FaceTime between Hikaru and representatives of Cygnus Moon. Hikaru complained about the safety issues—some type of radiation leaks. Mr. Choi from the Korean plant told them in halting English that they were "working on it."

Apparently, the plant had a history of "issues" during the manufacture of the grails and her mother's incident was their only breakdown.

She couldn't open the middle square. She tried again, and now noticed a big metal lock on the lid of a banker's box. It actually felt like the lock was hitting her smack dab in the forehead.

She skipped forward to the next box. In the middle row on the far right was the crime scene video shot from the lapel cams. She'd seen it before, but she was still shocked by the act of violence committed by her brother and his dazed expression. She also realized that the lapel videos shown by the cops had been edited. While the drone itself was not visible, she could now clearly see a light coming from above, like a spotlight shining on Denny.

"Denny," she asked out loud. "What happened to you that night?"

As if to answer her, her attention directed itself to the bottom row of boxes. A new series of images now appeared in her brain that appeared to have been taken by a hidden cell phone. Denny was now in his twenties was responsible for beta-testing the grails somewhere in the desert. Denny was clearly affected when he was near the grails, but apparently that was part of the testing process. The last square in the bottom right corner portrayed chemists taking samples of the Lake Holloman "water." Results came back as UN-KNOWN, NO EARTHLY MATCH.

Had aliens been dumping toxic waste in the lake? The more likely explanation was that the military was flushing their own rocket fuel there, but that didn't make her feel any better.

When she had finished with the bottom of row of squares, she tried the center one again. There was still that damn lock on it, and it hurt to think about it.

"I'm not getting anything more," Denise said. She opened her eyes. She had a slight headache from the lockbox. "I couldn't unlock the center square."

Hikaru touched his own forehead as if probing it. "I guess the center square isn't filled in yet. I must still be transmitting, and it won't open till it's done."

"When will it finish transmitting?"

"Probably when I'm dead. I told you that there's an implant in my brain that has some kind of regulator. It shows up in your vision as a "lock." Once the regulator is no longer in place, it will be unlocked. I'm sure there will be a final burst of data that will be released to the final box and you can access it."

"Well, I don't think we want that." She touched him on the arm. "You're going to have to testify in court about what you know."

He looked down at his phone. He didn't get a text, he got something else. "I don't think that's going to happen. I've got to get moving, like right now. I was in danger before, but by giving you this, they might try to *terminate* me. Terminate with extreme prejudice."

He took the grail and opened a thermos on his bike.

He poured fluid into the grail, fluid with the unmistakable odor of that lake. Without even a potholder, he held the grail over the fire for a moment, and the water boiled, and yet he was able to hold onto it without being burnt. If that wasn't enough, the grail suddenly disintegrated in a puff of smelly steam.

"Did you want it do that?" she asked.

"I think so," he said. "I don't want it to fall into the wrong hands. Let's just say I don't want to meet with my big boss right now."

He wiped some sweat off his brow with a bandanna. He pointed to the second bike. "Do you want to come with me? I'm going to try to bike down to Tierra del Fuego."

"The one in Argentina?"

"The end of the earth. It's pretty much a straight shot, but you have to take a ferry around the Darien Gap in Panama."

"What are you going to do there?"

"Take a ship down to Antarctica. Let's just say there's a classified, *independent* research station there that is doing some studies that might shed some light on our current situation. They found an *artifact* that might have a connection to our current situation."

Denise had a vision of this *artifact*, a frozen flying saucer containing well-preserved aliens buried beneath the Antarctic ice. Then again, she might be thinking back to the plot of a half-dozen episodes of forgotten TV shows. For a moment, she was tempted to ride along with Hikaru and uncover the truth. The truth was *down* there, so to speak.

But as she looked in the fire, a log broke apart and emitted a burst of sparks. A spark landed on her wrist and she swiped it away. She thought of her brother, he needed her. Needed her now. The truth could wait.

"I think I better go back and save Denny."

"I knew you'd say that," he said. "I respect you for that."

"Ummm... I *respect* you too."

He stamped out the fire with his feet, without burning himself. "I'll keep in touch while I'm on the run."

"I'd like that."

Without another word, he got on the bike and rode off into the darkness.

She stared at the smoldering ashes and wiped away a tear. Moments later she heard "I love you, Denise Song" echo off the mountaintops. And then there was laughter.

"I love you, Hikaru Yu," she said to the damp coals of the fire. She was about to add the word, *"kinda,"* but she realized that there was nothing "kinda" about it. It was the real thing.

Would she ever see him again?

She sat there for a few hours staring at the embers and *experienced* the information from the interface in her head, experienced it as if they were her own memories. Denny had been telling the truth. She typed the info from her brain into her laptop and actually arranged all her notes into the tic-tac-toe board, like a PowerPoint presentation. It was amazing, she could click on a square and get the information, even access the videos.

This would be gold if she could introduce this in court.

And then she realized even with the most relaxed rules of evidence, the PowerPoint of her vision would not be admissible without Hikaru to authenticate it. Without Hikaru, the truth was stuck in there.

Chapter 56
Thursday, August 13

It was after midnight when she got back in the Kia and took the road out from the cabin. She pulled over to allow some heavy military vehicles to pass. The aspen trees along the road shook from the vibrations. A branch fell down on the Kia. That sure was a lot of firepower to retrieve one unarmed man for a peaceful meeting with his boss.

She prayed that Hikaru was long gone in the darkness. Would they really terminate him with extreme prejudice? She didn't know what that meant, didn't want to know.

As she drove deeper and deeper into the heart of the desert night, she confirmed everyone's appearance in court for the next hearing—talking to Dew, Rayne by phone and text. She hoped Rayne would get a message to Rita who was probably asleep. Once she hit Cruces, she thought about visiting her mother again, but the exit to the hospital was closed. That couldn't be a good sign. As she hit Interstate 10, she drove at the speed of light back to Lordsburg. If there were drones overhead, she must have outrun them.

It was dawn when she arrived at the Last Palm. There was a text from Hikaru at the Rio Grande, probably Juarez. He was under a sign that said "*Bienvenido a Mexico.*"

* * *

Denise awoke midday on Thursday. Unfortunately, the PowerPoint now seemed locked in her computer. ACCESS DENIED came up over and over again. Had she lost control of her own memories without Hikaru?

She hoped Hikaru was alright. She noticed a text from an unknown number showing some pics of somewhere on the

Mexican Riviera. The sunrise illuminated a shadow of a bike and rider against the asphalt road. He couldn't have biked that far. Had he hitched a ride once he'd crossed the border? SOUTH BOUND! MEET ME IN ARGENTINA! I WILL TEXT YOU FROM MY NEXT DESTINATION.

Then again, he did have access to a high-speed helicopter. Maybe he could send it to pick her up.

Still, Tierra del Fuego would be a trek, even by helicopter. Taking a boat from there to Antarctica would be no picnic either. And then getting to the frozen artifact whatever it was sounded epic. She was glad he was safe wherever he was, and she hoped that she'd be able to see him again.

Chapter 57

Friday, August 14

At eight in the morning on Friday, Shakespeare street was still empty. Denise checked her phone. Hikaru had sent a selfie of him on his bike posing next to a "canal lock" on the Panama Canal. How did he get there? Denise guessed that he must have access to a helicopter, supersonic jets and maybe even a flying saucer. Good for him.

Here in court, some workmen were laying tiles on the courthouse roof. Another worker hung precariously over an open skylight. That was new. A worker dropped a tile that nearly hit Denise as she entered.

"Watch out!" someone yelled, then swore in some foreign tongue. Denise noticed some creepy looking figure in a black hoodie and sunglasses standing in the shadows of an alley, watching her enter the courtroom. She couldn't tell if he was human or an alien under all that covering.

Even worse, inside the courthouse all the bathrooms except one were "under construction." What the hell was going on here?

Denise hurried inside the courtroom, empty except for Dew, Rayne, and Rita. Above, the new skylight opening was covered by a mildewed tarp and was directly over the witness chair. A drip of water came down right on the seat.

"I hope I don't have to sit there," Dew said. She was actually dressed like the lawyer she had once hoped to become—black power-suit and turquoise top. She could pass for a shorter version of Hurricane Luna. Rita wore a turquoise blazer, breaking away from her usual red. Rayne also went with turquoise. The three of them looked like a woman's basketball team traveling in style—Rayne the center, Rita the power forward and Dew as the scrappy little point guard.

More tiles fell off the roof and Denise heard more swearing in that foreign language. Russian? Louder this time.

"I have a bad feeling about this," Rita said. "Who are these guys up there?"

No one seemed to know. Caliban the bailiff entered. "Has anyone seen Madam Dark?"

Before they could answer, a new jail guard brought Denny in and seated him at counsel table. His orange outfit had not been washed and smelled of mildew and bologna. There was another drip onto the witness chair. The bailiff hurried over and wiped it off the chair. A stain remained.

"That's gross," Denny said. "I sure wouldn't want to be sitting there."

"Don't worry," Denise said to Denny. "You're not going to testify today, so you're safe."

Jane Dark barely fit through the narrow doors. She pointed down at her belly. "Hopefully not today."

Without a sound, the judge materialized on the bench, *sans* robe. "It's official! I got the probation and parole job from the governor!" she said to the bailiff. She looked different, her piercings were gone, her tattoos covered by scarves and band-aids. "Head of the whole department with a cabinet level salary. And a car! I get sworn in on Monday!"

The judge covered her mouth as she realized that everyone in the courtroom was listening. She straightened up and did her best to adopt a judicial demeanor for her final day on the bench. "We will *finish* the case this morning. Does the defense wish to make an opening statement?"

"Yes, your honor," Denise said. "My client was clearly *impaired* when he allegedly committed these actions. He was affected by an unidentified flying object which caused him to be unable to form the specific intent required to be culpable for his actions. I would like to bring in the testimony of Dew Cruz, Rayne Herring and Rita Herring who can testify from personal experience about how these objects—these unidentified flying objects—can affect people."

The judge rolled her eyes. "Does counsel want to call

any witnesses in the dangerousness hearing to prove this ummm... hypothesis?"

"Yes, your honor, I will call Rayne Herring, Rita Herring and Dew Cruz."

"I will renew my objection," Jane Dark said.

"What are they going to testify to?" the judge asked.

"Your honor, these witnesses will testify as to how their personal experience with similar objects, drones, can cause otherwise peaceful people to become violent and not be responsible for their own actions."

"I'll allow it," the judge said. "This is going to be my last day as a judge, so I might as well go out with a *bang*."

Denise didn't like the sound of that, but she had a chance now. She called Dew first. Dew went up and immediately recoiled when a drip from the skylight fell on her blazer.

Back in their mock trial days, Dew had been the lawyer and Denise played the witness. It felt refreshing to turn the tables, and Denise felt good to be the one in charge. Was Dew actually looking at her with respect? After a few preliminaries, Denise turned to the money question.

"Did you have any recollection of a similar incident involving a drone?" Denise asked her. "An incident which showed how an unidentified object could affect someone's behavior?"

Unfortunately, if Denise had become a better lawyer, Dew was a lousy witness.

"At first, I didn't have any recollection of any incident," Dew said, looking downward. "But then I got hypnotized and it all came back."

Jane Dark objected immediately.

"Move to strike all testimony of this witness regarding any other incident," she said. "Do I need to go through Rule 11-403 on how this testimony was a waste of time due to her lack of personal knowledge or expertise under Rule 702."

The judge didn't look up. "I will strike her testimony. Next witness, counsel?"

"Strike one," Denny said, shaking his head.

Another drop from above hit Dew right on the forehead. She looked immensely relieved that she wouldn't have to testify any further and could get the hell off the stand. "Sorry, Denise," Dew said.

Denise hoped that she would have better luck with Rayne, who could talk about how she was directly affected by the drones which caused her to become violent.

Rayne went up to the stand. She too felt a drip, but Rayne was tough and didn't flinch. Denise went through the preliminary questions with her, and they were really flowing, as if the two were making music together. Rita was actually nodding along to the beat of her mother's testimony.

Denise stopped for a dramatic pause. Time to get to the climax. "Isn't it true that you were directly affected by a drone, or some other object floating above you."

Jane Dark didn't bother to rise. "Move to strike this witness's testimony as not being relevant and a waste of time under Rule 403."

If they'd been playing music, someone had scratched the turntable.

Before Denise could say anything on behalf of the defense, the Judge lifted her hand. "I will strike her testimony."

"Strike two," said Denny.

"I've got to make a call," the judge said. She started talking while still on the bench. Was she mumbling something about the color of her new state car—a choice between red or green? "If you'll excuse me," she said before she seemed to vanish off the bench.

"I've got to go to the bathroom," Denny said. "And there's like only one in the building that still works."

Everyone else in the courtroom looked at each other. As the court seemed to be in recess, they all rushed out in a race to the one public unisex bathroom in the building.

With an unexpected moment to spare alone in the courtroom as everyone seemed to be stuck in the bathroom line, Denise noticed a new pic of Hikaru on her phone. He was next to the famous Christ the Redeemer statue in Rio de Janeiro. Still on the bike, his arms were outstretched like the statue.

That was odd. Rio was a detour from a straight shot to Tierra del Fuego. Maybe one of the UFOs was flying him down south, although it was probably a helicopter. Next stop Argentina, or would he keep going down to Antarctica?

And then it hit her. Hikaru was probably not going to Antarctica after all. He had mentioned something about the "lock" on the final square being released after his death. Maybe this was Hikaru's way of saying good-bye. Maybe he was going to jump off of the statue of Christ down into sea.

Missing him greatly, she decided to look at all the pics he had sent her that she had saved in her phone's library. She frowned when she looked at her archives. Every single one of Hikaru's photos had vanished. Worse, there was no record of them ever arriving. All her texts back to him had vanished as well, as if he didn't exist.

Even the last pic of Hikaru under the Christ the Redeemer statue was gone, and for some reason that hurt her the worst as it might be the last image of him she'd ever see.

Had he sent them with his mind? Had he even sent them at all? Perhaps it was worse than that, the bad guys had caught up and deleted him and everything about him.

Maybe he was already gone... If you were going to jump off a cliff, Rio would be the perfect place to do it.

She tried to text him, tried to reach out with her mind, but it was like he no longer existed. She knew numbers could be unavailable, but could psychics?

The judge reappeared back on the bench, and everyone else hurried back from the bathroom line, most without accomplishing their objective. The door was still open as Rita bumbled in.

"Do you have any other witness testimony indicating that the court should not hold that Denny Song is dangerous and must remain in custody?"

Rita nodded at Denise. "We call Rita Herring to the stand," Denise said.

More footsteps coming from above.

"Are gorillas working up there?" Rita said.

Rita walked to the stand filled with excitement, like a gymnast about to tumble.

"What do you want to talk about?" Rita asked, after the judge swore her in.

"Are you related to the Defendant in this case?"

"He's my *father*, but I will tell the truth, no matter what."

"When did you find out he's your father?"

"Technically this week. But this might seem weird, but he's reaching out to me with his mind now that we know about each other. While he's a little paranoid, he seems like a decent man, a good man. I hope we can build a relationship in the future."

"Do you feel that he's dangerous?" Denise asked.

"No."

"And why is that?"

"Objection, lack of personal knowledge!" Jane Dark objected.

"She does have personal knowledge your honor," Denise responded.

"I'll allow it but be brief."

"Why do you think he's not dangerous?"

"Well, I saw the video and it looks like he was affected by a drone when he shot at the cops, I mean allegedly shot at the cops. But then I found out that my own mother was affected in the same way by a drone and she became violent. So, I think my dad isn't violent and should get out of jail, free."

"I love you Rita," Denny said out loud.

"I love you, *dad*," Rita replied.

"Move to strike," Jane Dark said. "Love is not relevant."

"Agreed," the judge said. "Both statements are stricken. There is no love in this courtroom. Please stick to the facts."

Denise wanted to disagree but kept going. "And how did you find out that your father is not dangerous?" she asked.

"Well I'm kinda psychic," Rita said. "I just know."

Denise sat down. "Pass the witness."

"You said you are some kind of psychic," Jane Dark asked Rita on cross-examination.

"I guess so."

"Are you sure?"

"Yes."

"Can you prove it?"

Rita closed her eyes. "You are going to name your daughter Jean Dark. Jean Dark's father is Judge Comanche, chief judge of the Second Judicial District Court."

Jane Dark was stunned. But Rita wasn't done...

"Jean will be very famous someday, the most famous lawyer in the world. And she and I will meet again. And she will be here when the aliens come back."

Jane Dark was blindsided by that. She had a few more pages to go, but sat down, abruptly.

Denise asked one more question on redirect. "Based on your interaction with your father, do you think the drone affected him and made him dangerous?"

"I do. I believe my father is not a dangerous man and it caused him to go crazy."

Jane Dark must have regained her mojo after sitting down. Maybe her daughter, the so-called greatest lawyer in the world, had told her mom not to give up. The lawyer looked down at her phone as if it was an instruction on what to do.

"Move to strike the entire testimony of this witness," Jane Dark said.

Denise stood up. "Young Ms. Herring does have personal knowledge of Mr. Song, even if it's not *direct* knowledge."

The judge interrupted her.

"I will strike that testimony," the judge said. "Don't waste my time any further counsel."

Strike three," Denny said. "Is that it? You gotta save me, Denise."

"Counsel, do you have any other witnesses?" the judge asked, her desk totally clear. "If not, I'm ready to make a final ruling on dangerousness."

Through the skylight, Denise heard an aircraft flying overhead. Was it a helicopter or a drone?

She closed her eyes and concentrated one more time. She felt a tap on her shoulder, Denny added his own spark to her energy.

"Fifth dimensional consciousness," Denny said. "That means you can send it back through time."

She felt Rita and Rayne helping out even if all they did was buy some time. She even felt someone or something else join in.

She kept her eyes closed for one more moment. Fifth dimensional consciousness. Why the hell not? She felt some kind of energy come from her and Denny and the others go somewhere into the universe... or maybe some... *when*.

Had it worked? Before she could check, the judge banged the gavel. "Counsel, please open your eyes in my courtroom!" the judge said.

Denise complied. The courtroom door swung open.

"Sorry I'm late, your honor," a voice said. *"Traffic was a bitch."*

Denise now remembered that was the line from that old film *The Player*—the line that was in every single story regarding her family.

Chapter 58

Hikaru was still in his bike clothes. Covered in sweat stains, he looked like he had finished a triathlon—running to Juarez, swimming the Rio and then biking to Lordsburg. His hair looked like it hadn't been washed in days and he smelled of the toxic lake water. He had a dirty black sweatshirt around his neck despite the heat. Still he was the most handsome man Denise had ever seen. He must have been the creepy guy in the hoodie she had passed earlier today.

He clutched his heart for a moment, but it was merely his phone in a breast pocket. He reached in and turned it off. He did have a tablet computer with him that he took up to the stand with him.

The judge stared at him. "So I can access my files," he said. She shrugged as if she didn't care.

Dew, Rayne and Rita actually clapped. "Team Turquoise," they said in unison. The judge banged her gavel. "Order in the court. Ms. Song, do you have any more witnesses.

"We call Hikaru Yu to the stand," Denise said.

"Let's finish this," the judge said. Outside, there was a rumbling on the stairs. Caliban went out, but the door did not shut behind him. "He's here. Hikaru must have been here all along."

Denise recognized the sheriff's voice in the hallway. "He's going to testify. Yeah, I thought he was in Brazil too." Was he talking to Caliban, or someone else?

The sheriff listened for another moment; he must be on the phone. "We need to go to Plan B, pronto."

As if on cue, the wet tarp above Hikaru was taken off. At least Hikaru wouldn't get dripped on. Still, Denise felt uneasy. Hopefully, taking off the tarp wasn't part of Plan B.

Hikaru was sworn in by the judge and then took the stand and looked up at the open skylight He then smiled at Denise, and then at Rita, Rayne and Dew. "Team Turquoise," he mouthed back at them, clenching his fist in solidarity.

"Please state your name," Denise asked.

"Hikaru Yu."

"How did you get here so fast?" She hadn't meant to ask this out loud.

"I've been here the whole time," he said. "You subpoenaed me, remember?"

"But..."

Hikaru glanced toward the closed door, and above to the skylight. Apparently, he wanted the powers that be to think he was somewhere else. Could they bug a psychic's phone?

Of course they could.

"How are you employed?"

"I work for a military contractor called Helmsman Associates. Well, I *worked* for them, my status right now is unclear."

"Tell us about Helmsman."

"Helmsman is a government contractor with contracts at various military bases and labs around the southwest. It was started by my father, Dr. Yu, when he was at Los Alamos. It was ultimately folded into a company called Cygnus Moon."

"How do you know my client, Denny Song?"

"He was originally a military conscript, but he was assigned over to our direction at Syrinx Testing Station which is part of the White Sands Military Range."

"*Our* direction?"

"Cygnus Moon corporation."

"Was he still in the military when he worked for you?"

"No, he received a *general* discharge. However, he was told that if he worked with us at Syrinx, it would be upgraded to an *honorable* discharge."

"And why was someone with a less than honorable discharge chosen for your program at Syrinx?"

"He was chosen for our team because he had special *abilities*. The rest is classified, and I am not at liberty to discuss that."

His phone beeped again through the cycling jersey. "My phone is off, your honor, someone is overriding it," he told the judge.

"You've been warned," the judge said. "Please continue."

Denise laid the foundation to establish Hikaru as an expert witness under Rule 702 with several questions about his qualifications.

"Your honor, we are submitting Mr. Yu as an expert witness."

"Objection," Jane Dark said. She was still looking at her phone as if it contained some information about Hikaru, but by the way she was scanning her phone, she couldn't find what she was looking for.

Denise noticed that he had slipped a few copies of his resume onto the table and she gave them to the judge and to Jane Dark.

"If this man isn't an expert, no one is," the judge said.

"Can I turn on my tablet?" Hikaru asked. The judge nodded.

She opened her laptop, and with some quick technical help from Hikaru and his tablet from the stand, she now had the access to her PowerPoint. With some direction from Hikaru, she was even able to get her PowerPoint displayed on the courtroom's big 72 inch Mondo Pad screen.

"Could you describe what this is?" Denise asked.

"It's a PowerPoint presentation that I made to convey the information I've developed over the years in regard to Denny's case, that I umm... transferred to you."

"Objection, hearsay," Jane Dark said.

"Your honor, we have relaxed rules of evidence. Since he created the interface it would not be hearsay and your honor, since he's been qualified as an expert, he can rely on hearsay information. In any event, there are relaxed rules of evidence."

It took a few moments of squabbling between the parties, but Hikaru was able to authenticate the PowerPoint presentation and the judge admitted it. She didn't even have to go into the fact that she'd seen it before via the grail. To the judge and the others in the courtroom, this was just another

PowerPoint on the big screen.

On the Mondo Pad, the squares of the board were labeled, and Denise had Hikaru go through each one and related the information contained within, square by square.

Hikaru was a bit nervous on the stand, but with each square, each answer, he grew more confident. She made it a point to skip the center square which was labelled "incomplete."

"Without going into the classified aspects of these experiments, in your expert opinion under Rule 702 would these experiments affect my client's mental well-being, his ability to form specific intent?"

Hikaru smiled. "They *would* indeed affect his mental health and his ability to form specific intent."

"How so?"

"They could intensify pre-existing emotions such that he would have no ability to control his actions."

"And let me clear this up, you didn't actually perform these experiments personally?"

"I did not. I was aware of them, but they took me off the project. They said I had too much of a vested interest in the subject."

"And what about the events on July 7 of this year?"

"Objection, lack of personal knowledge," Jane Dark said.

Denise laughed as Jane Dark had fallen into her trap. "Do you have personal knowledge of the events of July 7?"

"I do. I was there."

"He was? Why was he there?" Jane Dark asked.

The judge looked at Denise. "Counsel lay a foundation, please."

Denise was now going to ask questions that she did not know the answers to.

"Why were you there at the site?" she asked.

"I believe my superiors feared that something like this could occur, an incidence of violence. They wanted to have plausible deniability, to blame it on me."

Now with the tarp gone, sunlight was shining directly on him through the skylight, and he wiped away some sweat off his forehead. The roofers had left but the aircraft sound increased and seemed to funnel through the skylight.

"What was supposed to happen?"

"We had information that someone was going to attempt to touch the grail. That person's mere proximity to the grail would trigger the appearance of a drone, and I was there to monitor what happened next."

"So the appearance of this drone was actually part of an experiment then?"

"It was. One of a series of experiments."

"Did these experiments have something to do with the 24 Grails Contest?"

"I can neither confirm nor deny," he said. He clutched his chest, right over his phone. He wiped his forehead again.

Rayne, Dew and Rita were all whispering amongst themselves how pained Hikaru looked. Caliban the bailiff had to quiet them. Caliban glanced out the door and motioned to the Sheriff as if asking for reinforcements.

The sheriff and a new deputy entered the courtroom, and now guarded the exit.

Had Hikaru just aged a decade while on the stand? His black hair was now streaked with gray. Even the judge was worried. "Are you OK, sir?" she asked.

He was gasping for breath now. "I'm sure," he said.

"Ask him about the UFO!" Denny said.

Denise hesitated. "Perhaps if we move him out of the sun." Denise now wished that the dripping tarp hadn't been removed.

"I'm good," he said. "This is where I *need* to be at this very moment."

"So, what happened that night?"

"I arrived on the scene and was monitoring the situation from inside my vehicle. The officers knew I was there, and I let them do their jobs. Apparently, when I was inside the van, Denny Song came near the vicinity and this activated a drone."

"Could you describe the drone?"

She had Hikaru use his own tablet to create a rough diagram on the Mondo Pad. It was something that looked like a globe with wings.

"It's a UFO!" Denny said.

"Was the drone ummm... *alien?*" Denise asked.

"No, it was probably from *Alamogordo.* Holloman Air Force Base."

The judge laughed in spite of herself.

"Actually, while it might have been physically created somewhere off site, it might have been located under the cylindrical water tank at the top of the hill near the ranch."

"But the aliens were controlling it!" Denny yelled. "Ask him about that."

"I'll ask about it," Denise said.

"Did the drone have any *connection* to anything that was extraterrestrial or alien?"

Hikaru now looked even more uncomfortable. "I don't know."

Denise heard that something in the sky above coming closer. Hikaru looked up and shivered.

The sheriff still guarding the exit, was now whispering into his phone. "Plan B, plan B."

"What happened next?" Denise asked.

"I was actually in the van, there at the site, and I have to admit that I had dozed off."

The sound from above seemed to abate for a moment. Denise worried that Hikaru was wimping out. He had clearly been agitated by the sounds coming from up above.

She looked at him and their eyes seemed to communicate with each other. "You've got this," her eyes said to his.

He nodded. Did he just whisper I love you to her? "Even though I had dozed off, I did have a chance to look at our own audiovisual recordings of the incident."

Denise turned to the judge. "May I publish them to court?"

"I haven't had a chance to see them," Jane Dark said.

"How long is it?" the judge asked.

"Ninety seconds," Hikaru said.

"Just play it then," the judge said, clearly in the mood to get this over with and not wait on either side.

Under Hikaru's direction from the tablet, Denise played the tape on the Mondo Pad. The drone showed up as a mysterious light. Denny looked like a zombie and shot at the officers before the light went out and he collapsed. If anything, it made things worse.

"So what is causing the light above?"

"That's the drone."

"How would you describe my client's appearance in the video?"

"He appears to lack control, like he's a robot." He pointed at the screen. "Let me blow up his face right there."

Hikaru manipulated his tablet with a pinch, and the Mondo Pad did a close-up on Denny's face right as he was picking up his gun to fire. Denny indeed looked like a robot.

"By lacking control, what do you mean?"

"He didn't have the ability to form specific intent."

"What do you think caused this behavior, this inability to form specific intent?"

"Perhaps there was a technical malfunction because of the drone's interaction with the grail. The malfunction must have affected your client. Then again, perhaps the drone and the grail were supposed to make him act like this."

"Act like what?"

"His emotions were *amplified*. My suspicion is that he was angry toward the sheriff and the drone interacting with the grail somehow intensified his anger."

"How did it do so?"

"It's a little unclear, but it might be electromagnetic radiation of an unknown frequency."

The sounds audible from the skylight intensified. It sounded like the drones all right, that damn buzzing. Did this have something to do with the sheriff and his Plan B?

"So, in *your expert opinion*, when Denny attempted to shoot the officers, his actions could have been a result of these electromagnetic radiation waves from either the drone or the grail, or perhaps both?"

Denise realized that she had no idea what she was talking about in regards to "electromagnetic radiation waves," but since she said it with such authority, no one noticed.

"It could," Hikaru replied.

"Are you willing to say that we've established that by

clear and convincing evidence?"

"Yes, by clear and convincing evidence, in my expert professional opinion and in my *personal* opinion. I've known Mr. Denny Song personally and he was never violent. In the video, he appears like a different person."

"So, in *your expert opinion,* without the presence of the drone or the grail, Denny Song might *not be* dangerous?"

The whole courtroom grew dark except for a sunbeam spotlight shining on Hikaru. Denise desperately wished that the tarp was still up.

"Yes, it is my expert opinion that by clear and convincing evidence, Denny Song would *not* be dangerous."

"Pass the witness."

Denise looked around the courtroom. The judge had her phone down and was actually paying attention. Jane Dark walked slowly the podium.

Jane Dark wasn't intimidated by anyone. "You've been qualified as an expert, but your expertise is in astrophysics and not neuroscience."

"Rocket science is not brain surgery," Hikaru said with a smile, despite the sweat on his forehead. "But part of my work deals with how radiation from these drones affects the brain."

"So, he still might be dangerous, correct?" Jane Dark said. "Something else could set him off?"

"I have no way of knowing."

"And you haven't brought *any* of his military psychiatric records with you today, have you?"

"No, I have not. The records are missing. I have seen some, but I would not be permitted to share them with you."

"How convenient," Jane Dark said. "Other than this little video we've seen, the real records that would prove your conclusion can't be introduced into evidence today, correct?"

The whole courthouse was shaking. "They're already here!" Denny said. "Right above our heads."

"Again," Hikaru said. "I want to say in my expert and personal opinion, that Denny Song is NOT dangerous by clear and convincing evidence? What else do I have to prove?"

Everyone looked up. The deputies had their hands on

their guns, ready for Denny to give them a reason to open fire. Was that Plan B?

Jane Dark clutched her belly protectively and moved toward the state's table. "Pass the witness." She moved to an empty chair at the far side of her table as far away from the skylight as possible.

"Calm down, Denny!" Denise said, then put her hand on his shoulder.

He was fighting something within himself, but her touch was working wonders. "Thanks," he said, and nodded at her.

"What's going on?" Denise asked.

"They're coming back," Denny said. "That's their Plan B."

"May the witness be excused?" the judge asked.

Denise looked at Hikaru, who winced in pain as he nodded at her. She needed to ask him a question that she did not know the answer to, but she would have to lay a foundation first.

"You've seen these records?" she said.

"I have."

The judge looked up. "Can someone see what's happening on the roof? Maybe put the tarp back up?"

Caliban the bailiff hurried outside.

"So based on your experiences, was my client ever *violent* in these experiments?"

"He was not."

Time to take a leap of faith. "So what is the only thing that can make him violent?"

"The presence of *extraterrestrials*." Hikaru paused. "Well the presence of what he *perceives* as extraterrestrials."

Hikaru's phone rang, loud enough to be heard over the buzzing outside. That couldn't be good.

The judge said, "Didn't you say your phone was off?"

"I'm sorry, your honor, but my boss, well my ex-boss keeps calling me and *she* can override my phone in an emergency."

"Who is your ex-boss?" Denise asked.

Hikaru paused. He didn't want to give up the information, but he looked at Denise. Denise nodded at him. He looked up at the skylight shading his eyes.

"He's gonna say the name," the sheriff said, clearly agitated. "Plan B! Plan B!"

Hikaru took a deep breath. He was ready for Plan B, whatever it was. "My superior was Colonel Regan Herring, United States Air Force, (retired)," he said. "But you know her as Big Red."

Without missing a beat, Denny called out, "Regan was the daughter in *King Lear*, just like Cordelia."

Denise looked back at Rayne and Rita. Rayne looked genuinely shocked as if she had no idea of her mother's involvement. Rita nodded. "Duh," she said.

Rita looked out the window and put her hand over her eyes to cover the glare. Something was out there. Something was *up* there.

And then, Denise heard it. The hive sound above grew worse. No, it wasn't the roofers above who were causing it. Were they jumping off the roof?

"Auntie Denise!" Rita yelled. "You've got to save him! They're here, they're *really* here!"

Before Denise could figure out what was going on, Hikaru's phone let out a sudden pulse, like a shock wave. Denise fell over from the impact of this invisible force.

It was still the middle of the day, but the room went dark for a moment as if there was a total eclipse.

"Grab my hand," Denny said. "We're safe together, I just know it."

She grabbed his hand. Rita and Rayne hurried over and formed a protective circle. "*We're not going anywhere,*" Denise said.

Rita and Rayne joined in. "*We're not going anywhere.*"

"Hikaru!" Denise yelled, but he was too far away. He was stuck in the witness chair directly under the open air. Now she knew why she wanted the tarp to stay up there. She couldn't see him, and then there was a flash of lightning that came right through the skylight.

Everything went black again. Were they under attack? Somehow their circle of protective spark worked—it was like a forcefield against this tornado. Through the darkness, Denise swore that she saw Hikaru being lifted up through the skylight. But that was impossible, wasn't it?

Denise lost consciousness.

When she woke up, it was daylight in the courtroom again. She had no recollection of anything. Not again!

Where was Hikaru?

The courtroom benches were overturned. A baby cried. During the commotion, Jane Dark had given birth and was holding her newborn.

"It's a miracle," Jane Dark said.

The judge looked at Denise and then over at Jane Dark.

"*We* seem to be all right," Jane Dark said. "Somebody get an ambulance!"

"What just happened?" the judge asked. "I have no recollection."

It was all fuzzy for Denise too. What had happened?

"Where's Hikaru?" Denise asked. The witness chair was empty. The skylight was still open.

"Should we come back?" Jane Dark asked.

"Finish up right now," the judge said. "Closing arguments?"

"Your honor," Denise said, standing up, but too much in shock to go up to the podium. "I think you've seen how these incidents can affect people. They are unpredictable. I think we have no choice but to release my client and dismiss the case."

Jane Dark was looking at her little miracle. Denny's case no longer mattered to her. "You're going to be a great lawyer someday, Jean Dark, Jean Dark."

"Counsel?" the judge said, looking wonderingly at the newborn in Jane Dark's arms. "Ms. Dark?

Jane Dark didn't look up, didn't really care anymore. "I'll defer to the court."

The judge looked down at her phone. "I'm going to take this under advisement and email you my decision later in the day. I might have to send it to you from Santa Fe."

Rita dragged her mother out the door. "We got to see what's happening outside."

The guards started to take Denny away. "Thank you," Denise said to him.

"Thank you," he said. "No matter what happens, you're a great lawyer and a great sister."

* * *

The door closed behind him.

Denise walked out of the courtroom feeling triumphant, she was cautiously optimistic that Denny would soon be free. Yet, there was something about the air outside. It smelled terrible.

It smelled like charred flesh. It smelled like death.

There in front of the courthouse, she noticed a crowd surrounding a body on the ground. She pushed her way through and gasped.

Sure enough, it was Hikaru. He was a bloody mess, as if he'd been dropped from the sky.

"Is he dead?" Denise asked.

Denise felt like the sky had dropped on her. Hikaru, her great love Hikaru, was dead. A line from Shakespeare floated through her cloud-filled mind: "To die, to sleep; To sleep perchance to dream: ay, there's the rub; For in that sleep of death what dreams may come..."

She felt a pulling on her sleeve and looked down to see Rita. "My grandma did this. I just know it."

"I won't let her get away with it," Denise said. But what could she do?

PART V

LOVE'S LABOUR'S LOST

Chapter 59

It was almost an anti-climax when the judge emailed Denise moments later. She must have been texting and driving on the freeway as it took a few tries. But finally, Denise could ascertain from the texts that Denny Song's case would be dismissed *with* prejudice, and that Denny would be released forthwith.

Forthwith…

Still in shock, Denise had to look the word up again to understand that her brother would get out *immediately.*

Then again, it might take an hour or so to "process" his release. It always did. Despite all the effort and emotion she'd put into the case, Denny could wait. Denise stood in the parking lot until the EMTs took Hikaru's body away on a stretcher, his head covered.

Denise considered the thermos in her car. She knew that the Holloman lake water could save some people, but Hikaru's charred body was too far gone for that. Dead was dead sometimes.

She walked over to the rear of the ambulance and waved good-bye to the body. The EMT gave her a moment to look at the body, then slammed the doors forever shut. She gave herself a moment to cry.

She could have loved him. Hell, she did love him. He was her one great forever love. *Kinda.*

She went back inside the courthouse and threw up in the bathroom toilet, and then threw up again. When she emerged into the daylight a few minutes later, her phone rang. It was Denny calling from jail. "Can you pick me up?"

"Hikaru's dead," she said.

"You never talked about him, but I could sense that he

meant a lot to you. I'm sorry for your loss. I know he did a lot to help my case. So, I feel it too."

"Thank you," she said. The fact that her brother expressed concern made her cry even more.

"I can get Cordelia to pick me up," he said. "If you need some time, I understand."

"I'll pick you up," she said. "It's my case. You are my client. You are my brother."

Rayne, Dew and Rita stood by where the body had been, staring down as if Hikaru was still there. Denise took their hands. "Team Turquoise," she said.

"Team Turquoise," they replied. Did she hear Hikaru's baritone in the mix?

Rayne and Rita got in Rayne's car and drove off. Dew gave Denise a hug. "I'm so sorry, he may have been a wierdo, but he was your weirdo," Dew said. "What are you going to do now?"

"I'm going to pick up my brother," Denise said.

"I'm going home," Dew said. "I probably should go back to rehab, but I need to do some drugs first."

Dew got into her own car and drove away.

Denise now drove over to the detention center. Cordelia was waiting at the prisoner release door. When Denny emerged, he looked back and forth between the two women as if this was the finale of *The Good, the Bad and the Ugly*. Was she the good or the bad? Neither woman said a word, it was his choice.

There was something different about her brother. She had expected him to be jittery with excitement, but he was calm—as if he expected this all along.

"Take me to see our mom," he said to Denise. "Is she in the hospice yet?"

"If she was, they would have told me, right?"

* * *

On the drive to Las Cruces, Denny stayed quiet. Inside the automatic hospital doors, the ancient concierge stopped them before they were past the welcome mat. She summoned Piranha the security guard and then paged Dr. Patel.

"Make sure they don't go anywhere," the concierge said to Piranha.

"I'm free!" Denny said. "I want to see my mom now!"

Piranha didn't budge until Dr. Patel came down to greet them.

"Can we see her?" Denise asked. "This might be our last chance."

Dr. Patel checked something on her tablet and frowned. "Take a minute with your mother, and then come up to my office, there's something I need to talk to you about."

"Thank you," Denise said. "We won't do anything to upset her, will we Denny?"

"I'm all good," he said. Piranha followed them up, just to make sure they didn't cause a scene.

Inside the hospital room, Jen Song looked even more skeletal. Piranha nodded at Denny. "I guess it doesn't matter now," he said. "She's as good as dead."

"Why don't you give us a minute?" Denise said to Piranha. "Like you said, it doesn't matter anymore."

"Why are you such a dick to us?" Denny asked.

"Because every time you come here things get out of *control*," he said. "And my job is about controlling the hospital, so the doctors can save lives."

Denise was able to gain insight from Piranha's red face. She could literally read him like a book with his glare. Patients had indeed died here in the hospital—stabbings, shootings even—that were an extension of border gang wars and what not. With his law enforcement and military background, she sensed that he was brought on board to lay down the law. That didn't make her like him any better.

Denny went to the bedside and took Jen's hand. "I'm going to make you *so* proud of me," Denny said.

The skeleton didn't move.

"What do you want us to do?" Denise asked. "How can we save you?"

The beeping from their mother's machines increased. Hopefully, that was a good thing. Jen's eyes were moving rapidly under the lids.

"What are you saying, mom?" Denise asked. "Do you

know what happened today? Does it have something to do with that?"

Jen blinked her eyes again, one time. Without any prompting on Denise's part, her phone switched to a Wikipedia entry on Colonel Regan "Big Red" Herring. The colonel was indeed the CEO of an American affiliate of Cygnus Moon and thus Hikaru's boss. Was Big Red ultimately responsible for killing Hikaru? Was Big Red the key to saving Jen?

Or both?

"Why is the colonel so important, Mom?" Denise asked.

Jen's body shook as if even the effort of thinking about Big Red strained every muscle in her body, every muscle in her soul. And then it hit Denise. She remembered that she hadn't been able to unlock the center square of the interface she'd received from the Alpha grail. Hikaru had said she wouldn't be able to retrieve it until he was dead.

"Denny take my hand," she said. "There's something you need to see."

He looked both ways in the hallway. Piranha must be making his rounds somewhere else in the building. Dr. Patel was waiting for them in her office. Dr. Schwartz was probably cramming for finals somewhere. Denny shut the hospital room door.

"Why are you doing that?" Denise asked.

"Shouldn't she be a part of this?" Denny asked, pointing to their mother.

Denise was hesitant, but what could it hurt? She and Denny both touched their mother's hand at the same time and closed their eyes.

With her mind's eye, Denise could see the tic-tac-toe board and a black box in the center square. There was a lock on the box. Did she need a password?

"Hikaru," she said out loud. "I love you."

The lock disappeared. The box opened. Everything went black...

Chapter 60

"This isn't a dream," Denise said to Denny as they opened their eyes. "This is real."

It was strange, but Denise, Denny and their mother were still in her hospital room, but they were also present (in spirit?) at New Shakespeare Ranch, as if they were looking into the opened box. Jen Song was still lying in the bed, but she had lifted her head up, fully conscious.

"Can you talk, mom?" Denise asked.

Jen blinked twice. There was a mist on the top of the box. Denise sensed that Hikaru's consciousness was literally in the air. Somehow, he was helping them to access whatever was going on at the ranch.

Denise recognized some of the dozen or so people in the crowd below. The Groundlings, including Fally, were there. They now sported white tank-tops, displaying their tattoos of monsters and aliens. Some of those tattoos were writhing around the body parts. They stood around a campfire on a crisp desert night.

"We're to remain here pending further orders," a voice said. Denise knew that voice from somewhere. "Let me see if they are sending further instructions."

On the other side of the fire, Denise recognized Colonel Regan "Big Red" Herring, United States Air Force (retired), Board of Directors in Cygnus Moon Inc, CEO of Helmsman Inc, Candidate 3rd Congressional District (Independent). The colonel was addressing the campfire crowd, her hand holding the handle of the Omega Grail which stood on the boulder.

Their focus inside the box grew sharper as if Hikaru was helping them to get better reception until there was an extreme close-up on the colonel.

"I can *read* her," Denise directed a thought at Denny.

"*We* can read her," Denny thought back at her.

Jen, still in her bed, blinked once.

"Let's focus," Denise said. "Look directly at the colonel."

"Won't she notice?" Denny asked.

"I hope not."

By focusing on the colonel's forehead, they received a burst of information. The colonel was one of the last of the original settlers who came here to the New Shakespeare Ranch in 1947, the same year as the Roswell incident. The colonel was *human*, but it was unclear whether she was originally cloned, genetically engineered or any of that. Even the colonel didn't know.

There were only two of the pure bloods left from the Lordsburg incident in 1947: the colonel and the sheriff. After landing and finding out that they were near a place called Shakespeare, New Mexico, the "settlers" had received orders to take Shakespearean names as a "way of blending in."

From the Colonel's disdain etched across her face, it was clear these orders from afar didn't always make sense. The colonel was over a hundred years old, but she was not immortal. The third remaining original settler, Cordelia's dad, Dogberry Dunsinane, had died recently of "natural causes." Time was becoming an enemy in the settlers' master plan.

Denise looked out at the Groundlings on the other side of the bonfire. Apparently, the original settlers couldn't reproduce amongst themselves, but they could "mate" with humans. So, this bunch were the second generation. Some were even from the third. Unfortunately, the latter generations were all too human; they had a weakness for alcohol and drugs among other human vices.

She recognized Hotspur, the guard from the cemetery. He was one of *them.* So was Caliban the bailiff from the courthouse and desk clerk at the Holiday Comfort, and his counterpart Titus from the Last Palm. She recognized a few others from around town, even the cops that Denny had shot who looked surprised to be there. Was everybody in the town in on it and didn't know it till now?

It was as if Big Red's feelings had seeped out of the box

and into the hospital room. Denise sensed the colonel's existential angst, her disappointment in the subsequent generations, and almost felt sorry for the woman. Big Red alone among the group touched the grail and received the vision messages. Big Red alone had to interpret the cryptic messages from the great beyond. Because of the vast interstellar distance, she was never sure of exactly what was wanted.

"Still waiting," the colonel said out loud to the Groundlings and the others. "I'm giving them another minute."

"We're always waiting," Fally said. "And half the time the message doesn't make sense."

Denise, Denny and Jen Song kept staring down through the box on the scene as if watching a chess match, but these pieces were alive and moving.

"I'm getting *something*," Big Red said. "We can use *lethal* force if they come here. The Song twins were an experiment that is coming to an end. They will be coming here to get the grail."

"What happens when they do?" the sheriff asked.

"We can *terminate* the experiment," Big Red said. "Or as we said back in my old job, we terminate with *extreme prejudice*."

The Groundlings murmured in agreement. The colonel closed her eyes, apparently sending a message of confirmation back. "Over and out."

Colonel Regan "Big Red" Herring kept her hand on the grail for one last moment. "We've got to stand together; remember we are *family*."

She took her hand off the grail. The cloud disappeared. The box closed on itself. Denise, Denny and Jen were thrust out of the colonel's brain, out of the box and back into the hospital room. The box itself disappeared.

While her mom's head had been raised up, *conscious*, in the vision, it was back to its original position, her eyes opened, but staring into space blankly.

"Did you get that?" Denise asked Denny.

He nodded. They looked at their mother, who blinked one eye.

"What was that?" Denny asked.

"I think Hikaru had set it up so he—we—would see what happened when someone touched the grail."

"But he's dead," Denny said.

"I guess he could only have that connection after he was dead," Denise said.

"Was that ummm... live?" Denny asked.

"I don't think so. But it seems pretty recent." This wasn't quite live, but they were unsure how Hikaru had replicated this experience. His powers combined with his access to tech were more powerful than they had imagined. "I bet he could only get a connection when someone touches a grail, and only after he died."

"Well, the colonel knows we are going to get the grail, and they'll terminate us with extreme prejudice when we get there. What does that mean?" Denny asked.

"They can kill us. They *will* kill us."

Jen blinked at them twice, then did it again and again.

"But if we *don't* go, she'll die," Denny said.

Jen blinked again.

"So, if we go there and bring the grail back, we can save you?" Denise asked.

Jen blinked again.

Someone knocked on the door. They both jumped. "We have permission to be here!" Denny said.

It was Dr. Patel, backed up by Piranha. "I think both of you need to come with me."

"Are you gonna terminate my mom?" Denny asked.

Chapter 61

Dr. Patel's fourth floor office had a nice view of the lights of Las Cruces twinkling in the desert night. Denise was disoriented. There were also some lights going *upward* in the distance above the city lights, and Denise didn't know if they were coming from the missile range, the spaceport, or Lordsburg.

"Please have a seat," the doctor said to Denise and Denny and directed them to the plush chairs. Piranha stayed in the room, chewing on an unlit cigarette, which made the twins uneasy.

"Is something wrong?" Denise asked.

"I'm afraid there is," Dr. Patel said. "Your mother's condition is worsening. She had a *Do Not Resuscitate* form on file. However, we need another signature as an assurance per our malpractice carrier. I'm calling her POA to sign the form to take her off life support."

"But she just blinked!" Denny said. "She knows what's going on! She wants to live!"

"It was probably a random muscle contraction," the doctor said. "She's brain-dead."

"I'm her daughter, he's her son," Denise said. "I was there, she blinked several times, and nodded at us several times." Denise neglected to tell the doctor that this was in the psychic vision.

"I don't want my mother to die," Denny said. "I won't sign shit!"

"*We* won't sign sh… anything!" Denise said.

The Doctor lifted up a piece of paper and pointed to a signature. "That's not your decision. We have a medical POA that gives the ultimate decision to her cousin, Susie Song.

329

Susie Song returned to Korea to get your mother's affairs in order and is flying back on the next available flight to El Paso. As you might expect, that is not a direct flight. She said she will return here tomorrow to sign the form to take your mother off life support and let nature take its course."

"Why don't you two take a night?" Dr. Patel said. "You can come back tomorrow to say good-bye to your mother when your cousin arrives. You can all be here as a family for her passing. Your mother would like that."

"No, she wouldn't!" said Denny. "She would want to live."

Chapter 62

As they walked out to the parking lot, they were surprised to see Rayne and Rita pull up in the Regal and park in a handicapped space. Rayne gingerly exited the car, cradling a thermos in her left arm. She had a cane in another.

Rayne gestured to them with her free hand. "We only have a minute," Rayne said. "Let's talk in the light."

Under a flickering streetlight, Rayne and Denny had an awkward reunion. Denny went in for a hug, but Rayne offered a handshake. Rayne kept Rita behind her with her pointed elbow.

"Why are you here?" Denise asked.

"I want Rita to see her grandmother before she dies." Rayne said. "Her *other* grandmother."

"I have a right," Rita said.

"Did you know about the colonel?" Denise asked.

"I swear to you that I didn't," Rayne said. "I always sensed it though. I always knew she was disappointed in me. It's like she didn't trust me to bring me into the conspiracy."

"You should take that as a compliment, mom," Rita said. Still behind her mother's elbow, she wiped away a tear. "I like your mom, Auntie Denise. She was famous once for being a lawyer. I want a real grandma, not some crazy colonel who is probably collaborating with alien invaders."

"She *is* human, but she's like a collaborator with them alien invaders," Denny said. "And you guys are descended from them. No offense, Rita."

"None taken," Rita said. "But collaborator or no, I sure feel like a real little girl."

"You are a real little girl," Denise said. "No one said you're not human. Just that your mom is one of the bad guys."

"I'm still in shock about the whole thing," Rayne said. "I still haven't figured out if my mom didn't bring me in to protect me or didn't think I was good enough to be a bad guy. I do think she was grooming Rita to take over from her someday."

Denise looked at her tall, awkward niece. Rita would grow into greatness someday, she just hoped it would be for the right side. But how?

"Can you help us?" Denny asked Rayne. He looked at Rita. "I tried to call you so many times, but your mom never let me get through."

"I know," Rita said. "That was the colonel's doing."

"Are you on our side or her side?"

"My mother was always disappointed in me," Rayne said. "I was one of them in a way by birth, but I balked at belonging to them by choice. Did my own thing. Made my own mistakes."

She didn't look at Rita. Denny frowned.

"My real first name is *Rosalind*," Rayne continued. "After the girl in some play. I always went with my middle name because well, I liked the rain. But I'm on one side and I've always been on the same side, my Rita's."

Rita nodded. "Wow, thank you mom."

"How come Rita didn't have one of them Shakespeare names?" Denny asked.

"The colonel wanted to name her *Portia*, but I told her I didn't want to name my daughter after a *car*."

Denise got the reference to *The Merchant of Venice*, Denny's quizzical look indicated that he didn't. She could sense the awkwardness. Denny and Rayne had had a one-night stand years ago. Both had gone in different directions in life, and they only had one thing in common, Rita.

"I want my daughter to be proud of me," Denny said.

"You can be." Rayne frowned. "But right now, I've got a feeling that you're going to have to go against my family and I don't want to be there when that happens. Like I said, everything I do is for my little girl, to keep her safe. I don't know if I want either of you in her life right now."

Rayne opened the thermos she had been holding. By smell alone, Denise knew it was the toxic lake water.

"This stuff is keeping me alive," Rayne said. She chugged it. "Rita, let's get this over with and take you up and meet your *other* grandmother before she dies."

Rita tried to pull away for a final hug with her father and auntie, but her mother dragged her inside the hospital.

Denise and Denny tried to follow Rayne back inside, but Piranha was sitting outside the lobby door. "I have orders not to let you two back in until further notice."

"From Dr. Patel?"

"From Susie Song, the Power of Attorney. She gets in tomorrow; you can talk to her then."

"Is she scared we're going to rescue our mom?" Denny asked.

"I told her about you two," Piranha said. "Like I said, I've got to keep control of your mother, make sure she's alive when this Susie Wong or whatever gets here."

"We're trying to make sure she's alive too," Denise said.

"After that power of attorney chick gets here and signs the appropriate form in front of the doctor, it's beyond my control. She dies, she dies, it's not on my watch."

* * *

Denny and Denise sat down outside on the bench under that rickety light. An ambulance hurried into the emergency lane, lights blaring. On the other side of the hospital a hearse drove out.

"Now what?" Denny asked. "I have no place to go right now. I thought freedom would be better, but it's like even worse. I don't like being an experiment."

Denise looked at her brother and then at the hospital. She wasn't sure if she could pick out her mother's room above. She could still smell the lingering odor of the lake water from Rayne's thermos. She thought about Hikaru and the grail and had an idea.

"Well maybe the experiment is that we're supposed to save our mother by getting the grail," Denise said. "It's our destiny. We've got to go to the ranch. We sneak in and both touch the grail at the same time, and then fill it with the lake water. We then bring it back to our mom and pour it on her to make sure some gets inside her mouth so it can work its magic inside her body."

"My whole life has been for this moment, to meet my mom, to make her proud of me," Denny replied. "But aren't the bad guys waiting for us? Do you think they'll try to kill us?"

Denise frowned. "Maybe we do a distraction or whatever when we get there. Like, what happened with the Greeks when they tried to conquer the Trojans."

"A Trojan whore?" Denny asked.

"Trojan *horse*," Denise said. She touched Denny's hand as if that would help with the plan. "Do you have any idea on how we can do it?"

Denny now got excited. "We use like decoys in the front, so they don't know we're coming around the back. Maybe Cordelia can come."

"I don't know if that would work. Would she even be willing to do that?"

Before Denise could even ponder the efficacy of a plan out of a bad movie, Denny grabbed her phone. After five minutes of pleading, Denny smiled. "She'll do it. She might not be enough. We probably need more of a distraction than that. Do you know anyone else who can help?"

Denise thought for a moment. Cordelia would be a minor distraction, but not enough. They needed something, *someone,* bigger, more distracting? Was there anyone she knew who could literally stop the world?

Chapter 63

After some furious texting, Denise and Denny went down the street to Dew's complex. Dew had texted that she would be down in a minute.

"Are you sure about this?" Denny asked. "Why do we want to see your cousin? Cordelia said she wants us to pick her up real soon back at her motel over in Lordsburg or she ain't coming. I still think she'll be enough. She comes in through the front gate of the ranch, they go toward her and then we sneak in the back."

Denise would never trust Cordelia. "Wait one more minute. And who said we were waiting to see my cousin?"

Dew finally emerged from an apartment on the first floor, directly below her own. Dew was carrying her cat, Sahar. Sahar now had a little vest that said COMFORT ANIMAL. The cat held the plush laser cat toy in her mouth like a dead mouse.

"What is she going to do?" Denny said.

"It's not her, it's her friend."

"Friend?"

On cue, Petro emerged from the apartment. Denise almost didn't recognize him. He looked well... sober. He was wearing a loose Hawaiian shirt that had flying saucers hovering over the waves, with aliens on longboards. One of the surfers had a caption labeling him the "Aloha-alien."

"Hey cousin," he said to Denise. Denise didn't know if she wanted the Aloha-alien to marry into the family.

"You're that guy who went away to college to be an astrophysicist," Denny said. Petro was a few years older than Denny and knew each other only vaguely. Being an astrophysicist was the apex of professions in Denny's view. "Did

335

you graduate?"

"Do I look like I graduated?" Petro said.

"What is the plan?" Dew asked, clearly impatient.

"It's simple," Denise said. "We pick up Cordelia at her motel and she gives us the scouting report. And then Cordelia and Petro act as a distraction at the entrance to the ranch. All the Groundlings come out to greet them. Meanwhile, Denny and I sneak around the back, duck under the barb wire and touch the grail and bring it back. You and Sahar stay behind as a look out and getaway driver."

"Sounds simple," Dew said. "Is that it?"

Denise nodded. "Then we drive like hell back to the hospital, pour the lake water from the thermos into the grail and pour it on my mom's face so hopefully some gets inside. All before Cousin Susie pulls the plug."

Sahar purred. The plan sounded good to her.

"That is the stupidest thing I've ever heard," Petro said. "I'm in."

"Remind me to bring my staff," Denise said. "I'm driving everyone. We're taking one car."

Denise was starting to like being in charge, she liked channeling Hurricane Luna.

"Don't forget to pick up Cordelia," Denny said.

"I wonder how she feels about going back to the beginning of all this madness," Denise said.

Chapter 64

Saturday, August 15

Cordelia thought back to the night that started this whole adventure, overlooking the ranch when Denny went crazy. If only she had given Denny the phone instead of the gun. She wondered if she'd made the right choice.

She wondered if she was making the right choice now. She was going against her family now.

It was after midnight, and Denise's carload of people had just arrived. Cordelia was waiting in the Last Palm parking lot, all alone. She was in her usual cowgirl outfit but had gone with sneakers instead of boots. She might have to run for it this time.

"This car smells like shit," Cordelia said. "I was about to go back to sleep. Are you guys sure about this?"

"We're sure," Denny said to Cordelia. "Are you?"

"I don't know." It had been one thing when it was just the sheriff and his goons, but now the Groundlings were there. She'd never liked them. She had never really known what this was all about, although she'd always suspected something illegal. What was worse than illegal?

She'd seen some weird stuff when her father had his "meetings." She had always assumed that the meetings had something to do with the Klan or God knows what. She had given them all a wide berth. Hell, part of the reason she hooked up with Denny was to give her family the finger.

She remembered the magnetism—or whatever weird force it was—she'd always felt when the old timers had gathered with her dad and then closed the door. She could feel it through the walls even. Something drew her in, but through sheer force of will she had pushed it away. Perhaps it was the strain that led her to the drugs, led her to Denny.

Cordelia waited another moment and then squeezed herself in the back seat with Denny and Petro. She gave Petro a cramped hug.

"So, you know Petro here?" Dew asked.

"We're cousins," she said.

Petro nodded. "We used to be close. They run people out of town sometimes if we don't quite fit in. That's kinda why I drink and drug so much. It's a long story."

They drove in silence for another mile south of town until they came to the park under the cylindrical water tower, on the other side of the ranch.

"Drop me and Petro off here," she said. There was still time to run away back into town. She wanted to figure out what Petro would do first.

Her cousin Petro had been brilliant at one time, but alcohol and other drugs had dulled his senses, dulled his abilities. While many of her cousins had had drug issues and died, it was amazing that he was still alive. Then again, she was no stranger to drugs either. She was a miracle of survival as well.

They parked by the old military tank at the entrance to the park. Cordelia did not get out. "So, what's the plan again?" she asked Denny.

"You guys go in front and pretend that you're happy to see them," Denny said. "I'm betting that your spark or whatever Denise calls it, confuses them."

Petro looked confused. "Huh?"

Denny was not good at explaining the plan. Denise knew she'd have to take over. She made eye contact with Petro so she could penetrate his defenses. "You know how when you say, 'We're not going anywhere,' and somehow your sheer force of willpower can influence people?"

"I guess so," he said. "It's not like I'm doing that on purpose."

"Well do that," Denise said. "Do it on purpose."

"I don't know how I do that," he said. "I'm usually messed up."

Cordelia touched his arm. "We'll figure it out," she said. "I'll help. But what will you do while we distract them?"

"We'll sneak around the back and get to the grail," Denise said.

"That's not much of a plan," Cordelia said. "Don't you think that's what they're expecting you to do?"

* * *

Cordelia and Petro walked to the front gate as Dew parked. Petro started emanating his spark, and somehow that triggered Cordelia. She had been nauseous the last time, but this time she channeled the sickness, so it radiated outward rather than inward.

Dozens of the old timers came over to greet them when they arrived at the gate. Being so close to so many relatives, it felt familiar, it felt like home.

For one moment, she thought of telling her relatives the true purpose of her return to the ranch. Did she really love Denny that much to risk everything?

She didn't have to think about it. She did love him, loved him for what he could have become if it wasn't for all of this. She also remembered that she hated home. Hated her father, hated what he did to Denny. Hated what he did to her. Hated what all these people did to her and would do to the earth.

"*We're not going anywhere*," Petro said. He took her hand.

Cordelia thought of Denny one more time. She did love him. This might be the last best chance to save him.

"*We're not going anywhere*," Cordelia agreed.

Whatever they did attracted the Colonel's attention, but that wasn't necessarily a good thing. She stared at them.

"Welcome home," Colonel Herring shouted to Cordelia and Petro, clearly suspicious. She was hanging back by the grail. "Why are you here?"

Petro laughed. "Just here to do my part. Rally and regroup for the Shakespeare crew."

While the Groundlings gathered around Cordelia and Petro, the colonel stayed put and kept glancing around everywhere like her own radar. She gestured to the sheriff to stay alert.

"Why now?" the colonel asked. "And you still haven't answered me why are *you* here, Cordelia. You know you can't go home again ever since..."

"Ever since I hooked up with Denny," she said.

Before the colonel could reply, that damn drone appeared in the sky and the grail started to glow...

"There it is!" Sheriff Diamond shouted, adjusting his glasses. "Look up there over the water tower! Look sharp everyone, it's happening again!"

Cordelia suddenly felt a whole new part of her brain being accessed and she wasn't sure that she liked it. Still, it was all starting to make sense... She realized that all of them were in very great danger. The nausea returned, and for one brief moment, she shifted out of reality into a void and then back again.

The colonel reached for her sidearm. The object in the air was like nothing they'd ever seen before. It must have come from even deeper under the water tower.

Cordelia grew even more apprehensive this time. What would this new drone or UFO or whatever it was do to Denny?

The sheriff had a rifle, he wasn't going to delegate this time. Earl the dog had appeared out of nowhere and stood by his master's side.

While they might have distracted the Groundlings, the Colonel and the sheriff were ready to stand their ground, take out the twins and feed the roadkill to Earl.

Cordelia looked at Petro. She would have to choose a side. "We're not going anywhere," he said.

"We're not going anywhere," she replied. She couldn't help but look around her. Where were Denny and Denise?

Chapter 65

After they dropped off Cordelia and Petro, Dew and Sahar stayed in the car by the park and stationed themselves behind the old tank as if its rusty turret could protect them. Meanwhile, Denise and Denny walked up the hill to the cylindrical water tower to do some recon. Sneaking a peek around the curve of the cylinder, Denny pointed to Petro and Cordelia as they made it to the front gate down below.

His prediction was correct, Petro and Cordelia caused some kind of electrical disruption, and their opponents were momentarily distracted. Well, except for the Colonel and sheriff who were still on high alert.

Denny pointed to the break in the fence on the other side of the ranch. "We can go around this way and under that fence. We've got to do it now."

Was it too late? Denise heard rumbling from down below, and the sound of water rushing above their heads. That damn drone suddenly appeared in the sky over the cylindrical water tower. This drone was even bigger, more intimidating. Had it materialized out of the air or from another dimension? Denise figured that they had maybe thirty seconds, a minute max, to make it to the other side of the ranch, use her staff to part the wires and then touch the grail.

"It's happening again!" Denny said.

Down below, the grail emitted pulses of energy, waves that hit them directly. Denny started to close his eyes as if he was being possessed again. Denise felt the urge to vomit.

Denise tried to settle her upset stomach by sheer force of will. "Take my hand," grabbing his hand in hers. That gave her strength.

Denny opened his eyes. She could see the conflict inside

him as he struggled to maintain control.

"We're not going anywhere," she said. She squeezed his hand tighter and felt her spark combine with his. He blinked his eyes struggling to keep them up.

"Denny, stay with me."

There were a few more blinks and then Denny kept his eyes wide open. "We're not going anywhere," he agreed.

Still holding hands, they hurried around the outskirts of the ranch, hugging the fence, and made it to the arroyo. Above, the drone hovered, waiting for directions from the other side of the galaxy. The presence of the Groundlings, the Colonel and the sheriff combined with the newcomers all created a perfect storm. There was too much psychic energy, too much electricity, for anyone, for any *entity* to control.

The drone darted in one direction, and then another. It spun on its axis and wobbled overhead, and wild lightning emerged in all directions.

In the confusion, Denny and Denise made it around back without being detected. Denise parted the fence wires with her staff, and the two ducked under.

They were now only a few feet from the grail. That must have triggered the drone. The lightning coalesced into a single spotlight and that spotlight shined directly upon them. The Groundlings turned around and spotted them. "Over there!"

"Get them!" the colonel yelled.

The Groundlings now marched toward Denny and Denise, Fally was in the lead. Hotspur the cemetery guard held his taser at the ready. Caliban hefted his boomerang.

Caliban threw it at them, but the boomerang came back right at him. Denise and Denny wondered if they had done that with the force of their will or whether Caliban had thrown it incorrectly.

The Colonel took out her gun that looked like it was a laser. She aimed, but the drone was now hovering over the grail. The light was so bright she had trouble making out the twins.

"We've got to keep going," Denny said. Denise took hold of Denny's hand and stepped up to the grail, but hesitated.

"Are you ready for this?" Denise asked.

"I guess so," Denny said. "Oh shit, look at Cordelia!"

Cordelia was walking in lockstep with the rest of the group. With Fally in the lead, they were only yards away and closing. Petro was caught up in it too and fell in behind the others. Was the drone directing the action with instructions from across the galaxy?

The colonel was still blinded by the light and the reflection off the grail. That didn't bother the sheriff. He had been waiting for this for months. Time to take Denny down for good. He played with his dark glasses as if giving a salute. "I can take them!"

"They're mine," the colonel said. "That's an order, sheriff. That little asshole knocked up my daughter! Once I can see again."

"We gotta do this now!" Denise said.

"I'm ready," Denny replied.

The colonel retreated a few feet away. Now that she had reached a better vantage point, she was ready.

"Good to go," she said. "I got this!" She fired.

Despite being at almost point-blank range, she missed. The shot was somehow absorbed into the grail.

"The grail's got a mind of its own," the colonel said.

Denise smiled, held Denny's hand tighter. "We got this," she told him.

"I got it colonel," the sheriff said. Denny and Denise were reaching for the grail as he fired his Glock with a few inches to spare.

"Concentrate!" Denise shouted at Denny.

"I am," he said.

Somehow the bullets also disappeared into the grail. Denny's and Denise's combined spark—somehow augmented by the presence of the drone and grail—had protected them. They wouldn't be able to keep that up forever.

The colonel fiddled with her weapon again. "Just need to adjust the setting."

"Cordelia!" Denny shouted. "I love you!"

And yet time had slowed. While they were only a few inches from the grail, and reaching towards it, Denny and

Denise couldn't make the final contact. It was like they were reaching into the void.

If Cordelia was under the control of the colonel, Denny's shouting must have broken the spell. Cordelia had broken away from the group and was bearing down on Big Red and the sheriff. "Don't fuck with my boyfriend," she said. "Or his sister."

The sheriff aimed the rifle. He wouldn't miss again.

Cordelia tackled the sheriff before he could fire. "This is my land, asshole."

The colonel now looked ready to take one last shot, but she was frozen as well. She looked to Petro for help.

"Petro, help me," the colonel yelled. "We're *family*."

"I'm not going anywhere," Petro said, and he blocked the Colonel's line of vision from the twins.

"We're family too, bitch," Denise said.

"We are!" Denny said.

The colonel was surprised that someone wasn't following her orders. In that moment of distraction, Denny and Denise gave one last push and touched the grail at the same time.

Denise felt a wave of energy pass through her, but it was different than before, more intense. Both of them fell to their knees.

And yet somehow, they both still held onto the grail. Denise was getting a vision of someone, *something*, beyond their consciousness.

The experiment is a success.

Who said that? It wasn't a voice; it was more of a feeling that was wired directly into their brains.

The Groundlings vanished one by one. First the purple man, then Fally, then Hotspur, Caliban and the others, and finally the sheriff himself.

Colonel Herring remained, but she looked like she was vibrating between two planes of existence. The colonel aimed her weapon at Denise and Denny one more time, but before she could fire, her hand disappeared, then her arm, until only her face remained...

"You will see me again!" she said, before her face vanished in a flash of light. "And my family."

Some metal objects had fallen to the ground where the colonel had stood. "Where's Cordelia?" Denny asked the heavens.

"Help!" It was Cordelia, she was lying on the ground. Petro next to her.

Cordelia and Petro oscillated one more time and then they too vanished.

"They were half-breeds." Denny said. "I hoped that they wouldn't be affected. I hoped that she wouldn't be affected."

"Are they dead?" Denise asked

"No, they've been transferred to another dimension," Denny said. "They'll be back like the colonel said."

"When?"

"I don't know. I figure the planet they come from is fifty light years away, so maybe in like a hundred years. Maybe less."

"You're making that up," she said.

"I am," he said. "But it makes sense, kinda..."

It suddenly hit him. "She was the only one whoever loved me." He nearly fainted from the shock as if it hit him all at once.

"I love you, Denny," Denise said. "And I've got a feeling that Rita will love you too."

They hugged and let it linger for a while. Both kept one of their hands on the grail.

But then it hit Denise. "What about Rayne and Rita? They might be gone too. We've got to get back to Cruces."

Chapter 66

They hurried back to the Kia. Dew was sitting in the driver's seat, petting her cat and playing with her phone. Sahar, her laser geisha toy blaster still in her mouth, nodded at them as if she understood exactly what had just happened.

She purred as if to say, the coast was clear.

Dew looked at Denise and the determined look on her face. "You drive," she said. "Where's Petro?"

"I'm sorry, Dew. I'm driving." Denise shook her head and practically lifted Dew out of the driver's seat. Once they were settled, Denise drove due east, directly into the sunrise.

The experiment is a success.

What did that mean? Were her and Denny the future of mankind or the end of the beginning?

She sure didn't feel like a success. She was tired, she was hungry, and her eyes ached from squinting into the morning sun. Denise kept her foot down on the gas pedal and prayed she wouldn't vomit into the windshield.

They made the one-hundred-twenty-mile drive in a little over an hour and a half. At least she still had her spark to avoid cop radar detection, or maybe it was something more. They were emitting so much of a spark that it was sending the radar right back at the detectors.

When they arrived at Centennial Hospital, Rita was waiting on a parking lot bench. "My mom is sick!" Rita said. "They took her to the emergency room and won't let me stay with her."

"Follow us," Denny said. "I got a feeling that if we save my mom, we'll save your mom too."

That made sense to Rita and she nodded. Still holding onto the grail between them, and the thermos of lake water in her other hand, Denise and Denny entered the sliding doors of the hospital. Rita was in hot pursuit. Would Jen Song even be there?

It might not matter whether Jen was alive or not at the moment; they could see the shuttle with Susie inside pulling up to the entrance, so she wouldn't be alive for long.

Piranha was waiting at the lobby entrance, ready to bite. For one brief moment, Denise worried that he was one of the Groundlings who had somehow developed immunity.

But one look at his snarl made her realize something. He was a small man who got to *control* this very small kingdom. He wasn't an alien; he was just an asshole.

Denise noticed that the grail was emitting some kind of steam. Just breathing it in made her spark stronger. "We've got a right to be here."

Piranha must have felt a wave of electricity pass right through him and he didn't like it. He backed away and let them pass. Still, he picked up his phone and was clearly dialing for reinforcements.

They didn't have much time before the cavalry came to the hospital. Unfortunately, there was a line of people in wheelchairs waiting at the elevator. Denise pointed to the stairs.

When they got to Jen's room, they found the whole clan waiting in the hallway. Hurricane Luna and Aunt Selena were there with several people they didn't recognize. The doctors were there as well, going through the forms. "We still need Susie to come in person," Dr. Schwartz said.

"What are you two doing?" Dr. Patel asked.

"Saving my mom," Denise said.

"Saving *our* mom," Denny added.

"Call security," the doctor said.

Denise glanced down the hall. Piranha was striding toward them, and he had brought the rest of the pack, armed with tasers. Jen Song might be dead in a few minutes, but she wouldn't be disturbed on his watch.

"Let's do this." Denise and Denny went inside Jen's room and up to her bed. Denise opened the thermos and poured it into the grail. It bubbled for a second, then Denise poured it over her mom's face. Hopefully, some of it would get into Jen's mouth.

Denny and Denise grabbed their mother's left hand. Time stood still. Had they ruptured the space-time continuum itself?

Jen opened her mouth, and some of the fluid flowed inside. She spit some out. Had they choked her? There was a burp, and then silence.

"Is she dead?" Denny asked.

"Did it work?" Denise asked.

Jen Song opened her eyes.

"Sorry we're late, mom," Denise said. "Traffic was a..."

"Denise!" Jen Song said as she recognized her daughter. "Where am I?"

It only took a second for Jen to look over at Denny. "Denny?" she asked.

At that moment, Susie Song entered the room like the angel of death in a gray business suit. "I have the notarized documentation to take Ms. Jen Song off life support," she said.

Jen threw off the wires and tubing connecting her to the machines. "That's fine by me," she said.

There were some more moments of confusion when Rayne entered as well. Rita hugged her and then faced Jen. "You don't know me, but I'm Rita, your granddaughter."

"I have a granddaughter?" For one moment, it looked like the shock of all the excitement would kill Jen Song for real. The doctor and the rest of the family crowded into the room, with looks of shock and amazement on their faces.

Denise and Denny hugged their mom. Did Jen get younger with their touch?

Dew entered the room, holding Sahar. "What's going on?"

Everybody was silent for a moment. Jen took a few deep breaths, closed her eyes for a moment and then opened them. "A miracle just happened,' she said. "I'm back."

Luna smiled. "Boy are we a close family."

Jen laughed as she hugged Denny close one more time. "I kinda knew that you'd come back someday, Denny. Did I ever tell you the story of how I gave you your name?"

Chapter 67
Sunday, August 16

Denise had mixed feelings about attending Hikaru's memorial service back in Albuquerque. He could have been the one for her, and instead of saying "I do," she was now saying good-bye.

Denise drove the Kia; Denny sat in the front with Rita in the rear. They were doing their best to bond as a family. Denny and Rayne had nothing in common except Rita and that might be enough. Rayne had recovered but was still hospitalized in Cruces as a precaution. The toxic lake water really worked.

Denise would keep some in her thermos there in the trunk of her car forever, regardless of the smell. Eventually they all got used to it. Dew had recently mentioned setting up a website so that they could probably make a few bucks selling it online—lasergeishawater.com.

Dew's last website idea had worked out, so Denise hadn't said no just yet.

"How about the other aliens or whatever they were? Are they really coming back?" Rita asked.

"They'll probably come back in a hundred years," Denny said. He then went into a lengthy discussion about the speed of light, constellations, and wormholes. Rita hung on every word.

"I'll be ready for them," Rita said.

"You do that. I probably won't be here when they do come back," Denise said with a grimace.

Her spark was off and on today, and she had a splitting headache. She had missed a text from Dew who'd gone up to

Albuquerque the night before.

WHERE WERE YOU? Dew had texted. THEY MOVED HIKARU'S MEMORIAL BECAUSE OF RAIN."

COMING ANYWAY, Denise texted back.

Sure enough, the other mourners were leaving the cemetery as the Kia arrived. It was pouring in Albuquerque, which was a relief after a long drought. Dew gave her a wave from her Mercedes. Sahar, still wearing that comfort animal vest, pointed the laser toy at Denise with her mouth, but it was done with love.

Denny and Rita stayed in the Kia and let Denise pay her respects alone out in the rain, sans umbrella. There was already a brick for Hikaru on the memorial wall. It was right next to Marley's.

As she walked toward the wall, Denise received a series of pings that must have come from Marley. She felt three pings and then nothing. It was not an SOS; it was an *over and out.*

She turned and tried to communicate with him, but she might as well be talking to a wall. "Goodbye, Marley," she said. "Hope you've finally gone to a better place."

Suddenly she had a vision. It was an image of a cyclist reaching the South Pole overlooking some kind of vessel buried in the ice.

"Hikaru?" she said out loud.

"It's me. Kinda," the voice was coming from the brick.

"They changed the times," she said out loud. "Sorry I was late, traffic..."

"Don't go there," he said. "I've got a feeling we'll be able to stay in touch."

She smiled. "I'd like that."

"By the way, congratulations!"

"On what?"

"You sure you're psychic?"

Denise reached inside of herself, and for the first time, she felt another spark. Actually two sparks. "Oh my god, I'm pregnant.

"How does that make you feel?"

"I'm going to be a mother. It's amazing."

"Kinda," they said in unity.

They conversed for a few more minutes, without making a sound. And then there was silence on his end. Hopefully, they would keep in touch. Denise nodded to the blank wall, turned around and walked back to the Kia.

Rita was worried. "You OK, Auntie Denise? I can't tell if you're happy or you're going to throw up."

"I'm pregnant," she said. "From Hikaru."

Rita smiled. "I need all the family I can get. What would the baby be, my first cousin?"

"*Cousins*," Denise nodded. "Going to be twins," she said. "I can tell. Just like us."

"That makes me an uncle," Denny said.

Denise looked at him with wide eyes.

He laughed. "Don't ask me to name them."

EPILOGUE
Thursday, November 26

Even after a few months, Denise was still getting used to this whole double pregnancy thing, but at least the family was being well, like a close family, a real family. They had finally become the clan she had always wanted. She might be a single mom-to-be, but she wasn't going through this all alone. It would take this village to raise her children.

She wasn't wearing black anymore, or even charcoal. She liked her maternity blouses in blue and pink—in honor of twins to be, one boy and one girl.

Denise had enrolled at UNM Law School and it was far more laid back then her last school. There were no cheetah moms on the faculty. Dew was also enrolled, actually doing her homework on her own which was a relief.

Taking a break from UNM law school with finals on their way, Denise was spending Thanksgiving in the living room of her mother's new house in the Sandia Heights neighborhood of Albuquerque. The home had an Asian flair with an Albuquerque accent, much like Jen herself. The living room even had a *yin-yang* gong made out of gold and turquoise. The Spanish tiles of the patio looked over an expansive view of Albuquerque in the valley below, past a bamboo fence.

Denise had invited Wu to cater the affair and he had arrived earlier that morning. He was in the kitchen, directing his staff on something called a *tom ka turkey* with spices from all over this planet and perhaps *off* planet as well. It smelled incredible.

Her Aunt Luna was no longer a hurricane, but still a bit of a drip. Luna just got off the phone with her ex, Dan the

352

Rattlesnake Lawyer, who apparently was off preparing for his big trial on a new case. From the sound of his rattling on about his client—a nurse's aide accused of killing a rich woman at an assisted living facility—it sounded like Dan deserved a book of his own. She sensed that it would be a dangerous adventure. Hopefully, Dan would survive that adventure so there wouldn't be a rattlesnake funeral.

Jen herself sat with her cousin Susie and the two were making small talk about their new endeavor—a class-action suit for factory workers harmed by radiation by Cygnus Moon all over the planet.

"I am so thankful to be here," her mother said to her cousin. "Actually, I'm so thankful to be *anywhere*."

"Sorry again about pulling the plug," Susie said for the ten millionth time. She was dressed in golf clothes and had just come off the links. She too had recovered but wasn't swinging for the stars anymore. She was happy to make par.

"You're forgiven, Susie," Jen said. "I'm thankful to be here with family."

"Me too," said Denise. "That's why they call it *Thanksgiving*, mom."

"Any ideas on naming *my* grandchildren?" Jen asked her.

"I have no idea," she said. "But they will be names that they can be proud of. The last thing I want is to give them joke names..."

"You were never a joke to me, Denise," Jen said. "Nor your brother. I think you've gone your whole life trying to prove that—your brother too—but you should have known that from the very beginning."

Denise wiped away a tear. It must be the hormones from pregnancy, right? She quickly got a hold of herself.

"They still need names," Jen said. "I may not have been the best mother, but I will be the best *grandmother* on earth. Or anywhere else for that matter."

Susie looked up from her phone. "Cygnus Moon came from a Greek myth about Zeus in the form of a Swan umm... hooking up with Leda, and the offspring were the Gemini twins—Castor and..."

"I'm not naming my daughter Pollux, or my son Castor

for that matter."

"*Polly* wouldn't be that bad," Susie said.

"If she was already a hundred years old," Denise said. "And she wanted a cracker."

"Well, I promise that I'll teach your twins how to golf," Susie said. "I owe that to you, and to them. Swing for the stars. Well, swing for the *moon* at least."

"I'd like that," Denise said. "They'll love it."

There was a knock on the door, which opened before anyone could answer it. "*Annyeonghaseyo,*" Denny said perfectly, as if he'd been rehearsing all day.

"Where's my Denny?" Jen asked.

"I'm here, mom," Denny said stumbling in with excitement. "With guests!" Rayne and Rita followed behind. They weren't quite a comfortable family yet. But they were working on it.

"Smells delicious," Rita said. "I like your Thanksgivings better than the ones we used to have with my *other* grandma."

Rayne shushed her.

"Dew is *allegedly* studying so she didn't come with us," Denny said. "Finals coming up."

"Tell me about it," Denise said. "I used to be a snob about people going to UNM, but law school is law school. Law is law."

"Someone had better pick up my wayward daughter, the legal scholar," Luna said, hanging up another call. "Her Mercedes is broken yet again. She needs to learn to put oil in it before it starts smoking. You're drafted Denise. Hurry back, dinner is in an hour, with or without her."

"I'll get her," Denise said. She patted her belly. "Save a drumstick for me. Well, save three drumsticks for *us.*"

Denise went outside into the crisp November air and got in her Genesis; the most luxurious Korean car ever made. It wasn't a Lexus, but it was shiny black and dent free.

* * *

Dew lived in a rental home by the law school, with a view of the wooded UNM north golf course and out to the

Sandia Mountains beyond. It was actually close to the Mental Health Center so she could monitor her Crotaladone use and do a pre-hab if need be.

Dew was paying her own way, tutoring UNM students for their LSAT exams on the side. She'd even developed a computer program that taught aspiring law students how to work the logic games portion of the test while they slept. She was thinking of adapting the program for teenagers and maybe even younger.

"You can give your kids a head-start by listening to the bar review tapes while you sleep," Dew constantly told Denise. "They'll grow up to be lawyers, whatever their names are."

Denise felt homesick as she pulled into Dew's driveway. It was near the group home where Denise had lived with her late grandmother during the earliest years of her life. She sure hoped that her own children wouldn't spend their lives without their mother like she did. If Jen was going to be the best grandmother, Denise would keep her end of the bargain by being the best mother.

She touched her belly. "What should I call you both?"

They didn't answer.

"How about Sonny and *Daughter-y*?" Denise said. She felt a kick and then another. They didn't like that one bit.

Feeling a bit dizzy, she knocked on the door.

"Come in! I'm in the shower," Dew yelled from inside.

"Hurry up! Your mom said she'd start eating without you!"

"Luna will wait," Dew yelled. "By the way, how about *Yin* and *Yang* as names for the twins?"

"Racist, much?" Denise laughed.

"But you should go with names that both start with the same letter, like my cats, Sahar and Suri."

Dew had replaced the old Suri with a new cat—same coloring and same name. The new cat was making a deposit in the litter box, but it was the same old Sahar, who must be hiding somewhere...

The place wasn't quite a sty, but not much had changed since Dew moved to the big city. There was still a gigantic computer in the middle of the room, but it was surround-ed by law books and CDs for the LSAT students. Dew still claimed that computers would replace lawyers, but not anytime soon. There was a framed photo of Petro in his Alo-ha-alien surfing shirt.

"Just sit down on the couch," Dew yelled over the water.

Denise was so busy looking around at the mess that she didn't look down before she sat on a blanket. She heard a bloodcurdling squeal, and jumped right back up, realizing that she must have sat on poor Sahar under the blanket.

Denise was unsteady on her feet after her leap up off the couch. Worse, Sahar was startled, her green eyes unfocused, and the cat leapt up landing on Denise's bulging belly. They both toppled her over. As Denise fell over, Sahar scratched her while trying to regain her balance. Could cats have ven-om in their claws?

It was too much. Denise fainted. Would the twins be all right?

* * *

Denise wasn't sure where or *when* it was when she awoke and stood up. She couldn't tell if it was night, or maybe she was actually out on some distant planet. She saw lights streaking by, a thousand shooting stars were falling on this location.

"They're finally coming," a voice said.

Denise looked around. "Who are you?"

"It's me, *Sahar*," a woman standing in front of her said.

It took a moment, but Denise recognized Sahar by her green eyes. The cat had taken human form and the laser gei-sha cat toy weapon was now a real laser. The human Sahar appeared to be in her late twenties. Dew's plan to integrate cat DNA into her future descendants was apparently possi-ble in this world, wherever or *whenever* it was.

This Sahar was dressed in some type of white jumpsuit. She was standing next to Dew's father, Marlow, who hadn't aged from the image on the picture Denise had once seen on Dew's mantle. Didn't he die a few years ago?

There was also an old native woman in traditional Navajo garb sitting in a wheelchair. "*Jean* Dark," the woman said, introducing herself. Denise could see the resemblance to her mother Jane.

"I knew you before you were born," Denise said.

The old woman nodded. "My mother said great things about you."

"She was probably the best lawyer I ever knew," Denise replied.

"How do you like our place?" Sahar asked. "It just came on the market, and we snapped it up right as the world is coming to an end."

She was apparently a couple with the resurrected Marlow. That must be a story for another time.

"It doesn't smell as bad as when Dew lived here," Denise said. She scanned the area. They were in the same house, Dew's house, same planet even. But it was now covered by a transparent bubble that vibrated slightly. Was it a glass dome or an energy field?

To the east, she could see the same Sandias, but there was some kind of cylinder on the summit, reminiscent of the water tower back in Lordsburg, but this tower was made of gold and glistened in the starlight. To the west, she could see Albuquerque, but a modern Albuquerque with a thousand-foot skyscraper anchoring the downtown.

Jean Dark pointed to a hologram of Dew, looking well over a hundred years old. It was so lifelike, but Denise saw a death date of 2112 and the words, RIP, hovering below the hologram.

"How did she die?" Denise asked.

"It's a long story," Sahar said. "And not a happy one. But in the end, she did the right thing."

"You're here," a voice said. "You're *really* here." Denise recognized a very ancient, but spry Rita coming through the bathroom door. Rita had shrunk with age and was nearly Denise' size.

"And my brother?" Denise asked. "Your father?"

Apparently, there was some kind of holographic projector in the room. Rita pressed an invisible button in the air and the hologram shifted to life-size image of Denny with a death date maybe ten years after his release from jail, but he looked thirty years older.

"He got back on the drugs, relapsed," Rita explained. "He was a lot more damaged than you thought, more damaged than we all knew."

The hologram showed a ravaged Denny lying on a death-bed. He looked worse than when Denise had first met him in jail, thinner and with deeper wrinkles.

"I didn't save him," Denise said.

"You gave him a chance, a life. He was there for me through high school," Rita said. "He helped me get into college. You saved *me*."

"And me?" Denise asked.

"You went away, but you're here again," Rita said. "*Kinda.*"

It didn't make sense, had she died and come back? It was too much to try to try to piece together.

There was an explosion overhead.

"They're here," Rita said. She pointed to the sky. "They're *finally* here. And we're ready for them, Auntie Denise. My grandmother, and the rest of them are coming back."

Denise was confused. "My mother? Jen Song?"

"My *other* grandmother," Rita said. "The colonel. Big Red Herring."

The shooting stars kept coming down like something out of a video game.

"What's going to happen?" Denise asked Rita.

"We don't know." Rita pointed to a door. "But *they* do. They are the key to saving us."

The front door vanished and then reappeared after two more people entered, dressed in those metallic fashions. One male, one female, but it was hard to tell them apart. Some of their body parts looked robotic, but their faces were still human. They looked at Denise and smiled.

"We're ready for them," the two said to Denise in unison, "Mother."

If Denise had a spark, the twins, *her* twins had it a thousand-fold. She had thought that she and Denny were the chosen ones, but suppose the real Gemini twins were Hikaru's and her children? These two were there to save humanity from whatever was coming down from above, coming from beyond.

Well, at least she hoped that they would save humanity.

There was another explosion up above, more streaks of lights heading toward earth.

"You better go back," Rita said. "We'll be waiting."

And then Denise slowly regained consciousness. She could already smell the fresh cat shit in Dew's apartment assaulting her nose. She took one last look at the twins, *her* twins as their image faded from her mind's eye. She hoped that they could answer one question, the most important question facing herself right now.

"What are your names?"

Author's Note

I didn't choose to write this book with these characters; these characters chose me. Denise has been a bit player in other people's stories ever since her birth in my third novel, *Volcano Verdict*. She's grown up on my pages since then and she deserved a story of her own. As I've said in previous Author Notes, time flows differently in the Rattlesnake Lawyer universe—Denise's age doesn't always match up with the ages of the other characters.

It can be assumed that all events depicted in this book took place before the Covid-19 pandemic.

There's some revisionist Rattlesnake history here. Nastia was never mentioned in *Volcano Verdict* in the scene in El Paso where Denise and Denny were born. Still, Denise's mother, Jen Song, knew Nastia in *Conflict Contract*, a later book. It's a small leap of faith to suggest that Jen and Nastia knew each other in the *Volcano* era. We do know that Jen took a bus down to El Paso in *Volcano* while pregnant with Denise and Denny. It is certainly conceivable that Nastia rode the same bus and was present for the birth of the twins that night.

I wanted a few scenes in Roswell, where I began my job as a public defender and started writing the Rattlesnake Lawyer saga. The town has always had a special place in my heart. Denise's opinions of Roswell and Lordsburg are not necessarily my opinions. The Roswell museum portrayed in the book is not based on a real museum. I don't know if there's a women's prison art collective, but I sure hope there is one.

Denise could indeed practice as a clinical law student under Rule 5-110.1 of the Rules of Criminal Procedure for the District Courts but would probably not qualify under the strict guidelines of the program.

I've also attempted to have continuity with this novel and my science fiction novel, *A Million Dead Lawyers*, which is set in the year 2112. Jane Dark's daughter Jean, Rita Herring and Dew have already appeared (will appear?) in that story. I hope for a sequel to that book, tentatively titled *Two Million Dead Lawyers*. Events in this book will certainly figure into that book if and when it is finally written. And like in the movies, this book's epilogue will most likely tie into that one.

Lordsburg, New Mexico is a very real town, but some dramatic liberties have been taken. The opinions of the characters toward the town are not necessarily those of the author. The hotels depicted in the story are not based on any real hotels. There is no Chinese restaurant called *Shiprock Wok*, either in Lordsburg or Shiprock. The recipes are fictional but hopefully a chef can take my ideas and run with them.

There is indeed a "ghost town" called Shakespeare in Hidalgo County, but New Shakespeare *Ranch* doesn't exist. There was no Lordsburg Incident on July 7, 1947 that is somehow connected to the events in Roswell. There have been numerous reports of UFO sightings all over New Mexico, so it is certainly possible that something happened out there. I don't know if there's a spaceship buried in Antarctica.

The practice of Hidalgo County residents taking Shakespearean names is purely the author's dramatic invention. White Sands Missile Range is a real place, but needless to say, I don't know what activities take place in any classified facility. There is no such thing as "grail" technology as far as I know.

In New Mexico magistrate courts, court reporters have indeed become judges without law degrees. While there is a requirement that newly admitted attorneys practice for a few years before becoming *district* court judges, there are always vacancies in the remote areas, so it is possible that an inexperienced lawyer could become a *pro-tem* district court judge.

Denise's opinions on psychic energy and Denny's opinions of UFOs are not necessarily those of the author.

As for the mysterious phone call that Dan receives, I'm sure it will figure into a later novel, Rattlesnake Funeral. That novel will not involve the paranormal or UFOs but will feature the law practice in the Corona age.

All events in this novel are fictional and not based on real events with the exception of the leaking waffle batter dispenser incident in the hotel buffet line.

About the Author

Jonathan Miller is an attorney who has practiced in every judicial district of New Mexico. He began his New Mexico legal career in Roswell. His first book, Rattlesnake Lawyer was published in 2000 and his novel, Luna Law was a 2017 co-winner of the Hillerman award for fiction.

www.ingramcontent.com/pod-product-compliance
Lightning Source LLC
Chambersburg PA
CBHW071510260626
47170CB00002B/321